F

Stover, Matthew
Woodring.

Caine's law.

$16.00

DATE			

CAINE'S LAW

CAINE'S LAW

THE THIRD OF THE ACTS OF CAINE, ACT OF ATONEMENT, BOOK TWO

MATTHEW STOVER

BALLANTINE BOOKS · DEL REY · NEW YORK

A Del Rey Trade Paperback Original

Copyright © 2012 by Matthew Woodring Stover

Published in the United States by Del Rey,
an imprint of The Random House Publishing Group,
a division of Random House, Inc., New York.

DEL REY is a registered trademark and the Del Rey colophon is
a trademark of Random House, Inc.

Stover, Matthew Woodring.
Caine's law / Matthew Stover.
pages cm.—(Acts of Caine. Act of atonement ; book two)
ISBN 978-0-345-45589-5 (pbk.)—ISBN 978-0-345-53254-1 (ebook)
(print)
I. Title.
PS3569.T6743C33 2012
813'.54—dc23   2011048289

Printed in the United States of America

www.delreybooks.com

9 8 7 6 5 4 3 2 1

Book design by Liz Cosgrove

for the horse-witch

author's note

Several parts of this story take place before the events depicted in Act of Atonement Book I, *Caine Black Knife*.

Other parts of this story take place after. Still other parts take place before and after both. Some parts may be imaginary, and some were real only temporarily, as they have subsequently unhappened.

Around the hero everything becomes a tragedy; around the demigod everything becomes a satyr-play; and around God everything becomes— what? perhaps a "world"?

—FRIEDRICH NIETZSCHE, *Beyond Good and Evil*

A powerful-enough metaphor grows its own truth.

—DUNCAN MICHAELSON

CAINE'S LAW

one thin slice of forever

BELOVED OF GOD

BELOVED OF GOD

"The gods exist beyond the reach of time. When we draw Their Eyes, They brush us with Their Power."

—ANGVASSE, LADY KHLAYLOCK, 463RD CHAMPION OF KHRYL

*A*nd in this My Dream, Beloved, you know Me.

Through your eyes I watch your blunt and broken hands scrabble upon the marble stair: spiders maimed and bleeding on frosted glass. The blood in your beard and hair carries a hint of the peat from the incendiary brew spewed from the ragged gape of your late friend Tyrkilld's throat when you took his head. As you creep up through the mouth of encircling stairwell, out upon the final spiral span that leads upward to the Purificapex of the Eternal Vaunt of the Knights of Khryl, I wish again—as I always have and always will—that I might make you look to the side here. You don't, you never have and never will. Still, in My dream, you cast wide your gaze over the limitless slaughter that is the work of Our Hand, and find it to be good.

The icy lash of sleet on your bare back. The reek of burning hair twisting up from the fires in Hell. Sawing of broken ribs in and out of your punctured lung. The blaze of the mines, the smoke and haze from the burning city, the storm of battle among the estates. Screams in the distance. Thousands in agony and terror. Tens of thousands to follow. Then millions. Perhaps billions, but We will never know; they will scream long after We have vanished into eternal nothing. After you take Us there, My demon of blessed grace.

My angel of the damned.

I dream this dream though I do not sleep. I have dreamed this dream though I have no past, and will dream this dream though I have no future. This I dream forever.

I dream that you truly knew the bargain you offered. I dream you were willing, even happy, to pay the price of My Love. That you joyously offered up all you do as well as all done to you. As a gift. A wedding present.

A dowry.

All this is to be savored. It is well that We will share eternity.

When the stone stair gives way to the vast cap of platinum, when you find the summit of the Eternal Vaunt to be icebound under half a span of freeze, when another man would be defeated by unclimbable ice, by a punctured lung, a broken hand, and a compound fracture of the leg . . . you reach down for your last dagger—the one you had used to secure the tourniquet above your knee—and with your one half-working arm you chip handholds to pull yourself up.

And so, here at the end of days, you are as you have always been. Willing to die. Not willing to quit.

And this is the death for which you were chosen, Beloved. From this place you cannot flee, and there is no life for you beyond Our Consummation; not even I can save you now, should I somehow decide your life outweighs My death.

No, Beloved. Never. I have waited a thousand years for this—and each second of these My thousand years outlasts the age of the universe. Here it ends. Here you give your life to take Mine. Our own private suicide pact.

My infinite millennium forever ends with Our lovers' leap.

I feel the lick of flame along your nerves, and I feel the shreds of discipline that no longer entirely lock this pain outside your consciousness. I feel the numb burn of frostbite settling into the toes on your good leg, and the fingers of your broken hand. I feel the seductive chill of the ice you climb, how it cools the fire in your nerves, and I feel your overpowering lust to let go, to lie flat and sleep, to fall forever . . .

But you won't. You never do. You never have, and thus you never will.

And now you struggle to the platinum altar and try to rise, to go out on your feet. The effort gathers darkness in your eyes and you sag back down, helpless. Hopeless.

Defeated at last.

With your final exertion of will, you reach up to the hilt of the Accursèd Blade and ignite its power within the altar. With the touch of your hand, the Accursèd Blade becomes again the Sword of Man, and now the first spastic twitch of your tattered arm will slash the Sword free from its platinum grave, to bring the Eternal Vaunt itself crashing into ruin that destroys My Body as well as your own—to make of yourself and Me an ending that cannot be unmade.

It is for this I have created you, Beloved. To set me free.

It is for this I Called you here to Me with dreams of Black Knives and murder. It is for this I created the Smoke Hunt and unleashed its hunger upon the innocent.

It is for this I brought you down from the cross.

With your hand on the Sword, the moment stretches ever closer to the infinite, an agonizing extension of eternity. Have you always waited so long to do what you were born for? Has it ever been thus . . . or . . . ?

Is this—against all possibility, against the weight of Reality itself—somehow *new*?

And here then, now, for the first time forever, you cough your throat clear of the blood from your punctured lung. Scarlet sprays across your useless legs. You gasp against the ripping within your chest, and now, impossibly—

"I know . . . what You are . . . fucker." Your voice is rusted barbwire, yanked up your throat one word at a time. "*Who* You are. You . . . *hear* me . . . fucker? You understand? I *know*."

You *know* Me—? O Beloved, is this yet merely My Dream . . . ?

It must be. You don't say this. You don't say anything. You never have, and thus you never will.

You *can't*.

"Dunno . . . if You understand. Dunno if You can . . . even *hear* me . . . uh. Fucking listen . . . anyway. I know You're not just . . . the Smoke God. I know how Panchasell Mithondionne Bound You to this place, and I know why. I know You chose me for Your Unbinding . . . and there's something I gotta say."

Had I breath, it would be held for this . . .

"No."

What?

"You hear . . . ? Y'understand? No, fucker. No. Terms . . . terms of my bargain . . . a universe of pain . . . our own Caine Show . . . uh. Nothing in there says I have to . . . kill you. Not like this. Not at all."

This is not possible. This does not happen. This cannot happen. This has never happened and it never will.

"It's not . . . the people who died here. The Pratts. T'Passe. Kierendal. Not the people I murdered. Khlaylock. Tyrklld. It's not even that I . . . shot Angvasse in the face . . . blew her fucking *head* off . . . when all she was trying to do was *help* . . ."

How should I care why you choose to defy Me? How can you even delude yourself that you have choice at all?

"It's just . . ." You shake your head, and now tears roll free from your shuttered eyes. "It's everything. It's the fucking world. It's that slave woman in County Faltane . . . the one who died in the fire . . ."

I set My Will upon you: Draw the Sword. Give your life to Unbind the prison that is My Body. Now and forever, My Will be done.

And beyond reason, instead of the clench of hand and arm to Draw the Sword, I feel your lips pull back from your blood-salted teeth. "I *felt* that . . ." you murmur. "So You're listening after all. Well, all right, then."

Impossibly now strength returns to your shattered limbs, and you use the Sword to pull yourself upright, and climb to your feet, balancing on your unbroken leg. "Pirichanthe: by Name I conjure Thee: Hear my word. Pirichanthe: twice by Name I conjure Thee: Understand my word. Pirichanthe: by Name thrice I conjure Thee: Believe my word."

Panting, coughing, hacking up gouts of blood into the storm winds and thunder, your voice is scarcely a whisper, but I hear, and I understand, and I believe . . .

"You want me to draw this Sword and send you back to whateverthefuck Outside nonplace you came from? Okay. I can kill you. Happy to. But I'm a *professional*, fucker. I get paid for this shit."

Paid . . .

Your hand upon the Sword to Bind Us in the permanent now, you lift your blood-smeared wolfen grin to the burning sky.

"I want to make a deal."

introduction

FEAR BY DEFINITION

FEAR BY DEFINITION

Simon Faller adjusted his tie for the hundredth time. All his collars
were too big for him now; his appearance had become a compromise
between leaving his collar half-open like a drunk and cinching it tight like
a Temp in secondhand clothes. His image in the palmpad's default mirror
grimaced back at him. Swipes of exhaustion black as dried blood underlined his eyes. His hair—where he still had hair—straggled behind his
ears. His lips had gone grey as his suit. When the door beside him slid
open, he flinched and almost dropped the palmpad.

The aide was barely a third his age. "Professional? The Director will
see you now."

Faller tucked the palmpad securely into one armpit and followed the
aide through three layers of outer office. The new Director's personal office was unimpressive, as was the new Director, a small nervous man with
a permanent frown who was directing that frown toward his deskscreen.
He made a shooing motion with one hand without looking up. The aide
discreetly evaporated.

"Professional Faller. Don't bother to sit."

Faller forbore to mention that the Director occupied the only chair.
"Yes, Administrator. Thank you for seeing me on such short notice, sir."

"And don't bother toadying." The Director turned that frown toward Faller. "You were born Professional, I take it."

"I, ahh, I mean, yes. Yes, sir."

"My family have been Artisans for more than a hundred years," the Director said severely. "I was the first elevated to Professional. I am the sole member of my family, *ever*, to rise as high as Administration. Ordinarily I enjoy obsequy as much as the next Administrator, but this is not an ordinary day."

"Yes, sir. That's why I asked to see you." Faller licked his lips and extended the palmpad like a serving tray. "This—I mean, have you seen this? What I'm supposed to show him?"

"Of course."

"Please, Administrator, you must understand—this will *not* persuade him. Or intimidate him. It's exactly the opposite of how—"

"Only a moment ago I was onscreen with the Board of Governors making precisely that argument. The Board isn't interested in argument. They aren't interested in our opinions. They're interested in our obedience, and they will have it."

"Administrator—" Faller almost dropped the palmpad for the second time in five minutes. He set it on the Director's desk and backed away. "I'm not sure I can do this."

"And I'm sure you will."

"But—please, sir. I thought you knew him. I can't threaten his *family*—do you know what *happens* to people who threaten his family?"

"You won't threaten his family. Neither will I. Our task is to convey information. Specific information, conveyed as specifically directed."

"That's a—" Faller thought he was about to laugh; what came from his mouth was instead more of a despairing bleat. "Do you think he'll care about fine distinctions?"

"You're frightened."

"Of *course* I'm frightened," Faller said. "Have you not seen footage of the fire at Marc Vilo's estate? Have you never cubed *For Love of Pallas Ril?*"

The Director lifted a hand as though to massage a headache. The hand trembled, just a bit, and instead he wiped away pale sweat that had beaded above his eyebrows. For a long moment he sat, eyes closed, resting his head against his sweaty hand, then abruptly huffed a sigh and rose. "Professional Faller, the analysis I am about to share with you is speculation, nothing more. Despite it being nothing more than speculation, should you repeat this conversation in any context whatsoever, I will not only deny it, I will see you downcasted for corporate slander. Do you understand me?"

"I, ah—yes, sir. I mean, I understand, Administrator."

The new Director rounded his desk and perched himself informally on one corner. "I was a porter and part-time nurse's aide when Arturo Kollberg came to be Director of St. Luke's Ecumenical in Chicago. I found ways of bringing myself to his attention, and made myself useful in any and every manner he might so much as mention. He found me sufficiently useful that when he was hired by the Studio, he brought me with him, and sponsored my upcaste to Professional to serve as his private secretary, which I did for more than a decade. After Chairman Kollberg's breakdown, I served in the same capacity under the new Chairman, Administrator Hari Michaelson. Because the Board of Governors considered Chairman Michaelson to be unreliable and potentially treasonous, they requested I provide periodic updates on the Chairman's activities. My compliance with their orders led me to find myself *this close*—"

The Director shoved his hand so close to Faller's face that he could smell the man's sweat on its palm.

"*This* close to Hari Michaelson's *face*—close enough to count his *nose hairs*—while he advised me to remind the Board that the only thing he'd ever been good at was killing people with his bare hands."

Faller took a step back. He'd been that close to Hari Michaelson a couple of times himself. "What did you do?"

"I did my duty," the Director said though his teeth. "As I always have. As will you."

Faller noted for the first time that the new Director's eyes were underlined almost as darkly as his own, and that his chiton and chlamys both showed damp below his armpits.

The Director pushed himself to his feet again, and moved toward the window. "We're ready for him," he said. "As ready as anyone can be."

Faller joined him at the window. The blasted wasteland of the badlands around was pocked with artillery emplacements, bunkers, and hardpoints of all descriptions. In the far distance of the hard blue sky, five stars flickered silver as they fell into a curve that would bring them to the rooftop landing pad. Faller swallowed. His dry throat tried to stay closed.

Some of the field pieces and SAM units tracked the falling stars. The rest maintained their prescribed kill vectors. Four of those stars would be the latest generation of riot cars, packing enough firepower to take a serious chunk out of the emplacements outside. The other—the star in the center—would be a specially modified detention van.

All this for one man. One man who wasn't even conscious.

"You'll forgive me, Administrator, for feeling that the entire armed force of the planet could be out there and do us no good at all. We're bringing him *in* here. In here with *us*."

"The division isn't there to protect us from him," the Director said, bleak as a granite headstone. "It's to make sure he doesn't get out."

Faller stared. "That's . . ."

"I believe you're here for the same reason I am. It's not so much that we know him—there are doubtless thousands, perhaps millions, of fans and researchers and historians who know him better than both of us together ever could. My best guess is that we're here because *he* knows *us*."

The Director turned to him, his eyes soft with unexpected sympathy. "He knows us, and he doesn't like us."

Numb horror squeezed Simon Faller's throat. "So this—" He coughed, waving weakly at the palmpad. "—this *information* . . . the Board wants you and me to . . ."

"Because they believe if he gets loose, he's going to kill someone. Likely several someones," the Director said simply. "Ours are the faces he will associate with this . . . information. My feeling is that this is in accord with the Board's plan. I believe the Board has calculated that as long as he's trying kill us, he won't be trying to kill them."

"So—how are *we* supposed to—"

"Don't whine at me, Professional. You were an Actor. You know how this works."

Director Keller spread his sweaty hands. "Win or die."

the whole story

SCARS AND SCARS

SCARS AND SCARS

This is the axe from Kor.
This is the arrow from the Teranese floodplain.
This is the spike from my cross, and this the burn from
Crowmane's god.
This is the alley knife from home, and this the brick, and this
my father's fist.

—"CAINE" (PFNL. HARI MICHAELSON)
  Retreat from the Boedecken

A week or two after my seventh birthday, my father beat my mother to death.

I remembered it. All of it. Finally.

I remembered the way it was. The only way it'll ever be.

Listen to me.

Yes, you. Pay attention. This is important. This is the whole story right here. Everything else is just context.

Listen:

The Mission District's Labor free clinic . . . Dad and me and the old guy with the scars . . .

Dad and me, we sat together on a plastic bench, shoved up against the mildew-stained wall a couple meters in from the age-smoked armorglass of the street doors. A girl hunched next to me, twelve or thirteen probably, because to me she looked practically grown up. She was talking, kind of under her breath, and most of the time I couldn't understand what she was saying and the rest of the time she didn't make much sense. She was rocking back and forth with one knee hugged to her chest while her other leg jittered and bounced and kicked out sometimes and she didn't seem to notice.

On the other side of her was some ancient ragface, probably Dad's age even, lying on his side on the bench, snoring with his head on a bundle of rags, blowing pinkish bubbles of bloody vomit out his nose.

On the other side of me was Dad.

Elbows on knees, hands dangling limp between his thighs, he stared straight ahead, barely even blinking, and I knew he was looking at something inside his head instead of in the room. He got like that after an episode. Like he was dead, except for moving and breathing and stuff. He hadn't made a noise since we sat down. Over an hour.

Me neither.

The clinic waiting room was bigger than our whole apartment. Cleaner, too. It was late morning, so there were only fifty or sixty Laborers waiting to see the practitioner. Slowest part of the day. Most of them just had the flushed faces and thick gluey coughs that meant they'd caught the wheeze, which had started early this year. It wasn't even fall yet. The wheeze could be cured by taking a pill every day for a week or two, but somehow there were never enough pills. Nickles Porter, a kid about my age who lived on our floor in the Temp block, had told me his dad had come home from the clinic worse off than when he'd went in, and that the old man had spent most of the night choking to death.

I remember thinking, when Nickles told me about it, how it'd be pretty neat if *my* dad would come down with the wheeze, because once he was gone, Mom could maybe get us recast to Professional, and she could teach and we'd go back and live in our *real* house, the one on Language Arts Drive at the faculty compound in South Berkeley.

I sort of figured that Nickles and his mom must have done something like that, because a couple weeks later he wasn't around anymore. I thought this because I was still new. A few months along, I'd have a more direct understanding of how and why Labor kids disappeared from the Mission District.

Sitting there on the bench, I didn't worry about Mom dying; I wasn't *that* new. In the Temp blocks, you don't worry about what's coming so much as about living through whatever it turns out to be. If she died, it'd be one thing. If she lived, it'd be something else. Nothing I could do about anything either way. Except sit and wait. And try not to think about the rest of my life.

So that's what I did until the old guy showed up.

He came in through the street door like he had someplace to be, walking with one of those hollow plastic crutches tucked into his armpit, even though he didn't look like he needed it. Except maybe for being old. He looked older than dirt. His hair was mostly grey, and his eyebrows too, and his face was the color of an old paper bag. His nose was crooked and the scar that slanted across it was the lightest-colored thing on his face. He headed straight for the inner door.

"You can't do that."

He stopped and looked back at me. "What?"

"You can't go in." I pointed over at the vented armorglass reception window. "You check in with the window-lady, then sit out here until somebody calls your name."

"Sure, kid. Whatever. I'm not here to see the . . . oh." He'd looked from me over to Dad, and he stared the way you stare in nightmares when you can't quite figure out what you're afraid of, and he sounded like somebody was choking him. "Fuck *me* . . ."

He kind of pulled himself together, rubbing at his eyes with his free hand, but he'd gone pale except for that scar across his nose, which had turned dark red, and he didn't look too steady on his feet.

"You better sit down," I said. "If you fall here, there's nobody to pick you up."

"Yeah." His voice had gone hoarse and breathy. "Yeah, I remember."

I didn't know what he meant by that, so I didn't say anything. He looked at Dad some more, then he looked at me and he got this expression like he was mad but was about to cry anyway. Then he got over that, and just looked sad. "You're having a tough day."

I looked up at Dad, but he was still vacant, like an old building nobody lives in anymore. "I guess."

The old guy came over and lowered himself onto the bench between me and the muttering girl. He leaned his forehead on the crutch, like this was why he carried the thing, because he was too tired to hold his head up. "Your mom, huh?"

I looked at the floor. He knew stuff he shouldn't, and I knew better already than to talk to undercover Social Police.

"My mom's back there too," the old guy said.

I knew to keep my eyes on the floor, but I never learned to shut up. "You got a mom?"

"Everybody's got a mom, kid. And everybody's mom dies."

"My mom's not gonna die."

"Maybe not today. Remember what she says to you? About your dad?"

I remembered. Lying on her cot in the living room, all sweaty and bruised and still bleeding a little from the corner of her mouth. I remembered how her hand would shake when she'd grab my wrist, and how her grip had no strength anymore. "Take care of your father," she'd say. "He's the only father you'll ever have. He's sick, Hari. He can't help himself."

She used to say stuff like that a lot. About how it wasn't his fault, *how Dad really loves us and never wants to hurt us*, even though he did anyway. Sometimes bad enough you couldn't walk much for a day or two. It never made sense to me; who cared whose fault it was?

She also used to say how sometimes *he's just not himself*, which never made sense to me either, because if he wasn't himself, who was he? If Dad was *just sick*, why didn't he ever get better?

And who cares why? What difference does *why* make? A punch in the mouth is a punch in the mouth. Why's got nothing to do with it.

But Mom seemed to think all this was important for me to understand, so I always nodded and played along, because that was the only way to make her quit bugging me about it.

The old guy watched me like he was listening to my mind. "For there is nothing good or bad, but thinking makes it so, right?"

I looked down at the floor again. "I think you shouldn't be talking to me."

"Got that right." He leaned toward me just a little, tilting his head down and lowering his voice like he didn't want Dad to hear, which made me wonder if he might really not be Soapy after all, because if he was, he'd know who Dad was and what he was like after an episode already, and he'd know Dad couldn't do anything right now even if you shot at him. "Listen, kid, I want to . . . ."

He stopped and shook his head, and I could tell he was making a face even though I wasn't looking at him. "Just one thing, kid. One thing and I'll leave you alone, okay?"

I didn't answer because I was looking at his hands.

He sat forward on his elbows, the crutch leaning on one shoulder, hands dangling between his thighs. Which was kind of funny, because that's exactly how Dad was sitting, but his hands didn't look anything like Dad's hands, which were wide and strong and hard as a brick—when he'd start in on me, he'd knock me down without even trying. Without even making a fist. He was working on the docks, and we were still eating okay, and it seemed like he was stronger every day. Stronger than people are supposed to get. Dad's hands were scabbed and scarred and rough with callus, but they still looked like hands.

The old guy's hands looked like hammers.

Not deformed or anything—he still had fingers and stuff—but they were covered in scars and some kind of weird stripe of skin across the knuckles and along the sides, skin that was dark as old bruise, thick and rumpled until you couldn't even really see his knuckles at all. There might not even have *been* knuckles under there—even when he made a fist, all you could see was that the patch over the joints behind his first and second fingers was thicker and darker than the rest.

His hands were made to hit.

"Ugly, huh? That's what happens when guys like me get old." He turned them over so I could look at the scars and calluses on his palms too. Looked like his fingers didn't really work too well anymore; they were crooked and stiff and bulged at the joints. "It's a little late for me to take up guitar."

I felt like I ought to say something, and even though I knew I shouldn't even be talking to the old guy, I didn't want to be mean. All I could come up with was, "You sure have a lot of scars."

"Yeah. You too."

I didn't have *any* scars, not like his, just some nicks and cuts from fights after stickball and stuff. He was making fun of me. "Making fun of a kid is an *asshole move*."

I didn't know exactly what an *asshole move* was, except that the older kids said that when you were mean to somebody for no reason.

"I'm not teasing you, kid. There's scars, and there's scars." He sounded so serious, and so sad, that I looked up at him, and his eyes were extra-shiny, like they were a little more wet. He shrugged and he coughed and he looked down. "These on my hands here, they're one kind . . . well, hell, look here for a second."

He twisted around and tugged the collar of his tunic down off his neck, and he had a *real* scar on his shoulder, jagged as a lightning bolt, rippled and weirdly smooth and white as spit.

"Wow." I couldn't take my eyes off it. "How'd you get that one?"

"Guy hit me with an axe."

"For *real*?" I could just barely imagine it. "That is *so* cool!"

"Not at the time."

"He could of chopped your *arm* off!"

"Except he was aiming for my neck. Whatever. But look—" He held his arm out and kind of twisted his shoulder in a little circle to show that everything still worked. "That's one kind of scar. It's there mostly just to remind you something happened. Where he broke my collarbone here? It's stronger than the bone on either side. A lot of scars are like that. They heal back tougher than they were before."

"Cool."

"But if, like you said, he cut off my arm instead . . ." He shook his head. "That's another kind of scar. You can live through it and learn to work around it and whatever, but for the rest of your life you're gonna be a little bit broken. Or a lot."

I got the idea, but I didn't get what it had to do with me, and I said so.

"Not all scars are on your body, kid. But some of them leave you broken just the same. My mom . . . she died when I was about your age. You don't get over that kind of shit. Just . . . listen, kid. Don't ever miss a chance to kiss her good-bye. You never know which time is the last time."

"You're not a very good liar."

"Huh?"

"Your mom died when you were *my* age? How come she's in the clinic here, then?"

He looked uncomfortable. "It's complicated."

"My dad says if you're gonna tell lies, you better remember which lies you tell," I said.

"And he's right. But you better remember the truth too." He shook his head again, a little shake, irritated with himself, like Dad would do when he found himself talking off in the wrong direction from whatever he was wanting to say.

"Here's the gristle. You're gonna see me again someday. A long time from now. So long that you won't remember meeting me, or having this talk or anything, right up until you see me. It'll come back to you. When it does, there's something I want you to remember, all right? One thing."

I looked back down at the floor. Somehow I felt like I was in one of those fairy tales Dad liked to read to me off the net—the kind where if you agree to something, it's a trap and everything goes wrong forever. But still I couldn't help asking. I had to know. "What's that?"

"That I'm sorry, kid." His voice was slow. Heavy. "That I said I was sorry."

"For what?"

He looked down too, like he wanted to see whatever it was on the floor I'd been looking at. "Everything."

"I don't get it."

"You will." He shook his head and his lips flattened into a straight line. "I'd make things different if I could."

I frowned. "Make *what* things different?"

"Nothing. Everything. Fuck it anyway." He gave a heavy sigh and pushed himself to his feet. "Forget I said anything."

My ears started to get hot. "I don't think that's *right*."

"Yeah, okay. Whatever."

He went toward the inner door, and I jumped up, fists trembling against my thighs.

"What's that even *mean*? You're *sorry* but you're not gonna *do* anything." I felt myself blush, like always when I get mad. The blush climbs my neck like I'm a bottle filling up with angry. *"Everybody's fucking sorry!"*

He stopped like I had him on a leash, but he didn't look back. I knew I was in trouble, because *fuck* is a bad word even when you say it to other kids, but it's worse when you say it to a grown-up. Since I was already in trouble, I wasn't worried about *getting* in trouble, so I stood there and screamed at him.

"People were *sorry* Dad got *soaped* and people were *sorry* we got thrown out of our *house* and Mom is *sorry* I get in *fights* and Dad is *sorry* he beats Mom until all she can do is lie on the floor and *bleed* and *nobody* ever does the *first fucking thing* to make anything *different!*"

Now everybody in the waiting room was looking, and I was shaking and tears were streaming down my face, because I get too angry to do anything but cry, and then I'm crying because there's nothing else I can do.

"If you were *really* sorry you wouldn't even have to *say* it and the only reason you *say* it is so you don't *feel* bad about not *doing* anything! Saying you're *sorry* doesn't do anything except make you feel like you're not such a fucking useless fucking rotten fucking *fuck!*"

I felt Dad move next to me like a sculpture coming to life, and his hand found my shoulder. "Hari?" His voice had that kinda blurry sound, like I woke him up in the middle of the night and he's not sure what's going on. "What's wrong, Killer?"

But by then I had the full waterworks going, and I couldn't even tell him because I couldn't get my breath. So I just stood there and shook and cried and wished I was big enough to beat that old guy the way Dad would beat Mom. Till all he could do was lie on the floor and bleed.

Then Dad looked up and saw the old guy, and his face went white as foam. "*You* . . ."

The old guy nodded to him. "Duncan. Guess I don't have to ask how you've been."

Dad got a funny look on his face, like he was worried and scared and mad all at the same time. "You can't be here—you *can't* be here . . ."

me right out of sobbing, then faster than I'd ever seen a man move, Dad was on his feet and had dragged me behind him to put himself between me and the old guy.

"What do you want here?" Dad growled in his *tell me before I pound you to paste* voice, and he was a *lot* bigger than the old guy and he was younger than the old guy and stronger than a person ought to be and had those hands like bricks, and the old guy didn't look scared at all. Just kind of sad, again.

"What if . . ." he said slowly. "What if you could take back the worst thing you ever did?"

"What?"

"Would you? If you could unring a bell, just one time. Would you?"

Dad kind of leaned toward him and bent his knees a little. "Stay away from me. Stay away from my family." I could hear the clench in his jaw. "If I ever see you again—"

He didn't say *I'll kill you*, but he didn't have to.

"I wasn't exactly expecting to bump into you two today," the old guy said. "It won't happen again."

He leaned around Dad's shoulder and met my eyes. "Remember what I said. And always kiss your mother good-bye, kid. Don't forget. Always."

"What you *said*?" Dad's voice went all thick, like he was getting mad so fast it was choking him. "You . . . were *talking*? With my *son*?"

His hands went for the front of the old guy's tunic and I knew what was coming next: Dad would lift him up and shake him, hard, and if that wasn't enough, he'd hold on to the tunic with one hand while he used the other to beat the old guy bloody, because that was what happened when Dad got angry enough to put his hands on somebody. Except this time.

Before Dad could grab the guy's tunic, the old guy said, "Don't."

And Dad didn't.

The old guy looked about as harmless as an old guy can look without being actually broke-down, but there must have been some magic in that one quiet word because it stopped Dad cold—*real* cold, frozen, hands in front, close enough to grab or hit or whatever. But he didn't.

"Duncan. Pull your shit together," the old guy said. "You've got problems more serious than me."

When I think about that moment . . .

Dad and the Social Police. Dad and the Studio. Dad and the Board of Governors. Dad and the Leisurefolk and Investors who rule the Earth, and the Businessmen and Administrators who run it. Dad and Mom. Dad and me.

Dad.

Because now, all these years later, I understand what I saw that day.

In the book Kris Hansen wrote about me, he had Tan'elKoth tell the Board of Governors how to beat me. *We must teach him to think of himself as a defeated man.*

My father had been more than defeated. He'd been crushed. He had poked his head up out of the grass, and the boot of human civilization had stomped him flat.

Slowly.

And through it all, his degenerative neurological disorder had been inexorably transforming him into exactly the kind of man he had given his life to fight: stupid, erratic, and violent. And he *knew* it.

He never even got to forget.

All those years . . . every time he looked at me, he remembered every time he had hurt me. He remembered choking me. Remembered hitting me with his hands, or other things. Books. Chairs. Frying pans. Once, memorably, a pipe wrench.

Sometimes he had blackouts. Not many.

I'm pretty sure he remembered beating Mom to death.

We never talked about her. Never. But you could see it in his eyes. The memory would hit and his eyes would go empty. Wet marbles. Nothing there at all. Not sadness. Not even regret. He'd lose the thread of whatever we were talking about, and he'd be just gone. Gone like he used to be after one of his rages. Not like he'd go dead. Like he'd been dead all along, but once in a while he'd forget long enough to dream he was still alive. Or maybe the dream was that he'd died the way he wished he could have: that he'd given his life to protect her.

I have failed people I love. Failing them *destroyed* me. What it did to Dad . . . I can't even imagine. I don't want to imagine.

I know why he took it, though. Why he didn't kill himself and skip forty years of living death. I figured it out a year or two after I got him sprung from the Buke and moved him into the Abbey with Shanna and Faith and me. I figured it out from seeing how he looked at me.

Mom would come to him like Banquo's ghost, and he'd go dead . . . and when he'd come back, there'd be this look. When he looked at me. After a while I realized where I knew it from. I recognized the look because when I think about Faith, I see it in the mirror.

Every time he'd drag himself back from that dead place, he was making a promise. Not to me. That look in his eyes came from silently reminding himself that no matter how crushed he was, how helpless and sick and *guilty* he was, even if I denied him and spit on him and cursed his memory . . . there was still the thinnest shaved-bare chance that someday there might be something, no matter how small, he could do to help me. There might even come a day when I'd actually need him. The look was him swearing to himself that if such a day should ever come, he would be there. No matter what it cost him.

He'd be there to save me.

Even if I never needed saving. Even if all his endurance, all his suffering, if the rot chewing away his brain and the guilt clawing through his heart turned out to be for nothing. Even if there was never one goddamn thing he could ever do.

Because there would always be that chance . . .

Dad in the Mission District Labor Clinic, on his feet, a barbwire tangle of fury and terror. Because he saw in front of him a bad man. A casual killer who takes lives the way most people take showers. Dozens of lives. Hundreds. A man who could slay faster than Dad could blink, and for less reason. Knowing that any slightest twitch might, without warning, drop his bloody corpse on the waiting room floor, he had something he thought was worth dying for.

He got in front of me.

In that one long stretching eyeblink of violence gathering like a thunderstorm around us, the clinic's inner door opened behind the old guy, and one of the practitioner's aides stuck his head out. "Laborer Michaelson?"

The old guy turned like he thought the aide was talking to him, but of course the aide was talking to Dad. And me. The old guy just pushed the door a little bit farther open and walked on through. I'm not sure Dad even noticed him go.

Like the old guy said, we had problems more serious than him.

"Yes? I'm Prof—Laborer. I'm Laborer Michaelson," Dad said. "How is she?"

"Can you come with me, Laborer?"

All the anger drained out of Dad and didn't leave anything behind to hold him up. He swayed a little and caught himself by grabbing my shoulder. "I'm here with—this is our son . . ."

"It's very crowded back here, Laborer. Your son has to stay in the waiting room."

"You can't let . . . we can't even go in together . . . ?"

But I knew the look on the aide's face. I shrugged out from under Dad's hand and sat back down on the bench, because I could already tell what was coming next.

"Maybe after you come out, Laborer," the aide said. "Sorry."

Sorry. Yeah.

It is only now—*literally* now, as I compose these words on the far side of decades that feel more like centuries—that this finally strikes me as incongruous. That Dad could stare violent death square in the eye without so much as a blink, but couldn't stand up to a goddamn nurse's aide. At the time, it was obvious. Natural. It was the primary lesson of my life.

You can fight a threat. You can't fight the way things are.

That's what got us buried in the Mission District Labor ghetto. Because Dad had tried to fight the way things are. By the time we stood together in the clinic, the scars he carried from that brutal beat-down had him too broken to even raise his voice.

So I went to the bench and sat, and waited for Dad to come out and tell me Mom was dead.

And the old guy? He was right. I forgot all about him until I saw him again.

Which was—to the surprise of absolutely fucking nobody except my own dumb ass—in a mirror.

The mirror was an old mirror, almost as old as I felt when I dragged myself out of bed that morning. Bent nails clipped it onto a splintered wall over a rust-crusted washbowl in a crappy village wayhouse where everything was damp and the whole place smelled of mildew. Including the mirror: half the silver had peeled off the back, and black stains rimmed the patches remaining.

Every week or two I'd hit one of these crappy wayhouses in whatever crappy village we happened to be closest to, so I could pick up any supplies we needed, and then spend the evening in front of a fire wherever the locals gathered to jawbone, buy a lot of drinks, and find out if the world had blown up yet. And sometimes the horse-witch would come with me, because even she liked a bed once in a while. As a change of pace.

And because, as she never gets tired of reminding me, I'm not getting any fucking younger.

That particular morning, I woke up alone even though I hadn't gone to bed alone. And she'd been gone awhile even though it was barely dawn; her side of the bed was cold as a tombstone in the rain. And I hadn't felt her go, which was kind of weird just because of who I am, but also because I hadn't slept well. At all.

I had finally drifted off sometime midway between midnight and dawn, and even then I wasn't resting easily; I had a nightmare. Well, not really a nightmare. By then I could tell the difference. It was a sending.

I should say, a Sending.

In the nightmare/sending/whateverthefuck, I was Orbek. I was up in the Boedecken and I blew the brains out of some old hunchbacked ogrillo named Kopav, then adopted his son into the Black Knives. I mean, Orbek adopted him.

Just like he adopted me.

So I'd had a shitty night, and morning without the horse-witch looked to be worse, and then I mopped my face with the rotting rag that passed for a hand towel and saw the old guy in the mirror.

I had to stare for a while before I could make anything make sense. I'm not sure how long. Sometimes I'm fast with shit—usually how to hurt people, but let that go—and sometimes comprehending shit takes me roughly twice forever, and I don't even remember which flavor of shit this had turned out to be. For the longest time, I couldn't get my head around how the old bastard hadn't been lying to me.

His mom really had died when he was my age. She really was in the back of the clinic that morning. Too.

I didn't give the sonofabitch enough credit. Whatever else anybody can say about him, that old fucker was an honest man.

It was raining weird all over the damn place. Except this wasn't so much raining weird as it was a hurricane of fucking impossible. There's a reason it's not called the 2nd Guideline of Thermodynamics.

Because if that was possible—shit, more than possible, considering it actually happened—what else is possible?

What isn't?

I remember thinking about everything I've done. Everything I've seen. Everything I know. And I remember a wave of wonder breaking over me when I finally realized what it meant.

That's when I started to smile.

That's when I looked at my reflection in a ragged patch of silver and thought, *Fuck you too, old man. Everybody's fucking sorry.*

The difference between him and me?

Hard to say. He obviously didn't expect to find Dad and me in the clinic, which means I'll never be him, because he must not have had that memory. So my future won't be that. The horse-witch would say he wasn't me. He was somebody who looked like me. Somebody who had my scars.

But, y'know, the horse-witch isn't always right about everything.

Kris—Emperor Deliann, who also isn't always right about everything—would say that each of us is the sum of his scars, which is what has always made the most sense to me. Even if I never find my way to the clinic on the day my mother died, that old guy was Hari Michaelson. Caine. Jonathan Fist. Dominic fucking Shade, even.

If you have my scars, you're me too.

But being me didn't mean I'm him, or that I ever will be. You neither. Shit, I wasn't the same guy I'd been the night before. I'm not the same guy I'll be after I go back to the Boedecken. That's part of why the horse-witch has her thing about names. Sometimes your name is just a dodge to fool yourself into thinking you're the same guy you were ten years ago. Six months ago.

Yesterday.

Funny thing, though: the old guy didn't remember us meeting. That means at least something about his childhood had unhappened. His childhood had been warped by a Power into *my* childhood. He's who I would have been.

So—stick with me here—his childhood, the one that led him to that morning in the Mission District Labor Clinic, never existed. But I still remember him. I remember all of it. Even though *he will never exist.* He can't. He himself has unhappened, but he still exists as a feature of my youth. Existed. Language fails.

That scene couldn't have happened; it's an acausal loop, a self-canceling sideslip of history. Couldn't have failed to unhappen.

Except it did.

Time-binding is not accomplished lightly. There have been, according to Monastic Vaultbound Histories, only two human beings who could do it at all. One of them was Jantho of Tyrnall, called the Ironhand, who crafted the Covenant of Pirichanthe, created the Vaults of Binding, and founded the Monasteries. The other was his twin brother, Jereth.

He's the one we call the Godslaughterer.

That white plastic crutch . . . those things are hollow. And the old bastard didn't need it for walking. I *really* wish I could ask him what was inside.

I guess, unlikely as it seems, there's a chance I might find out.

And there was another difference between him and me. The big one. The biggest there is: I had something I could do about shit he'd been just sorry for.

Which was good because, y'know, save the world one goddamn time and it's your fucking job forever.

beginning of the end

BOUND

BOUND

"Do this one thing, and there will be agony beyond Your imagination. Only grant my one small desire, and I promise You a universe of pain.

"Just get me off this cross."

—"CAINE" (PFNL. HARI MICHAELSON)
Retreat from the Boedecken

My cell in the Buke had no way to measure time. Night was when they turned off my lights. Day was when they turned them on. Meals were delivered through a feeding tube attached to a nozzle just behind my collarbone, minimizing solid waste, so I couldn't even track time by how often I have to shit. It was actually kind of relaxing. Though still, it wasn't the kind of place I thought I'd miss, until I woke up somewhere else.

Apparently food isn't the only thing delivered through my feeding tube.

Some things haven't changed. I'm still stripcuffed to a restraint bed. I still have no feeling below my waist. The room décor is still general-purpose cell, just with walls of institutional green instead of white, and actual furniture instead of molded extrusions of the floor. There's even a window—or at least a very convincing imitation of natural light—behind me where I can't see, but low enough to cast my bed's shadow on the wall. And I can tell time here. When the steel doors slide open and Simon Faller's standing there with a jumbo economy-size palmpad, I know exactly what time it is.

Half-past the rest of my life.

He's in the same grey suit from before. The fit hasn't improved. He looks drawn, nervy, round-eyed. A fawn scenting wolves. From the look of his collar, he's lost more weight and isn't really keeping up with his laundry. He flicks me half a glance from the doorway, then steps aside to clear the lines of fire from me to six Studio Security spec-ops guys, who block the door open and cover me with smartgrip power rifles.

Six. That's almost respect.

Spec-ops secmen. Y'know, it never really struck me how weirdly wrong it actually is to have highly trained, highly motivated special-operations troopers—we recruit from the Social Police—to keep order in an entertainment company. On the other hand, considering the specific entertainment we produced, maybe it's not weird, or wrong either. These particular guys wear the shimmery cardinal-red body armor and the silver moiré helmets of Artan Guards—anti-magick gear.

Interesting. Because if you think you need a defense . . .

.Before I can fully parse the various implications, a couple of Workers roll in a cart that carries a small console with a screen and I.V. stands, like a morphine pump, except I have considerable experience with narcotic painkillers and I know for damn sure that a standard morphine solution doesn't look anything like the iridescent black goo that fills the four bags on the cart, and it's only when one of the Workers plugs a line into my feeding tube's shunt that I finally click on what that shit reminds me of.

Fuck me inside out.

"Simon?" He's out of sight in the corridor. "What's going on? Are we still on Earth?"

Because if that's what it looks like, it shouldn't even exist . . . but the secmen carry power rifles, which don't work on Home . . .

This is beyond me.

"Uh—" A wet-sounding cough as he comes back in. "Yes. Earth. Mostly."

I roll my eyes up at the bags of black goo. "And what's that shit?"

"I . . . have been told, I mean, they said you'd know what it is."

My eyes roll closed and my head drops back onto the pillow. "This just keeps getting better."

"I know it's upsetting—"

"Fuck upsetting. I thought I might be useful for something more than firewood."

"I—we, ah, I mean, nobody wants to do that. It's not supposed to kill you. It's not supposed to even hurt."

"Yeah, tell me another."

Faller gives a resigned nod that's barely more than essential tremor. He comes over by me and picks up the hand unit. "Here. You control it. Nobody else."

It really is like a morphine pump—just a handle with a button switch that'll dispense a measured amount of black shit into my bloodstream. "So, what, it's an assisted suicide thing?"

Faller gives me an exhausted shrug. "I don't know, Caine. Hari. I don't know anything. I just do what they tell me."

"And how's that working out for you?"

"Could be worse." He smiles, just a bit. "I could be the cripple strip-cuffed to a restraint bed with a crude oil I.V."

"There's crippled and there's crippled, Simon." He doesn't ask me to explain, so I don't. "What happens now?"

Another sigh. He's barely vertical, bracing himself on my bedrail. "Right. Ah, that offer you made to the Board of Governors—guaranteed permanent Overworld access in exchange for amnesty and a job—"

"Yeah, I was there. What about it?"

"Well . . . this is, uh—I guess you'd call it," Faller says reluctantly as he turns my bed so I can see out the window, "their counteroffer."

"Wow." I blink, and then I blink again, but it's all still out there. "I mean, wow."

The landscape's grim: blasted hills and rock bleached white enough to hurt my eyes and not one living thing except for about a division of Social Police manning hardened bunkers and pointing everything from radar-directed sea whiz cannon to railguns to turret-mounted sixteen-fucking-inch guns out over the dead moonscape or up into the empty sky.

Honest-to-fuck *artillery*.

And the sky isn't empty. Not when I really look. Way up high, it's actually kind of crowded, what with all the shiny pinpoints that are probably the latest generation of riot cars.

Faller coughs behind my head. "The, ah, Social Police are, I guess, hoping to deter a rescue attempt. Or, ah, escape."

"Somebody did mention to them that I can't walk, right?"

"They—uh, they like to be thorough."

"And escape to where? Jesus, look at that shit."

I nod out toward the ragged hills rising in the middle distance: only the colors of stone and dirt. "There's nothing out there. Not even sagebrush or cactus or any other goddamn thing. What the hell is this, the Korean Peninsula?"

"Ah, no. No, we're in North America. We, uh . . . this installation is in the Dakota Badlands."

"Holy shit."

"Yes."

"I've heard—but I never thought it could still—"

"It is. Even now. Hotter than the provincial authority has ever admitted. That's why all the slavelanes divert south. There is nothing alive here that we didn't bring with us."

"I better knit myself some lead underwear."

"Better knit yourself a tank."

Wait . . . the Dakota Badlands . . . holy shit again. Holy shittier. "It's the *dil. That's* why this fort's here. That's why *I'm* here. This is the Earth-side face of the *dil T'llan.*"

He shrugs. "No reason to deny it now. Neither of us is going anywhere." Well.

Well well well. Explains the anti-magick shit. And the black oil.

Back outside the window some guys are walking by—what the fuck? No armor . . . and they're *huge* . . . and that color isn't cammo, it's their fucking *skin* . . .

"Holy shit . . ." I can't seem to get my breath. "Ogrilloi . . . ? On Earth? Are you pulling my fucking *dick?*"

"The, ah, Overworld Company has been employing ogrilloi at this facility for, ah—" He coughs harshly, and again, and he wipes his mouth with a handkerchief stained with what looks like blood. "For a while. They, ah, are very reliable. And they need very little upkeep. Mostly meat and beer."

"Has anybody told them how all their little grills are getting slow-roasted every time they take a step out there?"

"Apparently some factor of their genetics makes them resistant. About the worst they can get here is sunburn. And I've never seen an ogrillo with a sunburn."

He's got a point, but—

"And you give them *weapons?* Jesus, what are you, suicidal?" Then I get it. How much damage can ogrilloi do with small arms out here in the Badlands? Kill a few Social Police, maybe an Administrator or two, and that's about it. But heavily armed ogrilloi on Home is a different fucking story. "Orbek's pistol . . . he really did get it in town."

Faller nods tiredly. "Relations have been . . . strained . . . with the Order of Khryl for a long time. Ever since we first opened the gate, in fact. The Board of Governors has been preparing, ah, a contingency plan . . . and following your, ah—the death of the Justiciar—well, as you can imagine, we anticipate that the Order intends to shut down our Homeside operation. Possibly even close the gate—the *dil*—if they can."

"So you cut a side deal with the grills?" It actually makes sense. Too much fucking sense.

The only reason anybody bothers to deal with the Order of Khryl in the first place is their military occupation of the *dil T'llan*. We have to play nice, because they're in place and they have power and they are not to be lightly fucked with—but a few thousand ogrilloi with state-of-the-art training and Home-friendly firearms could kick their armored asses right the fuck off the Battleground.

I don't care how much God loves you. Getting shot in the face with an anti-tank rocket is gonna leave a fucking mark.

With the Order gone, taking with it all that whole Justice and Truth and Knightly Virtue shit that must put a serious cramp in the Company's operation . . . Jesus, we don't even need ogrilloi to work the mines; once we have full control of the *dil T'llan* we can ship a billion Laborers—five billion, more—there practically overnight. No wonder they think they don't need me.

Well, fuck. This could be going better.

"So what's the deal?"

Faller hands me the palmpad. "The docs are in memory. You can read the details for yourself."

"Soon as somebody unstrips my cuffs."

His eyes shift, and his right hand fiddles with a loose button on his jacket, and for a second it's twenty-five years ago and we're waiting for the Black Knives and he's playing with that fucking platinum coin. "Maybe not just yet."

"It's that bad?" I twitch the pump's hand unit. "Worse than this?"

He sighs, scrubbing at his eyes with the heels of his hands. "I'm sorry. I really am."

"Don't. Just . . . don't." I hate when people say they're sorry. "Save that shit for the kiddie matinee."

He nods distractedly. "That story—that whole yarn you spun out for me to feed to the Board of Governors, about what happened in Purthin's Ford—was *any* of it true? Any at all?"

"Every word. True as fucking Gospel. Maybe truer. Whether that's a word or not."

He's too tired to even pretend to believe me. "All right. Um . . ." He drifts off toward the door. "Uh, Director? He's ready for you."

I look down at the palmpad in my lap. Somehow seems too damn light to carry news this bad. Which is when it finally occurs to me to wonder just how bad this news will be.

Something tells me we won't part as friends.

"Uh, Caine? This is the Director of Operations for this installation. I understand you know him."

I look up, and it's Gayle fucking Keller. "Son of a bitch."

Gayle fucking Keller in a full-on formal chlamys-and-chiton, no less. Expensive too. The price of his sandals alone could feed a Labor family for six months. "*Administrator* Keller, is it now?"

"Hello, Hari. I won't pretend I've missed you."

I'll give him that one for free. "You used to be afraid of me."

"I still am."

Huh. "That's . . . unexpectedly forthright."

He clasps his hands together behind his butt and spends a second or two staring at the floor like he's being sent up for life. "I know you disliked me, Hari."

"I won't deny it."

His eyes come up just long enough to register a small, slightly rueful smile. "I know you've publicly registered opinions of me that range from *smug weasel* to *unctuous lying little fuck*. But I don't think even you ever thought me to be stupid, or disloyal."

"You weren't fucking loyal to me."

"I didn't work for you. I was employed by the Studio and the Board of Governors—you may recall discovering you didn't have the authority to fire me. But even though I wasn't employed by him, I was loyal to Arturo Kollberg, because he recognized and rewarded loyalty. He valued me as an assistant and a friend, whereas you—"

Different words, same tune. I wave him off. "Been practicing this conversation for a while?"

Again the oddly sincere flicker of rueful smile. "Almost three years."

There's something off about him that I can't quite capture. "Is it as fun as you expected?"

"Not even a little." Keller sighs. "I won't try to tell you this isn't personal. I know you too well to hope you'll take it any other way. Please understand that I am acting under orders, and that it's not my intention to cause you distress."

"Nobody gives a fuck about your intention."

"I don't expect you to," he says. "You told me once that the only thing to which any man is absolutely loyal is his conception of the obligations of manhood."

"Did I say that? Deeper than my usual."

"Probably quoting someone smarter. But the idea stayed with me. I understand you, I think. In this context at least. Your absolute obligation is to those you love, yes? It's well known. Mine is . . . well, my absolute obligation is to my duty."

He visibly gathers himself. Deep breath, set jaw, white lips. "I have been given a position of considerable power and advantage, bringing wealth and social opportunities beyond my most fanciful dreams. This position also includes certain unfortunate necessities. The fact that these necessities are unfortunate in no way affects my obligation to accomplish them to the best of my ability. To do my job well is worth my life. It's the only thing that gives my life meaning, or even value. Does this make sense to you?"

"You'd have made a pretty good Knight of Khryl."

"I know you don't mean that as a compliment, but I take it as one."

He gives me a straight-on level stare, rigidly solemn, like he's clenching to control an impulse to flinch. "I've never been a brave man. That hasn't changed. Not much, anyway. Violence terrifies me. I'm afraid to be hurt. I'm afraid to die. Especially in ways you have hurt and killed other men."

"So okay, you're right about not being stupid."

"The Board of Governors has full confidence in the Social Police—more perhaps than the Social Police have in themselves. They are confident that you are no longer a threat to anyone, much less me." Again he sighs, and now he looks down. "They don't know you like I do."

Ah, I get it now: he's telling the truth. That's the thing that's off about him. Somebody gave him an integrity transplant.

Huh again. "Careful, Gayle. Keep that shit up and I might decide I don't hate you anymore."

"That's . . . sort of what I'm hoping for."

"What, you're worried I'll think badly of you?"

"I'm worried you'll kill me." He starts coughing and looks away, out the window somewhere until he pulls himself back together. "That's why I wanted to talk this through before we go any further. Because you once told Professional Faller, ah, *I'm not gonna wreck you just for doing your job, man* . . . mm, verbatim. I believe."

"Like that, is it?"

"I have no authority to make any threat or offer any relief. I am here to fulfill the directives of the Board and the Leisure Congress. As soon as I discharge my duty here, I'll go back to my office and do whatever is necessary to carry out the task I've been given."

"I told you, I get it. Look, Gayle, for what it's worth, I really won't kill you just for doing your job."

He catches his breath. "Thanks. Thank you, Hari. Even though I know you might find another reason. Or that there need not be a reason at all."

"I thought that was understood."

"Apparently it was." His smile is weak and kind of blurry, but it seems real enough. "Professional? Go ahead, please."

Faller moves close to my bed and touches a control surface on the rim of the palmpad. The screen lights up with a page of standard-looking contract shit. "Like I said, the documents are in memory. The Board of Governors has directed us to summarize it for you, and confirm that there is no misunderstanding. The summary is, well—the Board of Governors have . . . um, their counteroffer is, basically . . . no."

"I worked that out for myself."

"You will not be given the title of Director of Overworld Operations. You are, as of this notice, stripped of the title and privileges of Administration, and downcasted to Labor. You will not receive amnesty or immunity from prosecution for any activity you have performed in the past or may perform in the future. You will not return to Overworld—er, Home. Ever."

"That's a ballsy opener."

"The Board presented their resolution to the Leisure Congress. It was approved by acclamation."

"So much for my fan club."

"You closed Overworld," he says apologetically. "Even your fans want you hurt."

"There's more?"

He nods. "Laborer Michaelson, you are directed to consult on, and cooperate with, any and every Overworld Company operation that requests your attention until the Board determines you have successfully concluded your assignment. If at any time the Board judges success to be impossible, or that you have engaged in deliberate obstruction or sabotage of this project, or that you no longer have anything of value to contribute, you will be remanded to the Social Police for trial, followed by summary execution for Forcible Contact Upcaste in the murder of Leisureman Marc Vilo."

"A trial? Seriously?"

"It's a formality."

"Oh, that makes it okay, then." I look over at Gayle. "Don't these idiots remember what happens when they try to bully me?"

"I'm sure they do," he says. "I believe they don't expect you to be intimidated; I believe they only wish the parameters of your situation to be entirely clear. I believe they expect that once you understand, you'll choose to join them. Of your own free will."

"Seems unlikely."

"It's not my plan."

I'll give him that one too. "I've had more attractive offers. Slavery and execution kind of leaves out the whole idea of, y'know, sweeteners."

"My understanding is that it's not supposed to be attractive. Just the opposite. It's supposed to make the alternative attractive."

"Oh, there's an alternative now?"

"There always has been, Hari," Gayle says solemnly. "Here, though, it's a little more straightforward. You might say, *unexpectedly forthright*. Because the laws of physics here are just a bit different from most of the rest of Earth. Do this one thing, and everything Professional Faller has detailed goes away. We can all be friends."

"That seems more unlikely."

"The switch in your hand, Hari." Gayle nods at the I.V. pump. "All you have to do is press the button."

Eventually I manage to pick up my jaw. "You are batshit fucking insane."

"No. And I'm not joking."

"Do you know what this shit *is*?"

"Not precisely. Neither do you. I suspect our superiors have a more complete comprehension. I know what it does. And I have been told that if you don't accept it—that is to say, if you hit the button without fully consenting to the terms—the substance will kill you. In a spectacularly painful fashion. The specific phrase was, *if he does not say yes*. Do you understand?"

"Oh, sure. I get it. You know, the first time I saw this shit it was burning Ankhana to the ground."

"I'm familiar with the history."

"They want to make me into . . . whatever the fuck Kollberg was."

"One more thing you'll have in common."

"This was what you were talking about all along. You weren't talking about enlisting . . . you want to make me *part* of that sick hungry mindless fucking *thing*—"

"Your father called it the Blind God, yes. It's not, though. Blind. Not at all. Nor mindless, unless we allow it to be."

"It's not? *You're* not. That's what you mean. I can fucking smell it on you. It's in you. You're in them."

And that's the integrity transplant right there: he has no fear of shame, no fear of humiliation, no self-pity, none of the resentments and weaknesses that defined his life. Now the only way to hurt him is to *hurt* him. Physical fear is the only one he has left.

Kris said each of us is the sum of our scars. Dad used to say we are defined by what we fear. "Jesus to fuck and back again, Gayle—did you somehow miss what happened to Kollberg? How could you do this to yourself?"

"It was my duty."

"Holy shit."

"I'm not entirely sure why it frightens you," he said. "You don't get lost in it, Hari. I'm still me. But I'm part of something greater now."

"Tell it to Kollberg."

Even this Gayle takes with only a thoughtful nod. "Administrator Kollberg is not a . . . representative example. The events surrounding his breakdown left his mind, ah, fragile. Exceedingly fragile."

"It wasn't too sturdy before."

"The belief was that his expertise in Studio operations, and intimate acquaintance with your career, would on balance make him an asset. But—" He turns up his hands. "—everyone makes mistakes, yes?"

I turn the switch over in my hand. I imagine my face must look like I'm holding a handful of radioactive weasel shit. "The more I think about this, the more I'm liking the slavery-and-execution option."

Gayle nods to this too, with a tiny sigh of regret. "Professional Faller, if you don't mind—?"

"This is . . . the rest of their offer." Faller's grey as his suit. Dark swipes underline his eyes like smears of dried blood. He touches a control surface on the palmpad's casing. "Look at this."

The screen changes. At first I can't make sense of it. A tangle of tubes and wires go into and out from some kind of mannequin, a Halloween decoration–looking thing, a plastic ghoul, shriveled and corpse-white, hairless parchment skin glued over jutting bones, empty eye sockets sprouting twists of cable like fiber-optic tears. "So?"

"Look again. It's not easy to see," he says faintly. "Because . . . well, you don't *want* to, you follow?"

I look again. After a second or two, I catch motion: the image isn't a still—faint color-shifts flow along a tube here or there, and the white plastic eye sockets . . . *twitch* . . . the echo of a blink pressing flesh around the cables . . .

Acid creeps up the back of my throat. "It's alive."

"Yes."

"What the fuck is this thing?"

"It's a Worker."

"Yeah?" Workers aren't good for anything complex; the cyborging shorts out higher brain function. "What kind of work does anybody get out of that?"

"Data processing." Faller's voice goes thick, like he's trying not to gag. "I was told that . . . this *unit* . . . is part of the Social Police signal-filter complex."

My mouth's so dry I can't even swallow the up-trickle of acid. "This is the stick, huh? Wire me up so I don't have a choice?"

"It's worse than that. Michaelson . . . Hari . . ." Faller's voice falls like he's praying. Maybe he is.

Maybe his god is kinder than mine.

"You're still not *seeing*. Because . . . because like I said, you don't want to. It's your mind, not your eyes."

"What, some kind of, whateverthefuck, psychological defense mechanism or some fucking thing? Because if I ever had any, they broke a long time ago. Burned down, fell over, and sank into the swamp."

No answer. No response at all. The face on the screen . . .

There's something about the way the hairless brow arches down to join the cheekbone . . . if those wires weren't in the way, I would have seen it already. This Worker used to be somebody I know.

It's not all that easy to pick out a face, not when it's somebody dead. Who you think is dead. Someone whose head's been shaved, even the eyebrows and eyelashes. Somebody whose flesh has melted away with age and starvation and whose eyes have been ripped out to make room for cables, and my fingers go numb and my legs, they go numb too and their weight drags at me, hauls me down through the bed, through the deck, freefall into the earth. Into the bedrock. "Him? That's *him*? *That*?"

"I'm sorry."

When the Social Police came for him the final time, that night at the Abbey . . . standing on the marble threshold of my marble archway, helpless in the moonlight, watching them load him into the back of a detention van on my front lawn . . .

No good-byes. The digivoder that had been his only voice lay in pieces on the floor beside his bed, crushed under a soapy's boot heel . . . His nurse at my shoulder . . . I remember asking, faintly, my lips numb and clumsy—

How long do you think he has?

Bradlee Wing, faithful Bradlee, who I haven't thought of in forever, maybe not since that same night—*He probably won't even survive the cyborg conversion.*

Yeah.

If he survives the operation, though . . . they'll probably hardwire him for data processing. He might live for years.

One apologetic cough.

Not that you'd, uh, want him to, y'know. Not like that . . .

Out on my lawn, in the grip of the Social Police, he had rolled his head toward me. He had lifted his twisted hand—his last voluntary function, not quite destroyed by his disease—and he had touched his head, and made a weak patting motion, and then walked his crippled fingers slowly up the chrome bedrail of his travel couch. The last thing he ever said to me.

Keep your head down, and inch toward daylight.

He hadn't kept his down far enough, and now wires come out of his eye sockets.

"He's alive. Sort of," I murmur, numb and stupid, knocked flat sideways by the way shit seems to come at me from all over at once.

"Oh yes," Gayle says. "I have been instructed to emphasize to you that the network into which he is wired is the Social Police global data mine—that his brain is being used to filter electronic chatter and flag potentially seditious communications."

This time I can't make my mouth form my fading mental echo of *holy shit* . . .

Using Dad to track down everybody who is anything like what he used to be. It takes my fucking breath away. It's like Raithe. Like Raithe and Shanna. Worse.

It's a stroke of evil motherfucking genius.

Gayle nods as if he can read my mind. "You should understand that the ingenuity of their malice is functionally infinite."

I don't answer. I can't answer.

"While surrender is painful and humiliating, refusal will be worse," Gayle says. "Do you understand? They know your, ah, your absolute. Your obligation of manhood. And they are willing to use it in any necessary way."

This pulls me back up to the surface of the swamp in my head. "So, what, if I screw with them, they kill him? Some threat."

"No. If you don't cooperate . . ." He looks at me then, and his eyes go as dead as mine feel. "If you screw with them, they *won't* kill him."

Oh. Of course.

That makes more sense.

"In fact," Gayle says gently, almost delicately, just like Vinson Garrette, "they'll wake him up."

Sure. What else?

Didn't matter. None of it mattered. None of it changed anything at all.

Except . . .

Dad.

Of course Dad. It's always been Dad. How could I think it would ever be anyone or anything else? He was right: I am defined by fear.

My fear is him.

Not fear of him—I got over that before I was ten years old. Fear I might *be* him. Sick. Crazy. Locked inside a body that doesn't belong to me anymore.

Alone with my rage.

Maybe that's why I never gave a shit about tossing my life into whatever the next fight was. Is.

People who say there's no such thing as a fate worse than death should try telling that to Dad. I don't know if his ears still work, but if they don't you're out of luck. It's not like you can draw him a fucking picture.

Funny how they understand me so well.

I take a deep breath. "Okay."

Faller blinks. "What?"

"I said *okay*. Need me to spell it? Here, watch."

I jam my thumb onto the switch. Black oil rolls down toward my feeding tube.

It doesn't feel like anything at all.

"Hey, I've got one last question." I look from Faller to Gayle and back again. "Who's your favorite character in *To Kill a Mockingbird*?"

the now of always

WHAT DREAMS MAY COME

"I have this dream, y'know? More like a fantasy. That once, just once, somebody I care about is in trouble, and when I show up to help, they're actually happy to see me."

—DOMINIC SHADE
  Caine Black Knife

He walks through a universe of white.

Snow . . .

He can't remember the last time he saw snow.

It falls gently as a child's kiss. Flakes twist and tumble and alight with the hushy whisper of raindrops on tiptoe. With each footstep, he feels a crunch too discreetly crisp to make sound.

He feels this crunch because his feet are bare. His legs as well, and groin and chest and head—entirely naked—yet he feels no chill at all. A dream, then. He understands how this works. No matter how cold this landscape, he's warm in bed somewhere entirely else.

Obviously a dream. It's been more than twenty years since he last could walk.

He might so easily lose himself in the glorious play of muscle and bone and blood and breath, but he's dreamed of walking for years; he can't pretend he doesn't know what waking will inflict.

He's been walking a long time, and has come very far. How long and how far is, in the way of dreams, impossible to know, but now a shadow looms in the white before him and becomes a silhouette—a cottage-size round with a conical top.

His experienced eye automatically identifies it: a yurt, too tall and the roof too steeply pitched for Mongolian, and as he approaches it comes clearer and he nods to himself. More west-central Asian, Khazakh perhaps: lucky. His graduate study had required a thorough grounding in Old Turkic and its linguistic descendants; he can make himself understood to speakers of more than a dozen north-central Asian languages, from Altay to Uyghur, while the Mongolic group always seemed to trip him up.

The yurt rotates, or he circles it; either way, he understands that this has been his destination all along.

To end something, or begin something, or both.

The entryway moves into view, and night has fallen without his noting the change. Now his only light is sanguine fireglow leaking through a gap in the layered felt. Not Khazakh after all; no upland nomad would be so careless with his home's warmth on a night such as this.

He discovers he's looking forward to seeing who's within.

He draws breath to announce himself, but hesitates, obscurely embarrassed to speak before he knows what language is appropriate. So instead he reaches for the thin slice of light; the interior furnishings will tell him everything he needs to know.

"You can't go in."

He stops, frowning. The voice had been low, a flatly affectless growl, close behind his shoulder, but he doesn't startle. The frown deepens. He hadn't startled because he'd already known he was not alone.

Slowly he turns toward the infinite night. "You speak English."

"So do you." A shadow assembles itself from the darkness. "Come over by the fire."

The shadow shifts to his left. Beyond it now he sees what had limned this silhouette: a small fire within a ring of stones, beneath a hide canopy to shield it against the snow.

"I apologize," he says. "I did not intend to trespass on your land, nor to presume upon your hospitality, nor to give offense of any sort."

"You haven't." A shadow backhand lazily waves in the yurt's direction. "That's your place."

"Mine?" Again he frowns, as he considers this; it seems he had somehow known that too. "Then why can't I go in?"

"Because I said so. Come on." The shadow beckons him toward the fire. "Put on your clothes."

"I'm not cold."

"Clothes aren't just for warmth."

Under the canopy—bison hide laced together with leather thongs, he notes automatically without stopping to wonder at how this came to be when bison have been extinct for more than a century—he finds a small rack improvised of sunbleached ribs and thigh bones bound together with sinew, and on the rack hang a wool serape and breeches. Nearby are tough, well-worn leather boots.

As he clothes himself, he speaks with his face toward the fire. "Do I know you?"

"You think you do."

"Your voice seems familiar."

"It would."

The soft prickle of the fire-warmed wool against his skin is the most exquisite sensation he can remember ever having felt. "Thank you. I get tired of being naked."

"Everybody does."

Another pair of bone racks support a long spit above the flames. "Is there food?"

"Are you hungry?"

He gives this question solemn consideration. "No. But I think I will be."

"When you're hungry, there'll be food."

He nods. "Where are we? What is this place?"

"Complicated."

"I don't understand."

"I know."

"What are you doing here?"

"Waiting for you."

"You say that like it's been a long time."

The shadow nods abstracted agreement. "Mostly forever."

"Will you come to the fire? I know your voice. I *know* I know your voice. But somehow I need to see you."

"Sit down."

"What?"

"Sit down. Right where you are."

He looks down. A thick pile of skins and pelts lies at his feet. "All right," he says, and sits.

"That's your side." A form gathers itself from snow and night. "This is my side. You're not allowed on my side. I won't come onto yours."

He finds himself nodding. "So there are rules."

"There are always rules."

"All right. Good. Figuring out rules is what I do."

"Not anymore."

The form reaches firelight beneath the canopy and the strange place and strange clothing and the white in the man's hair and beard mean nothing at all because the face is one he knows better than he knows his own. "Hari!"

He lurches to his feet, to lunge across the flames and gather his son into his arms. "Hari, my *God*—!"

"Don't."

"But—"

"Rules." His voice is dark and flat and promises to match the death behind his eyes. "Look at what's between us."

He follows the gesture, and squints down at the spit over the campfire. Unlike anything else he has found in this place, it's not stone nor bone nor any other natural thing.

It's a sword.

Long and black and lethal, lacking art, lacking grace, lacking beauty: a purely functional tool for killing. "What the hell—?"

"Touch the pommel. *Don't* pick it up. Touch it."

He does—gingerly, because the blade has been licked by the campfire flames for an unknown span, and thus might be hot enough for third-degree burns, but it does not burn his fingers and wonder blossoms within him. "It's not even *warm* . . ."

More than that: it trickles ice into his veins and up his spine and now, finally, fully dressed and standing before a crackling fire, he feels the cold.

"I'm on this side. You're on that side. The sword stays between us."

"Until when?"

"Until I pick it up."

He shakes his head, baffled. "Help me out a little, Killer. This all—"

"*Don't.*" The word comes out flat and hard and final as the chop of an axe into oak. The scar across his nose flares red as blood. Bad temper runs in his family. "Don't call me that. Ever."

He goes still. "I didn't mean anything by it."

"My father called me Killer."

"But Hari, I *am* your—"

"My father's dead. Your son, your Hari, is . . . somebody else. If he exists at all."

"All right. Just calm down, all right? We'll sit, can we?"

"Yeah. Yeah, sorry." A long slow breath and a lowered head. "This isn't exactly easy for me either."

The two men seated themselves on opposite sides of the fire, the sword of black ice between them. "So what should I call you? Is it all right if I call you Hari?"

"I've been going by Jonathan Fist. Deals I make turn out badly."

"Jonathan . . ." he murmurs slowly, squinting, because he should recognize it . . . and then he catches the pun and it lights him up and sparks a grin. "Oh. Jonathan Fist. Nice."

"Should have figured if anybody'd get it, it'd be you."

"We read it together. Remember?"

"I read it with *my* dad."

"Is that a meaningful distinction?"

"If I say it is."

"Stubborn child. What, then? Am I your Mephistopheles?"

"More like the other way around."

"Oh, please. A rhetorical inversion so obvious barely rises even to the level of trite—and your carefully cultivated Outlaw Loner persona may impress the tourists, but remember who you're talking to."

"Stop. Just stop. This isn't anthropology."

"Are you sure?" He offers a preparatory chuckle. "You know what anthropology is?"

"Whatever an anthropologist says it is, yeah, I remember. But I didn't hear it from you."

He settles comfortably into his pallet of skins. Here and now he is as happy as he has ever been. He regrets only that eventually he'll wake up. "If I'm not your father, who am I?"

The other inclines his head just enough to send a skeptical look through the fringe of his eyebrows. "How old are you?"

"I don't know. What year is this?"

"It's not. How old do you remember being?"

He shrugs. "I remember my seventy-fifth birthday. The autographed Twain. I remember you reading to me."

"Look at your hands."

He doesn't bother. "Hari, being able to walk was clue enough. I only hope I remember this when I wake up—the imagery suggests a complexity of Jungian ideation I've never even—"

"You won't wake up. It's not a dream."

He chuckles tolerantly. "Of course you'd say so."

"And I do."

"You say I'm dead. Is this then some style of afterlife?"

"I said my father's dead."

"Ah, I see. I'm not him. Some comfort in that, I suppose. This is a bit bleak to be Heaven, and one assumes, pacé Sartre, Hell to be—"

"Look, I'll call you Duncan." He looks down at his own hands then, and muscle bunches along his jaw. "I guess you should call me Caine."

A shock like he's touched the sword again ripples through him and crests and breaks like a wave over his head. "I don't much like the feel of this now."

"It gets worse from here."

"I'm sorry." His eyes sting, and his voice is a naked whisper. "I'm so sorry, Hari. You should never have had to be Caine. I should have—"

"You and me, Duncan, we don't get should. We get is. We have to make do."

"If this isn't a dream or my afterlife, what is it?"

"Complicated."

He finds himself nodding again. "Maybe you should start at the beginning."

"There isn't a beginning. That's part of the problem." Caine meets Duncan's eyes across the flames. "There isn't a beginning because time doesn't work that way. Not anymore."

"It *has* to."

"Yeah, well, that's the other part."

"So . . ."

"I can't explain it. Language fails. The easiest way to think of it is that everything happens right now. Even though it doesn't. Consequences can precede causes. There are causes that have effects only when they never happen."

"Chaos."

"Something like that."

"I mean primordial Chaos. Mythological Chaos. The Void before the Word. Gunningagap. Tiamat."

"Yeah, okay, so exactly like that. Maggots on a dead cow, whateverthefuck. The universe is broken."

"Broken."

"Yeah. It wouldn't be too far off true to say I'm the guy who broke it."

He tries not to openly scoff. "You take such pride in styling yourself a legendary bad man."

"It's not pride."

"You've always insisted on the lion's portion of existential guilt. It's a romantic pose. More properly: a Romantic pose. A Byronically doomed anti-hero. A dual gold medalist in the Rotten Bastard Olympics, in the events of I Don't Give a Shit Who Gets Hurt, and Can't You See How I Suffer for You."

"And people wonder where I get my mean streak."

"The transactional persona you present is a slightly modified expression of a well-established literary trope. The Scourge of God. I'm surprised that isn't one of your epithets."

"Scourge of God. Huh, funny. I'd forgotten that one."

"Yet it's the foundation of your image nonetheless."

"Yeah, except no." He shakes his head. "It's not God's hand on the whip."

"So." Duncan sits up straighter, and crosses his legs in a tailor seat, hands resting on his knees. "The universe is broken. I presume this damage is related somehow to my being here."

"Yeah. But not in the way you think."

"So: granting it's broken, how do we fix it?"

"That's what I meant." A chuckle harsh and inhuman as the scrape of bricks. "Who said it can be fixed?"

Duncan finds he has nothing to say.

"We're not here to fix anything. We're here for me to ask a question, and you to answer it."

Duncan coughs the clench out of his throat. "All right."

"It's a simple question. A simple answer."

"Isn't it you who likes to say that when someone tells you a matter is simple, he's trying to sell you something?"

"Sure. I just usually put in *shit* and a *fuck* or two. The question's simple. The situation isn't." He shifts his weight and draws breath to speak, only to sigh it out without words.

And does so the second time he tries, and the third.

"It's all right, ah, Caine. I can see this is difficult for you. Take your time."

"It's not difficult. It's fucking terrifying. Look, you're hip to Schrödinger's cat, right?"

"Quantum superposition, yes. I recall you referencing that thought-experiment during the climax of *For Love of Pallas Ril*—and incorrectly, in fact; Schrödinger's quantum-mechanically threatened cat is alive and dead at the same time. In the context you meant it, a more appropriate metaphor would have come from chaos science, as you were adding energy to an unstable resting state in a chaotic system—"

"Yeah, yeah, sure. My early education suffered a little from my only teacher being batshit insane twenty-three hours a day. Except when it was twenty-four. Fucking sue me."

Duncan lowers his head. "If words could only express how—"

"Forget about it. It's not like it was up to you. It's not like it was you at all."

"I still don't understand what you mean by that."

"Look, where we are—what we're doing here . . . it's more like the *real* Schrödinger's fucking cat thing. You and me—and about fifteen billion other people—we're alive and we're dead. We're plucking harps in Heaven and getting ass-raped with red-hot razors in Hell. At the same time. Right now, right here, you and I, we're inside the box. We kind of *are* the box. So as long as nobody opens us, all consequences are only potential."

"But opening it—us—makes everything real."

"Yeah."

"What kind of consequences are we talking about?"

"Dunno." He frowns. "We can't know. That's kind of the point."

"Because we're the box. Your question and my answer—that's what opens us?"

"Pretty much." He shrugs irritably. "It's just a fucking metaphor."

"A metaphor." Duncan looks down into the fire. His frown is identical to Caine's. "None of the rules of this place preclude me taking time to think it over, do they?"

"No. And don't worry about what you say. This isn't one of your goddamn culture hero sagas. There's no trick. No trap. I just want to know."

"Uncommonly forthright."

"There's no advantage in deception."

"Interesting."

"Imagine for a second that you could take back the worst thing you've ever done."

Duncan's heart curdles, and his response is only an empty echo.

"The worst thing I've ever done . . ."

"Yeah. What if you could? Make it unhappen. Vanish it into the time-stream of shit nobody ever did."

Duncan jerks upright. "Do you mean it?"

Across the campfire, all Duncan sees in Caine's eyes is flame.

"I am serious as a knife in the nuts. This isn't a place for jokes. Or for lies."

"Worst on what measure? Worse in what terms? Do you mean sin? Evil? Regret? Harm to others? Harm to myself?"

"It's not that complicated. *Worst* is just a figure of speech. Pick something you wish you hadn't done, or one thing you wish you had. You don't even have to tell me what it is. One choice you wish you could reverse. If you could, would you?"

"At what price?"

"Ay, there's the rub."

"Oh, it's like that, is it?"

"Everything is. Th' undiscovered country, from whose borne no traveler returns and all that shit. Hamlet had it wrong. It's not death. It's the future."

"Still—what I would give if only I could—"

The other raises one scarred hand, palm forward. "Before you answer, I need to tell you that it's not just about you. You follow? Sure, trade your hope of Heaven for eternal torments in Hell, whatever. That's your business. But it's not just you. Or even mostly you."

Duncan tilted his head. "I am professionally skeptical of the prospects of an afterlife."

"It's just a metaphor, right? Or maybe it isn't. The choice you make might rip open the lives of millions of people who never get a choice of their own. The price might be bad for you, sure. It might be worse for everybody else. If you're wrong about the afterlife, you might be sending, say, a billion children to burn forever in a lake of fire. Or screw the afterlife, and just say those billion kids are instead afflicted with hallucinations of being tortured by demons so they tear at their own flesh until they claw their eyes out and die screaming of brain infections."

"I don't envy your imagination."

"Yeah. Imagination. That's what it is, sure. How about a new strain of, say, vaccine-resistant HRVP?"

Duncan goes silent.

"Or, say, *your* disease. Turn every one of them into an erratic nutjob who'll die trapped in a rotting body, festering in a puddle of his own shit."

He lowers his head and speaks to the fire. "Hari, that's not fair."

"Fair's got nothing to do with it. And I don't go by that name anymore."

"Caine, then. I still can't seem to make this make sense. Are these people at risk if I say yes, or if I say no?"

"Both. Either. That's the point."

"Then how am I supposed to decide?"

"Flip a coin. How the fuck should I know?"

"So your billion children example is . . ."

"It's a nice round number. Take the worst thing you can think of and cube it. That's what might happen."

"Might. Not will. If the potential consequences are the same either way—"

"They're not. The only thing they have in common is that we don't know shit about what any of them are. We *can't* know. You might destroy the universe. You might send every living being to an eternal playdate on the Big Rock Candy fucking Mountain. Or you might not do much at all, and we're going through all this shit for nothing. Or anything in between. And I mean *anything*."

Duncan nods. This is starting to make sense. "Choice as an absolute, then. Choice as a thing-in-itself. The Law of Unknowable Consequence."

"More or less."

" 'Fuck the city,' " Duncan says softly. " 'I'd burn the world to save her.' "

"Yeah . . ." Caine mutters, hushed and hoarse. "I had a feeling you might bring up that one."

"Isn't that what you're asking me to do?"

His gaze shifts down to his knuckles, as it always does when he's in pain. Or ashamed. "At the time, I thought I was telling the truth."

Duncan's mouth draws down at the corners. "I thought you were too."

"Except when it got real, it was the other way around."

"I don't like the sound of that."

"Me neither."

"Hari . . . what *happened*? Is she—?"

"A while ago."

"But how . . . ?"

Another shrug. "Instead of burning the world to save her, I burned her to save the world."

"You sacrificed *Shanna*?"

"Not on purpose."

"Hari, I'm so sorry—"

"Everybody's fucking sorry." His face twists and his eyes drift shut. "Yeah, um, look. Now *I'm* sorry. I thought I was a little more over it. It just—uh, it was kind of . . . vivid."

"Ah . . ." Duncan says. "Ah, I think I understand."

"Cut in half, pretty much." Caine nods into the campfire. "With a sword a lot like that one there. A piece of her fell on me."

"I'm sorry . . ." A whisper. "Hari, I'm so—"

"Yeah, thanks." Their eyes meet across the flames. "At least I didn't kill her myself."

Duncan lowers his head. He hugs his knees to his chest and rests his forehead on them. "I think I'm done talking for a while."

In time, morning gathers itself beyond their buffalo-hide canopy, the light colder, grey as the sky. The snow flees with the night, and Duncan can finally see where they are: on the lip of an escarpment, overlooking a panorama of raddled badland. Something about it—he can't say what—is familiar, and that mysterious familiarity draws him to his feet.

Cautiously he wades out toward the brink, moving slowly, feeling his way, conscious that snow cover might make the verge deceptive. He now can see down the face, and below is a curious jumble, too regular to be scree, sloping gradually out toward the badland floor. Had there been people down there, or even a few chimneys releasing smoke, he would have thought it to be some sort of cliff city, like the Anasazi ruins . . .

"Oh," he says. "Oh, of course."

This too he somehow must have known already.

"Hari—I mean, Caine. This is it, isn't it? The place. The vertical city in *Retreat from the Boedecken*."

The voice comes from just behind his left shoulder. "Yeah, it's the place."

"So that's what this is about."

"No."

"What you did here—"

"Is not what this is about."

He turns. "This wasn't the worst thing you've ever done?"

Caine's right behind him, only fractionally on his own side. His eyes are cold as the sky. "Not even close."

"Would you take it back, if you could?"

"This? Are you kidding?"

"Curious, more."

"You never did have a sense of humor."

"Still . . ."

"Sorry. Thought it was clear. The answer's no." Caine gives a head shake that's half eye roll. "More like *fuck* no."

"All those cubs. The infants. The juveniles."

Caine walks back toward the campfire. "You think if you just keep asking, eventually you'll get the answer you want?"

Duncan stiffens, stung. "An ungenerous sentiment."

"It's a lot more generous than *shut the fuck up*. Which is what it meant."

"You're angry."

"I always was. Just not with you."

"Are you angry with me now?"

"Just—" He lifts a *fucking stop it* hand without looking back. "Just don't talk to me like you understand. Like you know how it is to have done what I've done. To have survived what I've survived. Like you can even imagine."

"One of the things you survived was me."

"No." Caine wheels and slices the air between them with a near-invisible blur that is the edge of the hand he'd raised. "That's what I mean. It wasn't you."

"Feels like it was me," Duncan says softly. "Hurts like it was me."

Caine's eyes warm a little. His shoulders sag, and he nods. "Yeah, I guess I can see that. And I'm sorry. I'm not here to hurt you. Or to work out my leftover daddy issues. I forgave my real father years ago."

"Is that why I'm here instead?" Duncan wades toward the canopy slowly through the snow. "A father younger than you are. Bigger and stronger than you are. I'm not sick. And—as you keep insisting—the father you forgave isn't me."

"That's not what this is about."

"Are you sure? Are you sure I'm not young and strong and healthy to assuage some unconscious reluctance to beat the shit out of me? We both know I deserve it."

"I don't even know what *deserve* means. I know what people think they mean when they say it. I'm just not sure how it applies to real life."

Duncan spreads his hands. "This is real life?"

"Yeah, well, I'm not all that sure what *real* means either."

He nods. "In the twentieth century, there was a subbranch of analytic philosophy devoted to parsing the structural linguo-psychology of truth claims—"

"This isn't a fucking debate. Or a seminar. Jesus." He shakes his head. "I'd forgotten how fucking aggravating you are."

"You never knew in the first place. Isn't that what you keep telling me? I'm not the Duncan you knew. You're not the Hari I knew. You and I never met before last night."

"Be whoever you want. Answer the fucking question."

"But doesn't my answer have a sensitive dependence on who I really am?"

"Fucking academics. Quit stalling."

Duncan concedes the point with an apologetic nod. "So if I understand the question, the choice is either to leave the world—the universe, reality, whatever—as it is, in all its darkness and disrepair, or to make, ah, mmm . . . one thing . . . happen the way I wish it had happened." He recovers control of his voice along with his professorial detachment. "Knowing in advance that any consequences, for good or ill or otherwise, are wholly inconceivable."

"More or less."

"It's a Monkey's Paw choice."

"You say that like I might actually know what the fuck you're talking about."

"A short story, three hundred years ago or so. English author, W. W. Jacobs. 'The Monkey's Paw.' Three wishes—three chances to bend fate to your will, yet each brings only horrors. Changing destiny only makes it worse."

"Sure. Except destiny is bullshit, and *worse* depends on who you ask."

"I can see why you'd like to believe so."

"And that matters exactly fucking how?"

Duncan finds himself conceding a point again. "Of course. It's only that . . . I mean, I suppose . . ."

His voice trails away and he lowers himself to the pile of skins beside the campfire. Now he is cold. Weakness creeps along his limbs, and his left hand trembles, and he cannot speak with his eyes open, and so he closes them and gives himself back to darkness.

"I only want to know," he says, very, very softly, "if it's real. If it's true. If I choose to . . . to take it back . . . will it happen?"

His closed eyes burn. Tears trail down his cheeks. "That's all. All I want to know. All I need to know. If I decide to change it, will it change?"

"Maybe."

"Maybe? That's . . . all? After all this? All you can give me is *maybe*?"

"Duncan . . . I thought I was being clear. I guess I wasn't." Caine's voice is low, reluctantly apologetic. "It's not the change whose consequences are unknowable. It's the choice. One possible consequence of the choice is . . . might be . . . that your change can happen. That's all I can give you. That's all there is."

"So you're telling me my choice might destroy the universe . . . for *nothing*?"

"Not for nothing."

"Ah, I see. Of course. Betrayed by my early training." The tears roll thicker now, though his voice is detached and distantly calm, like a kindly professor who continues to lecture through even his most fanciful day-dreams. "This isn't a fairy tale."

"I wish it was."

"Easier for you," he murmurs. "You've never known a world without magick."

"What's that got to do with anything?"

"It's not important. And I don't think I could make you understand." He draws a deep, shuddering breath. "It really is just the choice. The thing-in-itself."

"Yeah. Would you risk the universe to change one thing?"

"God help me . . ." The calm in Duncan's voice chokes on his tears. "You can't . . . I'm only a man. You can't ask me to make this choice. Not if it really counts for something."

"Except I do."

" . . . gods . . ." He finds himself reduced to pleading with figments of other people's imagination. " . . . have mercy . . ."

"No gods here, Duncan. Just you."

He hangs his head. This is not a place for lies.

"Then yes."

His truth is barely a whisper.

"Yes, I would. For even a chance. For the *hope* of a chance."

"Okay. Thanks, Duncan. I appreciate your help. Sorry it had to be like this, but you're the only guy in either universe I can trust to give me good advice."

"What? Advice?" His eyes blink open. "Is that all this is?"

"No."

Caine holds the sword in both hands. If it burns his hands with interstellar cold, he gives no sign.

"Hari . . . ? Hari, what is this? What are you doing?"

"I told you."

Caine lunges with casually brutal expertise. The blade spears through Duncan's sternum and carves his heart in half, and as darkness falls upon his life, he hears only this:

"I don't go by that name anymore."

premise

TIMES THAT BIND

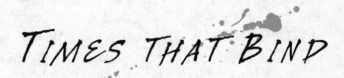

TIMES THAT BIND

"See, the whole point of being a god is that there's no such thing as consequences, right? You don't like how something turned out, you reach into reality and stir it around until you get something you like better."

— POSSIBLY SOMEBODY
Potentially Somewhere

This time, they sit together on a bench in the Railhead, Thorncleft's largest structure, and the headquarters of the Transdeian Heavy Rail Company.

"It's because I'm going to make a deal with your god."

"My god? Ma'elKoth?"

"No. The Black Knife god. Out in the Boedecken. I don't think it has a name."

"So? You say *going to*, hey? Then don't. *Y no hay problema.*"

"It's not that simple, big dog."

Usually, the young ogrillo leans back into a pillar with one leg up and resting on the bench between them, his other foot on the bulging bundle of his pack on the floor. Usually, the man leans forward on his elbows, stares off through the smoky gloom half-lit by dim greenish globes of coal-gas lamps, and speaks in a low, flat voice that draws no attention from idle passersby or the patient fellow passengers who wait there for the Thorncleft Falcon, the express train that speeds to Ankhana and back twice a day.

Usually. Not always.

In the past, this conversation has occasionally taken place in a haze of sleet below the Monastic Embassy in Lower Thorncleft. Several times it has happened among the vast stacks of creosote-soaked timbers waiting for transport to the Battleground Spur, still under construction. Once it was on a cliff-ledge at night, so dark the mountains around weren't even shadows; it might have been nowhere at all, except for the sweet copper scent of freshly spilled blood.

"The deal isn't the problem," the man says. "It might be the solution."

"So?"

"So it might blow up the fucking planet too. Or worse. Or nothing at all, or anything in between. I don't know. I *can't* know."

"You talk too much about what you don't know, little brother."

"Everybody does." A rasp of bitter chuckle. "The difference is I *know* I don't know. Everybody else is blowing smoke out their assholes and they can't even smell fire. See, the thing is, I shouldn't be able to make a deal at all. Not with a god. Especially not with *that* god. But I will. I already have. Even though it hasn't happened yet."

"And that's where you lose me every time."

"Yeah, that's where the mortal brain generally takes it in the butt. The Monasteries have some technical jargon and shit, but even having the right words doesn't help all that much. Look, in the Breaking—the Horror, right?—there came a, kind of, a turning point. I don't know what else to call it. Your guys had us all captured, and you were doing your usual shit, which was torturing people to death. An offering to your god, because the old Black Knives worshipped a demon that was Bound in the vertical city. *By* the vertical city."

"Demon? Just now you say god."

"Same thing. Well, not exactly, but there isn't time to recap the whole Abbey school Intro to Applied Deiology seminar. So look, the top bitches had me nailed to a cross, which is a slow and shitty way to die, and they were doing some other things that weren't much fun either, and I should have died there. All of us should have. Instead I escaped."

"You escaped? From being nailed to a cross? Nice trick."

"Fucking impossible trick." The man hangs his head and sighs. "What happened was, the head bitch took me down herself. Then I killed her and the Studio pulled me out and whatever. You know the rest."

"What, she just lets you go? And stands around while you kill her? How's that work?"

"It was the answer to my prayer."

"You pray? What, Tyshalle gets wet and sloppy for you all of a sudden?"

"No. I prayed to *your* god."

The grey-leather lumps of muscle that serve ogrilloi as eyebrows rippled and knotted. "And why does the Black Knife god give a shit for you?"

"That's one question, but there's one more important. The real one is *how*. Not why. Somehow the god made the head bitch do what I was praying for. That's what the Monasteries call an Intervention, and it's supposed to be impossible. It's exactly what the Covenant of Pirichanthe is supposed to prevent."

"What, gods aren't allowed to do miracles?"

"Exactly. *Exactly*. The power of a god can be expressed *only* through the intercession of a living creature. That's the fundamental principle that underlies the Covenant: a god can grant power or take it away and that's fucking well it. Again, it's complicated—the Monasteries call it *theophanic attunement*, and there's a shitload of variable specifics, but basically the more you're like what the god wants you to be, the more of its power you can channel. So the god doesn't even tell you what to do with its power, because the reason you have the power in the first place is that you're already the kind of person who'd use it the way your god wants you to. You follow?"

"Maybe. Maybe not. Better with nose than with brain, hey?"

"Interventions—what people call miracles—are direct actions by a god. Direct expression of the god's will. An Intervention literally changes reality. That's the problem with gods. Human gods. Ideational Powers, the Monasteries call them. Natural Powers are expressions of natural law. Outside Powers exist beyond reality. More or less in the middle are the gods of humanity. It's kind of like they're half Natural and half Outside. They don't dramatically violate natural law at any given moment, but they exist outside time. Some religions teach that to their gods, time is a dream, which is as good a way of thinking about it as any. A god can choose any moment—past, future, whatever, to them it's all the same—any moment they happen to feel like, then reach in and stir shit up to make something happen somewhen else."

"Somewhen."

"Yeah, I know." The man shrugs apologetically. "Say a god wants to destroy the Railhead here. Say it's pissed at me and wants to make the whole fucking building fall on our heads. Something really spectacular—an earthquake, a meteor strike, whatever—that takes a shitload of power. It's a hell of a lot easier to pick a couple seconds ten years ago and give some poor bastard a heart attack right when he was making some critical load calculation and so here we are, ten years later, and the weight of this ice storm finally overtakes its structural fatigue limits and the whole fucking thing collapses and kills us all. Control the past, control the future."

The ogrillo rolls his eyes toward the ice-packed armorglass vault above. "Just an example, hey? Serious-like."

"It gets worse when there's more than one. Say some other god wants us to live through it, or maybe just wants to fuck with the first one, so he reaches back ten years and has some other guy spot the dead guy's error and correct it, and then the Railhead's sturdy and solid and warm and here we sit. But then the first god can go back and kill the *other* guy, and we're back to being buried in rubble and glass.

"When an assload of gods are fucking with the past so they can control the future, shit goes crazy. Nothing is real. Not for very long. The only thing you can count on is that people are going to get hurt, because the stronger the god, the bigger changes it can make, and the strength of a god is a function of the number and devotion of its worshippers, so priests become evangelical and they start holy wars to burn down other gods' power and the other gods get pissed and shit goes back and forth until the whole universe is the worst fucking nightmare you've ever had. Except nobody never wakes up.

"That's what Panchasell Mithondionne saw coming. That's why he created the *dil T'llan*. But it was too little too late. There were too many of us here already, and when you put enough humans together, one thing you can count on is that pretty soon some smart fucker's gonna start a religion. I think that's why most human creation myths have reality being born from infinite chaos.

"Infinite chaos is exactly where we'd be without Jereth and Jantho of Tyrnall.

"Jantho Ironhand and Jereth Godslaughterer. Brothers. Twins, the story goes. They decided to stop the bullshit, and they were the guys to do it. They might have been gods themselves; some stories have it one way, some the other. In Abbey school, we're taught that their power was *time-binding*—that what made them capable of standing up to the gods was that shit they did was permanent. Even against the gods.

"Jereth carried a weapon they called the Sword of Man. Jantho never used a weapon. Two sides of the same power, right? Jereth the Destroyer. Jantho the Preserver. That's why, at the Monasteries, they want us to master the use of weapons, and to master ourselves, because the real weapon is the weapon we are, and a lot of other metaphorical mystic bullshit. So anyway, Jereth and Jantho take the fight to the gods up close and personal, and they start carving these fuckers up left and right, back to front and top to bottom. To the gods, this comes as a nasty surprise.

"See, the whole point of being a god is that there's no such thing as consequences, right? You don't like how something turned out, you reach into reality and stir it around until you get something you like better.

"So gods start dying. Dying isn't a big deal; lots of gods die and come back to life. Harvest gods, fertility gods, moon gods, sun gods, whatever. But when dead gods *stay* dead . . . well, that's a different thing.

"When the gods realize they might be in actual danger, the gloves come off. They get serious, and millions of people start dying—and dozens of gods, if not hundreds. The turning point comes when it gets so bad that the gods ask for a truce; they send one of their heavy hitters to negotiate terms. This heavy hitter is Khryl, the Lipkan god of personal combat, because the gods aren't stupid and they've figured that if gods Jereth kills stay dead, maybe if a god kills the Godslaughterer, Jereth just might stay dead too.

"Khryl, though, he's also god of honor and justice and virtue and shit. So he can't tell a lie. So the plan the gods come up with is for Khryl to offer his right like he wants to shake hands. *I offer my Hand of Peace. Let there be true peace between us,* right? So He holds His Hand out there without actually giving Jereth permission to touch Him, so when Jereth shakes His Hand, Khryl can punish his presumption by striking him down with a blast of deific spooge or whatever.

"Jereth, though, is a suspicious bastard by nature, and instead of shaking Khryl's Hand he whips out the Sword of Man and lops it off at the wrist. Khryl's Hand falls on the ground, Jereth says, *And I take your hand to demonstrate my wish for all you shitswallowing scumhumpers to fuck off and die. But I'm willing to talk peace. When there is true peace between us, I will happily shove this so far up your ass you can scratch the backs of your eyeballs.*" The man coughs. "I'm, ah, paraphrasing a little here."

"No, really?"

"So this is another nasty shock. Especially for Khryl, who discovers that He can't make His Hand grow back, and neither can any of the other gods.

"Now, there are a couple of conflicting stories about how the Deomachy ends. The Lipkans will tell you that their god of war—Dal'kannith Thousandhand, father of the whole pantheon, including Khryl, patron of Lipke and every fucking thing else—challenges Jereth to single combat to resolve the quarrel, Jereth takes Him up on it and after three days of furious combat on top of a mountain called Pirichanthe, Jereth's own treachery betrays him: the blood of Khryl that stains the Sword of Man eats the blade like acid, Dal'kannith strikes the traitor down, and then magnanimously decrees that the gods will honor an agreement he names after the Glorious Battle—the Covenant of Pirichanthe, which basically is an armed truce. Gods don't fuck with reality, and mortals don't fuck with gods.

"As you probably guess, the Monasteries' version is a little different.

"Our version is that the gods decided to gang up on Jereth all at once and just crush him with numbers. The Monasteries say that Dal'kannith picked up the epithet *Thousandhand* as a metaphoric reference to the thousands of gods he gathered to his side, hoping to slaughter the God-slaughterer without having to face the Sword of Man personally, because, y'know, a god could get hurt doing shit like that.

"Again as you probably guess, I favor the Monasteries' version.

"Jereth and Jantho know they're done for. They have an army of millions, but no mortal force can stand against the massed might of every living god. On the other hand, Jantho's every bit as clever as Jereth is suspicious, and he has this idea to stop the war, a trick that can bind the gods beyond the universe if only somebody can keep their attention long enough for him to pull it off.

"There are a lot of different things Jereth is supposed to have said then. I like to think he just lifted the Sword of Man to check its edge against the sunrise. *How long will you need?* and when Jantho tells him *Mostly forever,* Jereth only shrugs and says, *Done.*

"But, y'know, I made up that dialogue myself. I hate the flowery speech shit.

"What we do know is that Jereth and Jantho dismissed their army. Sent them home to their families for whatever time they might have before their lives are ripped apart into insanity and chaos."

"That's what this is? You send me off home because it's the end of the world?"

"Pretty much."

"Fuck home. My home is *you*, little brother. You think I'm letting you fight this alone?"

"It's not gonna be a fight. There's nothing *to* fight. This isn't something someone is doing. It's just how shit is."

"So? How's it end for your twin god ass-whippers?"

The man shrugs. "They faced the end of their war as they had its beginning: brothers, shoulder to shoulder. Giving their lives to save the world."

"Now, that part I like, hey?" the ogrillo says. "Brothers together."

"We're not them."

"Can die like 'em, though."

"It's a *story*, Orbek. It's not exactly factual."

The young ogrillo shrugs heavy shoulders. "What is it you tell me your sire says about metaphors growing truth?"

"Leave Dad out of it. Look, if fighting could fix this, it would have been over five hundred years ago. Jereth's Revolt would have settled it permanently. I would have died twenty-five years ago, on the cross in the Boedecken, and the Black Knives would rule there right now. But I didn't, and they don't. The whole second half of my life is about whatever fucking deal I'm gonna make with your god. You don't want to be anywhere in the neighborhood. And by *neighborhood* I mean continent."

"When does this deal supposedly happen?"

"Probably soon. I won't know till the god Calls me."

"And what's this deal do, hey? What do you give and what do you get?"

"I wish I knew. One of the things I get is off that fucking cross. I don't know what else. And I don't know what it'll cost."

"A lot you don't know, little brother. You don't know so much, how can you know it's gotta be such a catastrophe?"

"Orbek, Jesus Christ. Who are you talking to?" The man shakes his head, still looking only at the polished marble floor of the Railhead. "You're gonna sit here, Orbek *Black* motherfucking *Knife*, and ask how *I* know I'm about to set off a nuclear shit bomb? Seriously?"

"Maybe I can help."

"Don't. Just go. You got cousins and stuff, family you haven't seen in years. You want to die without ever seeing them again?"

"*You're* family."

"Yeah. That's why I need you to go. Orbek, please." His fists open and he hangs his head. "Please. One person I love has to live through this."

the now of always 2

POWERFUL ENOUGH

POWERFUL ENOUGH

"It's just a fucking metaphor. Don't beat it to death, huh?"

—CAINE

Blade of Tyshalle

*N*onexistence has no duration, and so it is that when Duncan Michaelson opens his eyes, no time has passed.

His son—the man who refuses to be his son—stands over him, silhouetted against a sky so featurelessly blue that it might have been a solid thing within the reach of his hand. Between him and the man who looks like his son stands the plain black blade with its simple crossguard and its salt-stained leather grip.

The blade and the guard and the grip belong to the sword his non-son had driven through his chest into the stone on which he lies, and still pins him there like an insect on a mounting board.

"Does it hurt?" His tone is perfunctory, but his gaze is not.

"Will it matter if it does?"

"It might."

Duncan pauses to examine, with his customary precision, exactly how he feels. "I can feel my sternum scrape up and down the blade when I breathe. I'm pretty sure that should hurt."

"Yeah."

"Mostly, it's cold. I recall from secondhanding your Adventures how cold a blade feels when you're stabbed, but this isn't like that. It's like cold is what it's made from."

" 'Cold is what it's made from.' Huh. I guess that's true enough."

He lowers himself to the snow on Duncan's other side. "Do you understand what's happening? What this place is, and what you're doing here?"

Duncan frowns up at the hilt of the black sword. He feels the beat of his riven heart against the metal. "Well, I'm pretty sure it's not Kansas."

"Can I just mention here how fucking tired I am of that joke?"

"Then you shouldn't use it so often." Duncan shrugs. "Some sort of shamanic dream quest or journey, I suppose. Except I can't actually journey until somebody pulls the sword out of my chest."

"That's the idea."

"What is this sword?"

"It's a metaphor."

"I gathered that. A metaphor for what?"

"Another sword."

"Oh, come on."

"Hey, it's not like I just make this shit up. It is what it is. Just like everything else."

"This other sword," Duncan says patiently. "Is it a metaphor too?"

"Since you ask, yeah."

"For what?"

Caine says, "Me."

"I'm sorry?"

"I know."

"No, I mean—there's a sword that's a *metaphor* for *you*?"

"Sometimes it's the other way around."

"You do understand what language is used for, don't you?"

"You'd be amazed what I understand."

"See? You're doing it again. You use words, but assign no content specific enough to be meaningful. How many times do I have to tell you this? What are words once abstracted from their meaning?"

Caine shrugs. "Music."

Duncan opens his mouth for a biting reply, then closes it again. "You've been saving that one."

"Like you said, you've had this conversation before. So have I." He draws his knees to his chest and wraps his arms around them. "My father told me once that a powerful-enough metaphor grows its own truth."

Duncan nods. "I remember. You asked about the blind god, after you were arrested by the Social Police. Right before they arrested me."

"After the arrest—well, let's just say a lot of shit happened. More than I can tell you about. What happened showed me a lot of the blind god, and it showed me more of me, and for a while I thought I had shit pretty well worked out. Who I was, how the universe worked. What it all meant, sort of. Not just me. Shanna. Faith."

"How is Faith? Is she well? Did you ever pry her loose from Avery Shanks?"

"You know about Faith and Shanks?"

"It was all over the nets the day you were arrested. Is she all right?"

"Mostly. Shanna's death hit her pretty hard, and what happened after hit her harder. But there's a lot of her mother in her. Nobody ever really understood how strong Shanna was. Not even me."

"And Tan'elKoth? A fine mind, and a formidable rhetorical opponent. Is he still at the Curioseum?"

"He's dead."

A dully freezing shock ripples through him, slow and low like a splash in a puddle of slush. Shanna and Tan'elKoth both? He tries to imagine how much that must have hurt him—but then he registers the hard flat grin Caine had turned out toward the brink of the escarpment, and a darker and colder shock breaks over him.

"It was you," he says slowly. "You killed him."

"That metaphorical sword we were talking about? I cut him in half, then jammed it through his face."

"Hari, I'm so—"

Caine turned a blackly glittering stare on him that freezes the word in his throat. "*Hari's* dead too. He died after Shanna. Before Tan'elKoth. And before you ask, yeah. I killed him too."

"Yes. Caine, then. I understand."

"You don't."

Duncan lifts a hand to touch the blade that stands from his chest. It's not even sharp. "You killed Tan'elKoth with this, didn't you?"

"Metaphorically."

"You said Shanna was—"

"Yeah. Same blade. The same blade Berne used to cripple me."

"Kosall?"

"Kosall was the literal blade, yeah. But that's just a detail. The one that counts is the metaphor."

"Which is you."

"That's right. Listen, things are about to get weird around here."

"Says the man who put a few pounds of steel through my heart and then sat down for a friendly chat."

"Yeah, okay. Weirder. Look, do you remember meeting me before? Not Hari, or even Caine. Me. This age. These scars. Forty-some-odd years ago."

Duncan frowns. "Not that I recall. Can you give me a specific context?"

"It was the day Mom died."

This hurts far worse than the sword could have, even were it not a metaphor at all. Hurts worse than anything he can remember feeling. He closes his eyes. "No. I—don't remember very much of that day."

"Okay. Here's the thing: *I* remember meeting me. In the Labor clinic. Some old guy sat down to chat with me—and that old guy was who I am now. Or looked like me, anyway. And my father almost got in a fistfight with him."

"A fistfight? With *Caine?*"

"It wasn't his best day."

"I hate to think what would have become of you if you'd lost us both that day."

"It could still happen."

Duncan goes quiet.

"That's what I mean about shit getting weird. People are going to start showing up here. Some of them might look like people you know, same as how I look like your son. These people will not be who you think they are. Some of them are not friendly. No matter what any of them say or do, don't let anybody pull that sword, all right?"

"How do I stop them?"

"Say no."

"No? Just no?"

"Here, yeah. It's the magick word."

"I thought that was *please.*"

"That's the *magic* word. The point is, that sword won't come out until you decide it can go. And you have to decide who draws it."

"Excalibur in the stone . . ."

"Something like it. Excalibur is another metaphor for the Sword."

"You say that with a capital *S.*"

"Yeah. And Durendal. And the Black Metal Sword. Sauvagine. Kusanagi-no-Tsurugi. Dyrnwyn. Stormbringer. I could go on. It's a long fucking list."

"Then I'm flattered to be stabbed with it."

"It's not a fucking *joke,* Duncan. What is done by the Sword is *absolute.* Get it? God Himself can't change the slightest fucking detail."

The names of legend have awakened Duncan's inner anthropologist. "Is the converse true? That is, as long as the Sword stays where it is, things *can* be changed?"

"Some." Caine hangs his head as if his sigh is a weighted chain around his neck. "It's complicated."

"Okay."

"Look, you need to understand what's at stake here."

"*End of the world* isn't specific enough?"

"The world ended a long time ago. What we're doing here is figuring out what comes after. Forever after, or near as fucking dammit."

"It must be a long story."

"Not so much. It's just that it doesn't always make sense. Or at least, not the kind of sense we're used to."

"You said *Causes don't have effects unless they never happened.*"

"Yeah. I can show you some things. Mostly stuff that involves guys who look like me. You need to understand that they're *not* me. Not yet. And they're not your son either. Some of them might be one or the other of us after the Sword is drawn, okay? But there's no way to know in advance."

"Huh." Duncan laces his fingers behind his head and turns his gaze to the limitless blue above. "Turns out to be a lot like one of my *fucking culture hero stories* after all."

"Maybe. Close your eyes."

And he does, and—

end of the beginning

MISTER GOOD-BYE

MISTER GOOD-BYE

"I sometimes wonder if one reason he so intractably resists conventional analysis arises of prejudice inherited from your European aesthetician Aristotle. His analysis of narrative structure in Poetics is invaluable for comprehending the elements of drama; because it is so valuable—and because a human being is after all primarily a creator of narrative—we reflexively reach for Aristotle's pen to etch our understanding of Caine.

"Aristotelian drama begins with the recognition that the world has become disordered; dramatic structure is the bringing of order from chaos. In tragedy, order is restored through destruction; in comedy, order is restored through marriage or reunion. What is fundamental is the conception that disorder is an unnatural state. Order is not created, but restored.

"I believe this is why we falter in the face of Caine.

"No single principle can capture him completely; as he likes to observe, all rules are rules of thumb—yet this in no way justifies abandoning our attempt. I have compelling reason to reflect upon Caine's mythometaphysical significance; as your viewers will recall, I was not only destroyed by his hand, but was in a sense created by him as well.

"Caine's life has nothing to do with the restoration of order. It has nothing to do with restoration of any kind. He sees nothing to restore.

"For Caine, order is delusion: a film of rationality we create to veil the random brutality of existence. His narrative arc leads *from one state of chaos to another. And this is related only tangentially to the Prince of Chaos twaddle promulgated by the Church of Beloved Children in Ankhana, which has made of him a convenient Satan to my Yahweh.*

"It is more accurate to see in him an expression of natural law: what your thinkers call the 2nd Law of Thermodynamics. Though this too is incomplete enough to be deceptive; there is nothing random or disordered in his actions. Quite the opposite: the supposed order he destroys is one in which those he loves are in danger or in pain.

"He does not seek safety; for him, safety is illusory at best, and the very concept is a dangerous delusion. He seeks only a more congenial chaos.

"This is, I believe, the root of his power.

"The concept of restoration limits most thinking creatures. We fear to do that which cannot be undone—to break the order that comforts us—because to do so lets chaos in. But because for Caine there is no safety and no order, there is nothing for him to fear. He does the irrevocable without hesitation because for him everything is irrevocable.

"Caine may be Earth's greatest living master of the absolute."

—ARTSN. TAN'ELKOTH (FORMERLY MA'ELKOTH, 1ST ANKHANAN EMPEROR AND PATRIARCH OF THE ELKOTHAN CHURCH), A RECORDED INTERVIEW WITH JED CLEARLAKE ON *Adventure Update*, FOR THE (NEVER AIRED) 7TH ANNIVERSARY CELEBRATION OF *For Love of Pallas Ril*

"Christ, shut up, will you? If I'd known I'd have to listen to you yap for the rest of my fucking life, I would have let you kill me."

—CAINE
Blade of Tyshalle

*T*he only one he said good-bye to was the horse-witch.

He rode out into the frost-crackled morning on Carillon. The breeze rolling down through the tree line was bleak with oncoming snow. He didn't bother to belt closed the serape draped over his hunched-down shoulders; the young stallion pumped out plenty of heat going upslope. With the village an hour behind, he found the witch-herd gathering below a sawtooth ridge, horses of a dozen breeds cropping scrub among shoulders of rock.

The herd parted around them like water. They knew him now. This was a good thing.

The witch-herd wasn't man-friendly, as wild horses sometimes are. The horses of the witch-herd were feral. Runaways, rescues, desperate escapees, whip-scarred and spur-scarred and brain-scarred, branded inside and out with every kind of damage two-legged creatures can inflict. Kind of like him.

Horses never forget. They can't. That was kind of like him too.

And it was exactly like her.

Carillon snorted at him when he slid down off the young stallion's back. He was careful to keep not only his motion but his whole energy smooth and slow; the horse-witch to this day teased him about being jagged as a cat, and it had taken him a long time to figure out she wasn't just teasing. She wasn't talking about a housecat.

Carillon nipped at the serape's hem, gave it a tug, and shook his head, ears twitching in opposite directions. This late in the year, he was in full coat; the pathetic human need for artificial protection against the weather tickled the shit out of him. The man went through his pockets for kober and hocknuts and bits of dried fruit, feeding them gravely one by one to the big dapple-grey, who just as gravely ate them.

Clothing is funny. Food, though, is serious, and sweets are absolutely fucking dire.

"Go on, go find a girlfriend. Go get lucky," he told the stallion with a *take a hike* toss of the head. "Somebody around here should."

Carillon gave his shoulder a farewell nudge and trotted away, quartering toward a tall sleek one-eyed mare with grey burn-scars down her neck below her missing eye, careful to approach on her sighted side.

He stood and watched the young stallion dance his way into a cautious courtship. He couldn't help remembering the reinforced stud-cell in the stables back at Faith's manor in Harrakha; if Carillon hadn't broken out with Hawkwing and Phantom, he would have grown up in solitary confinement. Never would have learned herd manners. Never would have learned anything except that he's huge and strong and has a dick like a fencepost, and that every once in a while Kylassi the stablemaster would let him out to rape a couple mares.

Now Kylassi was dead, and Carillon had become a seducer with the elegance and grace of Casanova; the mare spun and threatened a kick, but there was a sparkle in her eye and a playful arch to her neck and Carillon respectfully gave way . . . and just as respectfully sidled toward her once again.

The man shook his head. "I should be so good with women."

The horse-witch was above him on the slope.

She was in her traveling clothes, that sleeveless leather jerkin and long split skirt that looked like they'd been tanned in an old stump, her cabled arms bare, her long hard legs the color of oiled oak.

She never felt the weather.

On one knee behind a shaggy chestnut pony, one of its rear hooves resting on her other knee, her strong brown hand holding a curving flicker of soot-grey blade. Wild sun-streaked hair floated free over her downturned face and parted behind her neck, where the first faint tips of her own whip-scars gleamed like old ivory above the jerkin's collar.

He felt a sudden dark lurch in his chest that he just flat refused to consider the meaning of. He'd gotten pretty good at the whole refusing thing.

He'd gone out there with an idea of what he'd tell her: about his difficult relationship with God, and the Black Knives, and the ghosts riding his back these twenty-five years. He expected it to take a lot of talking. The weeks he'd spent with her, drifting with the witch-herd among the mountains and high plains and isolated villages and trading posts of the Harrakhan Marches, couldn't have prepared her for how deadly complicated his life could suddenly become. Shit, *he* wasn't prepared.

But the closer he came, the fewer words he had. By the time he reached her, all he could say was, "You were gone."

She didn't look around. He couldn't surprise her; she knew what the herd knew.

"So were you." A blurred flicker of her hand exchanged the hoof knife for a short rasp. She began scraping at the inner walls of the pony's heel.

"Maybe you might tell me what you mean by that."

"I felt you leave in the night." She still didn't look up. "How are you here talking to me, when you're already gone?"

Steel-colored flakes began to spin out of the iron sky.

"It's not like that."

"All right."

"It isn't," he said. "I'm not leaving you."

"All right."

"It's just—you know about God. Ma'elKoth. Home. Whatever. It was a dream." He shifted his weight. "One of His. Its. Somebody's."

"What's He want?"

"I was Orbek. He's in trouble. Or he's going to be."

"God cares about Orbek now."

"Not fucking likely." He folded his arms to tighten up the serape. He was starting to shiver. "He's just—y'know, just . . . bait."

He twitched a shoulder and tried to loosen his jaw. "A hostage."

She kept working.

"You maybe never heard about the Black Knife clan. About what I did."

"This is about what you did?"

"I'm pretty sure it is." He tried to swallow around the razor-knuckled fist tangled in his guts. "It's about what I did. And about what I didn't do."

"So you're going."

"When God calls you, His Voice can get real fucking loud."

"Are you sure it's Him?"

He spread his hands. "Is there some other god who yanks my chain?"

"That's what I'm asking."

A cold whisper went up his pants. It creeped the fuck out of him: like getting his balls licked by a ghost. A carnivorous ghost.

"Doesn't matter." Didn't sound real convincing, so he said it again. "It doesn't *matter*. I have to go."

"Don't pretend."

For a while the only sound was the scrape of the hoof rasp and the irritated snuffle of the impatient pony.

He looked up into the wind. "There's a debt up there."

He could feel that debt swinging loose and rotten when the razor-fist unhooked inside his guts: a corpse from a gibbet. "Not just to Orbek. Unfinished business."

"Business."

An empty echo, like his own voice coming back at him from the far end of a desert canyon.

"Home might not be Calling me at all." He wrapped his arms tighter. "He might think He's doing me a favor. If Black Knives are rising again . . ."

A cold scrape of the rasp.

"I can't let that happen. I *can't*. Not for Orbek. Not for anybody."

"It's still a choice."

His gaze went from the wind to the rocks, then he let his arms fall, and he looked down at his hands. "Yeah."

"So?"

"So it's a choice I made a long time ago."

Her neck bent a little more, lowering her face closer to the pony's hoof. She turned the rasp to the heel buttress. Her silences had a way of making him feel like a liar.

After a while, he said, "It's . . . complicated."

Her answer came from behind her hair. "Everything is, with you."

"Yeah."

"It's a desperate life, to be beloved of God."

He got interested in the snow-smoked distance. "Depends on the god."

"Does it?"

"Christ, I hope so."

His eyes followed the ascending saw-curve of the mountain's flank, toward its blunt, vaguely spork-shaped peak pewtered with last year's winter. He didn't know its name. He didn't know the names of any of these mountains, or the passes. Or the valleys that opened below them. Something about being with her let names slip away from him. Names are only words people assign to things.

He didn't know hers. She'd told him once that she'd never had a name. She didn't use his. Any of them. He'd asked her about it once. She only shrugged.

She didn't talk much, most of the time.

Eventually he figured it out. Took a while; he could be kind of slow about some things. Horses don't deal in abstractions. They have no use for them. She knew him. He knew her. Names are masks. They get in the way.

Like how all his names had gotten in his way, all these years.

What few names she had for him were nicknames, usually to mock his sillier poses. He had more than his share: affectations left over from his Acting career. She called him tough guy sometimes, and sometimes wolf king. More often, if she used a name at all, it was dumbass. He never minded. He usually earned it.

When she was mad at him, she called him killer. He never told her his father used to call him that. A lifetime ago. A universe away.

He looked down at the long fine curve of her neck parting the fall of her honey-streaked hair, and for a second his body hummed like a harp string tightened to breaking. He didn't let himself touch her.

"So," he said, eventually. "Where you headed?"

Her nearside shoulder lifted the thickness of the blade of her knife: a ghost-shrug that somehow took in the witch-herd, and the mountains, and the sky. And him. "Winter's coming."

This was why she didn't talk much. She didn't have to.

"Yeah." He looked up into the steel swirl; the wind had freshened enough that the flakes were starting to sting his eyes. "I'm going the other way."

She gave the pony's hoof a last few light scrapes, then set it down. She held out her hand and the pony shifted its weight; she touched its opposite hock and it picked up the other foot. "This is about the end of the world."

"Probably." He looked at his hands. "Orbek probably figured he didn't have anything to lose."

"He's very young."

"Yeah."

"The world didn't end, you know. It changed. Not for the better. It didn't end."

"Without the Covenant . . . look, the Deomachy isn't actually over, y'know? All Jantho did was engineer a five-hundred-year truce."

"What do you think you can do about it? Any of it. Even Orbek."

"Sometimes life surprises me."

"You hate surprises." She still hadn't looked at him. "Where?"

"Over the mountains, north of Thorncleft," he said. "Into the Boedecken. The Khryllian holdfast, now—they call it the Battleground."

He felt her nod more than saw it. "You still haven't said why you're here."

He shrugged into the mountains. "The herd'll be passing Harrakha on your way downland. I was hoping maybe you could stop at the manor and tell Faith good-bye for me—"

The pony jerked its hoof off her knee and bucked as it skipped away. The hoof knife clattered off a rock a foot or two past him. It had missed his leg by almost an inch.

Almost.

This was how he knew she cared for him: she did not miss by accident.

And she was walking away, stiff-kneed, arms folded like she finally felt the cold.

"Hey," he said, going after her. "Hey, c'mon, don't—"

"What do I call you today? Not asshole." Her voice was colder than the ice on the wind. "Assholes are good for something."

"*Hey*, goddammit. Stop." A suggestion; she didn't take orders any better than he did.

"You think this is easy for me?"

"You love saying good-bye, killer. It's who you are."

He stopped, stung. He didn't try to sting her back. She could smack his best snide right down the mountain. "It's not forever."

Her head bent over her folded arms. "Everything's forever until it isn't."

He thought about that for a second. Then another, and more.

"Is this what you wanted . . . ?" she murmured toward the sweep of bracken and scree below. "Did you just want me to be . . . to be still *human* enough to . . ."

"No," he said. "No, c'mon, it's not like that . . ."

"Or did you want me to be petty like your dead River Bitch? To say don't go? Choose him or me? Or Him or Me?"

It was like she'd stabbed him with a needle. A horse needle. Because he wasn't sure she was wrong. And Christ, she knew right where it hurt.

She lifted her head. "Would you make me choose between you and the herd?"

"That," he said solidly, glad to be back on firmer ground, "is a stupid question."

"Yes," she said. "It is."

He found the start of a smile.

"It still hurts," she said. "I'm still afraid."

"Talk to me." The dark ache in his chest pushed open his palms. "Tell me what I can do to make it better."

Her shoulders lifted half an inch. "Take me with you."

He chuckled. "Oh, sure."

A couple seconds later he discovered she wasn't laughing with him, and then it wasn't funny anymore. Not even a little. "No fucking way."

She kept staring downslope. He followed her gaze. Carillon wasn't having a lot of luck with his scarred mare either. "I told you how shit gets around Caine. I mean, you know about the Faltane County War."

"Better than I want to."

"This'll be worse. Goddamn Knights of Khryl are—you ever hear of the Knights of Khryl? They ever get down your way?"

She looked away from him, up into the iron sky. The sunstreaks of her hair began to frost with snow.

"These aren't just guys in armor. Their guys in armor—the Khryllian armsmen—they're the best soldiers on the planet, and they're just the god-damn grunts. Knights of Khryl are priests of the Lipkan god of *personal combat* . . . Shit, one of the three Actors ever to play a Knight of Khryl was this guy Raymond Story. He played Jhubbar Tekkanal. They called him the Devil Knight. We called him the Hammer of Dal'Kannith. Ever hear of him? He's the man who killed Sha-Rikkintaer. Took him three days. Nonstop battle. Against a *dragon*. He won. By *himself*. Are you listening to me?"

"Aktiri." She sounded bored.

"You don't get it. I can't fight these guys. Nobody can."

"They can't be killed?"

"Well—no. They just can't be fought." He flicked a hand through the snowflakes. "That's not the point."

"I know."

"I can't protect you up there—"

"You don't protect me down here."

He bit down on his temper. "I will not watch you die."

She stared off toward the snow-shrouded angle of a distant peak. "I die all the time."

"We've been over that."

"Then you need to decide what you want."

Christ, he hated when people started that shit. "Please, for the love of fuck, tell me you haven't gone Cainist."

"That depends. Do you want to be caned?"

He couldn't manage even a courtesy laugh. His only answer was to half surrender to the ache in his chest.

One hand floated free of the serape and laid itself along the bone-clenched muscle of her shoulder and she spun like a spooked mare and in the half second while he half expected her to belt him one, she folded herself against his chest and buried her face into the angle of his shoulder and neck and her cheeks were icy wet like she'd been standing in freezing rain, and he got it then, or thought he did: why she wouldn't let him see her face.

Something broke inside him.

Putting his arms around her he wrapped her in the serape, and he pressed his face into the wind-scoured tangle of her hair and smelled horses and aspen and ice and high mountains.

She was shaking.

"All right," he whispered into her hair. To say it ate him alive, but to keep silent would have killed him. "Come with me."

Her shaking became shuddering, then a huge sigh filled her and emptied her again. She said, "No, thanks."

"What?"

"I hate cities."

"Now, hold on, goddammit—"

She lifted her head just enough that he could find through the curtain of her hair the curve of a wicked grin. "A girl likes to be asked, dumbass."

He said nothing. He didn't want the idiotic stammer inside his head to leak out through his mouth. That shaking started again and she folded herself against him again but now he knew what that shaking really was. "You—" She could barely get the words out. "You are so *easy* . . ."

Eventually he managed a chuckle of his own.

"And you," he said into her hair, "are a rotten human being."

"I'm the horse-witch."

"I remember."

"Then why do I have to remind you?"

"Yeah," he said, still smiling, surrendering. "Yeah, okay, I'm a dumb-ass."

"Just remember," she murmured against his neck, "remember you're not getting any younger, tough guy . . ."

His smile opened like a flower. The first time she'd said that to him . . . where they'd been, and what she hadn't been wearing, and what she'd talked him into with no more words than those . . . and he nearly asked if she remembered, but he didn't have to.

She never forgot. Anything.

"I almost left this morning." He lifted his face from her hair. Her favorite mare, an elegant medicine-hat paint, tugged at a brush of scrub in a cleft of bone-colored stone nearby. A squeal of half-playful outrage came from somewhere downslope, accompanied by snuffles and snorts unspecific through the thickening snow. Hooves drummed on earth and rock, and he could feel the beat of her heart against his chest. "I was going to. Y'know: just go. I figured, you taking off like that, you must've had reason."

Her only answer was a tightening of her arms.

"But I—" He shook his head and huffed a tired sigh. "I couldn't, that's all. I couldn't go without seeing you. Without looking into your eyes again."

She chuckled against his shoulder. "Which one?"

He cupped her chin and lifted her face and brushed snow-damp hair from the creases that sun and wind and pain had etched across the sharp angles of her cheeks, and he kissed the pale scar that pulled one corner of her mouth down toward the subtle curve of her jaw, and she looked at him first with her right eye, as she often did—the one that sparkled warm and alive and brown as a doe's—then with her left, the witch eye with the grey-blue cast cold as dead winter ice, like she had to make sure both of them saw the same man, and he said, "Either of them. Both. I don't care. I never did. There's nothing about you that I don't—" but her hands had already migrated, one north to the back of his neck and the other south to the curve of his ass and she pulled him against her and brought his lips to hers again and her body spoke to his without words.

And then for a time the mountain was their bed, and the sky their blanket, and the snow nothing at all.

But only for a time; the witch-herd had to winter downland, toward the south and west, and she was who she was, and there was trouble in the north and east, and he was who he was.

She rode. He walked.

He looked back; but only in his heart. Because he was going into the Boedecken, and there would be Black Knives there, and he couldn't afford to bring anything along.

Everything's forever until it isn't.

the now of always 3

COMPLICATED

COMPLICATED

"Does this ever get less fucked-up?"

—JONATHAN FIST

History of the Faltane County War (ADDENDUM)

"With me so far?"

Duncan opens his eyes. "It seems straightforward enough, if a bit abrupt."

"Good. That's good." For a moment, Caine almost smiles. Almost. "It's just that—well, these are what I *want* to happen. These are how I hope it ends up being."

"Is this about this 'horse-witch' woman you're, ah, seeing?"

"Mostly."

Duncan recalls how it felt to be in love with someone who isn't dead. "She seems nice."

"Thank you."

Her voice gives him a lurch, as he only now realizes he is no longer alone with Caine. "Ah. Um, hello."

"Hello."

She is seated on the ground on the opposite side of him from Caine, legs folded, arms loose, exactly as she had appeared in the vision. Same sleeveless leather jerkin. Same farrier's skirt. Same hair.

Same eyes.

Caine says, "I'm glad you're here."

The smile she aims at him past the sword says more than words.

"Remember anything I need to know?"

She shrugs. "I remember what happens if I don't show up."

"And so?"

"And so I'm here."

With a trace of a frown, Duncan realizes that she's not sitting on the snow on which he lies—she's on grass, thin and pale but clearly alive. Some crocuses have poked blossoms up through the snow around her, and she picks a few and slides them into her hair.

He says, "You have power."

"Everyone does."

He thinks about this for a while, and while he thinks about it, the flowers in her hair grab his heart like a fist; in the next instant, he understands. Davia had loved the expeditions to Overworld even more than he had—and she had always made a point to wear flowers in her hair. On Earth, flowers were a ludicrously expensive indulgence. "You're my son's, ah—you're Caine's current lover?"

"You mean him?" she says with another smile past the sword. "More than current."

"More than—?" He catches the expression on Caine's face. "Don't tell me. It's complicated, right?"

"I can't even tell you."

"And the, ah, River Bitch?"

"That's what she calls Shanna when she's trying to piss me off."

"It works too," the horse-witch says gravely. "He doesn't like to be reminded that she is not a nice person."

"Is?" He looks to Caine. "You said—"

"She's one of the people who might be showing up here. If she does, remember that she is *not* Shanna. She's an Aspect of Chambaraya, and the elKothan goddess of the wild, and she is not on my side. Not even a little."

"And Faith—"

"Is somebody else too. But she is on my side. Usually. Look, forget about them. This isn't about them."

Duncan rubs his eyes. "How am I supposed to know what's important and what isn't?"

"He'll tell you," the horse-witch says. "He likes that."

"You're not helping."

Duncan squeezes shut his eyes and makes a deliberate choice to forget about what *he* wants to know, because what counts here and now is what Caine wants to show him. "So this Orbek you—I mean, he—spoke of? He's a friend?"

"More than. He's the brother I never had."

"*Like* the brother you never had."

"That's not what I said." He dismisses this with a wave. "You'll see. He's an ogrillo."

"Like the Black Knives?"

"More than."

"Wait—" Incredulity brings Duncan's head up. "The *brother* you went back to the Boedecken to save—that you came *here* to save—was a *Black Knife?*"

"Yeah. I'd say it was ironic if it, y'know, had anything to do with irony."

"You came back to where you personally wiped out the Black Knife Nation in order to save your brother who is a Black Knife? How is that not irony?"

"Because I didn't go there to save him."

"What happened?"

Caine shrugs. "Eventually you and I are gonna figure that out, but there's shit you need to see first."

The horse-witch says, "Told you."

end of the beginning 2

ASSBITCH OF THE GODS

ASSBITCH OF THE GODS

"The trouble with happy endings is that nothing is ever truly over."

—ARTSN. TAN'ELKOTH (FORMERLY MA'ELKOTH, 1ST ANKHANAN
EMPEROR AND PATRIARCH OF THE ELKOTHAN CHURCH)
Blade of Tyshalle

The Monastic Embassy on the island of Old Town in the heart of Ankhana—only a bowshot and change from the Colhari Palace itself—had been considered a uniquely hazardous post since the days of the Khulan Horde. It became substantially more hazardous some years later, after a Monastic assassin was implicated in the murder of Prince-Regent Toa-Phelathon. The Monasteries had maintained a queasy pretense of neutrality during the First and Second Succession Wars, but the actions of some renegade friars, during the events of the Artan assault now known as the Assumption Day Massacre, had convinced rival powers that the Monasteries had effectively become an adjunct of the Ankhanan Empire—an auxiliary, in fact, of the Eyes of God, collecting intelligence and performing covert operations.

This made the Ankhanan Embassy an especially tempting target for the Empire's rivals, as well as enemies of the Monasteries; it was popularly supposed that the Ambassador to the Infinite Court, though theoretically subject to the orders of the Council of Brothers, had become an independent authority with virtually unlimited power to command any and all

Monastic operatives throughout the continent, and that he did so in unabashed support of the Empire's interests.

Unlike the common run of popular suppositions, this one was entirely correct.

Thus the Monastic Embassy in Ankhana was among the most comprehensively defended structures in existence, possessed not only of a bewildering array of Artan weaponry, security, and surveillance devices scavenged and rebuilt from the wreckage of the invading force, but also a vast and detailed standing array of countermagicks to prevent all manner of thaumaturgic espionage. Not least among these defenses were the Walking Brothers—highly trained friars specializing in counterinfiltration operations—who in every hour of every day patrolled the embassy's every hall, corridor, and chamber.

These defenses had been so effective for so long that when a Walking team rounded the corner of a corridor on an upper floor and discovered a pair of their comrades—one bound and gagged, apparently unconscious on the floor, the other similarly gagged but standing upright, hands tied in front of her, making a very persuasive human shield for a middle-aged man who stood behind her, one arm crooked around her neck and with a small matte black knife against the soft tissue under her chin while his other hand leveled at them across her shoulder a very large, similarly matte black, powerful-appearing pistol—they could not instantly comprehend what they were seeing, and so merely stared blankly for a second or two instead of instantly raising alarum, and spent another second drawing weapons of their own and splitting to opposite walls of the corridor so that the middle-aged man's pistol couldn't cover them both at once.

This brief interval gave the middle-aged man time to say—

"I am a Citizen of Humanity and a Servant of the Human Future. I have broken neither oath nor law. I claim Sanctuary; by law and custom, Sanctuary is my right."

The Walking Friars exchanged frowns, then as one turned their frowns upon the middle-aged man. One said, "To be granted Sanctuary, you must state your name and abbey."

"Hey, go to the head of the fucking class," the middle-aged man replied. "That was just to give you an excuse to stop and think before you got stupid. I need to see Raithe. He needs to see me. Privately. I would've let myself all the way in, but you've upgraded your security and I'd rather not kill anybody."

The Walking Friars leveled weapons as well. "I don't believe the Ambassador to the Infinite Court receives callers between midnight and dawn."

The middle-aged man squinted at the friars' weapons—both shaped of wood inlaid with precious metals, shimmering with power—and shrugged. "You boys aren't Beloved Children."

"Of what possible concern to you is our religious faith?"

"None at all. Go get Raithe before I start killing people."

The younger of the two friars tightened his grip and sighted his weapon. "You will have no opportunity to—"

"Kid. Seriously. That's a nice piece you're holding. Just like the ones I took off these two. I'm pretty good with them. But they're not what's pointing at you right now." The middle-aged man tilted his head a centimeter to the right. "Why do you think that is?"

The Walking Brothers exchanged another glance.

"If I have to make moves in here, we'll all get bloody. You, go wake up Raithe. Tell him Hari's waiting to see him. He'll come with you."

"Hari?" He frowned like he wasn't sure if he was being kidded. "Of what abbey? In what land?"

"Hari of Do as You're Told in the land of And Shut the Fuck Up." He twitched the pistol toward the other one. "You, do all your buddies a favor and don't let anybody walk in here. I'll keep these two company and we can all part as friends, huh?"

One more glance between them, then one said, "What if he's telling the truth?"

The other shook his head. "There's no way to know."

"Sure there is," the man said patiently. "Tell Raithe I'm here. Let him decide whether to sit down for a chat or have me killed."

"*I have decided already.*"

The voice was soft, almost gentle, wholly deliberate and precise, and it came from the empty air behind the middle-aged man's left shoulder. The man jerked, stilled himself, then gritted through his teeth, "Someday you'll pull that shit and I'll just start shooting."

"*I trust you've been well.*"

"You knew I was coming."

"*I have a stated policy to hope for the best and prepare for the worst,*" the quiet voice replied. "*Thus I am never surprised to see you.*"

"Yeah, okay, funny. Raithe, we don't have a lot of time."

"*We?*"

"Everybody. The world."

"*This seems somehow familiar.*"

"It's not a big favor. Then I'm gone. Probably forever."

Silence.

Then: *"There must be a compelling reason for you to come to me for aid, instead of your . . . more amicable options."*

"There's an easy way to find out."

Silence.

Eventually: *"Rellen will guide you to my chambers. After you release Tamal, she can tend to Rastlin. Ansen will clear potential witnesses out of your way."*

"You won't regret it."

"Don't make promises you can't keep."

Raithe of Ankhana, Monastic Ambassador to the Infinite Court, received his visitor in the large office attached to his personal apartments. He stood to receive the visitor, but did not offer his hand. The last time his visitor had been in this office, he had murdered Raithe's predecessor.

The Ambassador was of average height. The whipcord physique he'd brought to this post had lately softened, a victim of the necessities of diplomatic work—especially diplomatic dining. His hair, never thick, had thinned until he'd decided it was useless to trouble with; now his head was full-shaven and glossy, the color of buffalo hide. Only his eyes had not changed: pale as winter sky, they still had a purity of focus one expects in the eyes of eagles but is unsettling in the eyes of a man.

His visitor too had changed in the three years since they had last met. His hair and beard had gone salt-and-pepper. His skin had darkened as much as his hair had lightened, and added decades of creases: the color and texture of an old saddle. He wore layers of loose-fitting clothing that Raithe knew concealed a variety of weapons, some perhaps more lethal than the large pistol he wore behind his belt. Raithe was not concerned with them; the man's real weapon was behind his eyes.

It was a matter of passing irony to Raithe, justly famous for powers of mind that could trap the will, blind the eye, or even slay outright, to contemplate that he had the second most dangerous mind in the room.

"How's the hand?"

"It hurts." Raithe lifted his left hand, frowning faintly at the darkening stain upon its wrapping of thick white gauze. "For more than two years, I've had to add dressing only every second or third day—rewrapping as the inner gauze dissolves and is consumed. Lately, I've rewrapped three or four times a day . . . and still must awaken in the morning dark to wrap again, lest a leak set my bed afire."

"That's why you were expecting me."

"Not that alone. There are . . . matters afoot. Subtle gestures of politics and power, a gathering weave into cloth of a pattern known to . . . interest you."

"It's been awhile since anybody talked about me and subtle in the same sentence. But you're not exactly subtle yourself." The man waved a hand, a slight, irritably dismissive gesture taking in the office where the two stood. "Look at this fucking place. You haven't even changed the rug."

"On which you stood when first we met, a decade past," Raithe said. "The night you murdered the man who was more a father to me than my own had ever been."

"I've done lots of things I regret." His flatly neutral tone did not indicate whether he counted this among them. He nodded toward the vast scarred writing table that dominated the room. "That's not even Creele's, y'know. It was Dartheln's."

"It belongs," Raithe said with dispassionate precision, "to the Ankhanan Embassy."

"Yeah, whatever. Can we not bicker? It's bad enough even being here."

"We meet here because I think we both can benefit from being mindful of the . . . context . . . of our relationship."

"Fuck context. You don't see me bringing up how you murdered my wife."

"Until just now."

"Can we wait to score debate points until after we save the fucking world?"

"Yes. Yes, of course. I apologize." With a sigh, Raithe settled into the large leather work chair at the table. "You caught me sleeping. My nights have been a long march through evil dreams. You'll forgive a moment of . . . irrationality."

"You don't need my forgiveness. Look, I just . . ." The man sagged, rubbing at his eyes, all of an instant very old and losing a desperate struggle against exhaustion. "I really need your help. There's no one else. Please."

Raithe found his own eyes stinging with fatigue. "This is about Assumption Day."

"Was that a mystery?"

"No. We are gradually coming to accept as established fact that *everything* has to do with Assumption Day. Ahh—how should I call you? The name Hari . . . awakens bitter echoes. And the more famous of your names . . . well, I find myself reluctant to speak that name aloud, as though evil powers will wake at the sound."

"If I really wanted to scare the crap out of you, I'd tell you just how right you are." He found a chair and sank into it, wincing. "Lately I've been going by Jonathan Fist."

"Of course. Is that the name you prefer?"

"It's an inside joke." He shrugged, looking away. "It's a legend of Earth—you know, Arta. He made a deal he couldn't get out of."

"I recall making a deal with you, once."

"And you got what you paid for."

"I did not imagine any price could be so . . . . painful."

"Nobody does." He waved off the subject. "So it's like this. I spent most of the spring down south, working into County Faltane and back."

"I've read digests of the reports. And the transcript of your interview in the Thorncleft Embassy."

Old pain scoured the other's face. "Of course you have."

Raithe allowed himself one thin, humorless chuckle. "And are you now so far removed from the Monasteries that you have forgotten who we are?"

"Not exactly. I just thought . . . well, I guess I thought my story was over. That's all. I've been getting comfortable with being nobody special."

"And yet here you are, having breached the most heavily defended installation in this hemisphere, brandishing an alien weapon and speaking of the end of days."

"Another fucking Armageddon," he said. "We should be used to it by now."

Raithe again ventured a slim smile. "Your friend J'Than occasionally likes to say, 'Past performance is no guarantee of future results.' "

Jonathan Fist only looked bleak. "You get reports on me. So you're probably up on our old pal Damon and his pet project."

Raithe went still. "How do you know of that?"

"If we both live through this, I'll tell you all about it. It's really true?"

He didn't move. Not even to blink. "What do you mean by *true?*"

"That pretty well sums it up, then. Okay, listen. You've read my original History on the Breaking of the Black Knives?"

"Of course."

"The night I escaped, just after Pretornio overloaded, when the head bitch—Skaikkak Neruch'khaitan—when we were struggling there by my cross, when she hit me and I blocked with the spike and her hand exploded—"

"I recall. You described the experience as being joined with her by the Outside Power. When you learned the location of Panchasell's Tear."

"Something like that. But that wasn't all of it. That wasn't most of it."

"Yes. Her name, and the names of—"

"No." He sat forward on his chair. He didn't look old anymore. "She was . . . nothing. Not even a speck. The Power—it knew me. It knew all of me. And for however long I was out, I knew all of it."

Raithe looked thoughtful.

"The thing is . . . well, you know. An Outside Power—a human mind can't even come close to comprehending that kind of consciousness. Mine sure didn't. But some things . . . I don't know, it's coming back to me. Somehow. Mostly little stuff. Some of it not so little. Some of it fucking terrifying."

"What is it you want me to do?"

"I need to know what I know, Raithe. The shit you can do with your mind—Raithe, I need to *know*. All of it. Everything lurking around the back of my brain. Now."

"Why do you not go to the Emperor? Surely his powers outstrip mine by orders of magnitude, and you are his closest friend—"

"He can't know anything about this. Not one thing. I have to stay out of his way. If I'm right about this, you'll have to stay out of his way too. And I mean out. No friendly hand waves at a state dinner. No chat on the Artan Mirror. Nothing. I know you're elKothan, but you're also the only guy I can depend on to keep his mind shut along with his mouth. Don't even *think* too loud."

"It's that bad?"

"Let me show you something." He reached toward Raithe with his left. "Give me your hand."

Raithe lifted his right. The other man shook his head. "Not that hand."

Raithe hesitated. "The bindings are soaked nearly through," he said, raising his bandaged fist to illustrate. A stain near the cup of his palm darkened as it spread. "It is why this embassy has an open tun of water in every room. Even a pinprick can ignite a fire in your flesh that will burn until the oil is burned away, and flesh with it. It can burn through your bones."

"Maybe. What happened the last time I touched that oil?"

"I—I mean . . ." He frowned. The chaos of slaughter, agony, and terror that was now called the True Assumption of Ma'elKoth had branded itself indelibly into Raithe's memory; this morning he would have sworn an oath that he recalled it in every detail, but now uncertainty muddied his recollection. His powers of mind allowed him to see previous events as clearly as he might see across this room . . .

Usually.

"I don't know," he said at length. "I don't remember that you ever did . . . but I'm not certain. You bear no scars from it."

"Let's not start about my scars. Where do you keep fresh dressings?"

Raithe pulled a large roll from a drawer in the writing table. "Yet still I—"

"Watch."

He took Raithe's bandaged left hand in both of his own, and gently squeezed it between them until the black oil soaked through to the surface. The bandage ignited with a whisperlike *whumpf,* and burned with the crackle of a pine-pitch torch.

He stepped back and spread his hands. They were coated with the oil, so thickly that he had to cup his palms to keep it from dripping and setting the rug on fire . . . but from his flesh rose not so much as a wisp of smoke. "How about this?"

Raithe stared in awe, the flames licking upward from his left hand forgotten. "That's impossible."

"You'll probably want to douse that hand."

Raithe did so in the water tun beside the table, soaked the rolled dressing in the water, and began to wrap it around his fist. "That oil burns *everything* . . ."

"Except you."

Raithe looked exasperated. "I'm different. You know I'm different, and you know why."

"That's kind of my point. What I want to find out is why *I'm* different."

Raithe picked at the white fringes of his dressing, adjusting how it lay even as he continued to wrap. "How did you know it wouldn't burn you?"

"I didn't. But it was a pretty good bet. Remember Kosall?"

Skin stretched tight around Raithe's winter eyes. "Vividly."

"You were there when I picked it up. When I pulled it out of the floor of the Pit. Remember?"

Raithe's eyes narrowed, and his lips drew thin. "Actually, no."

The other nodded, his face set and grim. "Me neither."

"How is that possible?"

"Here's another: who wiped the oil off the hilt? You?"

"No. No, that I would remember."

"Yeah, I would too. But I don't. Kosall's hilt was wrapped in leather. You'd been using it in your left. The leather must have been soaked. Remember how it burned my hand when I picked it up?"

"No."

"Because it didn't."

Raithe found himself blinking through his frown. Over and over again. "Why not?"

"Exactly. Why not *exactly*."

Raithe could only sit and stare, though what he saw had nothing to do with the scene before him.

"I figure nobody wiped the hilt. I figure most likely, I just grabbed the fucking thing, and the oil . . . went away. And everybody forgot it was ever there or something."

"Or something . . ." Raithe echoed faintly. "You're talking about Intervention. A miracle."

"I'm just getting started."

"It's a pity we can't examine the blade itself. If you and Ma'elKoth hadn't destroyed it—"

"Shit would be worse."

"Worse than this?"

"Believe it." He made a fist with his right hand, and the logs stacked in the study's limestone fireplace against the chill of morning now exploded into a blaze of white unnatural flame.

Raithe lifted an arm to shield his face against the instant blast of heat—and found that his left hand burned with an identically fierce white fire within a cloud of sudden steam. He spat an expletive he had not used since his boyhood on the fringes of the Warrens. "Caine—Hari—Fist, whatever you are called. Make it stop!"

"Kris always said fire was easy." He made the other hand into a fist, and the fires swiftly dwindled to ordinary red and yellow. "Extinguishing's trickier. Don't have the hang of it yet."

Raithe returned his hand to the water tun. "Where did you learn to cast fire?"

"Ma'elKoth. When we destroyed Kosall. And when He sent me back to Earth and I blew Marc Vilo's estate to the far side of fuck. Fire really is easy, even for me. All I need is focus. It's not like thaumaturgy. Thaumaturgy is limited by local Flow characteristics. It's limited by reality. This isn't Flow."

He opened his fists and turned his palms for Raithe's inspection. "It's the power of a god."

Every trace of the black oil was gone; the logs burning in the fireplace were the only evidence it had ever been there. Raithe's ears rang and his jaw hurt and he realized he was clenching his teeth hard enough to chip them. Very slowly, very carefully, he withdrew his left hand from the water and began to wrap the sodden bandages in fresh gauze. "A god who is your bitterest enemy. Who is the greatest threat to life on this world."

"I used to think so."

"And nothing has changed, except it's getting worse," Raithe said. "When I—when this happened to me—the oil was only corrosive, flammable rather than actively incendiary."

"Everything changes."

"I still don't understand how you can do these things."

"I'm hoping you can help me find out."

"I haven't the faintest idea where to begin."

"I have a theory—well, a guess, really, but it's an educated guess."

He looked down. "Applied Legendry. First day. Why does no one know where the Covenant of Pirichanthe was negotiated? Why does no one even know where the fuck Pirichanthe was?"

Raithe blankly offered the standard response. "So that no one land, nor one people, can claim the Covenant as their own, and so that every land and every people can claim the Covenant as their own."

"So Jantho Ironhand for humanity and Khryl Battlegod for deity forged the Covenant blah blah blah. Whatever. But they weren't the only ones there; each of the Great Folk sent witnesses. Remember who was there for the primals?"

"T'ffarell Ravenlock."

"Yeah. The son of Panchasell Mithondionne, who Bound a Power to seal the gates between Home and the Quiet Land. Panchasell wasn't afraid of ferals—us, I mean. The humans. He was afraid of our gods."

The corners of Raithe's mouth drew back and downward; his eyebrows drew back and up. "What are you saying?"

"I don't know what I'm saying. I just get the feeling I might know what Pirichanthe is."

"What," Raithe said warily. "Not where."

"Yeah, and it's not so much a what as it is a who. And . . ." He took a deep breath and released it in a long slow sigh. "And it's starting to look like I've been its assbitch for twenty-five years."

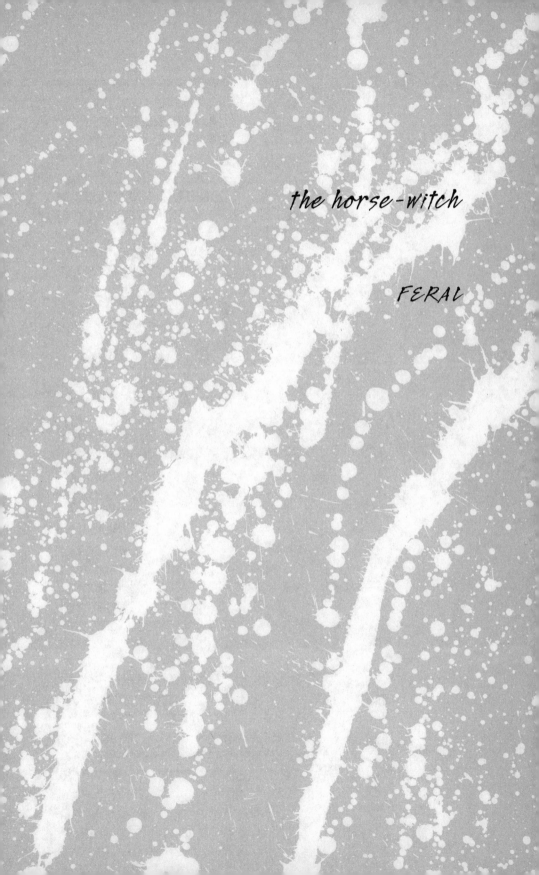

the horse-witch

FERAL

FERAL

"*In lands to the south, from Kor to Yalitrayya, the wise women say your horse is who you are without your name.*"

—THE HORSE-WITCH

   History of the Faltane County War (ADDENDUM)

*I*n the crosshairs, she looked pretty good.

With just the slightest tightening and relaxing of his fingers, he could keep the reticle centered on her chest as the big bay she was bare-backing moved slowly along the ravine floor, scavenging scraps of grass left behind by the vast herd. He couldn't guess her age; her skin was the color of oiled oak, and streaks of sun bleach coiled through her wild mass of hair. Her sleeveless leather jerkin looked like it had been tanned in an old stump, and showed off arms cabled with long muscle under half a tea-spoon of fat. Or less. Her legs were long and hard under a split skirt that divided into loose duster-style chaps. She rode with her heels out and her knees loose and nothing at all in her hands.

"Son of a bitch," he said. "They weren't pulling my dick after all."

Even after all the years he'd spent on Home, he still wasn't used to the way any random myth once in a while decided to jump out of the bushes and bite a chunk off his ass.

The ogrillo beside him, staying low, touched him on the ribs. "Let me see."

Slowly, carefully, he pushed himself, scraping back from the rim of the bluff. When he was sure none of the horses below would sense his move-ment, he passed the SPAR-12 to the young ogrillo. Nobody at Heckler-Colt had ever imagined their weapon in hands like his, but an enterprising stonebender had modified this one with an oversized trigger, a guard big around as a coffee cup, and a divot cut out of the stock so the ogrillo could sight the rifle without breaking off his right tusk.

"Mmm. Good enough to eat."

"The horse or the girl?"

"You pick." The ogrillo's trifurcate upper lip peeled back around his tusks. "They're down there, little brother."

"Yeah?"

He laid a talon along his wrinkled snout. "Nose of Orbek, hey?"

"Spare me the Great Hunter crap, citybred."

Orbek shrugged a couple dozen kilos of shoulder. "Can see Carillon from here. Looks like your boy's gettin' some."

The human snaked back up to the rim of the bluff and squinted into the broad shallow ravine. His eyes weren't what they used to be, but by following the angle of the sniper rifle's long black barrel he could pick out a black-dappled grey blotch that looked like it had mounted a chestnut blotch, and he nodded. If the big four-year-old was here, odds were Hawk-wing and Phantom would be too. Unless they'd run across a mountain lion or a griffin or a pack of hungry ogrilloi or any of the other dozen-odd large predators that roamed the southern foothills of God's Teeth.

"Any idea where we are?"

The ogrillo shrugged again. "Don't look like Kansas."

The human made a face. "Should never have told you that goddamn story."

"How many we gonna take?"

"Just the ones we came for."

The ogrillo gave him a look sour enough to curdle milk. "Long damn way for three damn horses. Specially when I'm hungry."

"Stay up here and keep the sights on her." He took a long last look down into the ravine. "I want to get out of this with nobody dying, but if it looks like I'm in trouble, drop her."

"Like you say, little brother."

The man slid down through the rocks to where Kylassi the stablemaster and the two grooms waited with the mounts. "She's down there: one twist in the middle of a herd of maybe ten thousand head. Maybe twenty."

Kylassi whistled. "That's a lot of horses."

"Forget about them. All we're taking is what's ours. Mine. Faith's." He made a face and waved a hand. "You know what I mean. There's a defile below to the south. Swing down there and come out slow. No screwing around. Go straight for Hawkwing, if you can see her; Carillon and Phantom will both follow her, right?"

The stablemaster nodded. "Maybe. Probably. What're you going to do?"

The man squinted thoughtfully into the slanting afternoon sunlight.

"I'm gonna have a word with this horse-witch."

He came out of the rocks on foot.

His boots made less noise through the sparse scrub than the horses' chewing. Only a couple actually looked at him, but they all knew he was there; the herd drifted outward from him, thinning and expanding and parting as naturally as a breeze parts a cloud. He kept his pace a step slower than theirs, giving them whatever distance they needed.

She sat her bay a couple hundred yards up the far slope of the little valley. Crumbling crags the color of bone shouldered out of the scrubfield that rose behind her. The slanting sun raised a curtain of shadow across her face, and she looked at him.

He kept walking. The same steady pace. Giving her plenty of time to think him over. Plenty of time to decide to get shy.

She just looked.

He could feel the tidal ebb of the herd around him in the curling shifts of breeze, the dry crisp crunch of horse teeth on fescue, the nervous jitter of a drumming hoof. The jitters rose to the occasional clatter and the chewing faded entirely away and the clean grass-sap smell curdled into a musk of sweat and piss.

Kylassi and the grooms had swung out to where the herd could see them, and were working their way out of the defile onto the ravine floor.

The breeze shifted to put the three horsemen downwind. The herd began to tighten up, like he'd known they would: now they could smell Orbek.

Horses on Home know what it means to be downwind of ogrilloi.

He stopped when he got close enough that he figured Orbek could hold both him and her in the sight.

"Hey," he said softly. "You got a name?"

She turned her head slowly to one side, then the other. One of her eyes was brown as a doe's, warm and sparkling; the other had a cast the grey-blue of dead winter ice. She looked at him out of each eye in turn like she was making sure they both saw the same thing.

"What's your name?" he said, louder. "Down the village, they call you the horse-witch."

She looked bored.

"Dammit." He felt like an idiot. "Do you speak Westerling at all?"

Her chest rose and fell briefly: a little huff of disappointment. "Not if I don't have to."

"Jesus Christ." He scowled and looked around. He could imagine the grin Orbek would be wearing about now, and it made him want to punch somebody. "Look. I don't want any trouble. I didn't come all this way to hang you, or arrest you, or do anything to you at all. I don't give a rat's ass about you. I just want my horses back."

"All right."

He blinked. She still looked bored.

"What do you mean, all right?"

"If they're your horses, they're your horses." She made him feel, some-how, as if he was lying to her.

"Well—" He shifted his weight. "They're my daughter's."

She nodded. "You don't like horses."

"What does liking them have to do with anything?"

"That's what I mean."

His scowl deepened. He shook his head and made himself unclench fists he didn't remember making. "I have a feeling talking to you is gonna piss me off."

She gave him her ice-blue eye. "Then don't."

He squinted up at her. The Automag registered weight inside the waist-band holster at the small of his back. He reminded himself that she hadn't actually given him reason to use it.

She looked over her shoulder. Something about the slope behind her was apparently a lot more interesting than he was. The big bay made a slow half pirouette; he found himself looking at her back and a quarter ton of horse ass. The bay flipped up its tail and squeezed out a turd as big as his head.

It plopped on the slope, black-green and wet and steaming faintly in the crisp air.

"And now I ask myself, why the fuck would I want to talk to a fucking horse-witch in the first place?"

"I could tell you," she said, still seeming to be interested in something above the crest of the slope. "But you wouldn't believe me."

"Yeah, okay." He glanced toward where Kylassi and the grooms were circling a small cluster of horses. He caught Kylassi's eye and lifted his hand in a small circle of *get on with it.* "We'll take the horses and be out of here. I'd say it was nice to meet you if it, y'know, was."

He felt her attention return to him. He had a sense for that kind of thing: a warm tingle lit up his back like carbonated sunlight. "It's not going to work that way."

"Want to bet?"

He could hear the big bay's hooves shuffling unhurriedly among the rocks. Coming toward him from behind. "Don't turn around," she said.

He went still. This wasn't a freeze; just the opposite. All tension flowed out from him, and he stood relaxed and balanced and if she wanted to get frisky within his arm's reach, that suited him right down to the road-rot between his toes. "Is there a reason why I shouldn't?"

"Don't look straight at him," she said, still with that tone of patient explanation that made him want to administer a boot-leather enema. "You have predator eyes."

"I bet you say that to all the boys."

"On the front of your head, dumbass. Binocular vision."

He ratcheted his head around to look up at her over his shoulder. "What?"

"Binocular vision," she repeated absently, gazing off toward where Kylassi was cutting Hawkwing out of the small cluster. "How predators see the world."

He was a long way short of giving a shit about details of taxonomy. "Did you just call me *dumbass*?"

From this close, weather creases around her eyes said she was probably closer to forty than thirty. Probably. "Were you being a dumbass?"

"I—" Dammit. "Maybe I was."

"Then why are you complaining?"

He shook his head in frank disbelief. "People have *died* for trash-talking me."

"Not lately."

He didn't ask what made her so sure; he had an uneasy feeling she'd tell him.

"That man." She lifted her chin toward Kylassi, still mounted, playing out rope on the lasso around Hawkwing's neck while the two sweating grooms, on foot, tried to get a halter on her. "He is master of the horses you want. The man you would call the trainer."

That was another thing he wasn't going to ask how she knew. "He works for my daughter. Maybe you've heard of her. The Marchioness of Harrakha. Those are her horses you stole."

"I don't steal."

"Oh, right. They ran away. Three weeks' ride. To you."

She was still gazing thoughtfully toward Kylassi. "Have you ever been whipped?"

"I'm sorry?"

"Imagine being enslaved. Imagine being whipped. Whipped for not doing what your masters want, but they won't tell you what they want. They just keep beating you until you figure it out for yourself."

He stared up at her. He had a really good view of the underside of her fine straight jaw and long, gracefully muscular neck, but he wasn't seeing with his eyes.

He was seeing a gnarled old slave wrangler in the Khulan Horde, from twenty-odd years ago: the run-up to *Last Stand at Ceraeno*. Three hundred fifty pounds of ogrillo weathered to the color of a granite cliff, one puckered eye-socket filled with old scar, in the other a lazily malevolent eye the color of dog piss. He was seeing the black lead-loaded tails of the grill's longcat draped over a fist the size of a human head.

He was hearing the half second of flat *whooshh* that was the only warning anyone got. He was feeling the loads in those leather straps smacking breath from his lungs. He was remembering a shot across his kidneys that'd had him pissing blood three days straight.

"Yeah, that's kind of familiar."

She nodded, still staring over at Hawkwing struggling against the noose, her whinnies scaling up from nervous toward black panic. Carillon had come out of the herd from somewhere; the big dapple-grey danced skittishly around Kylassi and the grooms. Even from here, he could see the whites around Carillon's nut-brown eyes.

"So what would you do?" she said softly. "What would you do if it was your mother he whipped? Your child?"

He didn't have to think about it. "Same as I did to the one who did it to me."

—the look in the wrangler's one good eye when his longcat tangled around an upraised arm that he'd thought had been securely shackled: a look smashed along with the eye by the impact of a pound of rock in the other less-than-securely-shackled hand—

She nodded again. "All right."

He was never sure exactly how it happened; later, the best he could reconstruct was that a sudden twisting lunge from Hawkwing must have shoulder-slammed one of the grooms off his feet while the other had wisely cleared the hell away from her rump as she swung around, ducking; her duck put unexpected weight on the rope Kylassi had wrapped around his fist, which yanked him half out of the saddle while both her hind legs shot out and up in a rising donkey kick that took him on the point of the chin, while behind him Carillon had spun and leaped into the air in the biggest goddamn capriole in recorded goddamn history, and the stallion's hooves had caught Kylassi at the base of the skull at the same instant the mare's had hit his chin.

Kylassi's head spun straight up into the air. The rest of him didn't.

His gelding screamed and bolted with the stablemaster's twitching corpse still in the saddle. A fan of blood from the stump of his neck broke into scarlet gemstones in the afternoon sun. The herd parted to let the panicked horse pass. Then it closed again.

The standing groom sat down. Hard. The other didn't look inclined to get up.

Kylassi's head hit the scrub and bounced.

The man looked at the severed head, and at the white-faced grooms. They were beginning to shake. Then he looked at the herd. Which now surrounded them, shoulder to shoulder.

Still and silent. Ten thousand horses. More.

Watching.

He looked up at the horse-witch. She looked down at him. He nodded down at Kylassi's head without taking his eyes off her. "That was a friend of mine."

"He wanted you to think so."

"What'd he do that's worth killing him for?"

She shrugged. "Ask the horses."

"Oh, sure. Why didn't I think of that? Oh, right, I remember. They're fucking *horses*. They'll tell me all about it."

"Not if you don't listen."

He put his hands on his hips, a position from which his right could slip under the back of his tunic and draw the Automag in about the same amount of time it takes normal people to blink. "Sure. Fine. So if I listened, what would they tell me about what you just did to them?"

"To them? Nothing."

"Oh, I get it. It was all their idea. Their cunning plan. Run all the way down here just so they could kill a guy they saw every day."

She appeared impervious to sarcasm. "They came to be with their own kind."

"There's wild herds a hell of a lot closer than this one."

"Horses in the witch-herd aren't wild," she said. "They're feral."

"I—" He stopped, squinting at her. "They—*all* of them?"

"Look."

He looked. For the first time. At the horses, instead of around them and past them. The herd had been just . . . well, context. Scenery. Local color. He'd been looking for the horse-witch and he just naturally assumed that when he found her, there would be horses around. Why else would people call her the horse-witch?

Finally looking at the horses themselves, he saw scars.

He knew a thing or two about scars. He knew what a whip scar looked like. He knew the difference between the scar of a knife and the scar of an arrowhead, and the difference between both of those and scars left by spurs. He knew the scar left when the skin rips around a club-blow, and the one when the flesh itself is crushed and destroyed. And he knew the look in the eyes when the scars inside are worse.

Every horse watching him and the grooms was remembering every time they'd been whipped. Beaten. Spurred. Clubbed. They were remembering being starved into submission, or penned in the sun without water. Remembering having chains pull their faces so hard that skin ripped to the bone. Remembering being tied down, screaming, trying to get away, to fight back, to do anything at all that might make it just stop. Remembering the bottomless nightmare that was their experience of humanity. Because that's what they did when they saw people.

Remember.

He knew what they were remembering because when he saw people, he mostly did the same. He said, very, very softly, "Holy shit . . ."

He looked up at the horse-witch. "I didn't know. I swear I didn't know."

"They believe you."

"What, the horses?"

She shrugged. "You're still alive."

"Uh. Yeah." He gave half a nod over his shoulder at the two grooms. "You two better go wait in the village."

They didn't need convincing. They scrambled to their feet and started toward the rocky slope where they'd left their mounts ground-tied. Ten million pounds of horseflesh closed across their path. Shoulder to shoulder. Not threatening. Just in the way.

The grooms recoiled. They looked back at him. He looked up at the horse-witch. "Can they go?"

She squinted over the heads of the herd. "Doesn't look like it."

"Come on, they're just kids. Let 'em go, huh?"

She tilted her head to watch him with her brown eye. "You don't understand what I am."

"Well, that's a fucking news flash. I don't give a shit what you are—"

"Except you do."

"—I just want to finish the day without anybody else dying, all right? Can we do that?"

She gave him half an apologetic shrug. "Seems unlikely."

"What gets us out of here? Come on, a clue, huh? Anything. Seriously."

"They don't like people," she said. "People are what they joined the herd to get away from."

"They seem to like you well enough."

"I'm the horse-witch."

"Okay, then, horse-witch, how about you witch some horses out of our fucking way?"

"That's not what I do."

"Another news flash."

She leaned a little forward, bracing herself against the bay's powerful neck, and angled her face to give him a full-on stare. "There are two things I do. Ruling these horses isn't one of them. Look at my eyes."

The one eye doe-brown, warm and gentle. The other milky bluish grey, cold as a glacier.

"Two things I do," she repeated. She touched her cheek below the brown eye. "Forgiveness." She moved the hand to the ice-milk side. "Permission."

"Forgiveness and permission? Forgiveness and permission for what?"

"It's not complicated. Forgiveness for everything bad that's happened to you. Permission to be who you are. Everything else is . . ." She shrugged. "Else."

He scowled up at her. He should probably just shoot her, grab the horses, and get out of here before Kylassi's blood attracted griffins. Or something worse. Who knew what kinds of predators might be stalking the fringes of the witch-herd? But when his hand closed on the Automag's grip, he discovered that he understood what she was talking about. A cold emptiness unfolded inside his chest, and he left the pistol where it was.

Forgiveness for everything bad that's happened to you.

Permission to be who you are.

She hadn't made the horses kill Kylassi. She hadn't made them do anything. She didn't have to.

Permission.

He looked at the horses again, then at the grooms, who were both white as the limestone bluffs. "Maybe you better walk."

"What about our horses?"

"They're not yours. Go."

They moved tentatively, sidling toward the wall of horses, and this time the silent herd drew away like an ebb tide and opened before them, and he reflected that she'd been right before. He did care what the horse-witch was. When he turned to tell her so, she was gone.

It never occurred to him to not follow.

the horse-witch 2

PROFESSIONALS

PROFESSIONALS

"His enemies are not demons, but are human beings like himself."

—LAO-TSE
The Book of the Way

*F*ollowing the horse-witch was easy.

He shrugged an interrogative toward the bluff where Orbek waited with the SPAR; a second later the young ogrillo skylined himself just long enough to wave in the general direction Kylassi's horse had bolted. He nodded and pointed with an open hand in the same direction along the rim of the bluff. Orbek waved acknowledgment and disappeared.

He started walking.

Horses drifted around him, giving him plenty of space without ever seeming to look up from industriously cropping the scrub. The herd thinned like dawn fog dissolving under the morning sun. The little valley opened into a broad rolling bowl a handful of miles across, and by the time he reached the mouth, he was alone in the open, the herd grazing disinterestedly behind him. The wind in his face smelled of pine, red clover, and oncoming weather. He didn't see her, and he gave another shrug up toward the jaws of the ravine. This time, Orbek held up both his arms, then crossed them into an X and pointed northeast.

Northeast, he caught a glimpse of something man-shaped that carried something bow-shaped in one hand as it slipped into a crease between two low knolls.

"Well," he muttered. "What ho, hail fellow well met and suchlike shit."

He faded back into the ravine mouth, then swung out along the base of the north face of the bluff. He moved like a ghost, a wisp of vapor borne by the wind: while it blew hard enough to cover his footsteps, he trotted through scrub that now thickened to grass. When it stopped, so did he.

A couple of horses were ground-tied ahead, one full-tacked, the other wearing only a halter and a lead-rope. He turned in pursuit of the bowman before the horses could take his scent.

The wind was still in his face. The bowman was staying downwind of his prey, which made it easy to stay downwind of him in turn. Fist gained steadily. Though he was no longer young, he had for some few years made a minor specialty of sneaking up on people.

He came around the shoulder of a rocky knoll to find the bowman on the summit of the next one above, no more than thirty yards away, kneeling among a jumble of weather-bleached stone. The bow was strung in an elegant reflex, short and thick and looking to have serious pop. The bowman had already nocked an arrow and extended his left arm and was drawing back the string.

"Don't do it."

He spoke just loud enough to be heard above the breeze. He didn't want to startle the bastard.

The bowman went absolutely still. His reply was no louder, and it carried the lazy twang of the southern steppes. "Don't do what?"

"Don't be a dumbass." Christ, now she had *him* doing it. "Lower your weapon."

The bowman slowly, carefully, slacked the tension on his bowstring and aimed the arrow at the ground.

"Now come out of there."

"May I turn around?"

"Sure, whatever."

The bowman edged back from the rocks, taking himself off the skyline before he stood up. The man nodded to himself: a pro.

The bowman had a closed, narrow face weathered as the rocks behind him, and slitted dark eyes that widened to discover the other man empty-handed below him. He shook his head. "And I would have sworn on my momma's hair that any man good enough to creep me would be smart enough to do it holding a bow of his own."

"I'm a crappy shot."

His dark eyes narrowed again. "Who are you?"

"You can call me Fist. Jonathan Fist, freeman of Ankhana."

"You ain't in the Empire now, freeman."

"No? Then where are we?"

"Someplace else. You alone out here?"

He shrugged. "Mostly."

"What are you doing in these hills?"

"Stopping you from shooting the horse-witch. What are *you* doing?"

"No business of yours, dead man." The bow came up.

"Don't point that at me."

The bow stopped. Old-leather wrinkles deepened around dark-slitted eyes. "Why not?"

"I don't like it. You won't either." The man calling himself Jonathan Fist tilted his head a couple degrees to one side and let it center again. "You'll get hurt."

"I'll take my chances." He drew back the string as he lifted the bow, and with a wet meaty *whap* an invisible fist smacked him spinning to the ground. The bow clattered away into the rocks. The arrow splintered against a random stone.

From the southern bluff above the mouth of the ravine, a thousand yards behind, came a faint crisp cough, like a healthy man clearing his throat.

Jonathan Fist said, "Told you."

He walked up the knoll. The scrub had given way to thick prairie grass almost knee-high that smelled weedy and full of sap. By the time he got to the top, the bowman was thrashing weakly. His boot heels scuffed gouges in the pale sandy soil as he tried to shove himself into the rocks without getting up. His rough-tanned leather jerkin was the color of pine bark except for a spreading patch of wet black around a small neat hole where his right shoulder met his chest. His left hand was over his shoulder as though it might be plugging a bigger hole in his back.

"What did you—how did you . . . ?" he gasped. His voice had gone thin and hoarse and shocky. Boneshots can do that.

"All you need to know is it can happen again."

She was a hundred yards downslope, the big bay peacefully cropping grass while she untacked Kylassi's horse. She finished ungirthing the massive high-cantled saddle, then she yanked it off and tossed it heedlessly over her shoulder like a soiled pillow. It bounced and tumbled down the slope and the bowman kept scuffling back from him and Jonathan Fist said, "How'd that feel?"

Still trying to scuffle back, the bowman blinked at him. "What?"

"You want another?"

"I, uh, I—" The bowman swallowed. "No."

"Then stay where you are."

The scuffling subsided.

She had one of the gelding's forehooves in both hands now; she was lifting it, bending the leg, working it slowly back and forth.

"What—what are you going to do with me?" The bowman's voice had gone even shakier. "I don't—I don't want to *die* . . ."

He kept watching the horse-witch. "Then quit trying to play me and give me the goddamn knife."

"Wh-what?"

Jonathan Fist sighed, and slowly turned, and looked at the bowman with eyes black as volcanic glass. "Remember what I said about being a dumbass?"

The bowman thought about it. The fear and shakiness drained out of his weathered face, leaving only the concentrated wariness of a deer hunter in bear country. His left hand came out from behind his shoulder holding a half-moon skinning knife with a split-finger grip: a fist with eight inches of blade for knuckles. "Can't fault a guy for trying."

"Can kill you for it, though." He made a flicking motion with the back of his hand. "Toss it down the hill. Easy."

"Into the rocks? Hey, c'mon—" The bowman looked distinctly offended. "You know what this knife's worth?"

"More than your life?"

"It's just—it's a hell of a thing, that's all." The wounded bowman shook his head. "It's a hell of a thing to do to a fine piece of steel. Look, I'll *give* it to you. All right? It's yours. What do you say? Just don't make me throw it into those rocks."

He chewed the inside of his lip for a second or two. "Set it in the grass, then. And the quiver. Push yourself away."

He didn't have it in him to make a pro disrespect his tools.

When the bowman had complied, he picked up the knife and held it in one hand while with the other he checked the man's wound. The bowman's face had faded from leather to old ivory, and the tremor in his hands was no longer faked, and when Jonathan Fist probed the wound, front and back, and felt splinters of bone within, the bowman shuddered and groaned against locked-shut teeth. When he was done with the wound, he looped the bowman's wide belt around the shoulder and cinched it tight: close enough to a bandage that it might keep him from bleeding out.

For a while, anyway.

The bowman got himself under control again. "How bad?"

"You might pull that bow again." A shrug. "Someday."

"Shit. That bow's my life. What else've I even got?"

"Get up."

The bowman was close enough to the rocks to pull himself to his feet. He leaned heavily against the stone, panting. "Well, uh, well—thanks for the patch, anyway. Not many out here'd bother."

"Didn't do it for you." Jonathan Fist looked down the slope. From below, she briefly met his eyes. Then she turned back to the gelding. "Come on, let's go."

"Go?"

"You're gonna meet the horse-witch."

"In a pig's asshole."

"You're gonna meet the horse-witch," he repeated, "and then you're gonna explain just why, exactly, you were about to shoot her in the back."

He helped the bowman down the slope. Slowly. The man's knees were going weak, and he didn't feel like carrying the bastard. He paused just before the knoll's slope would take them down off the skyline, and swung his arm in a wide circle, without turning his head.

The bowman frowned at the gesture, then checked the angle of the slope against a squinted measuring of the horizon that ended at the bluff. "You got friends out here."

"Worry about your own friends." Jonathan Fist steadied him down a broken shelf of rock. "Friends of yours out here will most likely bleed to death."

"I ain't sociable."

"How long before somebody shows up looking for you?"

The bowman gave a sigh that ended in a cough. "I guess we'll both find out together. Unless you want to turn me loose."

"Maybe later."

The bowman struggled down to a patch of dry grass. "This is about as far as I'm gonna make it on foot," he said, and Jonathan Fist believed him.

The horse-witch never looked up. She pried the steel shoes off the big gelding, one after another, and tossed them carelessly aside without bothering to watch where they fell.

"Hey."

She had produced a small hooked knife from somewhere and was thoughtfully sculpting the gelding's left rear hoof.

"*Hey*, dammit. You know this fucker was about to shoot you?"

"Yes." Her hands flickered, and when he could see them clearly again, the hooked knife had vanished back into whatever elsewhere it came from, replaced by a rasp that she applied to the hoof with the same absolute attention.

"Look, I'm sorry to interrupt. Hate to inconvenience you by saving your fucking life. Go right ahead on with what you're doing."

"All right."

And she did.

Again, he became conscious of the weight of the Automag on the back of his belt. "You think maybe you might be interested in, say, why? Maybe find out who wants you dead?"

"No."

He blinked. "Because you already know, or because you don't give a shit?"

She released that leg and moved on to the next. The rasp was gone and the knife was back. "You talk a lot."

"I'd talk less if you'd hold up your end of a fucking conversation."

"You mean side."

"What?"

"You're the end." She seemed to find something troubling in the hoof; a new knife, smaller, appeared in her hand. "Both ends."

"Whatever." He waved a hand. "Forget that, huh?"

"All right." She tilted her head to one side, then the other, and somehow he understood that she was examining the hoof with one eye at a time, doe-brown and milky blue-white in sequence.

His jaw hurt. He'd been grinding his teeth. "So, people try to backshoot you so often you're bored with it? Or what, you're arrow-proof?"

Her answer was only a distant shake of her head. The gelding had gone twitchy; the breeze had swung, and maybe he could smell the bowman's blood. She released his leg, squatting patiently beside him, as though there wasn't thirteen hundred pounds of nervous warhorse dancing around her.

"D'you think—" The bowman had gone white around the mouth. "Whilst you two flirt, d'you think I could maybe lie down?"

"Yeah, whatever."

As she calmed the gelding and picked up its next leg, he found himself watching the sunstreaks in her hair, shifting and gently twisting in the breeze. Made him think of dawn reflected on a rippling river. When he realized what he was doing, he shut his eyes.

Flirt. Son of a bitch. The bowman hadn't been wrong.

He might have to shoot her after all. Or himself.

He lowered himself onto a sand-colored outcrop a couple arm-lengths from where the wounded man reclined on the grass. The bowman lay on his back, his eyes squeezed shut. His forehead glistened with sweat, despite the spring chill and freshening breeze. Having considerable experience with grievous bodily harm, received as well as delivered, Jonathan Fist knew the bowman was only now getting a real taste of how much the rest of his life might suck.

After a minute or two he admitted to himself that even if the horse-witch didn't care about the bowman's story, he did. People in this part of the world don't travel alone. And questioning the man would give him something to think about. Something other than long, elegantly muscled sun-bronzed thighs, or a glance that could chill or warm or do both together but seemed in his mind to be trending definitely in the direction of warm. Maybe even hot.

He shook his head. He was, he reminded himself, old enough to know better. "Start with your name."

"Do I have to?" Hoarse. Going faint. Blood seeping out around the belt. "Talking makes it worse."

"I'd care, except ten minutes ago you tried to shoot me."

"If I talk . . ." He licked his lips. "You got water?"

"Not with me."

"But you can get it."

Jonathan Fist shrugged. The bowman still had his eyes closed, but he seemed to understand. "Listen, my horses are back there. I got three full skins. Hell, you can have one."

"I can have them all."

"Pardon me for saying, but you don't seem the type."

"Start with your name."

"Patch me real, can you? Better than this. Get me horsed and aimed on toward the rest of my life?"

"It's possible."

He coughed, and there was blood on his lips. Might have nicked a lung. Might just have bit his tongue when he fell. "You ain't as reassuring as I'd like."

"You tried to shoot me."

"Yeah." The bowman sucked in a halting breath, and he let it out with something like a shudder. "Folk who know me call me Tanner. My momma calls me Hack. Hackford, if she's mad."

"Still got your mother?"

"Sure. I ain't old as you. Shit, *she* ain't old as you."

"I'm younger than I look."

"You and me both, pappy." He coughed again. More blood. "It'll kill her to have to bury me."

"She won't."

He rolled his head a little, and one eye slitted open to examine Jonathan Fist's expression. Lack of expression. "That don't sound like a promise I'll live through this."

"It's still a promise."

"I guess." The eye drifted shut. He turned his face away. "What do you want to know?"

Tanner's story was depressingly familiar: something of value turns up where people can see it, so people, being people, decide to take it.

Ten thousand or more horses in the witch-herd, almost all of them already broke to ride, which was enough cash on the hoof to buy a good-size town. The local warlord does a rough cost-benefit analysis and decides it's worth paying twenty-five or thirty guys to collect the horses, and then five or six hundred more guys to use those horses to take over the range, cropland, and water holes belonging to warlords next door. The Lincoln County War with swords, bows, and magick.

And just like the Lincoln County War, the most interesting parts of the story were the hired killers.

None of them were anything resembling secrets. The local warlord, who called himself Count Faltane, wanted everyone to know just what kind of heavies he could afford. About half the witch-herd outfit was local, and the other half was a selection of imported hardguys and general-purpose psychos under a high-powered combat mage who called himself Bannon. Tanner was one of them. "I'm a hunter. Never miss a kill. Never spook the prey. First clue I'm there is an arrow in the back of the neck. Like being invisible."

"Not to me."

"Wasn't hunting you, was I?"

"And don't. Next time I won't be in such a gentle mood."

This outfit had been nipping at the skirts of the witch-herd for three days, but had only managed to carve off a few dozen aging, sickly, half-crippled nags. The rest of the witch-herd was smart and skittish, and always seemed to be a couple steps ahead of the men who were trying to chivvy them down into the flats. "Some of these local boys, they talk about this horse-witch, this twist who rides with the herd. Seems she's kind of a legend in these parts. The villagers leave out little gifts for her when the herd's nearby, and sometimes somebody turns around to find a horse coming up behind them like they already know each other. Story is, the witch-horses are half magickal or something, superstrong and supersmart, and if you treat 'em good they'll die for you. If you don't treat 'em good, it's you that dies."

"Sounds fair."

"Maybe it is. Except one don't seem to be enough for some folk."

"Somebody always gets greedy."

"I have been known to suffer a touch of that affliction myself."

Jonathan Fist pointed at some brown splotches on his pants leg. "This blood here? It belonged to a guy who thought he could grab some of these horses and drag them off this afternoon."

"Thought," Tanner said. "Not thinks."

"That's right."

"Well, I don't think, I hunt." Tanner shook his head and grimaced. "Hunted."

"Killing the horse-witch won't get you these horses. She's not your problem. Your problem is you."

"I suspicion that's true for a lot of people," Tanner said. "How about that water?"

"In a minute. Tell me again about this Bannon guy."

"He's the boss. Him and his pal Charlie. Bannon don't have a lot to say, but Charlie makes up for it. There's a man as loves the sound of his own voice. Good-Time Charlie, he says the girls call him, and he can tell a story, I confess. Show you the pictures too, just like being there—as pretty a sightcaster as I ever saw."

"Bannon."

"There's juice and a half in that one. On the trail out here, we flushed a K'rrx raiding party by accident—in full shell and big enough to do us the kind of harm as don't heal, *and* backed by a couple of them ghostsingers of theirs. Bannon didn't even get off his horse. None of us did. After about a minute, most of them was in pieces, and those as still whole was all over afire. I never even touched my bow."

Jonathan Fist had some experience with hostile K'rrx himself. "I'm impressed."

"You say that like it don't often happen."

"It's been a while."

"This is me returning the favor of you letting me live. People who get on the boss's wrong side come down with a bad case of dead. That *you'll get hurt* trick of yours is pretty nifty, but I don't recommend you try it on Red Bannon."

"Red?" Fist frowned. "That's his name? Red Bannon?"

"That's what we call him, 'cause of his hair and beard. Red as a fox, though on him it's more bear, as he's a more bear-size sonofabitch. Charlie calls him Lazz sometimes, but he don't like it. I don't even know if Bannon's his family or his given."

"Or just fucking made up." Fist looked at the ground, and allowed himself a couple of seconds of hoping he was wrong. "So Bannon's big, red-haired, and a bust-ass combat magicker. This Good-Time Charlie, the sightcaster who backs him up—he wouldn't be a hand or two taller, skinny as a straw? Laughs like a donkey getting kicked in the balls?"

"You know them."

"Not exactly." He rubbed his eyes, which turned into a futile attempt to massage away an oncoming migraine.

A few days tracking down his daughter's stray horses. Like a vacation. Camping in the mountains. Fresh air and spring water instead of smoke and whiskey. And instead of all that, he had somehow stumbled into another fucking meat grinder. Would have been nice if somebody could have posted a sign or something.

It's a little late to spot the grinder once your dick's already caught.

After a while, the gelding trotted off and the horse-witch came over to the two men. "Let's see that shoulder."

Both men looked askance. She said, "Well?"

Jonathan Fist moved out of her way. Tanner chuckled wetly. "Me dying ain't keeping you from something, is it?"

She uncinched the belt. One of those little knives was in her hand. She cut his tunic around his shoulder and peeled it back. "You're not dying."

"And if I was, would that have been important enough to get you over here before you finished trimming some goddamn horse feet?"

"No."

Tanner blinked, frowned, blinked again, and looked over at Fist, who opened his hands and turned his palms upward. "You asked."

"I guess."

The horse-witch reached inside her jerkin and brought out a big pinch of some kind of leaves that were dark and shriveled-looking, but still moist. She put them in her mouth and chewed thoughtfully, not unlike a contented horse with a mouthful of sweetgrass.

"You are nothing like a normal person," Tanner said.

She nodded absently and scooped the chewed leaves from her mouth with two fingers. After packing the leaves into the wounds, she plastered the sodden tunic back over them and rewrapped the belt around his shoulder. "You'll heal clean."

She stood and started walking up the slope.

Color was already returning to Tanner's face. "That feels . . . damn. Did you really just . . . ?"

His voice trailed off. She walked like she'd already forgotten about them both.

Fist went after her. "Hey, wait a second. Hey!" Dammit. "What the hell's your name, anyway?"

She paused at the crest of the slope. "They're worried about the blood," she said. "And there's an ogrillo up on the bluffs."

"Who's worried? And—" He squinted toward the bluffs. "You can *see* him?"

"The herd knows." She nodded toward the shallow defile where Tanner had left his two horses. "They're all right now."

Tanner's horses came walking cautiously up toward them, as though they'd been waiting only for permission. Fist stared. "I don't understand you at all."

She looked bored.

"If I hadn't stopped him, he would have *killed* you—"

"I get killed all the time."

"—and you're *helping* him, and what the fuck is I *get killed all the time* supposed to mean?"

She winked her ice eye at him. "Permission."

"Bullshit."

She started walking back through the rocks, heading for the ravine and the herd. "They love him."

"What, his horses? Are you fucking kidding me? 'His horses love him' means he's a good person?"

"Better than you."

"Well, no shit," he said. "Who isn't?"

She kept walking. The big bay she'd been riding rounded an outcrop and ambled toward her. Tanner's horses picked their way up through the rocks, nickering warily as if calling for him but afraid of getting an answer.

He beckoned to them, feeling ridiculous. "He's down there. It's all right."

They came on like they understood him.

He looked back downslope toward Tanner. "Your bow's up here. The knife too. Hell, even the arrows. It'll be a while before you're shooting again."

"If gratitude from me means anything—"

"Thank me by staying out of my way. Killing somebody after saving his life makes me feel like an idiot."

"Nobody wants that." Tanner waved his good hand. "Thanks anyway."

"Fuck off." He was already trotting after the horse-witch.

Again.

the horse-witch 3

PROPOSITIONS

PROPOSITIONS

"A girl likes to be asked, dumbass."

—THE HORSE-WITCH
HISTORY OF THE FALTANE COUNTY WAR
(Rev. Ed.)

He trotted after the horse-witch.

She was up on the bay now, sitting his big bounding trot like the horse was actually just her legs. He leaned forward and picked up speed. He ran without effort, and found himself wearing a fierce grin at how good it still felt when his legs did what they were told. The bay must have heard him coming; its trot lengthened until his *without effort* dried up and blew away. "Will you for fuck's sake please just *stop?*"

They did.

He caught up with them, puffing. "Finally. What changed your mind?"

"Nothing."

"Then—?"

"A girl likes to be asked, dumbass." She had her doe eye on him, and her unexpectedly gentle, good-natured smile made something in his chest lurch sideways.

"Yeah, all right," he said, shaking his head, looking away to stop himself from smiling back at her. "I should probably take notes."

"You're very rough," she said. "With you, everything's harsh. Jagged. You're always pushing. Shouting. Bullying. That's a bad way to come at a horse."

Or a woman, apparently. This one, anyway.

"Sorry," he said, surprised to discover that he actually was. "I've been living a life where manners don't count."

"That's sad for you."

"Sad doesn't count either."

She seemed to consider this for a moment. "I'm sad for you anyway."

"Don't be." People getting sad for him might lead him to getting sad for himself, which could be fatal in a multiplicity of ways. "Don't worry about me."

"You're ordering me to not be sad?"

"Lady, seriously, you have bigger problems than my shitty life."

"How do you know?"

"Will you stop that?" He lifted a hand. "Please. Don't answer. Listen."

Her gaze was patient as the bluffs behind her.

"That guy with the bow, he's not the only swinging dick out here to kill you today. There's more. A lot more. And compared to the guy running the outfit, I'm about as dangerous as a bag of puppies. The herd is what they want. They think killing you will get it for them."

"They'll be disappointed."

"Yeah, and it'd be nice if somebody could explain that to them *before* you die."

She nodded thoughtful agreement. "That would be nice."

"They don't want to come after you when you're with the herd, but if that's the only way to get you, they'll do it. Then horses will get hurt too. Killed."

"Very likely."

"You don't look too worried about it."

"That's not what I do."

"What, you don't worry about the horses? And you don't protect them or rule them, and really what the fuck *do* you do?"

She gave him both eyes. "Forgiveness—"

"And permission, yeah yeah, whatever. Forgiveness, permission, and the occasional hoof trim."

She smiled down at him, and spoke clearly, companionably, without the slightest trace of condescension. "Sometimes a horse has a problem I can help with—a sore foot, a cut, cactus needles. Other things. Many things are done best by someone with thumbs. Sometimes I have a problem a horse can help me with—when I must travel swiftly, or far, or need some-one to watch over me when I sleep. Many things are done best by someone with hooves. They don't do this because I'm the horse-witch, and being the horse-witch isn't why I do this. These things are what friends do for friends."

"Hey, wait." He frowned. That had actually made sense. "What happened? This is suddenly almost a real conversation."

"You're starting to understand what I am."

"I said *almost*." He waved a hand. "I'd like to understand you. I would. I was wrong before, when I said I didn't give a shit. But trying seems like a waste of time, when you'll be dead by sundown."

The crinkles around her eyes bespoke only impenetrable serenity and a reserved, patient compassion. "I'm never dead."

"What happened to *I get killed all the time*?"

"Being killed isn't the same as being dead."

"For most people, one follows kind of hard on the heels of the other."

A dismissive shrug. "People."

He knew this would piss him off, but somehow he couldn't help himself. "You're not people?"

"I'm the horse-witch."

"The horse-witch isn't a person?"

"The horse-witch," she said, "is me."

He opened his mouth to retort, then changed his mind and just lowered himself onto the rocks and sat, resting his forehead on the palm of his hand. "Never mind. I was having this dream, I guess, where I was talking with this nice-looking woman on a horse and actually *getting* somewhere. Shit was starting to make sense."

"You're getting farther than you think," she said. "I like you now."

"Excuse me?"

"I like you," she repeated. "When you're quiet. You get sane. You care. Even about me, though you don't know me. I wanted to like you from the instant I saw you. But you're difficult to like."

"So I hear."

"I hope I can keep on liking you, because I want you to like me. When I look at you, I think about sex."

He coughed, caught his breath, and coughed again. "I'm sorry?"

"You are a conspicuously beautiful man, and you're very fit, and strong, and competent in unexpected ways. You expect women to be attracted to you, and I am. When I look at you, I think about sex. With you. Sex with you will be very, very good."

He coughed again, but it didn't help. "Little old for you, aren't I?"

"Old?"

She laughed, and in her laugh was the creak of calving glaciers, the grind of rock along subterranean faults, the hush of surf and the soft, wet layers of decay that become the rich dark earth thundering under a billion years of hooves and feet and claws of creatures so ancient that all trace of them was gone from the world . . .

But not from her.

In her they still lived and ran and fought and fucked and called to her to come play with them in their vanished eternity.

He said, "Ah . . . ah, shit, come on, don't . . ."

She fixed him with her ice eye, and something in the back of his life broke open and left all of him naked to the winds of forever. They curled and twisted and raked his existence with whispers of razor-edged ice.

"Stop it. Stop it, *please*." He covered his eyes with his hands but it didn't seem to help. "Don't *do* that."

"Years mean nothing." Her voice was warm and human again, and when he saw the invitation dancing playfully in her eyes, warm and cold together, something inside his chest lurched again. One more time might break it altogether. "We're on horse-time."

"I don't know what that is."

"Sometimes eating an apple can last all day."

"So that's, like, a metaphor for sex?"

"Do you want it to be?"

"Uh . . . Shit. All right, I get it. Maybe. So I, ah, I mean—doesn't sex usually come up after we're, like, actually introduced?"

"I know you. You're getting to know me."

"I don't even know your name."

"What name?"

That one he wasn't even going to try to answer.

"I've been told I'm skilled," she said. "At sex."

"Uh, okay."

"Uniquely skilled."

"I can't even imagine."

"That's true." Her smile broadened. "It'll change your life. For the better. That's only an opinion, but it's informed. Well informed."

"Listen, uh—" He rubbed his eyes. He'd had some kind of lie ready, he was sure he had, but now he couldn't even guess what it might have been. He sighed. "When I look at you, sex is not what I think about. When I look at you, I don't really think at all. I sort of can't."

"Thank you."

"I didn't mean it as a—" He stopped himself, because he realized he *had* meant it as a compliment, and she knew it, and trying to deny it would just make him feel even stupider. "I like you. I do. But I'm not a, y'know, a casual sex guy. Besides, I'm kind of in the middle of something right now, okay? My life is a complicated place."

"You misunderstand what's happening here."

"You're not making a pass at me?"

"In your world, people say things to test, persuade, seduce, manipulate, deceive, or dominate others. But this is my world. I say things because I think they're true, and because I want you to know them. I want you to know that I like you, and that if I still like you when you decide you want to have sex with me, we'll be happy. Both of us. For a long time."

"And if I, like, decide to have sex with you sometime when you don't like me?"

"Then one of us will die."

"Um . . ."

"I can't be forced. Into sex, or anything else."

"Not that you need to worry—"

"I don't."

"But really? You can't be forced? Like in general?"

"Submission is not what I do." She gave him the winter eye. "People who try get hurt. Many die."

"But you don't."

"Sometimes. But I'm never dead, so I don't really mind."

"Just so you know? If you get killed today, forget about the sex. No matter what people say about me, I'm not into cold."

Her brows drew together just enough to hint that a line could someday develop there. "All right," she said. "Usually it's less trouble to let them kill me. But you might be worth it."

"Flatterer."

"I said *might*."

He smiled at her. She smiled back. The whatever-it-was inside his chest lurched sideways one more time, and this time it cracked, and he knew this was going to end in tears.

Being old enough to know better but still too young to resist mostly sucks.

He shook it off. "First, we need to find these fuckers. Orbek's a pretty good scout—"

"They're over there," she said, waving vaguely eastward. "Three dry washes come together. Lots of rocks."

She saw the inquiring look on his face, and shrugged. "The herd knows. Orbek is the ogrillo?"

"Yeah."

"Then he's already found them."

For the span of a breath or two, the wind shifted east. When it did, Jonathan Fist heard an irregular scatter of distant coughs, and saw flares of power swell upward from behind the hills that made an open question of who found whom, and without a word he lurched into a sprint. As he took his first steps, three blasts erupted over there, painting the sky with fire and shattered rock, and then the whole mouth of the ravine blasted into a living wave as the witch-herd boiled out and galloped for the open savannah.

He ran hard.

Those bluffs were barely over half a mile away; some tinkering in his blood chemistry with Monastic Control Disciplines would get him there flat-out. He'd be winded, but he'd be there, and he wouldn't have to catch his breath to pull a trigger.

Thunder rolled behind him, and when he remembered there hadn't been so much as a cloud in the sky for three days, he looked over his shoulder. The thunder was the big bay that carried the horse-witch, coming on at a gallop.

She extended a hand toward him and he had just long enough to get a really vivid picture of the bay, the horse-witch, and him hitting the scrub in a full speed face-plant, because she didn't have a saddle or a bridle or even fucking *stirrups* or any of the shit that makes this kind of bullshit maneuver possible, but she caught his hand and threw herself the opposite way over the bay's withers just enough to keep the horse and herself perfectly balanced as she swung him up behind her and he caught her round her slim hard waist and hugged her exactly as tight as he would have if he hadn't been thinking about having sex with her.

She nodded to him over her shoulder, and raised her voice to be heard over the wind and the bass-drum pounding of the bay. "*What friends do for friends . . .*"

He answered her nod with one of his own, and hung on.

Tight.

Apparently the herd had a good fix on the location of everyone in the area. The horse-witch brought the bay to a halt on a sunlit slope, just below the rocks that would force them to proceed on foot, and Jonathan Fist hadn't seen so much as a wisp of the raiders. "This way."

She led him on a winding course over the shoulder of that hill and up the southern slope of one that was taller, and rockier, and Jonathan Fist heard the sharp clatter of the SPAR-12 on autoburst. "Orbek!" he shouted. "*Orbek*, goddamn you sorry fucking excuse for a broke-down assbitch, what do you think you're *doing*?"

There came a brief interval of silence as the echoes died away.

"Um . . . hey there, little brother. Um, sorry."

"What part of *stay out of sight* do you not fucking understand?" Jonathan Fist strode up through the tumbled boulders. The young ogrillo lay prone in a natural barricade of jagged rock, still with his eye to the scope as he aimed downhill. "Put the goddamn rifle down."

"One second, little brother." *Crack* and somebody down there yelped. "Fucker."

"Orbek."

"Time to shift anyway." Orbek snaked backward from the firing point and rolled into a sitting position, rifle across his knees. "Hey."

"Fucking right hey, goddammit."

His grey-leather cheeks darkened. He looked down.

"They sneak me while I'm watching you, coming up downwind. Shifty breeze, though, good for me. If the breeze don't shift, I never know they're there. Can have take me with a knife. How's that for suck? Who wants to die embarrassed? But instead I nose 'em and shuck off for high ground, and one comes out and says *We got thirty guys down here! What you got up there?* and since he asks so nice . . ." He shrugged. "I show him."

Jonathan Fist rubbed his eyes. "How many dead?"

"None. I'm an amateur now?"

"That's what I'm trying to figure out."

"Winged some. What you humans call, you know, kneecapped? Three, maybe four, before they work their Shield. And then this fucker just now."

"Terrific."

"It's a nice shot on that bowman back there, hey? Pretty shiny, you gotta say."

Fist didn't answer. He moved toward a position among the rocks that might not get him killed.

"And hey, human lady—? Excuse my no-fucking-manners little brother. Orbek Black Knife: Taykarget."

She nodded gravely. "The horse-witch."

"Pleeztameetcha donwannahaveta eetcha."

"Likewise."

Fist worked his way around the outcroppings to take in the fire zone. The guy who'd crept Orbek would have most likely been another bowman like Tanner, flushing Orbek by accident while working his way up here to stand lookout. Now the ogrillo—who was gifted with any weapon, but especially with firearms—was up here with the SPAR, with clear shots for a long damn way down each of the three washes that were the only way in or out. The place was the sort of trap even a smart guy can fall into, if he doesn't know he might need to worry about such things as selective-projectile assault rifles.

But Orbek had a dragon by the tail; if he bailed, he couldn't hold them in the wash, and they could swamp him in seconds. Kneecapping instead of killing meant they'd have nonwalking wounded to look after, which would slow them down. It'd also make them kind of motivated to inflict harm of their own. "Christ, what a sandpaper clusterfuck this turned out to be," he said. "The grenades?"

"They got thaumaturges. Thaumaturges got Shields. Gotta knock 'em down somehow," Orbek said. "How come other guys always got thaumaturges?"

"For spare toilet paper. How the fuck should I know?"

"How come *we* never got thaumaturges?"

"Because I can't stand being around them. Shut up."

"Since when you can't? You *marry* one—"

"Did you not hear me say shut up?"

"And you're ass-pals with Emperor Deliann, who's just about—"

"Orbek."

"Sorry. Yah yah. Sorry."

Jonathan Fist rubbed his eyes again, then rubbed his forehead, then scratched all the sand out of his hair and finally he just said, "Screw this anyway."

He moved away from Orbek's last firing point. "Danny!" he shouted. "Danny Macallister! You down there?"

A distant voice echoed off the rocks. "*Who the fuck is Tammie Mick Lassiter?*"

"Danny, it's Hari Michaelson! Come on, man. Talk to me."

There followed a span of silence, which was finally broken by a different voice, deeper, and a lot closer. "No shit?"

Jonathan Fist nodded to himself. "You got Liam with you? Lee, hey, Hari Michaelson. Sing out."

A third voice, closer still. "Yeah, sorry, woulda said something already but I had to unswallow my tongue. Fuck me upside-down and sideways, Hari fucking *Michaelson*! Can somebody come wipe shit outa the seat of my pants? You're supposed to be dead!"

"I've heard that," he said. "Danny, Lee, we need to talk."

The horse-witch said softly, "You know these men."

"Not personally," Fist said, low. "By reputation. They know me the same way."

Danny's deep voice echoed up the hill. "What do we call you?"

"Jonathan Fist. You're going by Red Bannon, right? And Lee, you're this Good-Time Charlie I've heard about?"

"That's what the girls call me."

"Only ones who don't know you," the horse-witch muttered.

He decided not to ask how she knew. "Listen, Bannon, Charlie, there's no reason to go bringing our other handles into this, huh?"

"Depends. What is 'this'?"

"It's a situation that's gonna go better for all of us if we keep who we used to be out of it."

"Sounds fair. So. You wanted to talk? We're talking. What can we do for you?"

"It's more like what I can do for you, Red. But maybe you don't want what I can do shouted all the way to the fucking coast, you know what I mean?"

Orbek leaned close behind Jonathan Fist's shoulder. "Aktiri, hey?"

"Yeah."

"What's these other names of theirs, hey? Ones I maybe hear before?"

"Fucking be *quiet*." Fist turned to the ogrillo. His face was bleak, and he looked a decade or two older than he had earlier in the afternoon. "Good-Time Charlie? That's Morgan Blackwood."

Orbek's yellow eyes bulged, and a thin choking noise came from his throat. "Grh? So the other—he must be—"

"Keep it *down*."

"I'm shooting at Lazarus fuck me *Dane*?" Orbek's eyes rolled white. "Born lucky, I must be. Holy shit."

"Now you might understand why you better settle the fuck down while you still have a down to fucking settle."

"But—but Lazarus Dane, holy shit. Lazz Dane can take off the whole top of this top! Bottom too, and everything between, hey? Why's he wait?"

"The rifle," Fist said, grim and low. "He doesn't want to damage the rifle. Or the grenades. Or any other Artan gear that might be up here. He didn't know suchlike crap exists on this world. Now he does."

Orbek thought about it. He sagged against the rocks. "Shit."

"He can do a lot of shit just with magick, but quietly putting a shatter-slug into somebody's skull at two thousand meters isn't one of them."

"Yah . . ." Orbek echoed Fist's sigh. "Still, helluva shot on that bowman, though, hey?"

"Ask me again after we live through this."

"Hey, Michaelson, if you're just looking to walk out of here, we can dicker," Bannon called out. "Must be a nice rifle."

"It's a work of fucking art. Forget it. I've got something better."

"I could be interested in better, I guess."

"Crossed paths with your bowman Hack Tanner a span or two back."

"His momma'll be sorry to hear that."

"He's alive."

"Really?"

"So far."

"Well, that's the most you can say for any of us, I guess," Bannon said. "If it doesn't seem too cold-ass to ask, why didn't you kill him?"

"I didn't have to."

"Don't recall hearing about that stopping you before."

"Maybe I decided to start acting like a grown-up."

"Well, shit down the back of my neck. Everybody gets old, I guess. Even you."

"Guys like us don't get old," Fist said. "We get slow, then we get dead. And I'm already slow."

"And aren't you just a bushel of sunbeams."

"Your guy Tanner, he peeled the slim on you and your Count Fartface or whateverthefuck, and I'm thinking, Well, this Red Bannon we got here sounds game enough, but somebody pooched the pitch. I'm thinking, I might know who Red Bannon used to be, and I might know who his pal Charlie used to be, and if this Bannon and this Charlie know who *I* used to be, we could all aim higher than working as some assclown's fucking *cowboys*."

"Well, you know, yippee-tie home on the range and shit," Bannon called back. "The payout on this job sparkles all year long."

"So? It's still a fucking *job*. Come on, Danny—sure, there's money to be made doing other people's shit work. I'm thinking a smart bastard like you might want to be the guy who pays some *other* shithead to do *your* shit work. Am I wrong?"

Somebody else called out, "You ain't listening to this asshole, are you? I don't think the Count is gonna like finding out—"

The growing shadows in the dry wash were blasted away by a streak of green fire and a detonation that rang among the rocks for what seemed a very long time. There followed a silence that rang even longer.

"Anybody else?" Red Bannon said quietly.

Another long silence.

"Really," Bannon said. "Anyone else want to tell me how the Count'll feel when he *finds out*?"

A longer silence.

"Michaelson?"

"Fist," he said. "Still here."

Bannon switched from Westerling to English. "What's the proposal? You looking for work?"

Fist did the same. "Yeah, no offense, Danny, your corporate disciplinary policy is a little fucking harsh."

Bannon laughed. "The deal?"

"You probably heard about me and the Studio and shit, right?"

"Something like it. I hear after your wife took the drop, you blew up half of Ankhana. And made 'em line up to kiss your ass for it."

"Something like that. I don't think any of us is going home. Ever."

"It's been three years. I'm inclined to agree."

"There's none of us getting younger, Danny. Guys our age, we should be looking for someplace to retire."

Silence.

Then: "I'm listening."

"So, this Count Fartface, I hear he's got a pretty nice spread. Villages, handful of towns, nice capital. Big enough that he doesn't need any more land, he's just stirring shit up because he's an asshole."

"Yeah, but who isn't?"

"Well, there's assholes and assholes. There's assholes like him," said Jonathan Fist, "and then there's assholes like, y'know, us."

"Us." Bannon sounded thoughtful. "Well."

"Here's the thing: for two hundred miles around there's maybe only a handful of guys who know who I used to be. I could be the only guy down here who knows who you two used to be. Knowing what we know, I'm thinking that between us, we can persuade Fartface to settle his Count ass right down. Without hesitation, reservation, or fucking conversation."

"Do you practice that shit?" Charlie drawled, also in English. "Or are you just naturally verbalicious?"

"Screw the horses. Leave them. We don't need them, and without them Fartface won't be invading anybody this year, and maybe never," Fist said. "We don't work for the Studio anymore, Danny. We don't have to start a fucking war just to earn a living."

Silence.

"Red, he's got a point." This from Charlie. "If the war goes bad, all of a sudden the whole place is on fire and everybody's dead and it won't be such a nice spot for us to live."

"Risky. Real damn risky."

"Think about it, Danny. Instead of starting a war, we can end one before it starts. And retire as landed gentry."

"Not likely," Bannon said, grim. "Not while the Count's alive."

"Danny, Danny, Danny, come *on*, man." Fist grunted an ugly laugh. "Who are you talking to?"

Silence.

"You know, Red, that's another good point."

"Yeah," Bannon said slowly. "It surely is."

Fist laid one hard hand across Orbek's harder shoulder. He kept his voice down. "Take the supplies and the weapons," he said in Westerling. "Leave the extra clips for the Automag and a couple boxes of tristacks. Take the gold. Get those poor bastard grooms remounted and rekitted and kick them back toward Harrakha."

"Like you say, little brother."

"After that, stay with the witch-herd. I figure maybe a tenday, maybe two. Between now and when I get back, kill anybody who comes after the horses. Or the horse-witch. You okay with this?"

The ogrillo's fleshy brows drew together. "If you don't come back?"

"Worry about that when it doesn't happen."

He nodded. "Like you say."

"Die fighting, Orbek."

"Die fighting, little brother." He picked his way back down through the rocks toward the cache of gear. Full dark was coming on.

Fist turned to the horse-witch. "Look out for him, will you?"

"That's not what I do."

"Not as the horse-witch," he said. "As a friend."

"Then of course." She looked solemn. "This is dangerous for you."

He shrugged. "Everything's dangerous."

"I prefer you alive."

"Thanks. Me too."

"You place your life between dangerous men and horses, and you don't like horses. Between dangerous men and me, and you don't know me. Do you know why you're doing this?"

His lips drew into a thin flat line. "What does *why* have to do with anything?"

"I hope you know. That's all."

He was silent for a long time. He'd been right about this ending in tears. About that, he was always right. It always was tears and he knew it and he was old enough to know better but her hair smelled of sunshine and grass and wildflowers and finally the knots in his heart twisted so tight he could barely breathe.

"Is it all right . . ." He coughed, and swallowed, and took a deep breath. "May I touch you?"

"Of course."

He reached out with his left hand and she came to him seriously, solemnly, staring full on, her eyes of fawn and white into his of midnight. Instead of pulling her to him, he let his hand slide up her neck to the corner of her jaw, where the bone was a little crooked, like an old break badly healed. He slid his hand along her cheek to touch a small, almost invisible scar that tugged at her lower lip, and reached with his other hand to her ice eye, and to the pale thread of scar that snaked up from her eyebrow. He pulled her closer. His fingers found the back of her jerkin's loose collar, and there on her back he felt what he had known would be there: skin with the texture of silk layered over irregularly knotted cords.

Whip scars.

"Price of admission," she said. "Not just any girl can be horse-witch."

"Must have hurt."

"Some more than others. Some still do. But you know about scars. You especially."

"It's that obvious?"

"That's why you're welcome here. You always have been. You always will be," she said. "Come and go as you please. You're paid in full."

"I guess I knew that, too." He gave her as much of a kiss as the knots in his heart would allow: one chaste brush of his lips on her forehead. "I guess that's one reason why I'm doing this."

She gave him a smile like dawn breaking over mountains. "I still like you."

"Funny thing," Jonathan Fist said. "That's the other reason."

the now of always 4

ENTER HERO

ENTER HERO

"She's a hero, Ma'elKoth. A real hero, not like me—or you
either, no offense. She couldn't stand off and let innocents be
killed, and that's the only reason she's involved in this in the
first place."

— "CAINE" (PFNL. HARI MICHAELSON)
For Love of Pallas Ril

When Duncan reopens his eyes, another woman has joined them.
She is tall, clad in a full suit of gleaming tourney plate. Her short-cut
hair is dark auburn with red streaks of sunbleach. She stands, staring out
across the snow-softened badlands, a great helm under her right arm and
a shield on her left. He sees no sign of a weapon.

Duncan says, "Hello."

She turns and meets his eyes, then inclines her head in grave acknowledgment. "Dr. Michaelson. An honor, sir."

"Duncan, meet Angvasse, Lady Khlaylock." Caine now sits on the
other side of him, next to the horse-witch. "She used to be Champion of
Khryl."

Khryl . . . Interesting. He remembers another female Khryllian, from
several of Caine's early Adventures. And he remembers the name Khlaylock. "I believe the honor is mine, Lady Khlaylock. You'll excuse my not
getting up."

She inclines her head toward the sword. "Courtesy surrenders to necessity, Doctor."

"A gracious answer. And there's no need to address me as *Doctor*."

"I apologize, sir. I have been given to understand that this is a title you yet hold."

"Technically, I suppose, yes. It has been a very long time since I have practiced my profession, and even then, the customary honorific was *Professor*." He turns his head toward Caine. "Lady Khlaylock is another of the 'people' you spoke of?"

"Yeah."

"Since she doesn't look like anyone I know, can I assume she is who she appears to be?"

"Depends. Who do you think she appears to be?"

"Someone on your side."

"My only side, Professor," she says stolidly, "is that of my sworn duty. I have no other."

"Your duty? You have duty here?"

"Wherever I am. Simply put, I am sworn, in all ways and at all times, to reflect honor upon the Order of Khryl. Here I have an additional duty as well: to defend this place and all within it with every power at my command."

"You're here to guard us? From whom?"

"From whomever might seek to do you harm."

"Ah." He looks over at Caine, who has one hand resting on the horse-witch's knee. "Curious how much of your life is defined by your complex relationships with exceptional women."

"Curious for a guy who hasn't had a mother since he was six?"

"If you want to hurt me with that needle, you'll have to stick it somewhere else." He rolls his head back over toward Angvasse. "Lady Khlaylock, I hope you have been made welcome here. Please feel free to have a seat and relax."

"I do feel free, sir. I prefer to stand."

He turns to Caine. "A relative, yes? Daughter?"

"The woman she looks like is his niece. Might as well be daughter." He gives a *same difference* head-bob. "Raised in his household."

"The household of a man you maimed with a sucker punch."

"And killed him the same way."

Duncan is far past being surprised by such news, but still he finds the concept difficult. "You'd think after the first time, he'd know better than to get that close."

Caine shrugs. "Special circumstances."

"When did this happen?"

"Mostly now."

"And yet here stands his niece."

"Sort of. These are special circumstances too."

"This man did not kill him," Angvasse says. "Purthin Khlaylock dishonored himself, House Khlaylock, and the Order of Khryl. It was Khryl who took his life; this man had the honor of acting as Khryl's agent, no more."

"You managed to convince her you were doing God's work? You're smoother than I thought."

"I didn't convince her of anything. And that's not really her. You get that, right?"

"Well . . ." Duncan has been frowning so much for so long he's giving himself a headache. "I know I'm not really me in one sense, obviously; I know I'm not a twenty-something man with a sword through his chest. But otherwise—"

"Yeah, well, otherwise you're not really you either. None of us is."

"I am," the horse-witch says. "I'm never anything else."

"Except for the horse-witch. But she's a special case."

"I'm still not entirely sure exactly what she is." He nods to her. "What you are."

"I'm the horse-witch."

"And the horse-witch is . . . ?"

"Is the horse-witch," Caine says. "You get used to it. Here's the thing: this place is a real place, but it's also a metaphor, just like the sword is a metaphor but still a real sword. Just like I am. You need to understand that so are you. We're each here to represent something."

"Except for me," the horse-witch says.

"Except for her."

"Represent what?"

"If it were simple enough to be described in a sentence or two, we wouldn't need metaphors, right? Any answer I can give you will be just another metaphor. And anyway, each of us is kind of a special case too. Look, Angvasse there isn't the real Angvasse; she looks like her because the real Angvasse is the most profound expression of what this woman here with us really is."

"And who is that? Who are you really?"

"You seek another name?"

"I don't wish to insult you, but I do hope to understand you."

Caine looks disgusted. "I explained about anthropology, right?"

She nods. "There is no insult in the service of truth."

"So who are you, really?" Duncan repeats patiently. "Who just pledged to defend this place and everyone in it?"

"I did."

"And you aren't Angvasse Khlaylock."

"I am as much Angvasse Khlaylock as she can be Me. She is My Aspect in this place."

"Aspect?" A peculiar tingling seems to begin in the sword and trickles outward along every nerve and vessel. "You're a god?"

"You seem undismayed."

"My son was married to one."

"Ah."

"And so—if a Knight is your Aspect, you must be . . ."

"Yes, Professor Michaelson," she says simply. She turns to show him the back of her shield; with no hand to hold it, the shield is bolted to the stump of her wrist. "I am Khryl."

yesterday's tomorrow

MEAT PUPPETS

MEAT PUPPETS

*"It wasn't Tourann's fault that the god he served had murdered
my wife, and my father, mind-raped my daughter and made my
best friend into his immortal zombie meat puppet. Gods are
like that.*

"And what the hell: He's my god too."

—DOMINIC SHADE
 Caine Black Knife

The smoke choked out the moon and haloed the flames of tenements
around. It smelled of seared wool and burning blood, and of the thick
stinking lampblack that twists up from untrimmed wicks. The screams
were sporadic now; civilians in Purthin's Ford knew that screams draw the
Hunt, and no armsman would sully his honor by showing terror. Echoes
of gunfire boomed in the distance and nearby, random splatters of blast
accented by an occasional roar of *Dizhrati golzinn Ekk!*

The fires were a gift. Deep shadows flickered and twisted at the edges,
always in motion, masking his movement, and not even ogrillo eyes could
dark-adapt fast enough to see him beyond flame. He flitted across empty
streets and threaded ink-black alleyways. The supple suede of his soft boots
kept his footfalls no louder than the rush of flames and the swirling wind.

He followed the river until he could glimpse the street where they had
come out of the water. The street where the hostelry stood.

Had stood.

He found he had stopped without meaning to. He leaned on a white-washed wall and tried to unclench his jaw. "Not the hostelry, goddammit," he muttered. "It was the Pratt and Redhorn. At least fucking *say* it."

The timeline was hard to correlate, but he was pretty sure it had to be hours rather than minutes since Lord Motherfucking Righteous Markham Tarkanen had slapped him into a skull fracture. Five of the fucking Leisure-brat Smoke Hunters had still been upright and active.

Hours. Jesus.

He'd been trying to imagine some way it could have worked out okay. He hadn't come up with any. Five mostly indestructible monsters under the control of a pack of sociopathic teenagers. Who'd get extra points for killing everyone at the Pratt & Redhorn and burning the place to its foundation.

Kravmik Red Horn, who could roast a duck that would bring tears to your eyes with every bite, who had independently discovered the secret of Scotch whiskey. Lasser Pratt, the harried, hardworking head-of-the-family hosteler. Yttrall, his fierce and beautiful Jheldhi bride. Their infant twins. His son, the armsman nurturing hope of Knighthood . . .

It already seemed like a long time ago. In one sense it was. But only one.

In every other sense it had happened maybe an hour ago.

And he was too old, too tired, and too guilty to pick over the charred corpses of people he'd actually liked.

What was it about this place? If he raised his head, he could look up into the face of Hell and probably pick out the spot where he'd crushed Stalton's skull with a Black Knife war hammer, and he needed to stop this shit, because if he kept it up, pretty soon he'd be thinking about Marade, about her breathtaking courage and a toughness he could barely imagine, and that would get him started on *Race for the Crown of Dal'Kannith* and how she and Tizarre could survive everything except Berne. And that would get him to Shanna, and he didn't have time for that shit right now. It was this fucking place. Something in the air wouldn't let him just walk.

Jesus. Why did he keep coming back to this town?

Why did he feel like he'd never left?

He pushed off the wall and forced himself to keep walking. The alley, he decided. He could come at it from the alley. The alley where Markham had stood waiting for Calm Guy and Whistler and Hawk. And him. Sort of ease his way in, instead of having to face the fucking thing all at once.

And maybe there was something there, some kind of a clue, he didn't know, cigarette butts or peanut hulls or whateverthefuck people did on stakeouts in Purthin's Ford, a clue that might tell him something if he were smarter and sharper and actually knew shit other than how to kill people.

Besides, that's where he'd dropped the pistol.

Maybe nobody thought to pick it up. Maybe it was still lying where he'd dropped it. Maybe this time he'd get lucky. Maybe. That's how his luck seemed to run. Luck for him. Everybody else fucking duck and cover.

He found an alley mouth on the opposite side of the block and paced along it slowly, silently, giving his eyes a chance to adjust, pumping up his night vision which told him, predictably, nothing of value. No sign of the Automag. An ogrillo arm lay on the brick only a meter or so past the far end of the alley. If he moved close enough to look it over, he couldn't avoid seeing whatever was left of the Pratt & Redhorn. And he didn't need a close look. It was a right arm. He remembered the Smoke Hunter he'd blown it off of, how he had stopped in the street to pick it up and bring it along.

Packard. That was it. The kid riding the one-armed Smoke Hunter. Little fucking Packard, two weeks shy of his fifteenth birthday. Normal enough kid. Self-professed fanboy, mouthy and pushy and smart, figuring out how his pack could do something nobody else had ever quite accomplished.

Kill Caine.

The high point of his young life. His natural reaction. Just an extra boss battle. If you meet Caine in the road, kill him.

Because, y'know, children are the future.

This particular child had probably killed and eaten one of Lasser and Yttrall Pratt's baby twins. If he didn't, one or more of his friends did. Except for Turner, who no longer had a mouth. Or a face or a head at all.

Maybe the Khryllians were right. Maybe Earth really was where bad people go when they die. The True Hell. He could make the argument. How was the Smoke Hunt different from possession? How were Actors, doing violence, starting wars, crushing lives for the entertainment of their underworldly brethren, different from devils?

How was he different from a mythological hell-spawn, clawed up from Pandemonium to wreak suffering and death across the face of the world?

He remembered lying on the transfer platform in the Cavea, Kosall through his guts, Shanna with him, cradling his head, Berne's corpse beneath him. He'd seen it on Ma'elKoth's face. He'd spoken the words himself, in his Soliloquy, his Actor's internal monologue.

. . . he sees that his world, Overworld—that place of brutality and pain and sudden death—is the dreamed-of, sought-after paradise of this one, where now he's trapped.

I've brought him with me into Hell.

He knew something about monsters. Berne had been a monster. Kollberg had been worse. But there are monsters and monsters. Some monsters can be haunted by faces of their dead.

Once again he found himself leaning against a wall, head down, only his locked-straight knees between him and collapse, and he pushed off the wall and lifted his head and bared his teeth to the fire-lit clouds. "You fuckers won't break me. None of you. One at a time or all in a rush."

He was talking mostly to himself because he was more than one of those fuckers himself and if he broke himself there was nobody to put him back together. He shook the knots out of his shoulders, cracked his neck and all his knuckles, and walked out of the alley.

Where the Pratt & Redhorn had once stood, there stood a building that looked exactly like the Pratt & Redhorn.

He stopped in the street, frowning, blinking, unable at first to comprehend . . . until he saw the woman sitting on the boardwalk in front of the door.

She was on the high side of middle age, body thick and as square as her jaw, hair clipped short around a hand-size swipe of burn scar where she should have had a right ear. She sat calmly, even stolidly, a thick walking stick across her knees, and she was staring at him with no expression at all.

"Holy shit." He had to stop himself from running across the street and gathering her into his arms. "Holy *shit*, t'Passe! I'd kiss you, except you'd clock me for it. You are absolutely the last fucking thing I expected to find here. You saved the place."

"Not alone," she said tonelessly. "You are nigh upon the last thing I expected as well. I thought you were dead."

"Lots of people do. Where are the Pratts? Where's Kravmik?"

"Inside. It's worth noting that also inside are several Khryllian firearms, of which at least two are aimed at you right now, by persons who know how to use them and who have no stake in your continued health. They have no idea who you are."

He stopped. "Okay."

"I don't know who you are either."

"T'Passe, for fuck's sake—"

"Kravmik said Lord Tarkanen killed you and carried away your corpse."

"He was fucking close to right."

"You seem well."

"It's complicated."

"Of course."

He spread his hands. "Look, t'Passe, I don't care. I came back here thinking there'd be nothing left but cinders and burned corpses. There's some equipment I thought—"

"Like this?" She lifted a hand, and out from the sleeve of her robe appeared the Automag.

"Well, yeah, actually. Those are hard to come by."

"Yes." She pointed it at him. "I prefer that you keep your distance."

He raised his hands. "Shit, you can have it. I'm just glad the Pratts are safe."

"Safe enough. Lasser took a fighting claw to the chest that punctured his lung, and Kravmik's legs are broken. Yttral and the twins are fine. There are some others wounded, but no one you know. Nothing Tyrklld can't fix."

"You've seen Tyrklld? He's functional?"

"Yes." She seemed disinclined to elaborate.

"Look, I need him. Can you find him for me?"

"Yes." She tilted the pistol and righted it again. "The question is, will I?"

She was welcome to her Cainist crap this time. Shit, maybe every time. He was still astonished to be standing before an intact Pratt & Redhorn. "Wow. I mean, seriously. Wow and thank you, t'Passe. Really. Thanks."

"You're welcome." Her tone remained neutral. "Why are you thanking me?"

"You called out your Cainist cavalry and rode to the fucking rescue." He still couldn't believe it. "I mean, shit, how'd you even *know*?"

"Ah, I see the misunderstanding." Her expression softened, coming as close to a smile as he'd ever seen on her face. "Our defense of this establishment had nothing to do with your stay here. Lasser Pratt is a friend."

"You have friends?"

"He and Yttrall—and Kravmik, for that matter—are fellow Disciples."

"Right, right. Sure. I'd forgotten."

"In the two hours since you learned it?"

He waved this off. "I'm just glad they'll be okay."

"We gratefully accept the protection of the Order of Khryl, but we don't rely on it. The Pratt and Redhorn is our local emergency rally point. This city being what it is, emergencies are usually Smoke Hunts. Here we call roll, organize retrieval of the missing, bind our wounds, and stand to defend ourselves."

"Here?"

"It's sturdier than it looks. It housed the parish vigilry for decades, until the current Riverdock facility was built. And—" She shrugged. "—it's the best pub on the Battleground."

He nodded. "Okay if I sit?"

"Over there." She kept the Automag centered on his chest. "Then perhaps you can tell me who you are."

He lowered himself to the boardwalk a few feet away. "Jonathan Fist."

"Ah. And you are somehow distinct from, say, Dominic Shade?"

"It's complicated."

"To be sure. I am, ah, reliably informed that—ah, Dominic Shade, or his body, or yours—was taken by Artan soldiers, presumably to Arta—as you say, your Earth."

"You have a source inside BlackStone?"

"More than one. You seem surprised."

"The Eyes of God haven't managed to even pry open a window there."

"Eyes of God. Please." She snorted. "We're the Monasteries. We've been in this business five hundred years. Not all our instruments are blunt as yourself."

"Would any of your not-so-blunt types have details on their internal security?"

"It's possible. Such matters can be discussed after I become confident of your identity and intentions. Now: your escape."

He sighed. "I didn't escape. Haven't. Probably won't. That's kind of what I'm doing here: arranging my escape. Sort of. And a couple other things."

She sat very still, moving only her eyes. They flitted back and forth as though she was reading text inside her head.

Finally: "An Intervention."

"You would have found out pretty soon anyway."

"How, ah, how long ago is this night, for you?"

"There's no meaningful answer for that."

"Are you actively serving the Intervening Power?"

"One of them. More or less. But also not really. Look, once we get through this, I'll answer your questions. Any questions. Hell, t'Passe, you can interview me for your fucking book."

"Just not tonight."

"Yeah." He found himself smiling at her. "I'm grateful. Really. I owe you one. I owe you a dozen."

"I didn't do any of it for you."

"I owe you anyway."

"For what?"

"For reminding me that sometimes I'm wrong. That sometimes people are better than I expect. That sometimes shit comes out better than I even hope."

"Flattery."

"Why would I waste the breath to flatter you?"

"Cogent." She nodded thoughtfully. "And persuasive."

"You and I," he said, "will never get along. You aggravate the crap out of me, and my fucking existence is a constant embarrassment to you and your whole outlook on life. So, yeah, we can't stand each other. But you should know that I am your friend."

She blinked, blinked again, and then closed her eyes with a tiny shake of her head as though doubting he'd still be there when she opened them again.

"I mean it," he said. "I have profound respect for your intellect, your integrity, and your capability. And even more for your courage. If you need me, ever, the Eyes of God can find me, and the Monasteries usually know where I am. If I am alive, I will help when you call. I know you won't abuse the privilege."

Meaning she understood all too well how cataclysmic his help can be, and so wouldn't ask unless all alternatives were worse. "I don't know what to say."

"Just don't expect me to be nice to you."

"I lack the imagination."

"See? Aggravate the crap out of me. Listen, I told the Pratts to get out of town."

"I know."

"You can't protect them. I'd tell you to get out of town if you would. Since you won't, keep your fucking head down."

"How far down?"

"Purthin Khlaylock was behind the Smoke Hunt. So is Markham Tarkanen. I don't know who else on the Khryllian side, but there have to be others."

She nodded thoughtfully.

"You don't seem surprised."

"My sources speculate that the whole of the Lords Legendary are involved, and possibly the Champion herself."

"She's not in it."

"How can you be sure?"

He looked at her. Just looked. After a moment she looked away and sighed.

"The Monasteries have no official interest in how the Knights of Khryl maintains order among its slaves and civilians."

"The Monasteries should fucking reconsider. The Smoke Hunt isn't thaumaturgy. It's theurgy. Always has been."

Her eyes narrowed. "Then—"

"Fucking right, then. It's not riot control, it's a fucking crusade."

"Impossible."

"Just like it's impossible I'm here talking to you."

She let her eyes slip closed, and lifted a hand to massage her forehead. "I noted the verb tense you used in referring to the Justiciar."

"Yeah. And before you ask, it was me."

She coughed. She tried to say something but instead coughed again.

"Take your time."

She said, "You'll forgive me for restating, but I need to confirm you're telling me you intervened in a *holy war* by *assassinating* the head of the most powerful *militant religious order in the history of Home*?"

"It wasn't like that," he said, a little stung. "It was a fair fight. More than fair. He was fully armed and armored and at the height of his strength. I was naked, shackled, and had just woken up from a skull fracture."

"You caught him with a sucker punch."

"You say it your way, I'll say it mine."

"It's an overt act of *war*—!"

"In more ways than one."

"You have committed the Monasteries to *open war* with the Order of *Khryl*!"

"You mentioned that already."

"Do you have any *idea* how *catastrophic* this is?"

"Relax. You think I'd start a war without knowing how to end it?"

"Of *course* you would! You've done it at least three times I *know* of!"

Oh, sure, bring up the truth. "T'Passe, seriously. Take it easy. I've never seen you like this. You're almost, well, hysterical."

"Hysterical? *Hysterical?*" She finally registered the shrill edge to her tone. She sagged, then set the pistol on the boardwalk and rubbed her eyes with both hands.

"Yes," she said quietly. "I apologize. I have, ah, invested considerable . . . personal energy . . . in my position here; open war will be . . . unfortunate. For me. Personally."

"Personally? So like, what, you're banging a Khryllian?"

She only sighed.

He stared. Good thing he was already sitting down. "Um . . . you do know that was a joke, right?"

"Not for me." Again she sighed, then twisted to call softly toward the Pratt & Redhorn's front door. "Somebody tell the fat man I need him out here."

He frowned. The fat man? Was he dreaming *Casablanca* again?

His bemusement lasted only a second or two, at which point the doorway disgorged the bloodstained steel and dockhand's amble of Tyrkilld, Knight Aeddhar, who was very likely the only man alive who could amble nonchalantly while clanking like a steam boiler. "And here I am as ever, old girl, aleap at m'lady's faintest whim. Shall I dismember yon dire ill-favored apparition forthwith, or might I first occupy a board or two beside my fondest dream of paradise, that being the hope of brushing 'gainst the hem of m'lady's cloak?"

"Oh, my sweet suffering pigfucking god."

Tyrkilld managed an unstable sketch of a bow. "And up your Monass-dick, fuck you very much."

Fist could only shake his head. "You're still drunk."

"No honest man would deny it. But come the morrow I'll be sober, and you'll still be an assassassbite."

"It's the morrow already," t'Passe said sternly.

"Ah, fairly struck. If I might beseat myself to tend the wound—?"

"Christ, you're like a couple of teenagers."

He looked from him to her and back again, and some rusted-shut part of his brain kicked open. He felt like he should either cry or kill somebody. "*That's* how you knew me. You didn't know me when I kicked your ass at the customs lockup, but by the time I saw you in the Spire, you did—along with some half-assed story I didn't pay attention to. And you," he said to t'Pass, "sure, you were expecting me ever since you arrived in Purthin's Ford. Sure you were. Son of a *bitch*. It's a good thing I don't have to make a living by figuring shit out."

"A more generous man than my poor self might imply, in your defense, that your day has leaned a bit windward of eventful to be overconcerned with one's powers of deduction."

"I guess you probably heard that story of mine just now, huh?"

"Among the variety of tales to cross paths within my ear this night."

"Do you have to take me in?"

Tyrkilld gave a shrug that sounded like slipping gears. "No sane man would maintain the Lord Justiciar of the Order of Khryl might be struck down by your miserable assassassitude. Having, as I do, some passing acquaintance with the bewildering webwork of lies bewoven by your dishonest Monassbiteness, I can truthfully aver that I have no slightest cause to suspect the Justiciar enjoys anything other than his customary perfect health. Perfect saving peripheral vision, if you'll forgive. And depth perception, but nonetheless—"

Fist nodded. "And there's not a blessed thing wrong with the service of Khryl, saving only the company."

"Ah, you must be quoting a man of far greater wit than your pitiful—"

"Yeah yeah, okay, drop it. Look, what t'Passe said about me and starting wars . . . well, it's true. But this one's different. You can win it. You *personally*. Get with Kierendal and let her know the balloon goes up tomorrow at sundown."

"Sundown?"

"That's when Khryl's Justice ends, right? If Angvasse doesn't show?"

T'Passe frowned at him. "A Khlaylock fail to appear for Khryl's Justice? You have the wrong family, my friend. Not even the death of her closest living relation—"

"It might not be just a relation."

T'Passe and Tyrkilld traded grim looks.

"My distaste for the Justiciar does not extend to his bloodline. The Lady Champion's cut of different cloth entire," Tyrkilld said. "I will with all available force resist any endeavor to do herself the slightest hurt."

Jonathan Fist nodded. "I get it. I even agree. My source says she's not going to be there. Something's going to stop her. Maybe not me."

"And this unlikely source that whispers to your dishonest self is some variety of prophet?"

"Close enough. Look, Orbek versus Angvasse to the death is a pretty big show, even for the Battlground, yes? Living Fist of Khyl against the Last Kwatcharr of the Black Knife Nation? It's set for noon. If she doesn't show, the crowd will keep growing the later it gets. By sundown, *everybody* will be there—to either see the fight, or see Orbek go free. That's when Freedom's Face has to move on BlackStone."

"Your people," t'Passe said. "You want Freedom's Face to attack your own people?"

"Not exactly. We just need to hold the compound."

"Thus you asked about their internal security."

"Yeah. Tyrkilld, I need you to lead the assault."

"I? Still hoping to engineer my bloody demise, are you?"

"It's not a fort. It's not even military. It's just a fucking mining operation. Sure, they'll have some guys with advanced weapons, but it's all small-arms shit. Not much different from those riot guns your armsmen carry."

"Are they not a griffinstone producer? Belike to encounter ferocious magickal defenses."

"Yeah, and you have Kierendal. I know who my money's on." He leaned forward, resting forearms on knees. "Look, we need to control the *dil*. The gate to the True Hell, right? We need good guys in charge of this side, because otherwise bad guys will be coming from the other side, you follow? *Very* bad guys. Ask your girlfriend here about the Artan Invasion. Anyway, it has to look like a Khryllian operation. Win or lose."

"And why, prithee, would the Knights of Khryl undertake the seizure by violence of BlackStone, which is under Our Order's own protection by not only law and treaty, but the explicit command of the Justiciar himelf?"

"Well, let's see. Would this Justiciar be the same one who was murdered in the BlackStone governor's office? Would this BlackStone be the same place where the murder was covered up and the assassin, still dripping the Justiciar's blood and brains, was whisked away beyond the reach of Khryl's Law altogether? Hell, you don't even have to use the *whisked away* part—play dumb on that. Dumber. Because there's no reason you'd know about the gate . . . which means you can pretend the Artans are harboring the assassin. It's even true. They're just harboring me—him—somewhere else."

Tyrkilld looked thoughtful. T'Passe scowled into the distance.

"No need to involve the Monasteries at all, right? Where I come from," Fist said to t'Passe, "we call this 'Let's you and him fight.' Besides, I told Markham he was facing war with Earth. Wouldn't want to make me a liar, would you?"

"Hard to deny the scent of a certain rascally foxlike cunning," Tyrkilld admitted. "But for what gain? War with Arta—I make no pretense of being a Knight of notable honor, but to instigate a calamity of such proportion—"

"Which will never happen. If I pull this off, the war will end before midnight tomorrow, and the Artans will never trouble you again. If I don't, well, give them back their compound and apologize for the misunderstanding. Pay for the damages. That kind of shit."

"If you pull this off," t'Passe muttered darkly. "I hate when you say that. Pull what off?"

"I was telling you about the Butcher's Fist—ahh, Hand of Peace, whatever."

"How you thought it might be in the Spire."

"Yeah, except no. It's not in the Spire. But I know where it is."

"Four or five hours ago you weren't sure it exists."

"For fuck's sake, t'Passe, do we need to go over the whole goddamn situation again?"

"No—no, of course not," she said faintly. "Apologies. Eventful night."

"Yeah, wait till tomorrow. It's at BlackStone."

Tyrkilld lurched to his feet, and suddenly he didn't look drunk at all. "The *Artans* hold the *Hand of Our Lord of Battles*? I have but to sound an alarm and we will have it *tonight!*"

"You're a decent guy, Tyrkilld, and I know you're smarter than you pretend, but you need to work on impulse control."

"Am I in this so different from your miserable self?"

"Not usually. But we have to get this one right. I'm the only guy who can do it."

"Your will or you won't," t'Passe muttered bitterly.

"Cut it out. Listen, Tykilld, stop and think. How are you going to convince the Order it's really there? And then you have to explain how you found out about it. And eventually somebody's gonna ask how it got there in the first place, and that one's the bomb. Civil war will be the best you can *hope* for."

"How dire can one truth be?"

"You tell me," he said. "The Artans have the Hand of Peace because Purthin Khlaylock gave it to them."

Tyrkilld's eyes popped wide, and he sat down as abruptly as he had risen.

"It's what Khlaylock kicked in for the Smoke Hunt. His stake in the game." Jonathan Fist sighed, and shrugged, and opened his hands in apology. "You know I can keep a secret, no matter how somebody asks. Are you as sure of anybody else?"

Tyrkilld didn't answer. He stared at the street.

"And don't even think about blowing all this wide open. You'll only make it worse."

"Worse?" he murmured. "In what dark god's nightmare could it be worse?"

"Like I said: think it through. Were you listening when I said Khlaylock pitched in the Hand of Peace as his contribution to the Smoke Hunt?"

Dawning horror scraped his eyes even wider.

"So the real truth here is that the greatest hero of the Order in modern times took the single most sacred True Relic of Khryl Battlegod," he said, "and gave it to the Black Knives."

Tyrkilld only groaned. T'Passe set a hand on his pauldron, and they sat in silence for some considerable time.

At length, she sighed and looked back at Jonathan Fist. "You are," she murmured, "a perfect fiend."

"Thanks," he said. "Can I have my pistol now?"

He took another bite of blood sausage, peeling back grease-soaked paper around his fist, and chewed thoughtfully while he watched Khryllians lay out bodies in the street.

This used to be a tidy neighborhood, neat greystone townhouses and well-kept bungalows fronting the ways, identical truck-gardens fenced in behind. Clean flagstoned streets had radiated from this little plaza around a bubbling artesian fountain. Street signs carved into the corners of the buildings announced that the plaza, and the neighborhood around it, had been called Weaver's Square. On another world it would have been called lower middle-class: full of grocers and haberdashers, barbers and clerks.

Today all those grocers and clerks and barbers and haberdashers and their wives and their children were crowded around the plaza, white-faced and shocky, crying or whimpering or murmuring streams of half-comprehensible obscenities under half-held breath. Several of those neat greystones and well-kept bungalows were now smoking gutted hulks, choked with broken timbers and rubble. More were splashed with blood, and all bore scatters of fresh, bright white pocks on their stone faces.

Slug scars.

Last night would probably give this place a new nickname.

He didn't have a hard count yet. Too many armsmen milled around, taking pulses, binding wounds, and generally obstructing his view. Twelve or thirteen corpses.

More to come.

A pair of Knights stood praying in the improvised triage area they'd set up near the fountain. Here and there among the wounded, bloodflow stopped and yellow-lipped wounds zipped themselves shut, accompanied by bubbling groans and thin whistling gasps of agony. Those beyond Healing were turned over to the armsmen to be dragged into the ranks of the dead.

Four ogrilloi so far. A red-soaked pile of grey-leather meat. His mushy brain still stirred up occasional specks of detail like rat turds in oatmeal: he remembered taking most of those wounds.

Good thing he wasn't superstitious.

He watched with a clinically morbid satisfaction like scratching at the rim of an infected scab, cataloging correspondences between nighttime prophecy and dawnlit reality. That dream for him was a long time ago—a *long* time ago—but being here was bringing it all back.

That old woman—

He remembered smothering her screams with one grey-leather hand while he tore into her living belly with tusks and teeth.

The dismembered body parts nearby—

Had once been a pair of slim young men; two of him had found them in bed together and had ripped arms and legs from their bodies, cracking hips like wishbones, splintering knees and shredding shoulders, disjointing them while they shrieked until twisting off their heads had torn them to silence.

That middle-aged mother—

Screw it. He was already tired of this game.

Armsmen held back the crowd, those fancy inlaid riot guns slanted across broad hauberked chests. The eyes behind their helmets' nasals stared, grim and remote, over the heads of the throng they faced. Muscle bulged at angles of clenched jaws. Several of the bodies lined up in the morning sunlight wore armor bearing the sunburst of Khryl.

He recalled that the collective noun for ogrilloi is *massacre.*

That dead armsman, over there: one of him had snapped that man's spine with a blow of the fist. Finely worked chainmail hung in tattered shreds; he could remember tearing a hauberk with taloned hands as though it were rotten leather. The warhorse sprawled across the cobbles—it had kicked at him, and one of him had caught its hoof in the palm of one hand and splintered its fetlock with a twist.

That scarlet flame without heat or light had made these ogrilloi into more than ogrilloi. Even the dream-memory was an intoxicating fantasy of power.

A fantasy of being stronger than a Knight of Khryl.

Armsmen ranged the smoldering wreckage beyond the cordon. While he watched, another corpse was carried out: the shredded remnants of a young girl, maybe ten years old. He remembered the taste of her clean soft flesh. His daughter was just about that age. Most of the girl's hair was matted with brown-caked blood. One strand draped across the shoulder of the armsman who bore her, and it was fine and silken and golden. Like Faith's.

The sausage curdled in his stomach.

"Not my business," he muttered through his teeth. "Still not my business."

His business came walking out of a smoke-shrouded doorway with four hundred pounds of dead ogrillo over her shoulder.

Someone in the crowd shouted, *"Khlaylock! Khlaylock and the God!"* and her step hitched and her mouth twisted and her vivid eyes stayed on the wounded and the dead. He remembered hearing the same pious cheer twenty-five years before, from a different voice, for a different Khlaylock, in a different Boedecken.

Other voices echoed the call. *Khlaylock and the God!* Shouts swelled into a roar, and standing silently among them he could pick out individual voices: *killem Vasse! killemmall! killallafuckers!* Fists went toward the sky and men slammed each other on the shoulders and women shrieked into their hands, and the pious sentiment gave way to a hungrily choral chant.

Vasse! Vasse! Vasse!

There'd been a time when his own presence could quicken that ravenous pulse in any crowd on Earth. He could hear the echoes even now, and they could still raise a sizzle in his balls. He'd loved being a star. He'd lived for it.

Looked like she didn't.

Some voices—faint, scattered—did not join the chant. These had messages of their own: *Where was Khryl when they killed my daughter? Where was Khryl when my parents screamed? Where was Khryl last NIGHT?* These faint scattered voices joined, gathering strength and number. The choral *vasse vasse vasse* became blurred by a rising counterchant—

Where was KHRYL? Where was KHRYL? Where was KHRYL?

And there was shoving and flashing of fists that became snarling knots of struggle, and some of the armsmen began to advance from the line, using their long guns as crowbars to pry open paths into the crowd.

The Champion never looked up.

She shrugged the corpse toward a pair of burly armsmen who staggered under its sudden deadweight. She went to the artesian fountain and lowered her face into its cold boil; she scrubbed drying blood from her cheeks and forehead and fingerbrushed it from her hair, and the water shaded straw-brown where it rolled over the white marble spill-wall into the granite cistern below.

He watched her drift among the wounded and the dead. Here and there she knelt, reaching out to a hand or a forehead. The only notice she seemed to take of the roars and the cheering was how close to someone's ear she had to lean while she spoke soft words, and where she passed, light kindled in glazing eyes, agonized writhing stilled, blank shock released into clean tears.

In his vision, the arrival of the Champion—

Armor like a mannequin of convex mirrors. Walking out from the shadows of a street's mouth across the plaza, a massive two-handed morningstar propped casually over one shoulder. Reflected firelight dancing across the buildings. Three of him sprinting across the flagstones, smeared with the blood of the finest soldiers of Home. The Champion walking to meet the multiple him, casually removing her helm, shaking loose her hair. On her face no fear. No anger. Only a reserved, remote sadness.

Vasse Khrylget, they called her.

He had a pretty good idea why.

She moved a little bit apart from the triage area and spoke to a couple of armsmen. One of them nodded and moved away. The other stood respectfully behind her as she unbuckled the straps of her blood-smeared paldrons and cuirass, slid them off, and handed them to him.

The warm weight of the Automag dragged at the back of his pants. He could do it. Right now. With all the shouting, they wouldn't even hear the shot.

Her surcoat was shredded at the shoulder and rib, and was dark with blood; as she turned to examine the battered plates, the shreds of her surcoat parted and he glimpsed a white curve of breast striated with red. Pink keloidal starfish puckered the flesh over her ribs beside it. Their pattern matched the holes in her armor: probably buckshot. He carried dream-images of prying a couple of those fancy riot guns from the cold dead hands of armsmen.

Half an hour from now, you'd never guess she'd been wounded.

He nodded to himself: no point in going center-mass unless the slug took out her spine too. Khryl's Healing won't do a hell of a lot for damage to the central nervous system. As he knew from bitter experience.

A head shot was probably as close to merciful as he could afford.

In his vision—confirmed by the dark clots of blood she'd scraped from her face and hair—she'd fought without a helmet. Asking for major head trauma. Begging for it. Arrogance. Maybe a death wish. Maybe something else he couldn't even guess.

He wondered what she'd say if he asked her.

He stood and watched and felt the metallic solidity of the Automag's grip nudging his kidney, while she took the armor in her bare hands and started smoothing out the dents as though the chrome steel plates were only electrum foil. She sat on the fountain's rim to do the smaller details. He watched her bending shut buckshot holes with her thumbs, and reflected that he'd better take her from range. Long range. If he missed, he'd need a head start.

All he had to do was draw and fire.

And run. Better not forget *run*.

He slipped his hand under his tunic and slid it around to the small of his back to find the gun. His fingers closed upon the warm diamond-scored grip.

But—

The angle of her shoulders as she bent over her armor. The way the rising sun gleamed in the wet hair that screened her eyes. The long slim grace of her impossibly powerful fingers, and the thin line of inner pain described by her lips . . .

Forget that she was the chief headpounder of a theocratic police state. He never kidded himself. If you have to justify an action, you shouldn't have done it in the first place.

She was clearly a better person than he'd ever be. He could see it on her. She wore the warrior-saint thing like a crown of thorns. And he was about to shoot her for it.

Or not. Dammit.

Maybe that's what getting old really is: when you can no longer bear the consequences of being wrong.

The other armsman to whom the Champion had spoken passed among the crowd-control troops, and now they started gently but firmly expanding their perimeter. *All right, all over, go home. Excuse us, please. The area will be reconsecrated. Please be about your business. The public will be allowed to return by dusk.*

He didn't pay much attention to their polite insistence, and he didn't move as the crowd began to quiet, and part, and reluctantly drift away around him. He remembered how things had seemed the last time he'd been in the Boedecken. Perfectly straightforward. Run or fight. Die fast or die screaming. Simple.

Not anymore.

He regulated his breathing, emptied his consciousness of the hope and fear that blind mortal eyes and watched Weaver's Square fog with a chaotic webwork of night.

The vast spidery blur of energy-channels that resolved into existence around him was too complex to directly interpret. There are levels on which everything is connected to everything else, levels on which all existence is a single system linking the motion of each individual quark to the metastructure of galactic clusters. Understanding, on a human scale, required that he selectively blind himself: conscious perception is a filtering of reality, and it takes practice.

What he saw here was mostly how everything in this plaza was connected to him. Personally. On some level, everyone here was here because *he* was here.

And vice versa.

Oh, he thought, blank as stone. *Oh, crap.*

Having some goddamn Role to Play in the Grand Fucking Scheme of Things was a lot like having something spiny burrow up his ass.

Some of those cables of black were strengthening even as he watched: a gathering of energy into the threads that joined his life to theirs. His presence was already changing the lives around him. And black channels twisting outward from the pile of dead ogrilloi were thickening . . .

Some of the blackest, thickest channels tied them to him.

And tied him to the Champion.

It wouldn't have made any goddamn sense at all, except for the note on the cold-post board. And even that didn't help much. The longer he looked, the less sense it made.

He remembered a line from a book in his father's collection: when one eliminates the impossible, whatever remains — however improbable — must be the truth. But on Home, *impossible* is a slippery concept.

He gave his head an irritable shake. *Great fucking Detective I'll never be.*

Lacking superhuman resources of observation and inductive reasoning, maybe he should just ask somebody. When he turned back toward the somebody he had in mind, she was already staring at him.

Even from twenty yards, the Aegean dusk of her eyes took his breath away.

She laid her cuirass aside with her paldrons. With expressionless deliberation, she rose and gave him her back while she unbuckled her sabatons and the girdle-straps that held her cuisses high upon her thighs. She bent over as she worked her legs out of their steel sheaths, and he found himself staring at an ass that could crack walnuts.

He remembered Marade in the storm cellar, all those years ago. He remembered that nothing in the Laws of Khryl requires a Knight to be chaste. He remembered the white curve of the Champion's breast, pinked with healing scars . . .

He folded waxed paper around the blood sausage and stuck it in his purse, then shrugged and walked toward her. Just as he was about to step among the ranks of the dead, an armored hand fell hard upon his shoulder. "Your pardon, goodman."

A courteous tone. Respectful. Freighted with authority. "You must clear the area. For your own safety."

She had removed her cuisse-and-greave leggings. An armsman was strapping the various pieces of her armor together into a bundle, and she was already walking away.

"Lady Khlaylock!" he called. If she heard, she gave no sign. He couldn't blame her; being seen with him in public had to be pretty high on her *No Fucking Way* list. Admitting she knew him would be higher.

"Goodman." The hand on his shoulder tightened. "Be about your business. You are required to leave the plaza."

He could ask her to come back. He could. He could drop to one knee and beg that she might condescend to notice him. And right after that he could sprout wings and fly over the plaza farting fairy dust.

"Goodman, I must insist."

He'd made a career of looking for trouble. He'd had a gift for it, an instinct. When he couldn't find trouble, he'd made some of his own. He'd had a gift for that too. But that was long ago; mere years could not compass the difference between the Actor he'd been and the man he was. That's what he kept telling himself. But sometimes he forgot how old he was. Sometimes he forgot the scars he carried.

Sometimes he just got tired of being grown up.

He looked at the hand: a big hand, strong, sheathed in a butcher's gauntlet of interlocking steel rings. "People touch this body," he said, "by invitation only."

"I'm sorry?"

"I don't like strangers' hands on me. Please keep yours to yourself."

"Goodman—"

"I said please. I won't ask again."

The hand tightened and pulled to turn him around. "Goodman, I am required by the Law to inform you*ermgh*—"

The devolution of words into an animal grunt of surprise and sudden pain coincided with a smoothly unhurried wrist-lock that levered the armsman forward from the waist; the smaller man's thumbs folded the armsman's hand in toward his own forearm while a twist of his body kept the armsman's elbow locked.

The armsman's wrist made a squishy popping sound.

He twisted the armsman's wrist a bit more, drawing a strangled wheeze and forcing the armsman to one knee. "You don't like it much either, huh?"

"This insult," the armsman said in a voice thin with fury, gaze fixed on the flagstones a span from his nose, "will be requited in blood."

"You sure? Nobody's really hurt. That can change."

"By the righteous Law of Khryl Battlegod—" He sounded like he was chewing bricks. "I require that you arm yourself, and meet me upon a field of—"

"Maybe after your wrist heals." He pivoted, twisting until that squishy popping sound became a wet squelch. A low grunt forced itself through the armsman's grimace.

"You! Stop!" Armsmen swarmed toward him from around the plaza. A few yards away, he saw the Champion glance over her shoulder. The nearest armsman whipped out his riot gun and leveled it. "Unhand that Khryllian!"

"You want him any more unhanded, you'll have to lend me a knife."

"Release him and step away." The Khryllian's finger slipped through the trigger guard. "Do it. I *will* shoot you."

"We're having a discussion. That's all." He shifted his grip on the armsman's hand so that he could put one palm against the man's extended elbow joint, and held it there about five foot-pounds short of breaking the arm. "He thought it was okay for him to put his hands on me. I'm in the process of explaining that it's not."

Pain-sweat dripped from the end of the armsman's nose. He spoke through a locked jaw. "The goodman assaulted me without warning or Challenge. He has broken my wrist."

"It's just a sprain. Whiner."

The riot gun's muzzle came into sharp focus: steadied at the bridge of his nose. "To assault a servant of Khryl without warning is a serious offense."

He shrugged. "This *is* the warning."

The Champion slid among them, and laid one slim hand along the Khryllian's weapon to gently turn it aside. "Release him, goodman."

"Ask me nicely."

"Goodman, I am the—"

"I know who you are. It's not goodman. It's freeman."

"You are Ankhanan. Dominic Shade, isn't it?" She lifted her head and her expression cleared, as though this explained much. Maybe it did. He had to give her points for style. "Please, then, freeman. Release this man."

"Sure." He gave the armsman's shoulder a fatherly pat as he let him go. "Don't do anything stupid, huh?"

The armsman straightened, cradling his wrist. His face could have been carved from ice. "I will take my satisfaction on the field of honor."

"Honor. Yeah, okay. Sure."

Tiny crow's-feet etched themselves in the smooth skin above the Champion's cheekbones. "What is your business here, freeman?"

"A word with you, Lady Khlaylock. That's all."

She tilted her head toward the cold fury of the armsman. "You did this . . . to get my *attention?*"

He shrugged.

The Khryllian at her shoulder twitched his weapon. "Take a knee."

"Hm?"

"Take a knee when addressed by the Champion." His tone said: *Or I'll pound you.*

He looked into faces of the armsmen around him and found there a growing anticipation. Growing to eagerness. The Khryllian said, "Take a knee."

. . . black knives don't kneel . . .

He closed his eyes, sighed, and opened them again. "I am a freeman of the Ankhanan Empire. Maybe you don't understand what that means."

"You are not in the Empire now."

"Doesn't matter. Want me off my feet? You'll have to knock me down."

The Khryllian shifted his weight forward and poised his firearm like a short bo. Others did the same. "Do you think I can't?"

"I'm sure you can. The point is, you'll have to." He offered the Champion half an apologetic smile. "Don't we have something more important to do right now?"

Her indigo eyes went distant. She turned to the armsman with the sprained wrist. "You should withdraw your Challenge."

The armsman dropped to one knee as though his shin had been shot off. "With all respect, my lady: you may not lawfully order this."

"It is no order, armsman. It is advice. He is Armed as he stands. Do you wish to fight him here and now?"

The armsman palpated his sprained wrist and winced. "If I must."

Angvasse Khlaylock sighed. "I will Witness, should you so demand."

"Hey. Don't I get a say in this?"

"You do not. As an Armed Combatant, you are obliged to answer a Challenge from any Combatant of equal or lesser grade upon demand."

"Answer as in fight?"

"Or yield and confess your crime. Which carries a penalty of one year's labor upon the Estates."

"Shitty options."

"Which you should have considered before undertaking to put your hands on a sworn Soldier of Khryl. Did you not read your Laws of Engagement?"

"I've been busy."

She turned back to the armsman. "Before you begin, you might be interested to know that this man is here in Purthin's Ford under the name of Dominic Shade. Freeman Shade's customs examiner rated him grade six. As he stands."

The armsman's mouth twitched, and a muscle jumped at the corner of his eye.

"Freeman Shade is a Monastic Esoteric." Her indigo eyes darkened. "An assassin."

"I'm retired."

"You may be aware of the incident yesternoon in the Riverdock customs lucannhixeril. Where an unarmed inmate overpowered three armsmen and a Knight Householder, killing one armsman and severely injuring both others, as well as wounding the Knight so severely that only Khryl's Love sustained his life."

More muscles jumped, now along the armsman's jaw, and blood was draining from his cheeks. "Questions of combat are in the righteous hand of the Lord of Battles," he intoned grimly. "I have no fear."

"The Householder in question was Tyrkilld, Knight Aeddhar."

The armsman went pale. Really pale. Like only shame kept him from fainting on the spot. "Yet truth is truth, and justice is justice. My life is Khryl's."

"And it is for Khryl's sake I ask that you withdraw." She put a hand on his head as though calming an angry dog. "Please, armsman. Command this I cannot, but I do implore. Withdraw. Has this morning not seen bloodshed enough?"

"The crime—"

"Armsman. Please."

The armsman reluctantly ducked his head. "As my lady requests."

"See Lord Storyxe about your wrist."

"My lady." Slowly he found his feet. After a last lingering stare full of dangerous promise, the armsman rejoined his fellows. They slowly spread out, returning to the task of clearing the plaza, and he made his way toward one of the Knights in the triage area.

A surreptitious hand verified the Automag was still where it belonged. "Got some prickly bastards working for you."

"Speaking as an authority on prickly bastards?" For a moment the harsh planes of her face softened as though she might be about to smile. But only for a moment. "They do not work for me. They serve Khryl, as do I."

She lowered her voice, and barely moved her lips. "As do you, until the Smoke Hunt is quelled forever."

"Yeah, um, about that . . ."

"There is a problem? Since you have so cleverly engineered this pretext to speak with me."

"I thought Khryllians don't do sarcasm."

"And thus it is a day already for unexpected discovery. Tell me what is required, and I shall endeavor to provide." The arch of her eyebrows turned her lifted shoulder into a faintly apologetic shrug. "Anything that might prevent another morning such as this."

"It's not quite that simple."

"I have given up hoping anything will be simple. Just tell me." A fractional incline of her head managed to indicate not only the charnel in the plaza but the whole of Purthin's Ford below and Hell above and all the lands around. "I am . . . busy."

"Yeah, no kidding." Past her shoulder, he watched another Knight carry another dead ogrillo from the ruined building. "Look, the problem isn't the Smoke Hunt. Not directly."

He took a deep breath. "It's you."

"Your pardon?"

"Look, the cold-post board—the one that used to be over there. Somebody knocked it down last night, but a lot of the notes are still there. One of them reads *Rod, here's your box number.* And there are some numbers."

"And?"

"And I'm Rod. And there's no box. And that number is a date I asked a friend to look up for me. It's the date you became Champion of Khryl."

"You could have simply asked me."

"I didn't know I needed to know. Funny how you didn't mention it anyway. Last night on the Purificapex. Because it's kind of a huge fucking coincidence."

"And only that."

"See? You really aren't good at sarcasm."

"What bearing can it have on our current situation?"

"Oh, I don't know. Let's see, maybe we can parse this. So here on the Sacred Motherfucking Battleground, we find the Living Fist of Khryl up on the Hand of Peace, investing Ma'elKoth's One True Hand with the Authority of her *God,* and you don't think it's relevant that you won the title of Champion on the same fucking day as Ma'elKoth's True Fucking Assumption?"

She didn't even blink. "Perhaps you can explain to me the connection."

Explain? Shit. "It's, uh—it's kind of complicated."

"It seems everything is."

He chewed the inside of his lip. "Listen, have you eaten?"

"I'm sorry?"

"You've been up all night—" He gave half a wave toward the pile of dead ogrilloi. "—uh, working, and I haven't had anything to eat except half a hunk of blood sausage, and I was thinking maybe I could, y'know, maybe buy us breakfast somewhere. And I could try to explain some of the facts of life these days. Because they're not exactly what you think they are."

She looked vaguely astonished. "You wish to buy breakfast—? For me?"

"Well . . ." He spread his hands, feeling as astonished as she looked, but the more he thought about it, the better it sounded. "Yeah. Let's get some breakfast. Unless you just want to share my sausage."

"Share your sausage? Freeman Shade—" She inclined her head toward him, and that cool speculative appraisal flickered back into her eyes. "—are you flirting with me?"

"Am I—?"

Holy crap, he thought. *Am I?*

A hint of a mildly wicked smile tugged at the corners of her mouth, and the longer it took him to answer the wider her smile became, and before he could decide what the answer might actually be, let alone summon the faintest ghost of a clue what he should say to this insanely dangerous superhuman killer who was acting like she might be open to the idea of getting into him just a little bit, the Knight behind her threw the last ogrillo onto the pile of the grey leather dead.

And the world blew up in his face.

⌖

blank white discontinuity
permanently instantaneous

⌖

Eventually he opened his eyes.

Brown and grey and black swirled and billowed around him. Mist-blurred shapes loomed and receded, moving, shifting, doubling and tripling and shimmering back together in absolute silence.

This was not the morning he'd had in mind.

He should just go back to sleep. He couldn't think of anything else worth doing, and he couldn't remember ever having been so tired. This bed, though, must rank on some Top Ten Least Comfortable in Recorded Goddamn History: like lying on a pile of broken crates. He tried to shift toward a facsimile of comfort among the corners and edges, but his legs didn't seem to work. He couldn't feel them at all.

Now his day was fucking complete.

How many goddamn times had he woke like this? Had he crapped himself, as usual? Did he even want to know?

He felt a shiver under his back as though the jagged bed vibrated to some thump he should have heard; half a second later, hot rain splattered across his mouth and his tongue flicked out by instinct and the hot rain tasted a lot like blood.

He started to understand that what felt like a shit-rotten morning was actually a whole lot worse.

Where the hell was he, anyway? Why was it raining blood? The brown and grey and black swirl might have been some kind of smoke, but he still couldn't make his vision focus enough to be sure, and what the fuck was that smell, anyway? Was the kitchen on fire?

Smelled like duck.

He tried to sit up but something large and soft and maybe wet lay on his chest pinning him down, and his arms weren't working all that well either, but he managed to dig his elbows into the jagged pile of—boxes? rocks? bricks?—and lever himself up to where he could look—

There was a dead girl draped facedown across his lap.

What the fuck?

Shan—? Shanna? His numbly uncooperative mouth refused to form intelligible words. Was he actually talking? This was some kind of dream. Had to be: he spoke, but there was no voice.

Shanna—what did they—why are you—?

No—no, wait . . .

He remembered. His wife was dead. Sort of. A long time ago. Almost as dead as this girl.

Then who the hell was she?

His eyes still wouldn't focus, but he could squint the blurred haze of her into some kind of sense, and Jesus, she was a mess. The back of her skull was a swamp of bloody pulp, and her head flopped at a hanged man's angle. Her clothes were shredded.

So was her back.

Knobs of vertebrae gleamed red-streaked, old ivory lumped with yellow fat, dark red muscle peeled over ribs, a couple of bones sticking out of her back and he couldn't figure out what bones they could have been, because they were all at the wrong angles and anyway they were way too big to be human bones at all and before he could make any fucking sense of that a motion caught his eye and he looked up and his hard squint resolved a looming smear of shadow—

Into a mountain of ogrillo.

It came out of the smoke, wreathed in flame, head swinging, eyes down, searching the ground, and in its hand was an ogrillo-size version of the Khryllian morningstar and the morningstar came down and he felt again that shiver under his back, stronger now, still silent, and what the morningstar had come down upon was the steel-helmed skull of a man prostrate upon a litter of rubble and when the morningstar came up again blood and brains sprayed in fresh hot rain and the ogrillo's head swung—

And its eyes found his.

He got the feeling, somehow, that it knew him.

Trifurcate lips curled back from red-smeared tusks and its mouth worked as though it spoke though he heard no voice. It stepped toward him and the vast weapon came up in front of the scarlet pulsing wound of the smoke-veiled sun and he could only lie on the ground with the dead girl on his lap, gape up in blank uncomprehending stupor and wait to die.

He closed his eyes.

But instead of dying, he felt the dead come to life. The girl on his lap . . .

Moved.

When he opened his eyes again she had somehow come to her knees and even though her head rolled, dead limp and broken, one small fist punched up into the burning ogrillo's swollen burlap-clothed crotch faster than his eye could follow and the ogrillo's huge clawed feet lifted from the ground and he tilted over the fulcrum of her fist and toppled, face-first and writhing, into the jumble of broken bricks.

Oh. She was only *mostly* dead.

More like Shanna than he'd thought.

The dead girl reached over her own shoulder as though to give herself a pat on the back. Her hand closed around the joint-knob of one of those inexplicably huge bones that stuck out of her dorsal ribs and she yanked it bloody from her flesh. Its other end was a jagged break, splintered, serrated, and she pulled herself up the writhing body of the ogrillo and jammed that sharp splintered serrated end through the side of his neck. She used the bone like a handle to yank the ogrillo's head within reach, then ripped his head entirely off and cast it aside. Then she went on to rip away both his arms as well.

Fierce, he thought fuzzily. *Sincerely fucking fierce.*

He admired that in a woman.

Now her form and face limned themselves in the smoke with fire of their own: blue-shimmering fire that he could half-see and the other half sort of imagine—or hallucinate or dream or something—and the imagined hallucinated dreamed half of the fire snapped and snarled and grew into a searing arc-welder flame until the inside of his head went blind electric white.

But he could still see with his physical eyes, and what they showed his sizzling brain must have been some kind of imagination or hallucination or dream too, because what they showed was her broken neck straighten and the dent in her skull uncrumple.

She shook herself from head to hind like a wet dog.

Propped hands-and-knees on the dying ogrillo's torso, she looked at him with vivid indigo eyes and her bloody char-smeared mouth moved but only eerie silence rang in his ears. She looked at him, looked through him, and that imaginary blue fire sparked in her eyes and somehow he knew that for her he wasn't even there. Then she pushed herself brokenly to her feet and shambled off into the smoke.

He decided she was someone he'd like to know.

Nice ass too.

The sun brightened from crimson to scarlet, heading for orange as the duck-scented smoke swirled and thinned in some silent breeze. Empty eyes of shattered windows stared from blackened buildings into the haze. Clearing, it revealed a broad stone-flagged plaza, littered with human bodies. Most of them wore armor. A blast-crater big enough to swallow a couple cart-and-fours steamed: clear water drained into it through a jumbled gap in a broken fountain wall.

The words *Smoke Hunt* surfaced from muddy depths inside his head. He couldn't remember what they meant. All he had was silence and smoke and the taste of blood.

And the smoke was full of ogrilloi.

Six or seven at least, red-flaming specters pacing among the armored bodies with careful, methodical, deliberate intent, stopping here and there to smash a skull with huge mockeries of the Khryllian weapon.

And the dead girl reached the nearest of them and turned him with one hand on his huge grey arm and her other hand blurred and his huge grey chest folded inward around her fist and blood burst from his mouth in a spray that trailed behind him as he flew backward from her as though yanked by some invisible god.

Now the other ogrilloi stopped and turned and saw her.

They converged on her and she staggered to meet them and the first one to reach her died and so did the second but they closed around her and now they had her, because after all she was broken and dead.

Well, mostly.

Pretty soon to be all the way, because they had her now.

A grill held one of her arms and another held the other and a third swung back a huge steel morningstar like a golf pro in a morphine nightmare.

And one particular hard lump on which he lay—like a hunk of steel jamming into his right kidney—his hand slid toward without any prompting from his consciousness; his fingers closed around it and his arm pulled it out from under him and he discovered, to his mild astonishment, that his hand was full of big fucking gun.

He pointed it and the barrel fountained silent flame.

The ogrillo who'd lifted the morningstar spun and sprayed everyone around him with blood and shreds of flesh and bone that burst from sudden craters opening in his chest and the stump of his severed arm.

The others now turned. And looked *his* way.

A new burst unzipped another from balls to breakfast, and the girl yanked free and from there it was a settled question. She swung and stepped and swung again, and he reached out with streaks of silent metal that hit almost as hard as her fists: pelvis, knee, shoulder, spine. Shatter the bones to bring them down. Between his metal and her bone, every one of them died. More than died. Dismantled. Shredded.

None even tried to run away.

Each squeeze of the trigger pumped memory back into him. When it was over, he knew where he was, and how he had gotten here, and why.

He knew who she was.

And so when it was over, when she came back to him there among the broken rock and stood above him, her face blackened and solemn, her form a drench of clotting crimson, he held the muzzle centered between those vivid indigo eyes.

He needed both hands.

She didn't even look at it. She was looking at him.

Their eyes met over the sights of his gun, and her reserve dissolved. In her eyes, on her lips, in the angle of her head was some bleak shivering despair. How could he shoot that?

After a moment, her face swept itself blank, and she held out her hand for the pistol.

Ahh, Christ. He really was getting old.

He let her take it.

She cradled the weapon as though it were some exotic songbird that had died in her hand. When she spoke, he could hear only a thin singing whine that slowly strengthened as his stunned ears began to awaken. But he could read her lips.

Dominic Shade, she said, *you are under arrest.*

yesterday's tomorrow

INTERVENTION

INTERVENTION

"When the gods would punish us, they answer our prayers."

—ARTSN. TAN'ELKOTH (FORMERLY MA'ELKOTH, 1ST ANKHANAN
EMPEROR AND PATRIARCH OF THE ELKOTHAN CHURCH),
QUOTING DUNCAN MICHAELSON
Blade of Tyshalle

When he had washed her blood from his face and hair and hands, an armsman came to his cell to take the bowl and its rusty water away. "And the towel."

Beside him on the camp bed: thick bleached shag smeared clay-red, specked with clots—

He passed the towel through the bars, and the armsman folded it carefully, reverentially, then laid it into the water, soaking. He turned to go.

"Hey—"

The armsman stopped.

"My clothes, huh? It's freezing in here."

"Take it up with the Champion."

The armsman bore the bowl away in both hands as though it held something sacred. Maybe it did. His blood once had saved this world. Whatever they were hoping hers might save, he was pretty sure they were shit out of luck.

He watched the armsman leave, his tongue thoughtfully exploring the small flat pick and tension bar tucked back in his cheek along his gums; he'd coughed them up from his magician's half swallow after the Knights had finished their brutally thorough body-cavity search. He could go through the cell door without breaking stride, but he wouldn't get far running naked through streets full of angry Khryllians.

Besides, he was pretty sure the Champion would be along anytime now, and it might be worth his trouble to have another word with her.

No bones seemed to be broken, and he retained enough Control Discipline to induce reabsorption of serous fluid from his bruises. Most of the pain went with it. The rest he could handle with natural endorphins and dopamine. He'd pay for this later—glandular exhaustion is not to be lightly fucked with—but for now he had to be able to move.

He passed the time idly picking the locks on his leg irons, relocking them and picking them again: a fair-to-middling thumb-twiddle. Naked on the cot, he was mostly paying attention to the pictures in his head. Like the splintered knobs that had stuck out from her back.

Shrapnel. Wet bone shrapnel.

No petro-volatile stink. Not even the burnt-toast-and-bean-fart of gunpowder. Just overcooked duck. Not a bomb. Not chemical, anyway.

Magickal.

That's why with the eye of his mind he had seen energy gather around the dead Smoke Hunters. Each corpse thrown on the pile had brought the explosion a step closer. Magickal critical mass. An improvised timing device, to make sure the maximum number of Knights and armsmen would be nearby.

Worked, too.

Still, something was off. He couldn't quite spike it. No surprise—he didn't have much in the way of sharps after being blown up and all. Not to mention the whole fucking timeline thing. Funny: the guy whose wrist he'd sprained had been right. He should have left the square. For his own safety.

If Angvasse had been standing a foot to either side, he would have seen those splintered knobs sticking out from his own chest.

Luck. That's all. Lucky old man.

The man who'd become the god behind his eyes had sometimes said "*Luck* is a word the ignorant use to define their ignorance. They are blind to the patterns of force that drive the universe, and they name their blindness *science*, or *clearheadedness*, or *pragmatism*; when they stumble into walls or off cliffs, they name their clumsiness *luck*."

But with the eye of his mind, what he saw was exactly those patterns of force. And *luck* was still the only word he had.

Lucky old man.

Stripes of noonish sun slanted through the bars of the skylight. His cell was above the stable of a small subgarrison. The quiet here had an empty, echoic feel as though the place had been deserted for years. Most of the armsmen assigned to this particular subgarrison had been in Weaver's Square.

He was the only prisoner.

The street outside rustled with hushed activity. Resting his forehead on the bars of the cell's little window, black iron rough and cool against his skin, he watched armsmen drape open carriages in shimmering white silk chased with thread of gold, and harness carriage traces to immense thick-muscled warhorses. He watched a single white-clad drummer summon citizens from the houses and shops around with a slow bleak cadence.

Witnesses for the Last March.

One dead Knight lay alone in each carriage, hung on a mortuary board by large blunt hooks at armpit and groin. Their visors had been re-moved to display the blood-pudding remains of their faces. As the drum-mer rolled a solemn flourish, the mortuary boards were raised to vertical and fastened in place. Fallen Knights are borne standing from the field.

Slain armsmen rode in plain, practical wagons, six to a bed. They too wore their armor. They too displayed their death wounds.

He'd seen Last Marches before: here, twenty-five years ago, and in Ankhana, after Ceraeno. The Last March would wind through the streets of the city. The drummer's slow rhythm would stop traffic and trade, and line the streets with solemn silent witnesses. Citizens under the protection of Khryl are never allowed to forget the price of their safety.

Blood from the floor of the carriages and carts would be allowed to trail onto the streets over which they passed: a baptism, reaffirming the sanctity of this land. The living would march behind, in the blood of the fallen, leaving footprints of red dust and sand.

Blood prints in the Boedecken Waste. In what Khryllians called the Battleground, and ogrilloi called Our Place.

He watched her too.

Draped in white. A loose cowl over her hair and a veil erasing her face. He knew her by the square of her shoulders. By the angle of her head. By the deference of the armsmen as she moved among them with a word here and a touch there. By the way her presence alone seemed to give them whatever strength they needed.

While he watched her, inside his head he watched the bloody swamp that had been the back of her head uncrumple. He wondered in passing how long it had been since she'd last bothered to put on her helm. Khryllians stand to pray. She hadn't stood. She hadn't prayed.

Just as well he hadn't shot her. Probably would have only pissed her off.

Simon Faller had told him—would tell him, on Earth, in the Buke, a few days from now—that no one had seen Angvasse since the Smoke Hunt. That she never showed up to face Orbek for Khryl's Justice. And it might have gone that way too, if he hadn't started shooting Smoke Hunters.

Maybe it had nothing to do with him. Maybe it would unhappen. Sure. It was possible.

When one eliminates the impossible . . .

Hey, wait.

There was the other line his father had liked to quote, the one about the mystery of the dog who didn't bark in the night. Shanna used to say the toughest thing to spot is what *should* be there . . .

And that was it. That's what had been bothering him. What should have been there.

"Holy shit," he muttered. "Literally."

Assumption Day on God's Way in Ankhana. Ma'elKoth Incarnate, sliced shoulder to hip . . .

The man-god wasn't full of shit after all.

Neither were the Smoke Hunters.

Later she came to him, all in white as he'd seen her on the street: cape and tunic and skirted pants of bleached linen, gloves, cowl shrouding her hair and a semi-sheer veil softening the harsh planes of her face. She carried his clothing, laundered, still damp, folded; she laid them on the plain plank table outside the cell. On the floor beside it she set his freshly buffed suede boots.

He watched her silently. She didn't seem inclined to pass any of them through the bars. She wanted to do this with his dick hanging out? He didn't mind. He'd never been what anybody'd call shy.

She showed not an inch of skin from hair to toenail. He sucked on the inside of his cheek. Pretty clear which of them had something to hide.

She also carried a flat-folded wrap of smooth brown leather like a cook's cutlery-bundle; she drew the table across the splinter-scuffed floor and unfolded the leather on top beside his clothes, opening it like a map, smoothing it out with abstracted care, as though it were the setting cloth for a table she was dressing while her mind was on the far side of the world.

The soft brown leather did indeed hold knives. And not just knives. She lifted his Automag and weighed it in her hand.

After a moment, she said distantly, "I have seen only one other firearm of this design."

His Automag was a big brother to Orbek's. "Is that what this is about? What you're holding me on? A goddamn weapons charge?"

She didn't seem to hear him. "Nor have I seen a pistol that will knock down an ogrillo."

He sighed. "The rounds are tristacks. Sequenced bullets, three per shot." He flicked a hint of backhand. "Knocking things down is what they're designed for."

"And of these bullets, only splinters remain."

"They're called shatterslugs."

She nodded. "No overpenetration."

"Full kinetic transfer. What you might call maximum thump."

"Yes." She held it admiringly in the striped shaft of sunlight through the outer bars. "And against armor?"

"Dunno."

Her veiled eyes searched his. "Do you not?"

"I guess Orbek's did well enough." He shrugged and looked away. "Depends on the armor, probably."

"No doubt." She turned her gaze back to the gun. "Impressive."

"Like it? It's yours."

"Yes." She laid it back among his knives on the spread of leather. "As are all of these now. An astonishing array of prohibited weapons."

That didn't require an answer, so he simply sat.

She lowered her head as though the veil were not enough to hide her eyes. She picked up the telescoping baton. "And this," she said distantly. "Lovely. Perhaps not even illegal." She pressed the release stud and the baton snapped to its full length. "Effective against small bones, or thin. Fingers and wrist. Collarbone. Even the temple. To a cervical vertebra, perhaps a killing blow."

"You didn't come here to talk about my gear."

"Yes." She put the baton back onto the leather. She looked down for a moment, and her hands became fists, and her breath hitched. She turned farther away, and stepped to the bars of the window. "I find myself in a difficult position. As Khryl's Own Fist, my first duty is to His Law."

"And here I was hoping we could get through the day without another lecture on your fucking duty."

The shadow of her face shifted with the slow ripple of her veil. "I myself Invested you with Khryl's Authority."

"Um, yeah. About that—"

"I am sworn to defend the Battleground and its people with my hand, my heart, and my sacred honor."

"We need to talk about you and Orbek. About Khryl's Justice."

"Have you crushed the Black Knife insurrection? Have you secured Orbek's submission?"

"Not exactly."

"Then there is nothing to be said."

"I'm not going to make a lot of progress on either as long as my naked ass is locked in this cell."

"We both know you'll walk out of here seconds after I depart for the Ring of Justice. Setting men to guard you would result only in needless bloodshed."

"Likely be some anyway."

"And I will be helpless to prevent it, as I was last night. As I was this morning. As it seems I will always be."

"Except it's about to get worse."

"Peace. I did not come here to listen to you expound upon the obvious."

"Then why the fuck *did* you come here?"

"After . . . Weaver's Square . . . I sought my uncle's counsel," she said softly. "I could not find him. Eventually I . . . persuaded . . . Lord Tarkanen to reveal my uncle's fate."

"Uh . . ."

"Are you the man?"

"It's complicated."

"*Are you?*"

He sighed. "Yes. Close enough, anyway."

"*Why?*"

"Look, 'why' isn't gonna tell you anything you need to know."

"Tell me."

She wanted it straight? He could do that. "It was the job."

"The job? Our deal? In pursuit of the outcome with which I tasked you?"

"Yeah."

"And your weapon . . . the Hand of Light? The Authority of Khryl with which I myself Invested you?"

"It was all I had."

She nodded solemnly, and left her head down. "A harsh judgment upon my uncle's life. I had believed better of him."

"Well, hey, I mean—he was an asshole, sure, but I think he was trying to do the best he could with the job he'd been given. If that means anything."

"It doesn't. This will stain his Legend until the end of time." Her voice went even softer. "As Khryl has decreed, His Will has been done. You were only His vessel, as am I."

"I wouldn't go *that* far—"

"You have gone too far already. But my uncle's dishonor is not what has brought me to you now. I only . . . I wish you might . . ."

She finally moved: a slow twisting half collapse that she caught against the table's edge. She held herself there, shapeless silhouette haloed by the sun. One hand came up along the front of her gown, and it trembled as it slipped within her veil.

"I want you to tell me—" Her breathing hitched. "I only want to know . . . need to know . . ."

"Yeah?"

She lifted her head, and her hand came from her face, and with it came her veil. Her vivid eyes were smeared with red, and tears tracked the curves of her cheeks.

"Why didn't you *shoot* me?"

It was his turn to go still. Silence yawned between them.

Her hand slid behind her head to massage the back of her neck, and she returned to the window.

He watched her. Only watched. Without blinking. Without breathing. Without even thought.

"That was your intention, wasn't it? To shoot me dead." She spoke to the clear sparkling sunlight between the bars. "That was why you came to Weaver's Square this morning. Why you carry this formidable pistol. Why you aimed it at my face."

"I was . . ." He shook his head as though he were only now awakening. " . . . kinda foggy. The blast—well, you know. When I woke up I didn't know what the hell was going on."

"This is no answer." She turned back toward the cell and leaned on the edge of the table. Wood groaned in her grip. There was a shimmer to her stillness: a suggestion of trembling ruthlessly suppressed. "Speak truth."

"What truth do you have in mind?"

"Any you might offer."

His shrug apologized for useless honesty. "I was planning to."

"Yes."

"It was the best idea I had. The only idea. Assumption Day . . ." He met her scraped-raw gaze. "Shit that happened on Assumption Day shouldn't have. Including you."

"And yet—" The plank at the table's edge tore free with a short harsh squeal. She lifted the splintered wood as though she didn't understand what she was seeing, then let it fall at her feet. "And yet—"

"Yeah."

"You saved my life." Her flat tone softened into faded melancholy. "You saved my life."

Well, sort of. Maybe. A twitch of his shoulder. "Seemed only polite."

She lowered her head so the edge of her cowl shaded her reddened eyes. "Please—" she said softly, "I have asked you an honest question. I wish to know why you handed me your weapon, instead of using it. Please respect my desire for an honest answer."

There was no reason why he should. Not a goddamn one.

She waited.

Finally he sighed. "Maybe you remind me of somebody."

"Ah."

Motionless in white: a pillar of salt.

"And was this person . . . special to you?"

"Yeah. I guess she was." He found himself staring at his battle-scarred hands. "Not as special as she should have been."

An infinitesimal lift of her head. "She's dead, then."

"A long time ago."

"Did you kill her?"

"Fuck off."

"I only wish to—"

"Let me translate, huh? *Fuck off* is Artan for *I'm not gonna talk about that.*"

The trace of a nod, a drift of her chin to a lower angle, and he felt like an asshole. But he was used to that.

She stared through the window bars. For a time there was only the breeze and the slow beat of the drummer, the creak of cartwheels and the distant clap of hooves on flagstones.

After a while, she said, "This woman, of whom you say I remind you—was this by any chance Marade Sunflash? Marade, Knight Tarthell of Kavlin's Leap?"

"Um—" He squinted at her, surprised, even more wary. "Yeah, actually."

"I had hoped it was." Again she leaned her cowled forehead against the window's bars. "Knight Tarthell was betimes a guest at my uncle's manor. I admired her extravagantly. Her Legend is well regarded within the Order; in her day, she was considered a fair prospect for Champion herself."

He felt smaller. "I remember."

"She would bring gifts to me from exotic lands, and of course tales of her adventures reached mythic proportion among children my age— though we were forbidden to have any direct knowledge of them. For reasons I'm sure you can imagine."

He could. For a couple years he'd been one of those reasons.

"When I was finally old enough to be permitted access, her Legend of Breaking the Black Knives made, ah . . . riveting reading. As you can perhaps imagine as well."

He coughed as though something had caught in his throat. Better than trying to answer.

"It was Knight Tarthell herself who encouraged me to train for Khryl's Own."

He faked a swallow. "She was like that. She had a—way about her, I guess. A way of making you believe you could do anything. Just from that smile of hers."

"Hence her epithet. Not only for her reknowned beauty, but for her nature. There was no one warmer, or kinder, or who enjoyed more a joke, yet her wrath was legendary; like the sun, she could kiss or she could burn. A magnificent woman, and a very great Knight."

"Yeah."

"So you must guess how flattered I am to bring her to mind." She turned away from the window and came to the bars of the cell door. Her eyes were raw as bloody eggs. "Do you find me so very like her, then?"

Ohhh, crap. He knew enough about women to understand that this conversation had instantaneously transmogrified into a slippery slope above a lake of burning shit. "Uh, well . . . yeah, I mean—"

"And how would that be? Do you find me so warm? So kind?" Her tone sharpened. "Am I humorous? Or is it my lovely *features* that draw her to mind?"

Inside his head the turd-smoke thickened. "Look, I just—"

"I do not bear an epithet, did you know that? Other than those cast at my retreating back, when they think I cannot hear. Hatchetjaw. Gloom-crow. Steelcunt. Do you know that I no longer wear my helm?"

"I've heard—"

"I have not put it on since the day I overheard a pair of citizens sniggering together. 'It's true, Knights are supposed to wear full armor into battle, but one look at *her* face, you can see the helmet's not so much a rule as it is a guideline,' and the other replied, 'If she were as smart as she is strong, she'd leave it off in battle and wear it to bed.' "

Jesus, what gets me into this crap? He glanced through the ceiling. *I blame you.*

He looked back at her and decided to hit the lake of burning shit face-first. "Y'know, for a girl raised by people as relentlessly, ruthlessly polite as you Khryllians, you should have better manners."

She jerked as though he'd slapped her.

"When you ask a guy a question, isn't it simple courtesy to shut up long enough for him to answer?"

She stood at the bars, her raw eyes staring unapologetic challenge. Whatever answer he gave her had better be good.

He discovered he did have a good answer. Better than good, it was useful: he could use it to work her. The best part?

It was even true.

"It's because you're so unhappy."

Her raw challenge faded to quizzical melancholy. "Oh," she said softly, but then her brows drew together and her chin came up and he knew what she was about to ask.

"I don't know," he said. "She never told me."

"But—she seemed so . . ."

He took a long, slow, deep breath. "All I know is that she had . . . issues. Emotional problems. Deep ones. The kind nobody can really do much about. Being Marade—the Marade you knew, the *parfit gentil* Knight of Reknown, mirthful, valorous, surpassingly puissant and all that crap—that was her answer to her problems. That's how she survived whatever was eating her from the inside. I think that's why she was so good at it. It was the only answer she had."

She looked down at her hands. "And how, then, did you know all this?"

"I didn't. Well, I did sort of, but I pretty much didn't care." Not as long as he could use it to get between her legs. He shrugged, not much liking the feel of this particular scar. "I was just a kid. I had problems of my own."

Her hands tightened on the bars. Iron groaned. "So this insight came to you . . . too late."

"They mostly do."

"In her pain," she murmured, bowing her head until her cowl veiled her eyes once more, "she could only create herself anew."

She seemed to find sad satisfaction from this, as though it was the answer to the last puzzle she'd ever solve. "The sole escape from her pain was . . . to be someone else. Someone who would never feel . . . feel such . . ."

Ah. He knew what page they were on now. "That's something a lot of us try."

Her reply was to turn her back on him.

"Sucks when you finally discover it doesn't work, huh?"

With a faint sigh, she sagged against the bars, reaching up to hold on to them behind her head. "And how—" Her voice was muffled. Blurred. "—how did Marade handle . . . this discovery?"

"She didn't. She . . . couldn't, I guess. It was too much for her." The memory burned even now. Working her was working him too. "She . . . did something stupid, and got herself killed."

"In Yalitrayya. Searching with you for the crown of Dal'kannith Thousandhand."

"Yeah."

"Were you with her when she died?"

"No." He had to look at the floor. "I was late."

Days late. Remembering made him dizzy with nausea.

"Her Legend is . . . silent . . . on her death."

"It was ugly." Whatever hell Berne was burning in wasn't half hot enough. "Worse than the Black Knives. Worse than you can imagine."

"Would you . . ." Her voice had faded into a faint, sad yearning as though she called to him from far away. "Would you have saved her, if you could? Not from her death. From her pain."

"Oh, shit . . ." he breathed. "Jesus suffering Christ, what a fucking idiot I am . . ."

Obvious. So obvious a blind man could have seen it from the other side of town.

When she'd figured out who he was, it must have seemed like a gift from Heaven. A secret meeting, alone and unarmed, upon the holiest sanctum of the Order. Bathed in the blood of heroes to wash her sins away . . .

Handing a loaded gun to a man who had killed just about every kind of creature that flies, walks, or crawls in the fucking dirt.

And when he didn't . . .

The deal. The deal with a man who had killed a god. A win-win.

Because she knew that jobs he takes tend to get done, and people who hire him tend to end up dead.

Jesus.

He tongued the pick and tension bar out of his cheek. This might be kind of tricky.

He cleared his throat, then coughed the tools into his fist.

"For Marade? I would have done just about anything." He started on the left shackle, working by feel, talking to cover any metal-on-metal clicks. "Whatever your uncle told you about me, I'm not a monster."

"I hope I have seen that already."

The shackle opened in his hand, and he set to work on the other. "I don't know her Legend. I don't know what she said of—well, of us. There was a . . . moment . . . in the dark."

"She wrote that you refused to take her life."

That was one way of putting it. "Yeah."

"She wrote that the darkness let her say things—do things—that she never could have said or done in the light. It made her see herself without eyes. She said it was a test. Of her virtue, her courage, and her faith. The direst test she ever faced."

Her voice hushed to barely a whisper. "And that the only reason she passed it was you. Your faith in her gave her faith in herself."

He had that taste in his mouth again. "It wasn't like that."

"It was for her."

"Okay. Okay, yeah," he said like saying that could make it hurt less. "I guess she wouldn't lie."

"Of course not."

"It's just . . ." He had to look down. "I wasn't trying to help her. I was trying to fuck her."

"This might explain why this memory is for you only painful, where for her it inspired greatness."

Yeah, okay. He'd had enough of beating his skull against every cobble on memory lane. "So I wouldn't do that for her. That's the point. I wouldn't take her life to save her from pain. Not even for Marade. Not even facing what we faced."

"Ah."

"So what in the fucking universe makes you think I'd do it for *you*?"

She made a sound like she'd been punched in the throat.

He pitched his voice low. Gentle. As kind as he could make it, which wasn't very. No practice. "He can't read your mind, y'know."

Her back stiffened. "What?"

"Not unless you're thinking *at* Him. Almost subvocalizing. Otherwise, He has to guess, based on what He can feel you feeling." He chewed the inside of his lip while he got the right shackle open. "Yeah, you probably know that already: you're pretty good at talking around shit."

"I—" Her voice went thick, half-gargled. "I—"

"Can't even tell me about Him, can you? Can't tell me how He's in your head. What He makes you do. Can't tell anyone. Somebody might stop it."

"Don't—"

"I know you can't ask me. And I can't save you. Not in the way you want." One shackle in each hand and the chain between them, he rose. "But I might be able to help you, if you'll let me."

"Stop—*stop*—you don't *understand*—"

"Can you *not* do things? Will He let you?" He moved toward her, his bare feet utterly silent on the scuffed plank floor. The chain hung without swinging; he measured the back of her cowl through the bars. "Will He let you not move?"

With a shuddering gasp she burst away from the bars, invisibly fast: frames cut out of the film inside his head. She flattened herself against the wall across from him, trembling.

Nodding, he dropped the chain, and showed her his empty hands. "Listen to me. I know some things about being godseized, all right? Not just Monastic shit. I know what's happening to you. I even have a pretty good idea how it feels."

He went to the cell door. Across the walkway she shivered against the stone. "I don't need to know how it started. What damage somebody did to you. What made you think it'd be worth it. I only need to know how much you can do for me."

"*For* you? For *you*?" Her voice went shrill. Her gloved hands crushed chunks from the wall. "Why did you have to *speak*? If you even *hint*—I'll have to . . . have to . . ."

She squeezed shut her eyes. "I might have to, anyway."

"How about you walk out of here? Turn around and just walk away."

"I . . . can't. I can't. You've said too much. Too much already." Her shivering deepened toward tremors.

"Angvasse, listen to me. I will not harm you. Ever."

"We both know your word means nothing."

He knew *we both* didn't mean her and him. *We both* meant her and Him. "Everybody knows lots of shit about me. Some of it's even true. Like, for example, mercy killing isn't my thing."

"*Mercy* isn't your thing."

"Yeah. I'm not the guy who puts you out of your misery. I'm the guy who makes your misery worse. Khryl knows it. That's why He let you hire me."

"To *torture* me?"

"Gods are what they are because we are what we are. There's not much you can do about it."

"Do you want to *see*?" Tears now streamed from her swollen eyes. "Do you want to see how much I can do?"

"Okay," he said, low. "Okay, it's okay. Relax."

With that invisible speed she snatched up the Automag, thumb on the trigger and her mouth wide open, and when she lifted it blue faerie fire flared from her shoulder to her wrist, and one inch shy of pointing at her face, the muzzle froze.

The air around her shimmered. Hummed with power. Veins bulged in her corded neck and spidered across her forehead. A spray of blood burst from her nose and her face was turning black and he said, "Okay, *stop* it, *enough*, for shit's sake!" and she dropped the pistol back onto the table and half fell against the wall behind her, gasping.

"Do you *see*?" Her sobbing was open now. "I only wanted . . . it wasn't supposed to be like this. I only wanted . . . to be *good* at it. I didn't even need to be a great Knight. Just a good one. And now . . . and now . . ."

She sagged on the wall, her face twisting, tears streaking the blood from her nose. "There is . . . so little left of me . . ."

"Fuck me," he breathed, and she startled him with a sharp bitter laugh.

"That I can still do," she said, straightening. "That is nearly all I can do."

"Um, hey, y'know—"

She pushed herself off the wall and leaned toward him, a dangerously manic light kindling in her eye. "Is that what you want? You want me to *fuck* you?"

He stepped back. "It's a figure of speech."

"How did you get those shackles off, I wonder?" Her hands now gripped the bars of the cell door near the lock. Without any sign of effort she gave the door a wrench that split open the lock with a brief hoarse squall. "Were you not searched? A poor job we did of it, then."

Way too soon he found a cold stone wall against his back. "Look, you don't really want to do this—"

"Marade Sunflash herself gave her virtue to you. How can I do less?"

An eyeblink brought her to him and then her arms were around him and her hands were on him and his ribs groaned inside him like the cell's bars had in her hands. Her face met his and her breath tasted of mint and honey and she crushed her lips against his teeth and drew them off with blood.

"*Stop* . . ." Breath crushed out of his lungs and black clouds bloomed in his head and he fell back on instinct: a quick snap smashed his forehead into her nose and blood sprayed down their faces and she moaned.

Not in pain.

"Fight me," she whispered. "*Fight* me, Caine . . ."

Something in how she said the name brought blood thundering to his ears. And not just his ears. She pulled her face back so that her eyes of indigo could gaze into his while her splattered nose rebuilt itself and she murmured, "And where did you hide those lock picks?" and her gloved fingers began to force open his asshole.

"Fucking *stop* it!" he said, but he could say no more because her mouth was against his again and her tongue forced into his mouth. He bit down, hard, blood and live meat between his teeth, and she released his mouth, moaning as her tongue knit until she could gasp, "Yes . . ."

He worked one arm up between them, the back of his hand brushing a bullet-hard nipple, and hooked two fingers into the notch of her collarbone. Slow steady pressure forced her gagging backward enough to let him talk. "Angvasse—this is rape. You understand? *Rape*. Is that what you want?"

She released his ass and slid one hand around to his penis.

He looked down. He was hard as drop-forged steel.

"You want me," she murmured. "You do."

He couldn't deny it. "Maybe a guy likes to be asked."

"Is that it? You find me insufficiently *polite*?"

That and he was a little down on sex with suicidal superhuman killing machines.

"Please, then, Caine. Please," she said, and dropped to her knees in front of him and slid her mouth slowly, firmly, inexorably, down over the length of his cock.

He nearly lost his concentration right there, because he was remembering something Tourann had said about Khryllians and their firearms.

They don't do autoloaders here.

"Well, when you put it *that* way . . ." Gently, he teased himself back out of her mouth. He said, "Wait. Wait, Angvasse. Get the gun. It'll be better."

She frowned up at him.

"Do it. You'll like this. I promise."

She got up and reached through the bars for it. He followed her and slid an arm around her from behind. Her breasts were small, almost hard as muscle; his other hand slid down the back of her pants, and she shuddered. "That button by your thumb. That's the clip release. Press it."

She did, and the clip of tristacks clattered to the floor. "And now?"

"Give it to me and pull down your pants."

She twisted to face him. "What?"

"Come on." He gathered her to him and found her blood-smeared lips with his mouth. "Come on. It's what you like, isn't it? I'll hold it on you while I fuck you. I can hold it to your head." He slid a hand between her legs. "Or you can take it in your mouth."

She shuddered against him and clung to him with arms that could crush his bones to powder. "But—but He—"

"It's unloaded. He won't stop you. Why should He?"

"Yes. Yes, of course. Unloaded." She brought the barrel to her mouth, tentatively, testing. Then her tongue flicked out along the brushed steel. Her eyes drifted closed. "Oh, yes. Oh, Caine, *yes*—"

"Go on, try it," he murmured against her neck. "Let me watch you try it."

He took half a step back as she slid the muzzle in between her lips. Her other hand slid inside her pants, and she squeezed the trigger.

Her head exploded.

Didn't even make much noise: a soggy handclap, no more. Her torso twisted and her legs buckled and she fell into a heap of white and scarlet and he stood over her corpse with shreds of her face dripping down his chest.

He said, "You're welcome."

Firearms were new around here, and autoloaders were unknown, and neither she nor her god had understood how an autoloader, once fired, carries the next round in the chamber. Live and learn.

Well: learn.

He knelt beside her, scrubbing blood and tissue from his face and hair onto her cloak. Then he took the Automag from her hand, slapped in a fresh clip, and racked the slide. By the time he stood again, her corpse was wreathed in blue flame.

"See you," he muttered, and slipped out of the cell.

The shattered rags of flesh at her temples were already blunting and folding themselves back together. The larger hunks of skull and brain sprayed across the cell still looked fresh and solid, but smaller blood spatters disappeared and the larger pools shrank as though they were evaporating.

He pulled on his pants and slipped his tunic over his head and jammed feet into his boots without bothering with socks. He safetied the Automag, tossed it onto the leather wrap, and bundled his gear together, and even though he had some time before the god could Humpty Dumpty her head, he ran down the stairs, cut through the stable, and trotted away along the alley as fast as he dared.

This was shaping up to be a busy day.

He didn't even make it a block.

He got to the alley's mouth and stopped and stood, breathing harder than he had to. He stared out along the street, but what he was seeing was the inside of the subgarrison cell. What he was feeling was the warm plash of a woman's tears on his bare chest, years ago, when she held him in her lap in a room dark beyond the memory of day, and spoke gently of people they thought they'd never see again.

He had to run. He didn't even have time to be standing here. He sure as hell knew better than to go back.

He had to leave her. Had to.

He was still telling himself that while he was trotting back up the alley.

He turned aside for a moment into the subgarrison's tiny stable. Only two horses were still inside. One had a bloated gut that read as borderline colic, and the other was trying to keep his weight off his right hind.

He pulled open their stall doors. "You're free. Go if you want. Stay if you want. You pick."

Neither seemed inclined to leave; like most professional cavalry, Khryllians take good care of their horses. He went into the stall of the lame one, stepped to his left side, and looked deeply into his eye. "Change of plan. I'm not waiting. I can't. I have to go for it. Today. Sometime around sunset."

The horse's eye had clouded over, turning pale and milky as late winter ice.

He wished he could somehow reach out and touch her now, but words were all he had. "Tell Faith I need her mom. And have her get Deliann, because I need Ma'elKoth here too. And Raithe. Raithe of Ankhana—the Monastic Ambassador to the Infinite Court. You remember. If everything goes well, I'll see you tonight. If it doesn't . . ."

And now even his words ran out. "Take care of yourself," he said softly. "If you get a chance to take care of me, I hope you'll do that too. I have to go."

He left the stall doors open.

He slipped back inside the cell and lowered himself to the floor beside Angvasse Khlaylock's corpse, and he hugged her shoulders and her blue fire-crowned head to his doubled legs, and when the god had healed her enough that she began to breathe, her first few whooping gasps settled into quiet choking sobs, and by the time she had eyes she was already crying, and for a long time she clung to him and wept into his lap.

"So, y'know," he said gently, "this was the other reason I didn't shoot you."

Later, still lying across his lap, she was calm enough to remember her duty. "Khryl's Justice . . ." she said faintly. "I'm late . . ."

"Khryl's Justice can wait. You have till—what, sundown, right?"

"Yes. Sundown. As Knight Accusor, it is my duty."

He stroked her hair. "We might be able to manage that."

"We?"

"You and I have some things to talk about. Like, the ogrillo you were gonna fight? That's not Orbek. Not really."

"Who else could he be?"

"Someone like you."

"Like—" She sat up slowly—probably some uncertainty in function with her newly regenerated motor nerves. Just as slowly, she twisted to face him and squinted her eyes into focus. "Who—what—do you think I am?"

"Not human."

Her lips pulled into a thin flat line.

"You must have suspected," he said. "How many times can you wake up from getting your skull bashed in before you figure out you're not like other people?"

"I don't—" She lowered her head. "Whatever I am, it is what Khryl has made of me."

"And what you've made of yourself. Mixed in with your parents and schoolmasters and probably your uncle."

"Then—"

"It's not that you're not you. It's that you're not the you that you think you are."

"Is there any way in which any of this makes sense?"

"Technically—in Monastic jargon, at least—you're what is called an autotheurgic proto-Aspect fetch." He raised a hand. "I know, that doesn't help. Look, it's simple enough in concept. A fetch is a created duplicate, all right? It can be a duplicate of a living thing, like how Dal'kannith Thousandhand could make himself into an entire army. Or it can be a duplicate of something dead, like Deliann—the Ankhanan Emperor. Ma'elKoth built him out of a big pile of shit—not literal shit, just, y'know, stuff—that people brought from all over the Empire. Hell, Ma'elKoth was a fetch too, technically—He created that body for Himself with the power of Da'Kannith's Crown. It takes the power of a god to pull it off. So he wasn't the duplicate of a living creature, he was the duplicate of His fantasy-self, but it's the same general thing. With me so far?"

She nodded silently, still staring at the planks on which she sat.

"An Aspect is what we call a body created or taken by an Ideational Power—a god like Khryl—to express his will. Autotheurgic is just a fancy way to say that you are the answer to your own prayer."

Muscle jumped along her jaw.

"Just a guess," he said. "I imagine there was a full Tourney under way, and all you wanted was to do well, right? So you prayed that Khryl might make you . . . oh, y'know, that He'd lend you His Strength and Skill of Hand and Eye and shit. Something like that."

"Yes."

"And when you won, nobody was more surprised than you were."

Fresh tears spread splotches below her bowed head. "I was unworthy," she said faintly. "Was and am."

"Khryl doesn't agree." He laid a hand on her shoulder. "Neither do I."

She shook him off. "Your word means nothing."

"You'd be surprised what my word means." He offered her half a shrug. "You think you were the only Knight praying to Khryl that day?"

"I—of course not. We all pray. It's traditional."

"And you were the Knight He chose."

"And how far I have fallen . . ."

"I don't think so. I don't think you *can* fall."

"What I did to you—"

"Almost did."

"*Almost* only by grace of your cleverness."

"Listen, it's not like I forgive you. It was a shitty thing to do. To yourself as well as me. It was an act unworthy of you, and of the office you hold . . . but I understand too, that's all. Making somebody kill you isn't easy when you can't come right out and ask for it. Especially when you're, y'know, you. And if you could be killed by a mortal weapon, you'd be dead now."

She shrugged off his hand. "And thus my unworthiness is compounded by cowardice—to hazard battle when I cannot be slain—"

"You can be slain. I can do it. A couple other people I can think of might manage it too."

"But not with any weapon I have yet faced in battle or tourney. Cowardice. Worse than cowardice: concealing sin beneath a mask of virtue."

"Oh, for fuck's sake, Angvasse. Get over yourself."

Her head came up. Her face turned toward him, and her eyes were raw. "You dare?"

"Sure I dare. That's what people like about me." He drew up his knees and swiveled to meet her bloody gaze square on. "I know you feel bad about yourself. People who don't suffer from self-loathing are people who should. Doing one rotten thing doesn't make you a villain any more than doing one good thing makes me a hero."

She looked down again. "*Hero* is no word for either of us."

"Without getting too far into more mystic technical shit, all the training and praying and all—even Khryl's Law and your Knightly Code and shit—that's what we call *Theophanic attunement.* It's to make you as much like Khryl's ideal as you can be. He chose you. It takes the power of a god to create a living fetch. That means you are closer to His vision of a Champion—His image of *Himself*—than any living creature. Probably ever."

"Is that a compliment to me, or an insult to Khryl?"

"If you can't say something nice about yourself, shut the fuck up." He lurched to his feet. "I've known more than my share of Knights. I've only met two I didn't despise," he said, harsh. Flat and brutal. "One of them was Marade."

He held out his hand. "The other's you."

She drew back. "Now you mock."

"Usually. Not now."

She still refused to look up.

"Marade was a hero. A *real* hero. I cared about her. Even loved her, as much as I could love anybody back then. Enough that I've never gotten over how bad I treated her. She was a truly great Knight and a fucking magnificent human being, and she wasn't a tenth of what you are."

"How can you *say* that—?"

"Oh, you know, lips and tongue and shit. The usual."

She pressed her head lower. "Why do you even care?"

"Well, it's not out of the goodness of my fucking heart. I need you."

Now she did look up. "You . . . *need* me—?"

"Not like that. Not that I wouldn't, y'know, want you," he amended hastily. "You know I would. I do. You saw. I'm not gonna deny it. But I'm with somebody."

"A woman? A *human* woman?"

He decided she wasn't trying to insult him. "You should meet her. Seriously. She could do you some good. You need her. I need you."

"But why? And what? What do you expect of me?"

"I need a hero," he said simply. "You're the only one I know."

"And why would . . . a hero . . . help you?"

His lips stretched until his teeth began to appear. A lot of them. "What if you could take back the worst thing you ever did?"

She stared at him. For a long time. Expressionless. Finally she blinked. She gathered a long, deep sigh that lifted her chest and brought her shoulders up and then down, and then she took his hand.

"Cool." He pulled her to her feet and clasped her hand to his heart. "I know your truthsense doesn't work on me. Which makes us like regular people. You can choose to trust me, or you can choose not to. All I can do is ask you to look in my eyes and believe I will never willingly do you harm."

She did look in his eyes. For a long time. Then she touched his cheek. "For the memory of Lady Tarthell. For the honor of Marade Sunflash."

Better than he deserved. "Now we need to get you cleaned up."

"What do you hope to do?"

"We."

"Very well. We."

"We," he said, the spark of a smile igniting his eyes, "just might change history."

the now of always 5

LOVE ABSOLUTE

LOVE ABSOLUTE

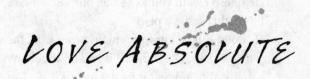

"We were at war, Caine. We both fought for what we most loved."

—HOME (AKA T'NALLDION, THE ASCENDED MA'ELKOTH, ET AL.)
  Blade of Tyshalle

It's snowing again, except on the horse-witch.

For the others, snow falls in fairy-tale flakes, light and beautiful and carrying only enough chill to be refreshing. The day has turned to night, and no fire has been lit, but around them and out some ways into the whispering white is a soft and gauzy illumination that casts no shadow. When he'd inquired about it of the man who looks like his son, Caine had only shrugged a nod toward Khryl. "Sun god."

"Oh, of course. Sure. I should have remembered."

"Never really dark when He's around."

"Must make it difficult to sneak up on people."

"You have no idea."

Not long after this, Caine became restive, shifting his weight, clenching his jaw and frowning even more than usual. Shortly he rose and stalked off toward the darkness. Now he is only a shadow that gathers and dissolves and gathers again as he paces at the limit of visibility.

Duncan looks at the horse-witch. "He seems worried."

"He is worried. Whenever he has time to worry, he worries. It's who he is. What should worry you is when he stops worrying."

"I think I actually understand that. So what's wrong? He seemed to be in control of everything."

"It's an act. He's an Actor."

"He was."

"He doesn't control. It's against his nature. When he tries, things break. People bleed. Usually him, but sometimes others. Mostly they die."

"Ah."

"He doesn't want you to be one of those others."

"I thought he has a plan."

"He does. But he knows his plans never work the way he hopes. Mostly, things turn to shit. Deep shit. But he's an excellent swimmer."

"I recall. Why doesn't it snow on you?"

"I don't like snow."

"I love the snow," Duncan says. "I always have."

"That's probably why it's snowing."

"He's doing this for me?"

She shrugs. "It's hard to say for sure who's doing what for whom. Especially here. Might be you."

"How would I control the weather?"

"That's harder to say. If you're making snow, you're doing it some time that isn't now. Can you think of why you might do it, if you could?"

He lets his head fall back into its cool cushion of fairy-tale snow, and now he has tears.

"Ah." The horse-witch nods. "It reminds you of your wife."

Duncan's eyes drift closed. "Everything reminds me of my wife."

"That's sad for you."

"Sometimes. Usually. It was snowing the day we admitted to each other we were in love."

"Sad and happy together, then."

"A writer from Earth said there is no greater grief than to recall, in misery, times when we were happy."

"Dante Alighieri."

Surprise opens his eyes and lifts his head. "How do you know that?"

"A man who looked like you told me once. I don't forget."

"Someone who looked like me?"

"We met before their son was born. I also met the man's partner—the woman he would marry. She was very beautiful."

"Yes," he said faintly. "She was. Very beautiful. Lucky that Hari favored her more than me. Did wonders for his career."

"Your son must be very handsome."

"He was. He is. Probably. Whoever he actually is."

"You're proud of him."

"Very. But I can't tell him that."

"He can't bear to be admired."

"You know him well."

"Very."

"I am also, well . . . I'm in awe. He's killed people, and saved people. He's fought monsters, and he's fought men who became monsters. He's saved kingdoms and toppled empires. Now he has set himself against the gods to save a universe . . . and I used to change his *diapers*. I used to yell at him to make his bed."

"You used to beat him so hard all he could do was lie there and bleed."

Some few moments passed before he could respond.

"He said you know right where it hurts," he said, slow and thick. "I should have believed him."

"He told me once that every time you look at him, you see only where you hurt him. Is that true?"

He laid one hand over his eyes. "Why would you ask me that? And why would I answer it?"

"It's what I do. Answer, or not, for whatever reasons please you, or for no reason at all."

"Then not. I can't talk about this."

"You should know: you're not here because you beat him."

"*He's* here because I beat him."

"That's a matter too deep for me. He brought you here because he wants you here. He thinks he needs you here."

"I can't imagine what he could need from me."

"Are all the men in your family obtuse? You're here for the same reason I am. And Angvasse or Khryl or whoever she wants to be."

"He thinks I can help somehow?"

"You're here because he loves you."

And this, somehow, is a wound deeper than the last.

"I'm not even his father. Even if I was, I wouldn't know him. Not really."

"Do you think that means he doesn't know you?"

Duncan finds he has no reply.

"It's not simple," she says. "Nothing about either of you is simple. I don't know how well he knows you, or even how well he thinks he knows you. But I know he loves you. And I believe you love him."

"It's . . . difficult."

"It's difficult for me too. He's a difficult man. It's a good thing I can afford to be patient."

"I'd imagine so."

She reaches over to take his hand. "I'm not always right, Duncan. But when I say something that's not true, it's because I'm mistaken, not false. I don't tell you this as part of his plan, or any plan. I tell you because I believe it's true, and I want you to know it."

"Why do you care?"

"Because he does."

Duncan is silent again.

"He cares about all kinds of things," the horse-witch says lightly. "Some of them are much more unlikely than you. He loves in the same way he does everything else. Any time he backs away from the brink of a cliff, it's only to get a running start."

"Most people think he doesn't love anything but himself."

"And they're exactly wrong. His whole life is about who and what he loves. It always has been. For him, love is absolute."

"Until he met Shanna, he never seemed like he cared much about anything except his career."

"Some of the things he loves are not nice things. At all. But he loves what he loves."

"I apologized—tried to apologize. If I had been a good father—even a better father—he never would have had to become Caine . . ."

"He loves being Caine. His love for being Caine is just as absolute. Like I said: some things he loves are not nice."

"How can he love being . . . that? Being what Caine is?"

"Because he's an asshole," she says. "You must have noticed."

middle of the end

THE MOCKINGBIRD TEST

THE MOCKINGBIRD TEST

"Just the other day I killed a better man than you'll ever be, for doing less than you did. Did you really think I'd let you live?"

—"CAINE" (PFNL. HARI MICHAELSON)
  For Love of Pallas Ril

*T*he oil trickles into my blood without pain, without heat, without any sensation of power at all. Only an intimation gathering into a certainty that I am loved.

Loved by a power greater than my mind can conceive.

Looking over at the armored secmen, their power rifles at slant arms, I know that Studio Security isn't a job. It's an assignment. They're not retired Social Police, because Social Police don't retire.

And now I understand why.

Gayle's frowning at me. *"To Kill a Mockingbird?"*

It seems like a year since I asked the question. "Have you read it?"

"I—well, I suppose I . . ." He frowns, squaring his shoulders and stretching his neck like he can't quite figure out if I'm pulling his dick. "It's only—that was my mother's favorite book. She used to read it to me, a few pages at a time, for bedtime stories. After I started school, we used to read it together. She'd help me pronounce the words, and explain the things I didn't understand. Why do you ask?"

"It was my father's favorite book too. For Dad, *To Kill a Mockingbird* was the Bible. More than the Bible. Dad used to say you can learn most of what you need to know about somebody by finding out his favorite character." I nod toward the palmpad in his hand. "Dad's kind of on my mind right now."

"I had nothing to do with that."

"Simon? Ever read it?"

Faller shrugs. "Sure. Long time ago."

"See, Dad had this idea because, y'know, just having read it says you have a brain and some idea what it's used for, and that you read fiction, and that you have at least a theoretical appreciation for the classics. But beyond that, well—most people who read that novel like to imagine themselves being like this character or that one, because those characters, it's like they're more real than you are. Y'know, some guys identify with, say, Tom Robinson, suffering injustice with dignity. Some guys go for Jem, the big brother. Shanna liked Scout—obvious, sure. Dad told me once that my mother favored Maudie Atkinson. And if you know somebody, sometimes you don't even have to ask who their character is. You, for example, strike me as a Dill guy."

Faller stares, blinks and stares again. "How can you know that?"

"It's obvious. Dill's thing is that he knows stuff, right? So smart it's scary, not strong but charming and resourceful and inventive . . . and a little sad. And you grew up to be a necromancer. Tell me I'm wrong."

He shakes his head. "You're not wrong. I just don't get where you're going with this."

"Gayle?"

"It's plausible, I suppose. It still seems to be, well, a little abstract."

"Sure. Don't take it wrong if I'm off. I think you liked the sheriff. Heck Tate."

"Well . . . my mother and I used to talk about how the sheriff had to enforce laws he didn't always believe in. And how he knew everybody and liked everybody, and everybody liked him, even though he was the local authority. But he wasn't the only one."

"Yeah? I'm thinking, maybe, Calpurnia? Becoming part of a family through devotion and diligence, more to her than meets the eye . . . ?"

He flushes and looks down like he's suddenly interested in braiding his fingers together. "That's—well, I mean . . ."

"How much do you know about my father?"

"I don't—well, I guess, the usual. Your—uh, Caine's—promotional pack included a, I suppose, a sanitized profile. You spoke of him once in a while, while we worked together. He was living with you, wasn't he?"

"Yeah. Simon?"

Faller shrugs. "I studied Westerling from the Michaelson text, forty years ago. More. And *Tales of the First Folk* is required reading in the Conservatory's Battle Magick program."

"*My* father's favorite character was—" I have to swallow to clear my voice, and just thinking about it is making my eyes hot. "Dad's favorite character . . . *is* . . . Atticus."

Gayle nods thoughtfully. He's caught up in the game now. "Plausible. Even obvious. Unconventional single father, educated, intellectual, philosophical turn of mind, exemplary moral courage—"

"That's not—" I choke on it. "That's not why."

And now the stinging in my eyes threatens to spill over into moisture trickling onto my cheeks, because I guess when you come right down to it I'm still that seven-year-old kid.

Sometimes the rage is too big for anything but tears.

"My father wanted to *be* him. My father wanted to be *exactly* him. He pledged his life, his love, his skill and hope and heart in a cause that can't be won, that he *knew* can't be won, because Atticus fucking Finch made him believe there were things more important than winning."

"You sound like you're angry about it. Him. Atticus. Like you hate him."

"I'd gut that fucker like a rabbit."

It's the truth.

This is truth too. "Atticus Finch made my father believe that *how you lose* can change people, and that changing people changes the world, and you saw that fucking screen. You saw Dad's prize for fighting his good fight."

Again his fingers get interesting. "Hari, I—"

"You *saw*. Both of you."

"I—yes," Gayle says warily. "Yes, I saw."

Faller just looks away.

"My father wasn't—isn't—a sane man. He couldn't match his behavior to his ideals, but it wasn't because he didn't try. He believed, *believes*, in the rule of law. He believes in civilization. He believes rational discourse can make the world a better place. He believes everything Atticus Finch believes. He couldn't live up to his hero, but who ever does?"

"I'm still unclear on the significance here."

"So who's *my* character?"

"Yours?" His eyes go distant. He's thinking about it. "Not Atticus. You're no fan of civilization."

"I believe in civilization. I just don't buy the rational discourse part. People are exactly as civilized as somebody forces them to be, and that's the whole fucking story. Front to back and wall to wall."

He squints at me. "Jem? He's not afraid of anything, and—"

"Here, look. The theme of that book—the message that most people take away from it, maybe even the theme intended by the lady who wrote it—is basically what Dad got out of it, you follow? That love and hope and courage and patience and reason can right wrongs, or at least show people what the wrongs are, and nudge the world in the direction of justice and peace. That's what you got out of it, right?"

Faller shrugged. "That's what the book's about."

"Not for me."

"My mother," Gayle says slowly, with a thoughtful look over at the Social Police pretending to be secmen, "said it was about the consequences of losing sight of your place in society. That how clever you are, how good you are—how *righteous* you are—doesn't matter. At all. Violate the social norm and society will destroy you."

Faller looks skeptical. "Hari?"

I shrug. "What I got out of it is that Atticus Finch is a fucking idiot."

Faller gives me a distantly appraising squint that I recognize. That was how he looked at me up on the bluffs above the vertical city: like I'm some kind of exotic bug and he's trying to figure out how dangerous I might turn out to be.

He's about to find out. Everybody is.

Me too.

"Oh, sure, great guy, Atticus. Deep thinker. Gentle, kind, and rational. Civilized. Good for him. Bad for everybody else," I say. "All his fine qualities accomplish a grand total of getting his client shot and his children knifed."

"That's not . . . I mean, that's a little extreme . . ."

"When the kids are attacked—when some asshole with a grudge decides he's gonna murder them both—Atticus is off somewhere being civilized. Law enforcement is off somewhere enforcing the law. Civil society is off being civilly social. When the real fucking world comes after two kids with a hunting knife, who's there for them? Who's the only fucking one who gets it? Who's the only one paying attention to what the real world really *is*?"

"Really?" Faller's eyes are still distant, but he's lost the squint. He trades frowns with Gayle. "Boo Radley?"

"You're fucking right Boo Radley. The monster down the block. That's what *I* get from that book: when the real world comes after everything you love with a knife, you civilized fuckers better pray there's a monster looking out for them. Fuck Atticus Finch and fuck his civilization. The only reason civilized Atticus has the luxury to *be* civilized is because he's got a monster watching his back."

"Boo Radley's not a monster."

"Well, yeah." The hair on the back of my neck prickles, and there's a faint whisper of crackling, like static electric discharge. "That's the main difference between him and me."

Okay. Remember that *It doesn't feel like anything at all* thing I said before?

I take it back.

It seems the physical substance of the blind god trickling into me is kindling my blood. Not in a good way.

"Hari? Are you all right?" Gayle looks genuinely worried, but maybe not about me, as he's currently edging backward to clear the secmen's field of fire. "Is something wrong?"

Now I'm up against it and I still don't know how to put words to this. There's too much. I look over at Gayle again. "I want to say something. I want to say something to the Board, or the Leisure Congress, or whoever the fuck it is wiggling that hand up your ass. They'll want to hear me. Believe it."

Gayle frowns judiciously. "No harm in asking, I suppose."

He reaches over to take the palmpad, carefully avoiding the reach of my stripcuffed arms, then steps back to fiddle with the controls. "Give me a moment."

"Simon," I say softly while Gayle tinkers with the palmpad. "Run."

His head snaps up and his eyes goggle. "What?"

"Run. Now."

"But—I don't—"

"No time to explain. Remember the story I told you? The talk with t'Passe?"

His eyes go distant, looking inward. "Even your lies become truth . . ."

"That's exactly fucking it."

"I don't understand."

"You will. If you live long enough. How long will it take you to get your ass in the air and pointed toward home?"

"I—I can't. Not now."

"Don't even think about staying. You need to get your family away. All of them, if you can. Yourself too. You might have twenty-four hours, but I wouldn't bet your grandkids' lives on it."

"Get . . . *away?*"

"Hide. Dig a hole and pull it in after you. Bury yourselves somewhere far enough from the rest of the world that you and yours have a chance to live through this."

He looks blank. "Live through this what?"

"The usual. Dead rising, seas boiling, moon to blood, you know the list. John the Apostle's greatest hits."

"You're joking."

"I live for comedy."

"You can't possibly—"

"You don't have to believe me. The only reason I'm telling you this is so I won't feel quite so bad after the Social Police torture your grandchildren to death."

"They . . . But Michaelson . . . Hari—" His eyes bulge and his lips work like somebody tied a plastic bag over his head. "I *can't* leave. We're in lockdown. Nobody goes in or out while you're here—and it's a no-fly zone. Even if I can make it to my car, the Social Police will shoot me down."

Of course. That would have been too easy.

"All right. Go to your quarters. Lock yourself in and don't come out. For anything. And screen your family. This is probably your last chance to say good-bye."

"Caine—Caine, *please*—"

"Gayle? We don't need Faller anymore, do we?"

He looks up from the palmpad with a frown. I give him a *come on, take care of your people* toss of the head. "Give him a break, huh? Look at the guy—he's dead on his feet. And he's not looking forward to watching this, you know? Shit, Gayle, he's known me half my life."

"I don't believe anything about this should make him feel—"

"Gayle, for fuck's sake, put down the Company Man shit one minute, huh? To hell with what he *should* feel. Let him go."

Gayle swiveled his frown over toward Faller, who pulled himself up unsteadily in a credible I'm Not Hurt good-soldier attitude. "Administrator," he said faintly, "I'll stay if you need or want me to. Don't worry about me, sir. I'll be all right."

"No," Gayle says abruptly. "You're done for the day, Professional. With my thanks."

Faller sways. "Thank you, sir."

"Nothing to thank me for. Good work today, Faller."

"Thank you, sir." Faller ducks his head with a hint of flinch, just long enough to send me a look, then he stumbles for the door.

And there he goes.

There are three people still alive who knew me in my twenties. One of them is an immortal zombie meat puppet, another has wires where his eyes should be, and then there's Faller. "So what is it? Cancer?"

Gayle is back fiddling with the palmpad. He's not listening.

"He's been coming back and forth here for a couple years, right? Before you types built shielded structures, the radiation must have been pretty harsh."

"Mm?" He flicks me a look and then seems to recall what I'm talking about. "Mm, yes. Unfortunate. He's a good man."

"So it's magick scary cancer, huh? You can't cure him?"

"My impression is that upper management feels heroic measures aren't likely to produce acceptable return on investment."

"Jesus, Gayle, Ninth Circle of Hell much?"

Wrinkles flicker at the corners of his eyes. "This from a man made rich and famous by killing people for entertainment."

"And that makes you less of a scumbag?"

"Less than you, at least."

"Gayle. I am what I am. What does that have to do with what you are?"

He lowers the palmpad for a moment, frowning. "I too am what I am, I suppose."

"Are you? Where's that loyalty and friendship when Faller needs it?"

"We're not going to have this argument, Hari." He goes back to fiddling with the pad.

"How much longer?"

"I'm told they are attempting to assemble a quorum. You may be surprised to learn some of the wealthiest men and women on Earth have lives that aren't spent waiting breathlessly for your next word."

"Yeah, except they are. Waiting. Listening."

I know they are. I can *feel* them.

The oil—they're *inside* me now . . .

And I should have a speech ready, but I don't, because I guess I'm just as stupid as they are. I guess I still believed it wouldn't go this way. Or hoped, which is worse, because I fucking well know better.

Hope is for losers.

It's like they forget, y'know? A few years go by, and they think I'm not that guy anymore. And what the hell: they're right. I'm not that guy.

Funny thing, though: must be nobody sat down and really thought about it. Not one of them sat down and asked himself, "So if he's not that guy anymore . . . what guy *is* he?"

An unasked question is a fucking dangerous thing. Since they didn't ask that question, nobody made it to the next one. The real one.

Nobody thought to ask, "What if the guy he is now is worse?"

raining weird

GOOD AND EVIL

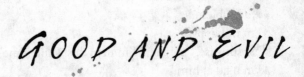

GOOD AND EVIL

When somebody starts talking about good and evil, keep one hand on your wallet.

—DUNCAN MICHAELSON

The witch-herd moved north with the spring; when spring edged into summer, the feral horses ranged the middle reaches of the eastern slopes of God's Teeth, keeping to the high scrub above the tree line and below the snow. As the days stretched toward a month, the witch-herd had become increasingly restive. Irritable. Tense. Dominance challenges between stallions got bloody, sometimes lethal. Fights had broken out between rival mares. Three geldings and a stallion had been pushed over the lip of a cliff by a scuffle that had become a general brawl during a sudden thunderstorm. All but one gelding had been killed outright by their crash into the rocks below; the one that hadn't had screamed in agony through too much of the storm. Violent winds and jagged ground-strikes of lightning delayed the horse-witch's arrival; not even the horse-witch can sprint down a rocky mountainside in a black blind downpour. Hundreds of horses were screaming by the time the horse-witch could reach the injured gelding, and calm it, and send it beyond the memory of pain.

The witch-herd began to lose its cohesion, carving itself into smaller and smaller clusters that skittishly avoided contact with others. The horse-witch herself grew snappish; her fraying temper shortened with every passing day. One night when Orbek came into her camp for some of the jerky, beans, and cornmeal the local villagers had left out for her, he saw her suddenly backhand one of the old pots off the fire, spraying boiling water into the night, and he heard her snarl an obscene profanity that would have made even his human brother blush.

"Hey."

She crouched with her back to him, a black silhouette ringed with fire. "I'm sorry you saw that."

"No problem."

"I'm unhappy."

"No surprise," he said. "I'm here this whole time, hey?"

"I'm mad at him."

"Happens to everybody," Orbek said. "It's how he is."

"How he is sucks."

"Want more water?"

"I worry for him."

"Me too."

"But I shouldn't worry. I *never* worry."

"Should's nothing like is." Orbek shrugged. "Don't mind me saying, because he saves my life couple-three times a month and I love my brother and everything, but you carry a damn big load over some guy you meet one afternoon a month ago."

"I didn't worry before. I didn't even remember how it felt. I don't like it," she said. "It's not what I do."

"It's what friends do for friends."

"Human friends suck."

"You just now figure that out?"

She didn't answer. Cold whispered down from the snowcap. Evergreen branches in the fire popped and spat sparks.

"I'm coming back with water, hey? I'm hungry."

Her silhouette finally moved: she lowered her head. After a moment, she said, "Thank you."

"Friends for friends, hey?"

"Friends for friends."

In early summer in the God's Teeth, night can fall with startling speed. The sky goes from blue to indigo sprayed with stardust, and the shadow of the mountains feels even darker than the coming night. At just this moment, Jonathan Fist came out from among the trees, squinted up at the scattered witch-herd, then shifted the bulging saddlebags draped over his shoulder and began to climb.

He moved slowly, and frequently paused to catch his breath. When he could walk, he did so with a slight limp that would steady out after a few minutes, but stiffen up again after each brief rest. His clothing was new, rugged leather and heavy brocade. His boots still had a gleam of polish across their uppers, though it was gone from the toes and heels. His hair was barely a whisper over his sunburned scalp, and one patch of that scalp above his left ear still showed the dark smear of a partially healed burn.

He climbed silently, but still he heard the occasional nicker and hoof-drum as horses saw or smelled him and retreated. Eventually, the clatter of retreating horses diminished, leaving only the unsteady clop of a horse that instead approached, picking its way over the jumble of boulders.

He stopped, waiting. The moon was still in first quarter, casting just barely enough light that he could identify the hulking silhouette of the rider. "Fuck me upside down," he said. "How'd she get *you* on horseback?"

"He's better'n me on the rocks. And I'm exhausted waiting for you."

"Ogrilloi *eat* horses."

"Humans too."

He looked around. She wasn't here. His chest tightened, and his mouth tasted of vinegar and ash.

"She's not coming," Orbek said. "She's mad at you."

He frowned to himself. The tightness in his chest began to ease. "I guess that's good news," he said. "Been thinking about me, huh?"

"You got no idea."

He guessed that *wasn't* good news. "Things quiet?"

"Some days."

He nodded. "Listen, there's a guy behind me. See him?"

Orbek moved only his eyes. A first-quarter moon was to him no darker than a cloudy day. A thousand yards below, a slim human moved from shadow to shadow, climbing slowly but steadily, parallel to the course Jonathan Fist had taken. "Yah."

"How's he armed?"

"Crossbow. Big one."

"How about the rifle?"

"He sees us. Good enough to know I can maybe see him." Orbek sighed. "And he knows about the rifle."

"How do you figure?"

"Shadow to shadow. Cover to cover. Looks before he moves."

"You're a smart bastard, you know that?"

"Yah, maybe." Orbek's upper lip peeled back in a grin that even Jonathan Fist's merely human eyes could see in the moonlight. "There's also that he don't use his right arm so much."

"Oh, for shit's sake." A month of deception, murder, and hard travel piled itself on his shoulders. "I am such a fucking idiot. All right. I guess probably a pitch-out. You game?"

"You need to ask?" Orbek's grin expanded in all directions. "Got a little time to kill, huh?"

"That too. Just don't lose him. I've been shot with crossbows enough for one lifetime."

Orbek shifted his weight on the horse's back, an absolutely natural settling-in that also left him facing toward the man below. "How does the Count and the war and all play out?"

"Let's skip the details." He tried to massage some knots out of the back of his neck, but there were more knots than there was neck. Shit, he really was tired. Really was too old for this. He slid the saddlebag off his shoulder and held it up for Orbek. "Mostly provisions, but there's a thousand royals in there too."

The ogrillo hefted the bag judiciously. "Nice."

"Five men-at-arms—heavy horse—escorted me up here, and when we parted they expressed the new Count's eternal gratitude for my assistance in this difficult time, as well as the undying affection of every subject of his realm, and reminded me that if I ever go back they'll drop me down a well headfirst." He released a tired sigh. "They weren't specific about the rest of my body."

"Business as usual, hey?"

"And then when they left, they took my horse."

"Fuckers. So, a new Count? Your work?"

"Turns out that the late Count's younger son is a decent-enough guy. Inclined to mind his own business and leave his neighbors alone. An orderly succession was arranged."

"Orderly is good."

"At least I didn't have to get orderly with his mom."

"What about Dane and Blackwood?"

"Retired."

"Retire as in they retire, or retire as in you retire them?"

He shook his head. "How we doing with Crossbow Guy?"

"Couple-three minutes. So: Dane and Blackwood?"

"Forget them."

"You can't make this one of your, whaddayasay, teachable moments, hey?"

"Drop it."

"You worry about my virgin ears?"

"No." He took a deep breath. It didn't make him feel any better. "It wasn't thrilling. It wasn't funny. It wasn't brave or heroic or even particularly clever. It wasn't anything worth telling. Shit needed to be done. Let it be."

"Don't get like this, little brother. I'm making conversation, that's all."

Jonathan Fist stood there in silence, trying to think about something other than the faces of his dead and the skin-crawl of his back anticipating the impact of a crossbow quarrel. A wisp of cloud drifted toward the moon. Thicker clouds crept behind. "It's about to get a whole lot darker."

Orbek nodded. "If he sees with magick, that's his window."

Fist stretched a knot or two out of his shoulders and moved a pace or two to the side, so if the fucker missed, Orbek wouldn't eat the bolt. "It's not gonna be too dark for you?"

"One way to find out."

"Don't wait for him. With that arm still bad, he'll brace the crossbow on a boulder."

He didn't need to say that this would put everything below the fucker's nose behind a big slab of rock; Orbek had learned a lot these past three years. Fist put one hand to the side of his head and cracked his neck, then he put his hands on his hips and arched as though he was stretching his back, which he was, but that wasn't why his hands were there. "Call it."

Clouds rolled in, and the night went black. "This'll do."

In a single fluid motion, so smooth it didn't look fast, his right hand slipped from his waist to under his tunic to the grip of the Automag, gently tossed it underhand up toward exactly the spot he'd last seen Orbek's right hand, then he closed his eyes and stuck his fingers in his ears.

Thunder ripped past. When it stopped, he heard only a high thin whine. He took his fingers out of his ears, opened his eyes, and looked down the mountainside.

"Do I get him?" Orbek was on the ground, the Automag in his hand weaving threat in the general direction of down. His horse was clattering away somewhere above. "Is he down? I'm blinder than fuck."

His voice sounded distant.

"Haven't been shot yet." Fist turned to feel his way down toward the pursuer. "That's encouraging."

"What? My fucking *ears* too—I *hate* shooting in the rocks."

"Bitch, bitch, bitch."

"I got your bitch right here, little brother. You know you only have three fuck-me rounds in this fucking clip?" Orbek said, still waving the empty pistol as though he might be able to summon ammunition by force of will. "Three fuck-me rounds!"

"I explained about the orderly succession, right?"

"Three fuck-me rounds and you want a *pitch-out*? How come you don't *tell* me you got only three rounds?"

"I didn't want you to worry."

Orbek made a noise like he was strangling a cat.

"See? That's exactly why."

Clouds slid away from the moon. A boot stuck out from behind a fold of rock, toe down. He couldn't see well enough to be sure it had a foot in it. "Tanner?"

A low, gurgling moan.

"If you want to shove that crossbow out here, I can help you go easy."

More gurgling, including an attempt at speech that Jonathan Fist interpreted as "cock-whore."

"Yeah, okay. It's not like I need to watch you die. See you in Hell, Hack."

"Garrh . . . uh. Fuck it. I'm done."

"That's what I'm trying to tell you."

"You can make it easy?"

He didn't answer.

"Jonnie?" A wet cough that was half vomit. "Jonnie, you'll help, right?"

"Changed my mind." He settled into a resting crouch and leaned on the rock. "It'd be just like you to have some little fucking hold-out and take me with you."

A gurgling laugh. "Guess you got to know me pretty well, this past month or so."

"I knew you on sight."

From up the mountainside, Orbek called softly, "You square? Need a hand? Maybe a firearm?"

"Stay where you are. I'm pretty sure he's alone, but it'd suck to be wrong."

On the other side of the rock, Tanner chuckled. It turned into a wet cough. "Told you before I ain't sociable."

"And I told you to stay out of my way."

"How long . . . guh. How long since you nosed me?"

"Two days."

"Gahhh, the fucking notch pass. Goddamn shit. I *knew* that was a bad idea. I knew it. Fucking skyline."

"Guess you're not as good as you thought."

"Next closest pass . . . two days south. I knew . . . that sonofabitching notch pass . . . bad risk. Bad."

"And you did it anyway."

"Had to. *Had* to."

"I'm sure it felt that way at the time."

"The Count, his eldest, the other guys, whatever. Life on the frontier. Even Bannon, he was a son of a bitch and nobody's gonna shed a tear. But Charlie . . . how you did him . . . how you left him. I never seen a guy die that hard. Most of it was screaming. The rest sobbing and moaning in some language I don't know, but I'm guessing *momma* means the same as in Westerling."

"I'd say I was sorry if I, y'know, was."

"Charlie was a friend of mine. Friend of yours too, Jonnie, goddammit. I couldn't let it go. Let you go. Couldn't."

"Yeah."

"Somebody who'd do . . . that . . . to a man he *knows* . . . a man he's eaten and drunk with. Fought beside. Laughed at each other's jokes. And you just . . ." Another round of wet coughing. "You are one cold damn evil cock-whore. You need to die."

"People keep telling me that."

"Someday it'll catch up with you."

"Not today."

"Charlie wasn't a bad man. Not like Bannon. Shit, not even bad as me. What'd he ever do to you that you'd leave him like that?"

"I mostly kill people for what they're going to do."

"But *Charlie* . . . ?"

"He would've come after me. For how I did Bannon. Just like you have for how I did Charlie. And no offense, he was an assload more dangerous than you."

"Huh. Hadn't been for . . . that fucking notch . . . you'd know something about me being dangerous." More wet coughing, and another weak splash of vomit. "But . . . but Charlie . . ."

"I left him like that so he could tell all you bastards not to come after me. And show you why."

"Oh, sure. You were . . . doing us a *favor* . . ."

"Some. Mostly it was because I didn't like him."

"Everybody liked Charlie. How could you not like Charlie?"

"Hard to say. You'd probably have to ask everybody who died at Hooker's Leap. Or who used to live in Tabletop, back when there was still such a place. If you can find any who survived."

"Tabletop . . . ? Wait, come on. That . . . gahh. Tabletop was Dane and Blackwood. Everybody knows that."

"Yeah."

"Charlie in that outfit? I don't see it. Everybody knows what kind of fuckers those fuckers are."

"Were."

"Come on. Charlie with those guys? You can't expect me to believe—"

"Nobody cares what you believe."

"Why would you even tell me such a thing?"

"You asked. I'm just passing time until you bleed to death."

More coughing. Voice half-strangled. "Like that, is it?"

"Unless you drown in your own blood first."

"You won't . . . not even . . ." He choked, coughed, and choked some more.

"You were warned."

"I'd do it . . . for you. Do it for . . . an *animal* . . ."

"I'm not you. A few minutes from now, you'll be dead. I won't. And I know where your momma lives."

"Gahhh . . . ? My *momma* . . . you promised . . ."

"First I'll cut off your head. Then I'll take it to your momma's house and show it to her, and I'll tell her you died the same way you lived: crying and begging like the whiny back-shooting pustule of festering weasel cunt you are. Then I'll cut off your face and make her eat it. And when I'm done, I will take your dead faceless skull and I will, my hand to God, jam it up her ass."

"Nahgg . . . come *on*, Jonnie . . . !"

"It's not a figure of speech. You understand me? She won't survive."

"Huh. Huh huh. Huh huh huh huh."

Tanner was laughing. The bastard was actually laughing. "'Scuze me for saying . . . but Jonnie, come on. I *know* you. You ain't the type."

"Charlie and Bannon knew me. When you get to Hell, ask your pal Good-Time Charlie who did him like that. Ask Bannon who I am. Want to know the name they'll give?"

"Yeah, all right, come on, Jonnie, don't try and—"

"They'll tell you it was Caine."

Silence.

"Still funny, fucker?"

A hoarse rasp of breath. Rock clattered somewhere upslope. A veil of cloud made the night absolute.

Finally, faintly, barely more than a fading cough: " . . . *Caine* . . ."

"Think about it. Think about me. Then think about your momma. Take that with you into the dark."

Wheezing. The rasping struggle to exhale. Then a whisper: "*Jonnie . . . Jonnie please . . .*"

"No Jonnies here, fucker."

" . . . *why would . . . why would you do something so . . .*"

"Because you made me feel like an idiot. And I don't like you much better than I did Charlie."

After that, there was more *huh huh huh*, but it didn't sound like laughter.

He crouched there for a long time, leaning against the rock face, listening to Tanner die. Thinking about his name. Names.

He had a lot of them.

He had other things to think about too. Like blood, for instance.

The Automag had been loaded with shatterslug tristacks. Three rounds, nine slugs, and a guy bleeding out around the fold, and he didn't smell blood. Which didn't actually prove anything; evening breezes flow down from the snowcaps, and Tanner was downhill and downwind both, and Fist had never had all that great of a nose anyway. But that wasn't the only thing.

The other was that Jonathan Fist had taken a little time to chat with Morgan Blackwood—Charlie—in between taking him down and leaving him to die. Charlie, never a brave man, had been forthcoming about what he knew about those in the outfit who'd survived the orderly succession, in exchange for the prospect of a swift and merciful death. Tanner and Charlie really had been pretty good pals, as such people go. They drank together, whored together, told each other jokes and swapped stories in the still of the occasional midnight, over the embers in the campfire pit. Charlie had a considerable fund of tidbits about his buddy's life story. One of them was that Tanner's endless yammer about his momma was an inside joke, to amuse himself and those who were in on the gag.

Tanner's mother died ten years ago.

After a while, the gurgling turned into a rattle, then went quiet. The clouds passed away from the moon. He looked around the area on the moonlit side of the fold. There were plenty of chunks of rock around. He picked out one slightly larger than his doubled fists, then took off his broadcloth tunic and knotted it around the rock. He tied the sleeves together at the cuff, then slipped them over his head so that the rock hung down the middle of his back. "Tanner? You dead yet? *Tanner.*"

He waited a few seconds, but there was only the hush of night breeze and the occasional skittering of stones shed by the mountain. "Ten more minutes," he said softly, as though to himself. "It's not like either of us has anyplace we need to be."

Then he scrubbed some of the dry, sandy grit into his palms and turned to the face of the rock fold. Finding cracks and projections by feel, he slowly and deliberately pulled himself upward.

He climbed to three times his own height, and waited for the clouds to veil the moon again before he traversed the spine of the fold to look down at Tanner. All he could see was a pool of night, dark as a well.

He focused his concentration, controlling his breathing and allowing his eyes to defocus; the outline of a man began to gradually resolve itself from the darkness. This man crouched near an empty boot that lay half-exposed to the uphill side, and he held a crossbow at low ready, and just when it struck him that he suddenly was seeing Tanner entirely too well, the bowman whirled and fired without seeming even to aim, but the nonaiming was only seeming, because when Jonathan Fist realized that he'd been so busy with his Control Discipline that he hadn't noticed the clouds passing away from the moon and his stupid fucking amateur ass casting a shadow where Tanner could see it, he instantly kicked off the rockface in a headlong dive for the ground, and so got a spray of stone shrapnel across his back instead of a half meter of steel through the sternum.

Fucker could shoot.

Jonathan Fist had discovered early in life that the difference between a pro and an amateur isn't that a pro doesn't screw up. Everybody screws up. What separates the pro from the amateur is that the pro fights first and gets embarrassed later. Get embarrassed first and there is no later.

He flipped forward in the air, yanking the tunic sleeves from around his neck in time to avoid strangling himself on impact, but the rock threw off his balance and to be perfectly honest it had been an unfortunate number of years since he'd actually done any aerial tumbling, as a result of which he overrotated and sprawled face-first across the ledge, shredding his forearms, and his pants at the knee, and before he could even turn over, Tanner was at his side and the crossbow was coming down at him like a pickaxe, because the spring-steel lath could be considered a reasonable-enough facsimile thereof that his spine would never know the difference.

Fist rolled out from under just barely fast enough; the lath ripped opened a long gash on his side but glanced off his ribs instead of breaking them, and because Fist was a pro first and nothing else made it as high as fifth, he had rolled toward Tanner instead of away, and now used all the strength of his arms and the torque of his roll to whip his rock-laden tunic like a flail directly at Tanner's balls.

The bowman saw it coming and twisted to take it on his thigh instead of into his groin, but it was still a lot of rock moving at a respectable clip; the impact disrupted his balance enough that Jonathan Fist could come up to one knee as he whipped the rock once around his head and fired it straight at Tanner's kneecap with considerable confidence that this fight was over. Except the kneecap wasn't there.

His rock-loaded tunic was met with a sideways swipe of the crossbow. The tunic wrapped around it and Tanner stepped back again, yanking on the crossbow's butt with both hands, and Fist, knowing a losing position when he was in one, let go of the tunic as it pulled him forward and turned his fall into a shoulder-roll that brought him to his feet, moving straight into Tanner with both of his hands full of boot knife. He jammed one angling up for the underside of Tanner's chin to draw his eyes while he hammered the other ice-pick-style toward Tanner's femoral artery, and somehow the crossbow was there *again* and his knife and hand went between the lath and the string and the crossbow twisted to lock his knife and hand right there while the stock came over the top, deflected his other knife and caught him square in the nose hard enough to make his head ring and his eyes blur and wouldn't you just fucking know that shooting wasn't even the best thing Tanner did? He could fight almost like a—

Almost like nothing; he was. Had to be. Monastic. An Esoteric. A good one. Too entirely good.

This was a shitty place to come up against somebody more dangerous than he was.

He leaned into Tanner, using his lower center of gravity to drive the taller man back while he reversed the grip on his other knife and used it to trap the stock against his forearm. He forced Tanner skidding toward the lip of the ledge until Tanner collapsed his legs, dropping flat for the back-throw, and Fist only barely managed to wrench his weight sideways in time to avoid being tossed out into empty space that was bottomless in the moonshadow. He raked his knife hard up along the stock and was rewarded with a wordless snarl and a couple inches of skin and muscle off the side of Tanner's thumb that flopped on the ground, scattering little dust-clots of blood.

For a moment they struggled, locked together by the crossbow between them. A handspear doesn't need a working thumb, and Tanner jammed his into Fist's throat hard enough to make the older man's neck spasm and clamp down on his trachea. Tanner paid for the strike by taking a slash across the gut from Fist's other knife, maybe deep enough to kill but not deep enough to stop him from killing, and they both struck and hooked and gripped with knee and foot, hands and blades and the crossbow itself, trying for anything that might harm or slow or control the other man, and Tanner was younger and stronger and better trained and the outcome wasn't in doubt, especially considering Jonathan Fist couldn't breathe much at all.

Shit, he should have stayed back with the rifle and sent Orbek down here. This was a stupid way to die.

Tanner stripped his left-hand knife with an expertly executed corkscrew of the crossbow. He twisted to pin Fist's right hand with his knee, then slammed the bow stock down, equally expertly, onto Fist's immobile forearm. A wet crunch spread numb deadness up and down his arm. He knew the sound too well: Tanner had broken his wrist.

On the other hand, if he'd sent Orbek, Tanner would have killed him and Fist would have had to fight the fucker anyway.

Tanner slammed a knee straight into Fist's abdomen below the belt, and he must have liked the result because he did it again and one more time—on the last, throwing his weight behind the strike to lever himself up into a mount that straddled Fist's hips. He lifted the crossbow straight up in a two-handed grip, said, "I planned on taking you with this. Glad it worked out," then brought it down to crush Fist's skull with the butt—but in that second or so Fist had remembered how Tanner kept that half-moon skinner he liked so much in a thigh-sheath and Tanner was right-handed which put the sheath about six inches from Jonathan Fist's working hand.

When Tanner brought down the bow Fist jabbed upward with the skinner, gouging a curled shaving out of the bow's tiller and damn near taking Tanner's right hand off at the wrist, but clever fuck that he was, Tanner saw the blade and let go with his right, and the crossbow came down and just clipped Fist's forehead and ripped his ear and Fist couldn't breathe and his coordination was gone and his strength was going, but he hacked at Tanner with the skinner with everything he had left, no skill, no art, nothing but a blind snarling lust for harm. Tanner blocked the blows easily, contemptuously, with the crossbow.

"You're pathetic, you know that? You—son of a *bitch*! *Fuck!*" he screeched when he realized that each knife-blow he blocked was chopping chunks out of the crossbow's tiller and stock. "This is my best *bow*!"

He threw himself off his mount with a back-roll to his knees. A hack with the bow sent the end of the steel latch into Fist's ankle and the foot went dead but Fist was already coming for him, pivoting around his hips, reaching for Tanner with the blade, and the younger man scrambled back, coming to his feet. "Sure, all right, pappy. That's how you want it? Come and—"

He was interrupted by a crisp *whap*. It sounded very much like the noise made by slapping an open hand against a man's chest. A sliver over a second later: *whap whap*.

Tanner staggered, not unlike a man who has taken some unexpected body-blows, but then recovered his balance, frowning as if unsure what could be happening. His frown deepened when he tried to recock the bow and discovered that his hand didn't want to grip the cranequin, and once he finally got hold of the lever, he couldn't actually draw it. He peered down at his arm, then at the spreading patches of black that stained his tunic, and only then realized that he was standing fully in the pale moon-glow, out of the shadow of the mountain's fold. "Fuck."

His knees buckled and he pitched forward, catching himself with the crossbow, leaning on it from his knees. He looked into the shadow at Fist. "You fucker," he said, more in reproach than in anger. "Same fucking trick."

He crumpled forward, facedown across his bow, and went still.

The older man didn't answer; he still couldn't force more than a thin whistling wheeze through his spasming throat, and he didn't get up because he didn't know yet whether his ankle was broken. He set down the skinner and massaged his throat with his good hand. Shortly after the other man had slipped all the way to the ground, a great gasping whoop of air opened his trachea—just in time to aspirate half a lungful of his own vomit.

Coughing, gagging, and coughing some more, he struggled to the lip of a low shelf—so he wouldn't have to kneel in his own puke—then leaned out and let fly, vomit splattering across the dirt and scrub grass a meter or two below, because it's just better that way. Get it over with.

Didn't make his balls feel any better, though.

"Hey, little brother!" Orbek called from upslope. "Want some help?"

"Stay where you are," he rasped through his raw throat, then said it again, louder. "Stay where you are, and for fuck's sake keep your sights on him."

"He ain't dead?"

"No."

"Looks dead to me."

"Do as you're told. And quit making me *shout*, goddammit!"

Using his good hand and good foot, he slowly managed to push himself over to his knives, which he returned to their boot-sheaths. He also collected his tunic and shook the rock out of it; pressed to a wound, the rough texture of the brocade would promote clotting, and he had very little blood to spare.

Inch by inch, he made his way over to the stone of the fold, and rested his back against it.

Taking some time to manage his breathing, he focused on his Control Disciplines to suppress the pain that grew now steadily in proportion to the fade of his adrenaline. He looked over at Tanner. Tanner looked at nothing. He lay facedown, eyes glazed and fixed on some impossible distance within the mountain's heart.

Knowing what Tanner was made shit different. It wiped out coincidence and chance, and like an incantation over a scrying pool, it brought everything into focus.

Almost everything.

"Holy shit," Orbek said when he peered around the fold, rifle tucked under his arm. "Does he kiss you down?"

"What part of *stay where you are* do you not fucking understand?"

Jonathan Fist sat with his back against the rock wall. His face was painted with drying blood, both from his nose and from a slanting gash across his forehead; his left eye was already in the process of swelling shut, though that was due less to his nose and forehead than it was to Tanner's devastating straight right. Fist's arms could pass for hamburger dropped into a gravel pit. In his lap he kept his right arm, already swollen to twice its size. With his left hand, he explored his ankle through the gash the crossbow's lath had chopped into his boot.

"Guess I should learn how to follow orders from somebody who's not you. So, like I say, does he kiss you down?"

"What are you talking about?"

"Him." Orbek nodded at Tanner's body. "Does he kiss you down before he fucks you up?"

He could feel something sharp in the ankle wound. Chipped bone, and maybe worse. "Orbek, my hand to any god you pick, if I could get up right now I would knock your punk ass right off this mountain."

"You mean pun'k ass, hey?"

"Cut it out. Or I'll cut it out of you."

"You use that one already, little brother—couple-three times, even. How's the pain?"

"I can suppress awhile. Not long. I'm a little out of practice." The boot would have to be cut off, and he didn't have another pair, and it was still spring enough at this elevation that walking barefoot would suck, and even that was a generous assumption, given that he didn't know whether he'd actually be able to walk anytime soon. He'd given up optimism twenty-five years ago. "If the horse-witch can't fix my ankle, I'm likely to have a shitty couple of months, though. Maybe a season or two. You got water? I could really use water."

"Up with the horse."

"Shit. You might have to carry me up there."

"Just like old times, hey? Back in the Pit. And we have a water shortage then too, hey?" He came over for a closer look.

"I just need to rinse out my mouth. In the process of pounding the fuck out of me, he tagged me two-three good ones in the stones."

"You eat too many vegetables, little brother. Bad for your stomach."

"Yeah, and they don't taste good the second time either."

Orbek looked Tanner's body up and down. "He don't seem so tough."

"Not anymore." Tanner's boots were in good shape. Given the difference in height, they'd likely run a little big, which was better than the reverse. "Last time I fought somebody this good, he was the favorite son of a Monastic personal combat instructor. This guy here might be even better."

"Yeah? For real, or for excusing why he kicks your ass so bad?"

"Both."

"Who's he when he's at home? I like to know when I kill somebody famous."

"All I know is he's Monastic. Esoteric, and good at it. I rode with him half the month and never caught a whiff. Fucker never broke character. Never. Even tonight, he made the climb without using his right arm. Look at my eye to see how well that arm works. But he played wounded, because he knew I might be watching. Hell, he played wounded for *days*. He knew that was how I'd recognize him, and he knew that being underestimated is a shitload safer than being mysterious. That's quality work. This guy's a motherfucking artist."

"One of yours, you think? Like Dane and Blackwood?"

Fist shook his head. "I would have heard of him. Probably would have met him. Listen, I'm gonna need his boots."

"In a minute. First you tell me how this guy's such a motherfucking artist and still you beat this motherfucking artist guy."

"I didn't beat him. You did. I admit it, okay?"

"Yeah, and you have to admit it later too. In front of witnesses."

"I will," he said. "You saved my life."

"Second time this month, hey? Ties my personal best. How do you get him out from cover?"

"If he hadn't been beating me to death, I'd have thought of it sooner." Fist gave an irritable wave toward the crossbow that lay pinned under Tanner's chest. "He's a little too attached to his tools, that's all."

"Nice crossbow," Orbek allowed. "Too bad about the chop-outs."

"Didn't do the knife any favors either."

"And so now, what am I waiting to hear you say, hey? Since you live through it?"

Fist sighed. "Hell of a shot, Orbek."

"Yah?"

"I should say *shots*. Both times. Great shots. Really great."

"All right, then."

"Completely pooched the pitch-out, though."

"Hah?"

"Didn't even nick him, Super Sniper."

"No? *You* fuck-me try a pitch-out a hundred yards downhill in the dark, smart bitch. With a fuck-me mostly empty pistol too."

"I'm not saying I can, I'm saying you didn't."

"And I'm saying screw you."

"Don't take it hard. There's a rock or two down there that'll never kill again."

"Maybe I come back and check on you in the morning. If I can find this place in the light. Do I ever mention there's khoshoi in these mountains? And that maybe I like this nice crossbow and want to take it with me, hey?"

"I wouldn't," Fist said. "Get close enough to touch it and he'll kill you."

"Hah?"

"I'm serious."

"He's not dead? He looks dead. He smells dead."

"He's really, really good at faking."

Orbek rolled his eyes. "More fuck-me Monastery crap-ass."

"Also why he's not bleeding much. He would have killed me already, except he knows that if he moves you'll shoot him again."

"Maybe I shoot him anyway."

"Let's try talking one time."

"You can talk him back from being dead?"

"Could be." Jonathan Fist cocked his head. "So when you chew down to the gristle, Brother Whogivesashit," he said, "this is all about the girl, isn't it?"

After about ten seconds of motionless silence—long enough that he began to wonder if he might be wrong—Tanner released a long, slow sigh, and said, "Fuck."

ALL ABOUT THE GIRL

ALL ABOUT THE GIRL

"Fuck the city. I'd burn the world to save her."

— "CAINE" (PFNL. HARI MICHAELSON)
For Love of Pallas Ril

"If you move very, very slowly, he probably won't shoot you again," Jonathan Fist said to the dying assassin. "That can't be comfortable."

Very, very slowly, Tanner rolled himself off his crossbow. "You'll excuse me not getting up."

The front of his tunic glistened with blood, black in the moonlight. "What do you fuckers want to know?"

Orbek leveled the rifle. "How about one reason we shouldn't torture you till we get bored, then shoot you in the head?"

"Please yourself," Tanner said. His voice was cold as the stone he lay on, and had the flattened urban whine of Seven Wells. "There's nowhere I have to be."

Fist sighed. "I liked you better folksy."

"Well, whatever suits you just tickles me plumb to death."

"Yeah, like that."

"Maybe start with your name," Orbek said. "Also why you're trying to kill my little brother."

Tanner lifted his head and frowned at Fist. "Did he say *brother?*"

"It's a long story."

"It would have to be."

The young ogrillo took a step forward and peeled his lips away from his tusks. "Your *name*, fucker."

"Orbek. You're too close."

He looked at Fist. "What's he gonna do? Bleed on me?"

"Well, shit, Orbek, what the fuck would *I* know about it? It's not like I know shit about *fighting* or anything. You want to put your grey leather ass inside the reach of a guy who just now came within an ace of beating me to death while armed with nothing but an empty crossbow and a bad attitude, you go right the fuck ahead. I'll just sit over here with my broken wrist and my broken ankle and cheer you on until my fucking eyes swell shut, huh?"

Orbek glowered, but took a step back. Then another. "Guess it's no trouble to shoot him from over here."

"It was no trouble to shoot him from a hundred yards uphill. Which is where you need to go back to," Fist said. "Really. Right now."

Cords bulged in Orbek's neck. "First he says his name."

"Y'know, I was lying there wondering why a grill would carry knives. Didn't make sense," Tanner said. "But now I see you favor long sleeves, and that pretty much answers—"

Orbek snapped the rifle to his shoulder. "The next you say that ain't your name—"

"Oh, for fuck's *sake*," Fist said. "Don't you assholes realize you want the same thing?"

They looked at him. He was too tired to make a joke out of it, and some of the pain had begun to trickle through his Control Discipline. "He wants to shoot you. You want to be shot. Both of you need to back the fuck off and give me some room to work."

Tanner looked skeptical. "What's in it for me?"

"If you want to find out, quit fucking around."

"Is that how you always play it?"

"Only with you. And only when I've got you bleeding out. Orbek, take a fucking hike. If you spot the horse-witch, let her know where we are."

"Easy peasy. I tell my horse."

"Your horse?"

"You don't know this? What you say to the herd, she knows."

"Huh."

"You be careful, little brother." The big ogrillo backed his way into the darkness, rifle still covering Tanner.

Jonathan Fist watched him go, then nodded to the fallen assassin. "If it's any consolation, you are better than anybody I've even heard of. Not just better than me; you're better than people *think* I am. I feel like I should know who you are."

Tanner's snort sounded more like a wet cough. "Only fuckups get famous." He flicked an apologetic hand. "No offense."

Fist waved it off. "Listen, I don't care what your real name is—"

"You can call me Heywood, Lord Jablohmie, Marquess of Jammit and the Eleventh Earl of Upyourass."

"Yeah, okay, what are we, twelve years old?"

"How's your wrist?"

"Broken. How's your sucking chest wound?"

"Oh, serve one up, why don't you," he wheezed. "Let's just say I've got things under what our folks call Control."

Fist nodded. "Like I was saying: I don't care about your name, or what abbey you're from. I'm not even going to ask about your mission, because, let's see, we're already through the revenge-for-your-friend story. Next would be a freelance bounty."

"Grateful as the Young Faltane is for all your help in this difficult time, you did smoke his father."

"And the one below that is probably a Council of Brothers shoot-on-sight for Aktiri."

"Damned gentlemanly of you to take out Dane and Blackwood for me. And once you're over, I get your thousand royals too."

"Three layers of story is standard. You've probably got six more. Forget that shit. The only story that interests me is something like the truth."

"Good luck with that."

"It's the girl. The horse-witch. You're the one who put together the outfit—you just let Dane run it because it kept him and Blackwood oc-cupied. Out of your hair."

Tanner closed his eyes. "You know I won't tell you."

"Rounding up the witch-herd would have been your idea too, though I bet you had the Count thinking it was his; we both know the late Count didn't have many sharp spears on his rack. Which got you an excuse to bring an assload of hardguys into the hills to watch your back while you hunted down the horse-witch."

"She's right about one thing," Tanner said. "You talk a lot."

"The legend of the horse-witch centers in the lands around Faltane's county; the farther south I went, the more people knew about her. The shoulder wound worked out good for you—got you out of the red work, which left you plenty of time to talk to the people down there. About the horse-witch."

"You've got a thing for her," Tanner said. "I get that. Me, I like mine extra-curvy, but whatever waxes your banister, you know?"

"You didn't make a mistake at the notch. You wanted me to know somebody was on my track, because you knew I'd make for someplace quiet where I have backup and you don't. You figured that place would be somewhere in the vicinity of the witch-herd, and once my pet sniper and I were out of the way, there'd be no one between you and her."

"Charmin' story."

"Hangs together pretty well, given my recent guided tour through your festival of blunt force trauma," Fist said. "Notice how I worked through that whole story without asking any questions you won't answer?"

"And nicely worked it was."

"I know there's no way to force information out of you. But I'm getting to a question. I know you're going to lie. But while you come up with your lie, there's some shit I want you to keep in mind."

"You must be the talkiest damn killer east of the Teeth."

"I came up through the Monasteries, same as you. Trained for and entered the Esoteric Service, same as you. And I swore, without deception or mental reservation, our oath to uphold and advance the Human Future. Same as you."

"Except I never broke mine."

"Yeah, well, if I were as good a man as you are, we wouldn't be having this conversation."

"This ain't a conversation, it's a goddamn filibuster with occasional sardonic commentary."

"Do you get that you and me, we might really be on the same team?"

Tanner stared at him. Muscles bulged at the hinge of his jaw, and Fist could see a tightness thinning the skin around his eyes, and decided he'd better jump to the kill, because it looked like Tanner could lose his concentration sometime in the next few minutes. Once his Control Disciplines slipped he might bleed out in seconds.

"If we're enemies . . . well, it's not complicated. The Monasteries will send other guys. I'll kill them. They'll send more guys. I'll kill them too, then I'll kill the men who sent them. If I have to, I'll kill the entire Council of fucking Brothers. I will burn down every fucking Monastery in the world and salt the earth on which they stood. Look in my eyes and tell me I'm just kidding."

Tanner didn't. He turned his face away, and whispered into the night. "The Monasteries are . . . aware . . . of the facts surrounding the True Assumption of Ma'elKoth."

"If we're not on the same side, you've lost nothing. If we are, you've won everything."

"You have the damnedest way of interrogating a person I ever heard of."

"I know who you're after. All I want to know is why. What is it about her that the Monasteries want her dead?"

"It's . . ." Tanner scrubbed weakly at his face with one hand. He pressed the other to two of the holes in his chest. "Look, it's a capture, not a kill. The arrows, the quarrels, they're all charged with Hold. Even the one I shot at you. Nonlethal."

"Which was why you just about put it through my heart."

"You startled me."

"And then you decided to open my skull with the lath."

"Look at it from my side," he said. "Here I am trying to creep my friend Jonnie Fist and give him a nice nap—just long enough for me to get in, get the girl, and blow. Then all of a sudden there's flashes and thunderclaps and something hits the rock so close to my face that my hair's still full of granite chips, and my friend Jonnie's around the corner telling me he's not Jonnie at all, he's the single scariest motherfucker in the entire recorded history of scary motherfuckers, and he wants me dead. Except he wants to hurt me first, and hurt my family after. What would *you* do?"

"Lie my balls off, just like you," he said. "Get the girl and blow where?"

"Someplace dark and quiet would be my guess."

"She'll die first."

"I know." Tanner tried to settle himself into a less uncomfortable position, apparently without success. "I've killed her twice myself."

Jonathan Fist tried to think of something to say more intelligent than, "Huh," with a similarly unsatisfying result.

"Hence the nonlethal, you follow?"

"Is it a coming-back-to-life thing?"

"She doesn't. It's more like replacements. We've got remains of at least five of her already. "

"Five."

"Five confirmed. Verified kills. A couple dozen probables. As near as we've been able to tell, there's only one of her at a time, but somehow the world never seems to run out."

"I don't get it."

"Me neither. It's not my end of the business."

Fist rubbed his forehead, which reopened a cut, and Control Disciplines or not this was all starting to really fucking hurt. "So what is she?"

"That's what we're trying to find out."

Fist nodded, which made his head hurt even more. "Have you tried asking her?"

Tanner stared.

Fist shrugged. "Unless you'd rather lie there and bleed while we guess some more."

"Well, when you put it that way . . ." He shrugged. "There's a guy on the Council of Brothers who's pushing a crazy theory, but at least he's *got* a theory. Damon of Janthogen Bluff."

"I know him. He's not the crazy theory type," Fist said. "He's probably the sanest guy I ever met."

"He thinks it's spontaneous theogony."

"Come *again?*"

"Spontaneous theogony. That's when—"

"I know what it means, goddammit. Seriously?"

"She is nothing like an ordinary person."

"She's not much like a god either." He tried to shrug. It hurt. "That's an informed opinion."

"So I hear," Tanner said. "Things do start to get strange in her vicinity, though. In the vicinity of any of them."

Any of them. Fist let his head tip back to rest against the rock wall. "There's more?"

"Looks like it."

"Horse-witches?"

"Nah, other kinds of nothing-like-ordinary types—you know, a jack-o'-the-green here, a Wild Hunt there. It's raining weird all over the damn place."

"Has anybody correlated timelines?"

Tanner shrugged. From the spasm of pain that crossed his face, his shrug had been a mistake too. "That's not my end of the business either. They tell me tales of the horse-witch predate the Deomachy. They tell me we've got an unsourced Lipkan translation of the West Branch of the *Danellarii Tffar* that claims she was here already when the damn *elves* got here. That's, what, like thirty thousand years?"

Fist scowled. "Was she human then?"

"Is she human now?"

"You know what I mean. That long ago, there weren't any humans. Not on this world."

"You want to go argue with a ten-thousand-year-old elf saga in person, I can tell you where to find it."

"What happened to the fucking Covenant of Pirichanthe?"

"You happened," Tanner said. "That's what Damon thinks, anyway. You and your pal Ma'elKoth."

"Bullshit. Who's doing the counterfactuals?"

"Supposedly Damon's got Inquisitors and Reading Brothers all over the world working the Vaults through a timeframe of three or four tendays. A few months shy of three years ago. That date strike a gong, pappy?"

He let his eyes drift shut. "Fuck me inside out."

"Can't be that much of a surprise, can it? You had to at least suspect, considering you hooked Ma'elKoth a physical Aspect your own self."

"I guess I've been kind of hoping the Covenant doesn't apply."

"Then hope crashes into reality and people get hurt."

"Too fucking right." He shook his head and sighed a time or two. "If you'd told me what you were really up to a month ago, you wouldn't be dying here right now."

"And if you'd told me who you really are a month ago, I wouldn't be dying right now either. Because instead of me coming up this mountain, it would have been ten or twelve Esoteric strike teams. And maybe a dragon or five."

"Stop. You'll make me blush."

Tanner stared, squinting through the moonlight like he wasn't sure what he was seeing. "You don't know, do you? You really don't."

"So these, whateverthefuck, sorta-kinda-demi-semi-gods—the horse-witch and all the whateverthefuck others. They have anything in common outside of being basically impossible?"

"Probably should ask yourself that question."

"How the fuck would I know?"

"No reason, I guess," Tanner said. "Except you're one of them."

His back against the cold, night-damp stone, he waited for the horse-witch.

He'd pushed himself farther upslope, away from Tanner. No sense taking chances. The unconscious assassin lay where he had fallen, his breath hitching and shallow, his eyes rolled up until only white slits showed in the moonlight. He was pretty sure Tanner wasn't faking this time, but it'd suck to be wrong.

While he waited, he tried to fit it all together in his head, but he just couldn't. This had somehow become something so much more than he'd ever guessed. Than he could have dreamed. He got lost in it. In what and why. When. Even how. Who, on the other hand . . .

Then came a clatter of rock, closer, and then there was someone at his elbow. In a flicker, faster than thought, an arm was seized and yanked even through the screaming of broken wrist and a head wedged against rock and a knife in a hand stopped just short of gutting a torso, then dropped free to clank on rocks.

"Goddammit, don't *do* that! I could have *killed* you," he snarled. "Say something when you're coming up blind. Anything. *Hey, dumbass, I'm here* would work."

"Hey, dumbass," the horse-witch said. "I'm here."

He sagged back down to the ledge. "Jesus suffering Christ."

His knife lay where it had fallen, a dull smear of reflected moonlight. He couldn't pick it up. He couldn't look at it. He couldn't look at her. "Orbek says you're mad at me."

"I am."

"So you punish me by making me kill you?"

"I'm not here to punish you, dumbass."

"You say that like it's my name."

"It isn't?" The cloud-filtered moonlight made her witch-eye shimmer like a snow opal. "Do you want it to be?"

He shook his head, cradling his wrist. "And all this time I couldn't stop thinking about how much I wanted to see you again, and now I can't re-member why."

"I could tell you—"

"—but I wouldn't believe you, yeah, I remember. Except that's not it. Just the opposite."

"I was going to say," she murmured, "I could tell you, but you don't want to know."

And just as he opened his mouth to remind her—in the most color-fully emphatic terms he could devise—how incredibly fucking aggravat-ing she was, the last of the clouds parted around the moon and he could see her smile then, her sly sidelong look-how-much-fun-we-have-together smile, and some stopcock inside him finally twisted loose, just a little bit, and some of his permanent sick black rage began to trickle out, as if it might just drain off and wash away.

Like it wasn't permanent at all.

And because it had never seemed to do anything like this before, he discovered that he didn't really know how he felt about it. Except he was pretty sure it wasn't a bad thing.

That was as much as he could manage while the moon gleamed in her eyes. Maybe he'd figure it out later. When he wasn't looking at her.

"So, okay, uh . . ." He coughed. "Uh, hi."

"Hi."

"Nice to see you."

"Thanks. I'd say something nice, but I'm still mad at you."

"Okay. Uh, listen—if you *weren't* mad at me, y'know . . . Uh, do you think maybe you might tell me what the nice something would have been? Y'know. If you weren't mad."

"I'd say that since we met, every day without you is a thousand years, and every night without you is forever."

He gaped until he decided to close his mouth before he started to drool. "Uh. Mm. Well."

She shrugged. "If you don't want to know—"

"Yeah, yeah, right. I should probably write that down."

"Don't be frightened. Beginnings are difficult."

"You seem to manage."

"This isn't my beginning. And it's not our beginning. Only yours."

"I, uh . . . I, uh . . ."

"Sh." She touched his lips with her forefinger. "Talk later. Work now."

"Work? Horse-witching, or whateverthefuck?"

She touched her face with two fingers, pointing at her eyes, and he understood what she meant.

Forgiveness. Permission.

"I still don't get it."

She had a waterskin slung over her shoulder, which she now passed to him. "Wine," she said. "Rinse your mouth."

He barely quelled an instant, astonishing impulse to tell her that he loved her, because he wasn't sure it wasn't true. "Um, when you're not mad anymore—"

She walked past him without another glance. "I'll let you know."

He worked loose the stopper and squirted wine into his mouth. It was sharp and resinous, and it awakened an astonishing array of cuts and tears inside his mouth by stinging them savagely, and it was fucking magnificent. He spat and rinsed and spat again, and after that, he kept rinsing, but without spitting, because he hadn't had a drink in almost a tenday and he'd earned this one.

She reached inside her tunic and brought out about half a handful of wilted, soggy-looking leaves. Her other hand filled itself with a small pouch of some kind of powder. She shook a judicious amount of it into the leaves, then returned the pouch to whatever nonpocket she'd taken it from— probably next to the one where she kept those knives—then rolled the powdered leaves between her palms until it all turned into a darkly gooey ball. When the ball began emitting a nasty-smelling smoke, she slapped it onto the face of the stone fold as high as she could reach. "Don't look straight at it."

He shaded his eyes with his good hand as the goo crackled and spat magnesium-white fire. Even shaded, the glare hurt his eyes. When he could see again, what he saw was the horse-witch looking at Tanner, and at him, at the ruin of their clothing and at the crossbow and all the blood they two had spilled.

She said, "Now do you believe what I said?"

"About what?"

"That it's less trouble to let them kill me."

Over the course of the month since he'd last seen her, Jonathan Fist had repeatedly promised himself that if he ever found her again, he would stop and think for a second or two every time he was about to open his stupid goddamn mouth.

"I believe that you think so," he said slowly, "and I believe I understand why. But I disagree. Strongly. I probably always will."

"I know," she said gravely. "I feel the same about you. That's why I was mad at you."

"Was? Is this you letting me know you're not mad anymore?"

"No, I am. But for a different reason now." She squatted beside him, inspecting his wounds. "I want you to take better care of yourself."

"I'll try," he said. "I will."

"I believe you." She palpated a rip over his eyes that he'd gotten from the butt of the crossbow, frowned, and nodded to herself. "You've changed the way you speak."

"Blame it on a woman I met."

Her fingers dug into the swelling of his broken wrist hard enough to prickle beads of sweat across his face. "We need to set the bone. It'll hurt."

"Okay."

"I can give you something for the pain. It'll still hurt, but you won't mind."

"Will it make me sleepy?"

"Usually."

"Then not now."

"Uh," Tanner said, coughing like a heavy smoker awakening from sleep. "Would it be rude to point out that he's not actually dying? And that I am?"

"Not at all," she said without the slightest flicker of a glance in his direction. "Did you think I didn't know? I can see how you might make that mistake. You assume that I don't know and do care. The truth is the other way around."

"Always the charmer."

"I don't have to be polite to people who murder me."

"Well, when you put it that way . . ." He sighed, and coughed some more. "Guess I'll go back to sleep. Wake me or bury me. You pick."

She stayed in front of Jonathan Fist, gazing steadily into his eyes with her head cocked just a bit, to hold him in her eye of grey-blue ice. He said, "What?"

"Will he live?"

Fist shrugged. "You tell me."

"No," she said. "Decide."

He got it. "Yeah. Sorry. This has been kind of a tough night."

"I know. You still have to decide."

"Yeah. Yeah, okay, in a minute." He closed his eyes. "He wants to know what you are. The people he works for want to know."

"I'm the horse-witch."

"I think," he said slowly, "the real question is why there would be a horse-witch. At all."

"There isn't. We're all just pretending there is."

"Okay."

"You get confused by names," she said. "Most people do."

"Um . . ."

"People call me the horse-witch," she said patiently, "because they find me strange. Witchy. And because they find me among horses. But I'm found among horses because I like horses, and horses like me. We understand each other. We share power with each other. Most horses deserve me. Most people don't."

"I guess the forgiveness-and-permission-witch doesn't really scan."

"Some things are difficult to explain because they're complicated. Other things are even more difficult to explain because they're simple. *Forgiveness* and *permission* are words, and abstract. What I do is concrete and specific."

"Yeah, and maybe you can explain it to me. Small words, huh?"

"I can use words, if I have to. You seem to need them."

Her ice-eye opened like a flower before him, and in its depth he saw horror he could barely imagine. "Everything that lives understands punishment: the pain of having done wrong. We're born knowing it. It's what pain is for. A smack on the wrist for stealing sugar. A burn from touching hot iron. A slap for approaching a woman the wrong way, or a beating for approaching the wrong woman. But deep inside, in the places we can't look, punishment is the source of *every* pain. All pain. So when we are enslaved, when we are whipped, when we are raped, when we are maimed and tortured and slain—in that dark place inside us, *we know we deserve it.* Because if we weren't bad, bad things wouldn't happen to us."

"But that's not—I mean, y'know, you grow up and you find out that's just not—"

"But you never believe it."

"Well, I guess . . . I mean, sure, some people can't seem to let go of—"

"You're not *listening.*" Her face had gone dark and savage, and behind her eyes smoldered a fury that threatened to burn him down and maybe the mountain too. "I said, *you* never believe it."

He went still.

For a long, long moment, he could only blink.

Slowly.

She said, "Was it *concrete* you don't understand? Or was it *specific*?"

"No," he said, blank. Numb. "No, I get it. But—I just . . . the kind of shit I've done—"

"Has nothing to do with me," she said. "You might face justice some-day, if there is such a thing, and if it's unlucky enough to find you. Absolu-tion is between you and your god."

"Then you—" He shook his head, still blank. "I guess I don't get it after all."

"Listen to me now," she said intently. "I know you call yourself a bad man. I know you have harmed people who were no threat to you. I know you have left a trail of horrors that scar the face of this world. I know all these things, and many more, and I don't care. They have nothing to do with me. They're not what I do."

"Maybe if you started with what your work is, instead of what it's not."

"My work is your father's madness," she said gravely. "My work is your mother's murder. My work is pain, and fear, and having to be a parent to your parent while still you are a child."

"How do you . . . how can you possibly *know* . . ."

She laid a hand on his arm. Her touch was warm and cool together, and it unspooled eternity inside his head. "What you call yourself, what others call you, what you have done—these mean nothing to me. I know you. You met me a month ago. I have known you since the world was born. Everything you are is what you should be. Everything you should be is what you are. I know all of you, and there is nothing in you I do not love."

The abyssal depths of forever were too dark for him to gaze into; he flinched back as if she'd burned him. "Don't—don't *do* that . . ." but she held on to him and drew him close until she was everything he could see, everything he could hear or smell or taste or touch and she didn't say it, she didn't say anything, but she didn't have to.

child

you are forgiven

It was too much. It would always be too much. "You can't *do* that— I don't deserve—"

"What you deserve has nothing to do with me."

"Lucky for me, I guess." He pulled back his arm, and grunted at the sudden pain. He'd forgotten that his wrist was broken. With his other hand he scrubbed at his eyes. "You know, I'm . . ." He had to cough his voice clear. "I'm way too old to fall for touchy-feely hearts-and-flowers shit."

"Do we need another talk about age?"

"No," he said. "Really. I remember."

"What I say to you is what I said to Orbek. What I will say to this dying killer. What I say to every damaged horse who struggles into the witch-herd." She leaned in and whispered, her lips brushing his ear. *"Be not afraid, child. Be what you are."*

He looked over at Tanner, who lay silently, eyes closed, breathing ragged and shallow.

Except you're one of them, he'd said.

The horse-witch smiled. "It's all right, you know."

"What?"

"The world does not require that we kill our friends."

"Friend, my ass." He glared at her. "And I had a pal named Stalton who'd tell you different."

She only shrugged.

He looked at Tanner, and couldn't tell if the assassin was alive, let alone conscious. "Fuck the world. I don't need an excuse to kill him. I don't need an excuse to let him live."

"That's what I'm trying to help you understand."

He turned to her, frowning. "Permission . . ."

"Is a word," she said.

He blinked. Then he blinked again, and when his eyes opened he saw exactly what she meant. "Tanner," he said slowly. "Tell your Abbot—no, tell Damon. Personally, if you can. Tell him I have the horse-witch."

"I'm sorry?"

So he was awake. And listening. Go figure. "Tell him I have her. Tell him I'll report what I learn. And tell him I don't need any fucking help."

"Um . . ."

"Tell the Council of Brothers we can have peace, if they leave the horse-witch alone. If they don't, we'll have something else."

"I get it," Tanner said. "Everybody knows your something else."

"Tell them the horse-witch is family now. My family. They'll understand what that means."

"I kind of do myself."

"I hope I'm right about you. I hope you're too smart to mix in my business again."

"What, no third time's the charm?"

"Third time's the slab, Tanner. Believe it."

"I wouldn't presume to doubt. Hey, if thanks from me means anything—"

"Don't."

"Yeah, all right." Tanner relaxed, and let his eyes drift closed. "Family, huh? Family since when?"

He looked at her. She looked at him.

"Apparently," he said, "mostly forever."

RELIABLE SOURCES

RELIABLE SOURCES

*"Everybody spends their whole lives pretending shit isn't
random. We trace connections between events, and we invest
those connections with meaning. That's why we all make stories
out of our lives. That's what stories are: ways of pretending
things happen for a reason."*

—CAINE
  Blade of Tyshalle

The entry hall of the Monastic Embassy in Thorncleft was wide and tall
and comfortably warm after the spring chill outside. In accordance
with Monastic custom, the embassy had been constructed with local ma-
terials; in Thorncleft, just below Khryl's Saddle, this meant stone, mostly
varieties of granite like the walls of polished porphyry that gleamed dark
rose in the afternoon sun.

There was the usual complement of a dozen or so novices dusting and
scrubbing and polishing pretty much anything that couldn't get up
and run away; his practiced eye tabbed four of them as covert Esoterics,
and there were two more who very well could have been, which meant
they were the dangerous ones. Even four covert Esoterics in the front hall
would be overkill for this embassy—a small installation in the sleepy capital of a small, peaceful nation—if the Monasteries indulged in overkill,
which in his experience they did not. So they were wary, watching for
trouble. Likely violent trouble.

They might be expecting him. Specifically.

Several of the novices and two of the Esoterics looked up when his
boot heels clacked on the marble floor. One Esoteric's eyes widened in

shock, and his mouth fell open, and when he drew breath for an exclamation, he was interrupted by the sudden appearance of a large matte black pistol whose muzzle was centered on his right eye.

"You. Shut the fuck up."

"Your pardon, sir?"

"There's a time to bluff, kid. This isn't it." He looked over the group. "Don't talk. None of you. Not a fucking word. Now, everybody here who knows who I am, raise your hand."

Both of the probables raised their hands, as did two of the obvious ones and three of the regular novices. Sometimes being a celebrity kind of sucked.

"All right, go over there. Stand by the Duty Master's office and keep your mouths shut."

They kind of looked at one another like they were trying to decide between obeying, stalling, or blitzing. "You know who I am," he said patiently. "You know you should do as you're told."

They did.

He looked at the remaining novices. He pointed the pistol at the head of the last Esoteric. "This guy knows who I am, but he didn't raise his hand. I haven't decided yet if I'll kill him for it. So if every other liar owns up and raises a hand . . . ah, fuck it anyway. All of you. Over there with the others. You, get the door. We're going in to chat with the Duty Master."

The office was small and plain, its only furnishings a writing table and a small wooden stool. On the writing table sat a large volume of cutgrass paper bound in what might have been dragon skin. On the stool sat a small plain man of indeterminable old age, who held a large reading glass in both hands. He lifted his head and silently regarded his visitors with a squint notable for its expressionless concentration.

He showed the pistol to the Duty Master. This elicited no reaction. "You know who I am?"

The small still man said, "Jonathan Fist."

He blinked. "That's . . . impressive."

"Thank you."

"How do you know that name?"

The small plain man set down the reading glass, closed the book, and stood. "All of you stay here. Keep the door closed and make no sound until I send for you."

All twelve of them clasped their hands behind them and settled into parade rest. The small plain man tucked the book into the crook of his elbow. He nodded to Jonathan Fist. "The rest of this conversation should be private. Please follow me."

"And they'll just stand here?"

"Yes."

"I wouldn't."

"Then we're both fortunate you're not on my staff. Shall we?"

"The only conversation I need is with the Reading Master."

"I am the Reading Master." He hefted the book. "You may be interested to learn that this is our archive's Unbound History of Faltane County, including a fresh transcription of the Faltane County War."

"Tanner filed already?"

"I know of no one by that name."

"Me neither. Interesting reading?"

"Unexpectedly so."

"And why in hell would *you* read it? Why would you even have one? Faltane's weeks from here; there are two abbeys within a three-day ride. How come they're not keeping this History down there?"

"They are," the Reading Master assured him. "The report on the events of the recent war has rendered the History of Faltane County subject to a specific protocol, requiring that one volume of each new edition be Bound in Thorncleft's Vault."

"Yeah? Why's that?"

"Because you're in it." He nodded toward the door. "Brother Jonathan? Please."

The embassy's kitchen was in the basement, kept warm and cheery by charcoal-fired ovens and wood-fired stoves. On the way down there, the Reading Master had explained that the protocol in question had been originally enacted by the previous Ambassador, Raithe of Ankhana. It remained in force simply because so much information had accumulated over the years that the Thorncleft Embassy had become the Monasteries' principal archive on the acts of Caine.

"Still a fucking celebrity."

"I'm afraid so."

They'd stopped briefly at a robe cupboard, and chose for him a traditional earth-toned design, with a hood. "You can put away your weapon. You won't need it."

Fist had looked down at the pistol in his hand and shrugged. "It's not loaded anyway."

"Indeed?"

"You might not believe it, but I was really hoping to make it through the day without killing anybody."

"Of course I believe it," the Reading Master said with an occulted tightness around his eyes that might have been a hint of smile. "Belief is my profession."

In the kitchen, the Householding Master bustled about, boiling tea and checking ovens, scrubbing utensils, and generally keeping himself busy. Jonathan Fist sat with the Reading Master, the History between them, at a small round table that from its scars must double as a butcher's block. "This is private?"

"The embassy has other guests, who may desire my attention. They're unlikely to seek me here."

"What about your chef, here?"

The Reading Master smiled. "You may speak freely in front of Master Ptolan."

"Oh, you certainly may," the Householding Master said. "Though I don't know much, I do know how to keep my mouth shut."

"And occasionally he proves it."

"Oh, pooh. I have one more thing I would say to our guest, if Your Grumpiness permits." He came close and lowered his voice. "Though I'd be the last friar in the world to speak ill of a Brother, I thought—and think—that the previous Ambassador treated you *very* badly."

"Which is a pretty fucking mild way to say he tortured the shit out of me after he murdered my wife, but let it go."

"Perfectly dreadful," the Householding Master said dolefully. "I hope you understand that no one on the embassy staff here approved, or willingly cooperated."

"Long ago and far away." Felt like it, anyway. "I'm as close to over it as I'm ever gonna get."

"Well, you're very kind. Just between you and me, I never liked him. Not one bit."

"I'm pretty sure nobody liked him."

"And then he was *promoted*—Ambassador to the *Infinite Court*! On my heart, I wonder sometimes if the Council Brothers have five grains of sense between them."

"Not their fault. I picked him for that job myself."

"I beg your pardon?"

"I picked him. All the Council did was confirm it."

Master Ptolan blinked, then shook his head. "Would you be offended if I were to say that I don't understand you at all?"

"I get that a lot." He looked over to the Reading Master. "I need an hour or two in your Vault of Binding."

"I'm afraid that's impossible."

"What, it's broken? You locked it and lost the key?"

"It's perfectly functional. You can't go in."

"The hell you say."

"The Vault is in use by the guests I mentioned, who happen to be an Inquisition research team. You should avoid them."

Fist scowled. "Did my name come up?"

"Not yet."

"Yet."

"They don't know you're here."

Fist sighed. "That was kind of the point to how I came in. I don't mind people knowing I've been here as long as I'm gone before they find out."

"Then time presses." He opened the book and turned it so that Fist could read. "This is about the horse-witch?"

"Shit, you *are* good."

"Oh, he does that all the time," Master Ptolan said. "It's impressive right up until he tells you how he knows."

The Reading master flipped a few pages in the History. "There are references to the horse-witch here going back more than four hundred years, since the founding of the closest abbey, which is Chanaz'taa, two days south of Faltane. The earliest Historians considered her to be a particularly well-established local myth, given the vast herds of wild horses roaming those plains. The first confirmed sighting was two hundred eighty-seven years ago, followed by another confirmed sighting one hundred thirty-five years ago. Though the descriptions match, the similarity was merely noted, as there was no way to determine if they were the same entity. Verification was apparently very difficult—the narrative is unclear on this—as she was not confirmed as a being-of-interest until about two and a half years ago."

Fist's face went hard. "After Assumption Day."

"The True Assumption, as it is now known. Yes."

"What about here? The witch-herd roams this far north. Farther. What do you have on her?"

"In our Vault? Two Bound copies of this same volume."

This was bad. He had a feeling it was about to get worse. "Nothing else?"

The Reading Master sighed, and began paging through the History. "Of course, the primary Archive for her area is Chanaz'taa. This is where the matter becomes troubling."

"We jumped troubling a while ago. This is the road to plain fucking scary."

"The earliest Vault-bound confirmed reference to her in Chanaz'taa is *also* a copy of this same volume."

"Same as in *same*?"

"Identical."

"As in she didn't actually fucking exist until *after* the war? Because when I met her—"

"I said earliest confirmed. There is one previously Vault-bound report that may reference her," the Reading Master said with quiet precision. "Not by name. A woman answering her description seems to have perished in the Faltane County War. A slave, killed in an attempt to rescue horses from the manor's stable fire."

"Wait—see, that's not right. Nobody died in that fire. I was there. All the horses were already gone. And how the fuck would Tanner know about it anyway? He was on the far side of the county—shit, he chased off the horses himself."

"The Vault-bound Prior of the Faltane County War doesn't mention anyone answering his description. Our analysis suggests that this report is of an event that has unhappened."

His fingers and face went numb. Most of the rest of him too. All he could really feel was the pile of broken bricks where his guts should have been. "An Intervention?"

"It's difficult to formulate a plausible alternative."

Tanner had told the truth after all. Fist closed his eyes. "It really is the end of the world."

"Was the end of the world. Yes."

"Was?"

"Our analysis suggests that our world—the world as we knew it—ended on Assumption Day. The world we're in now is . . . different."

"How different? And different how?"

"That we are still trying to determine."

"What are we—you—doing about it? Anything?"

The Reading Master turned up his hands. "We're open to suggestions."

Resting his spinning head on his hands did not seem to slow its whirl. "So . . . wait. Okay. So if Tanner wasn't there in Faltane the first time, who was? Who wrote the Vault-bound Prior?"

The Reading Master tilted his head a millimeter or two. "You did."

"You did not just say that."

The Reading Master replied only with a sympathetic sigh.

Jonathan Fist tried massaging his eyes. It didn't help. "Please say you're kidding."

"Oh, his sense of humor is legendary," Master Ptolan said dryly. "He's the life of the funeral."

"This slave woman made a considerable impression; you confessed candid admiration of her ferocity. Apparently she stabbed one man-at-arms in the throat and slashed the femoral artery of another, killing them both. With a table knife that seems to have been crudely sharpened, possibly on a flagstone. You intercepted and disarmed her, and attempted to prevent her from entering the stable. She responded by biting you on the face, near your left eye—inflicting what you wrote may be a permanently disfiguring wound—then managed to struggle free. Several horses were rescued from the fire, due partly to your assistance, before the stable collapsed."

"So when you couldn't stop her, you helped her?" Master Ptolan said. "Even though she hurt you? That doesn't sound like you."

"I get that a lot too."

The Householding Master's eyes clouded with tears. "Those poor horses . . ."

"Horses, Master Ptolan, who are *currently* safe and whole."

"No." Jonathan Fist lifted his left hand, and laid his fingers lightly on his cheekbone below his left eye. He could feel it. The wound. Her teeth. A sense-memory of something he'd never experience. Echoes of words unsaid. "It doesn't work like that. They're still dead. She's still dead."

"I'm sorry?"

"They burned to death screaming. Screaming that they were sorry. That they knew they were bad but if someone would only come and set them free they'd never be bad again."

The Reading Master leaned toward him. "You remember?"

"She died because she stayed with them. The ones she couldn't save. Burning with them was the only way she could think of to show them it wasn't their fault."

Master Ptolan looked worried. "Are you all right?"

"No. It's . . . shit, I don't know. I know it happened. Because she knows me, and I'm getting to know her. She says . . . the horse-witch says that nothing in creation loves like a horse loves."

The Reading Master frowned like he'd gone somewhere other than his planned destination, and he didn't yet know how dangerous this undiscovered country might prove. "Brother Jonathan—"

"It makes sense, you know? The other animals people have—dogs, cats, cattle, hawks and falcons and whatever else—we use them in ways that work with their natural instincts, right? Hunt or chase or breed or eat—we don't force them to violate their essential nature. But horses are prey animals. Eyes placed for maximum field of vision. To watch for predators. You know how a horse knows a predator? One of the first things she said to me: eyes on the front. Binocular vision. Dogs and humans are natural partners. Horses and humans are natural enemies. For a horse, a predator on its back is death. Every time a horse lets you up onto its back, it's giving you its life. Every time."

The two Masters exchanged wary looks. "May I get you something?" Ptolan said. "Mug of wine. Cup of tea. Anything."

"A horse can weigh more than a thousand pounds. Some a *lot* more. Horses have reflexes half a dozen times faster than a man's. They can kill you before you can blink. But they don't. They give their lives to us. Because they love us."

He looked down. He saw only what was inside his head. "We whip them. Starve them. Chain them. Break their spirits. Break their minds. Still they love us. Still they offer up their lives without hesitation. Because when a horse loves you, it's fucking absolute. And all they ask is that you love them back. Most of them never get even that."

He lowered his head. "That's what she did. Does. She loves them back."

The Reading Master reached toward him hesitantly, as if he did not quite dare to touch him.

"If you knew her, you'd understand," Jonathan Fist said. "She'd do it. She'd give her life just to show them they're not wrong about us."

"Please, Brother Jonathan," Master Ptolan said. "Is there anything at all we might do for you?"

"Why do you keep asking me that?"

The Reading Master laid that tentative hand flat upon the tabletop, and said with gentle precision, "Because you're crying."

"The hell you say." But the hand he lifted to his cheek came away wet. "Son of a bitch."

"You began to weep when you spoke of the fire; horses and love seem to be unexpectedly emotional subjects."

He'd known it would end in tears. But it had barely even started and the tears were already here, and already his. Couldn't be a good sign.

He wiped his eyes on the sleeve of his robe. "Doesn't mean anything."

"Perhaps not to you."

"There is a tradition in the oldest oral histories," Master Ptolan said, "that in the Quiet Land, from which we were taken by the First Folk, horses and humans had been together since the beginning of time. That it was the horses who gave humanity the gift of civilization. And that in the end of time, when the gates of Hell are broken and stars fall to set the world on fire, it is the horses who will come for us. All of us. They'll come to take us home."

"Can we move on to something else?" Jonathan Fist had to look away. "Keep that shit up and I'll be crying again."

"Ahh, I'm sorry," Master Ptolan said. "It's only that I find it a lovely conceit. The vast bulk of tales and traditions that survive from humanity's youth are filled with war and slaughter and horrors that beggar the imagination. But the return of the horses seems so lovely—almost not human at all. As if it could be the lullaby horses whisper to us when they nuzzle our ears."

"You're pretty fucking well read for a Householding Master."

"Ptolan is also the embassy's Keeping Master." The other Master tilted his head and righted it again. "We are a small post. Masters are needed more urgently elsewhere."

"Yeah? What's your other job?"

"As perhaps you surmise, I am the embassy's Warding Master," he replied blandly. "If I may revisit the story of the slave, Brother Jonathan, I do find it curious that you didn't find a way to restrain her."

"Me too."

"Even speculation would be a welcome addition to my commentary. Does your unexpected . . . insight . . . offer any clue?"

"I can't even guess."

"You might have rendered her unconscious, mightn't you?"

"I don't carry sedatives or paralytics, which pretty much leaves tying her up—bad idea when the manor house is burning down around you—or breaking her leg. Also a bad idea. And I don't like to hit women."

"Really? Because in your personal History—"

"I've hit women. I've killed women." He shrugged again and looked away. "My father hit my mother. She died. I don't like it."

"This is your Artan family, yes? That is, Duncan Michaelson and Davia Khapur, as opposed to the blacksmith and his wife in Pathqua?"

"I'm not Pathquan. That was just my cover narrative when I began training at Garthan Hold. The blacksmith never existed. Even if he did, he sure as hell wasn't related to me."

"That," the Reading Master sighed, "depends upon whom one asks."

"Oh, come *on*."

"Our Vault-bound archive is extensive."

"It'd have to be, if it's full of shit that never happened."

"*Never* is a word that, in this instance, may not usefully apply."

"You're telling me the story I made up about my background was, what, somehow true? Previously true?"

"Possibly. *True* is a word very like *never*. Perhaps the easiest way to think about it is as a truth that has been unmade. Some of our theoretical thaumatologists have speculated that unhappened events cast a shadow on reality—an echo—that might be expressed as fiction, or legend, or myth."

"Maybe I should come back some time when I can get in that Vault. Sounds like I could learn all kinds of shit about myself."

"I'm afraid that can't be allowed."

"Huh?"

"The edict has gone out worldwide, via Artan Mirror. You will not at any time be admitted to any Vault of Binding. Ever. Your entry is to be opposed by all available means, including lethal force. Including, if necessary, the destruction of the Vault and the Abbey where it resides. "

"Son of a bitch." He could barely get his mind around it. "So the extra security out front *was* about me."

"I proposed the ban myself over a year ago; it was confirmed by the Council of Brothers as soon as the Vault-bound Prior of the Faltane County War was discovered."

"You proposed it. You. For what fucking reason?"

"You can never be allowed to enter a Vault of Binding because, quite simply, no one on Home has any way to predict what might happen if you do."

Fist stared.

For a long time.

Eventually he said, "I used to think my own personal permanent shitstorm wasn't really about me. I thought the shitstorms were already wherever they were, and I'd get dropped into the middle of them all the time because that's how my masters got their jollies."

"There may be," the Reading Master said carefully, "more to it than that."

"Oh, you think?"

"I recommended the ban after spending more than a year researching the True Assumption. Something didn't feel right."

"A hunch?"

"I felt considerable unease, both concerning the account of the Assumption itself, and concerning the accounts of the various investigations we have performed. It was only after your Vault-bound Prior surfaced that

I was able to formulate exactly what was so disturbing. There was a question left unaddressed—not even acknowledged—in any account or investigation."

"What, one unanswered question? That's all?"

The Reading Master came close to having an actual expression on his face: a compression around his mouth, a tightening of the skin around his eyes, a blotch of flush at his temples. "Not answered—yet—but that isn't the issue. Unasked. Unasked by everyone, including me. A question that is central to the True Assumption, and central to the peril the universe faces as we speak. A question so plainly essential to understanding the event that our failure to ask it may itself arise of an Intervention."

"Holy crap."

"Here we have the single most significant event since the Deomachy; Monasteries all over the world investigating; thousands of reports, millions of words, written, reviewed, criticized, revised and edited, and in the nearly three years since the True Assumption, no one seemed capable of realizing it *was* a question, and now it's too late."

"Don't keep me in suspense."

"The question?" The Reading Master gave an infinitesimal sketch of an apologetic shrug. "How did you survive?"

Fist stared. He blinked. He stared some more.

Blank. Numb.

Empty.

He should be arguing, or mocking, or raging, or interrogating, or doing basically anything other than sitting like a boil on his own ass. All the ways in which his life was fucked had become too tangled for him to comprehend, much less formulate any idea of an appropriate response.

"Ah," said the Reading Master. "I see you haven't been asking that question either."

"No."

"You can appreciate the issue."

"You think I didn't. Survive. You think I'm not really me. That I'm some kind of fetch."

"It is difficult to formulate—"

"A plausible alternative, yeah." He squeezed his eyes shut, scratched his head, and scraped the broadcloth robe across his eyes. "I have another question."

"And that is?"

In his other hand was now the matte black pistol. "How many people do I have to kill to get out of this place tonight?"

Both Masters froze. The Reading Master said, "You don't want to do that."

"Oh, I really think I do."

A wisp of fleeting frown passed over the Master's face. "You want to put the pistol on the table," he said with gathering force. "You want to put it *down*. Now."

"There are some kinds of magick that work on me," Jonathan Fist said. "That isn't one of them."

He rose and backed toward the door. "A nice line, about the research team. You're pretty smooth, you know that? You tell me about Inquisitors so I won't notice the fucking Inquisition is who I'm talking to already. Smooth. Really. A better interrogator than I ever was."

"Interrogation wasn't your specialty," the Reading Master said equably. Though neither Master moved or even altered expression, the heavy bolt on the kitchen door behind Jonathan Fist clacked into place.

"Wait, what *was* my specialty? Oh yeah, I remember." He pointed the pistol at the Reading Master's forehead. "Do you really want to do this with me?"

"Your pistol isn't loaded."

"And you know that because your truthsense works so much better on me than your Dominate."

The Reading Master accepted this with a sigh. "I did say that you wouldn't need your weapon."

"And *my* truthsense would be all over that. If I had one."

"Everything I have said to you has been true."

"If nobody tries to stop me—or follow me—there's no need for killing, which would be nice. It's worth remembering that if nice is not the option, I don't really mind killing. Both of you. Everybody in this embassy."

"I apologize for the misunderstanding," the Reading Master said quietly. "I have advised the Council of Brothers—and generally the Inquisition—that it's better to be your friend than your enemy. Especially now. No official decision has yet come down, but I believe in taking my own advice."

"That'll be more reassuring after this door's unlocked."

The Reading Master inclined his head and the bolt clacked open. "And in the spirit of this friendship, I see no reason to mention, in my report, that you fabricated a confrontation in hopes that a dramatic exit might obscure the fact that you're considerably more adept at interrogation than you pretend. So adept that neither of us noticed how you learned a great deal while revealing nothing we didn't already know."

"Never kid a kidder. You told me what you want me to know. The pistol—" He shrugged. "That's in case you don't like how I took the news."

"Ah. You may trust we'll do nothing so rash as an attempt to restrain or harm you. As I said, our archive on you is extensive, and liberally planted with accounts of such attempts, each of which seems to bear painfully bitter fruit."

"Maybe anyway we should get the Ambassador down here to walk me out, huh? Just to make sure nobody gets stupid."

The two Masters exchanged a glance, and Master Ptolan gave an *okay you caught me* bob of his head. "Oh, I'm the Ambassador too," he sighed apologetically. "We really are a very small embassy."

"So the private kitchen thing was just a dodge."

"I'll see you out," the portly Master said. "Please keep the robe; the evening has turned cold, and it's begun to snow."

Jonathan Fist almost asked how he knew, but then decided his luck had been pushed enough for one day. For one lifetime. Or two. Or however many he was actually living.

He found Orbek waiting down the street from the embassy, tucked into a shadowed corner, shoulders hunched against the spit of sleet on bitter wind. Spring comes late to Transdeia, and later still to Thorncleft, high upon the eastern reaches of the Gods' Teeth.

"Ain't you cold? Holy shit," the young ogrillo muttered, low and surly. "No point having balls if I freeze 'em off, hey?"

Fist put a hand to his eyes and brought it away, a sleepwalker awakening. "It is cold," he said. He hadn't noticed. "You have the gear?"

"Right in front of you."

He looked down. It was.

"Where else do I put it? Since you don't bother to tell me which inn."

"I didn't think it'd take this long," he said. He hadn't thought a lot of things. He wished he could have kept it that way.

"They fix your arm, huh?"

He looked at his right wrist. It looked to him like it belonged to somebody else. He flexed his hand and made a fist. "As a courtesy. No charge."

He picked up his pack and began climbing the steeply rising street. "Come with me."

Orbek came after him, puffing. His pack was six times the weight of Fist's. "You know there's these new inventions, hey? Porters. You pay them. They carry shit."

"I don't have money."

"What happened to your thousand royals?"

"In your pack."

The ogrillo stopped, frowning. The man kept climbing. After a moment, the ogrillo shook his head, his frown darkening, and followed.

The air got colder. The wind trickled to nothing. The sleet became snow, a shroud of white falling silently on the stoneworked streets and gathering on eaves and garden gates. Orbek stopped again. "Tell me where we go, hey?"

"Keep up."

Orbek sighed and climbed faster. "I hate when you get like this."

"Me too."

They climbed into what once had been called Lower Thorncleft, though now it was the center of a much larger city; it had become a bleak gaslit tangle of railroad tracks that spidered out from the Thorncleft Railhead: a vast dome of glass, stained black by coal smoke, built over and around the formerly fashionable homes that now housed the offices of Transdeia Rail.

Orbek's scowl deepened when the structure came into view. "We taking a trip, little brother?"

"You are."

He stopped. "Alone?"

The other kept walking.

"Don't like traveling alone," the ogrillo said. "Maybe I don't go."

"You're going."

"Maybe you give me a reason. And take your reasons are for peasants horseshit and pack it in your ass."

He stopped. "Orbek, goddammit—"

"No. *No*, fucker." Orbek unslung his pack and threw it on the ground. Veins twisted in his neck. "You say carry me around the Pit. I carry you around the Pit. You say come with me. I come with you. You say stay with the girl and I stay with the fucking girl. You tell me stand in the fucking *street* and *wait* for you, and where do you fucking find me? I'm assbitch to you *three years*. You want to send me away by myself, you fucking well *talk me into it*. One time, hey? One fucking time."

The man unslung his own pack, dropped it and sat on it, leaning into his hands, massaging his forehead. "You don't understand."

"Make me understand."

"Yeah, good plan. Except I don't understand either."

"Then what problem we got, hey?"

"It's not like that, big dog. Since the fight with Tanner. Since we met the horse-witch. Something's going on. Something's *not* going on. I can't tell which. But if it's going on, it shouldn't be. If it's not, it should. All I know is that whatever it is, it's wrong. It's been wrong for a long time."

"And how come you and nobody else gotta fix it?"

"I'm not fixing it. I *am* it. Part of it. Something chose me."

"Chose you for what?"

"That's what I'm trying to figure out. All I know is that it's gonna suck. For everybody. You remember Assumption Day?"

"No, shit-for-brains. Remind me."

"Everybody within two hundred yards of me died. Everybody. You would have too if Raithe hadn't pulled you off that rooftop. They found me at the bottom of a twenty-foot-deep *crater*, for shit's sake. Ma'elKoth fucking *vaporized*. There was nothing left but me and the sword."

"So?"

"So what do you call a guy who stands at ground fucking zero of a nuclear shit bomb and walks away with just some new scars and a limp?"

"I give up."

"You call him Caine."

The ogrillo's eyes narrowed, and he did not reply.

"I think whatever chose me, that's what it chose me for. Everybody else dies. I go off to the next pack of fucking idiots who don't have enough sense to run like hell when they see me coming. Jesus, Orbek, if you could have seen Faltane you'd be running right now."

"So what do you do about it?"

"All this time, it's been like . . . like I knew all this, but I couldn't actually *think* about it. It's like a Cloak—the thaumaturge is right there in front of you, but he's stopping your mind from registering that your eyes can see him. This is like a Cloak for ideas. For concepts. Dad used to tell me that the next best thing to knowing something is knowing who to ask. But you can't ask anybody anything when you don't even know there's a question."

"And your horse-witch, she got answers?"

"Maybe. If I figure out how to ask."

"This don't have to do with her looking tasty, even if on the lean side, hey?"

"It might." He offered half a shrug. "If everybody around me gets killed, and the only everybody in the neighborhood turns out to be a nice-looking lady who can take getting killed and shrug it off with a nod and a wink, well . . . you get what I'm saying."

"Sure." Orbek shrugged equably. "Pallas Ril probably gets it too, hey? Not to mention Ma'elKoth."

"Sure. Cheer me up." He sighed and heaved himself to his feet. "Let's get out of the goddamn snow."

He shouldered the smaller pack. Orbek lifted the other. "You got some candidates? For who's maybe choosing you for his nuclear shit bomb?"

"Yeah. I do." He started walking toward the Railhead. "Your sire lived through the Breaking, right? The Horror?"

"Yah. Why ask?" he said to the man's retreating back.

"Because there's some shit we need to talk about. About who the Black Knives used to be."

The wind kicked up. Sleet began to sting. Orbek only faintly heard the rest.

"About the Black Knife god."

the now of always 6

CONSIDER INSANITY

CONSIDER INSANITY

"What if you could take back the worst thing you ever did?"
—CAINE

Caine looks even more worried as he tramps through the snow back toward Duncan and the others. "Angvasse—Khryl, whatever—if Ma'elKoth shows, I need you to distract him. I just need his attention elsewhere until I can figure out why Kris isn't here yet."

Duncan says, "Ma'elKoth? He's not dead?"

"He's kind of God now."

"He was kind of a god before."

"Not a god. God." He makes a face as though the word stings his mouth. "It's complicated."

"Apparently everything is. Who is Kris, and why do you need him here?"

"An old friend from school. Kris Hansen."

"I remember the name—killed on his freemod training, wasn't he?"

"He's the current Ankhanan Emperor. And he's the Mithondion."

Duncan can only shake his head. "He's fey? How could he have gone to school with you?"

"That's complicated too."

"I met the Mithondion—must be fifty years ago now. T'ffarrell, his name was. The Twilight King. He bore an epithet—the Ravenlock, for a streak of black in his hair, very rare for feyin. Davia and I interviewed him at considerable length for *Tales*—he was exceedingly gracious and patient with us, and seemed quite determined that we should depict his culture accurately. Do you know, he mentioned that we were only the second meeting he'd had with humans since the Deomachy?"

"I've heard that."

"If your friend Kris Hansen is the Mithondion . . ." Duncan sighs, captured by memory of brighter days and regret at how swiftly they had passed. "T'ffarrell was well beyond a thousand years old, of course, but still youthful and strong. Something terrible must have happened."

"It did," said a soft and unfamiliar voice from beyond his head, where he could not see. "It was us. We happened."

At this, all Caine's tension washes away and leaves no trace of its passing. "Kris. Damn, it's good to see you."

When Kris steps into Duncan's field of vision, he looks like a man with the face of a fey; he is dressed only in a simple shirt and pants of white linen. He wears no shoes and bears no weapon, and his platinum hair spills unbound to the middle of his back. "Hari. It's been too long."

Duncan reflects privately, and somewhat sourly, that apparently Kris can call him Hari without getting stabbed for it.

Caine gathers him into a hug, then releases him again and looks him up and down with a smile that, astonishingly, looks like he's actually happy. "Yeah, well, whenever it hasn't been too long, it's been too fucking short. So, what, you were hiding?"

"Some. I'm having a little trouble with a death cult, and just because a Call sounds and looks and feels like you doesn't mean it is. Especially once I get here, and find you standing around a man with a big black sword through his chest."

Caine nods. "Deliann Mithondionne, meet Duncan Michaelson."

"Duncan Michaelson," Kris says thoughtfully. He crouches on Duncan's right and offers his hand. "I've been told you're dead."

"I've been told that too," Duncan says, and shakes Kris's hand. "Deliann Mithondionne—wait, are you the Changeling Prince?"

"I was. How have you heard that name?"

Duncan smiles. "I had a lot of time on my hands and nothing but a net reader for company. Feature stories about prominent natives."

"When you were in the Buke. Hari told me."

"So, the Changeling Prince wasn't a changeling at all, but an Actor?"

"I was born on Earth, but I am not an Actor. I never was."

Caine says, "And this is the horse-witch."

"Ah. A pleasure."

"Thank you. He speaks highly of you, and thinks of you more highly than he speaks," she says. "He also doesn't want to tell you that he knows the Eyes of God have been checking up on him."

"Oh, for fuck's sake," Caine says. "Now they're gonna be twice as hard to spot."

"Not for us."

"Well . . . yeah, okay. Just for me. Not for us."

"Then what are you complaining about?"

"You see what I have to deal with every day?" He waves a hand. "Her over there? That's Angvasse Khlaylock, give or take."

She nods greeting to him. "Emperor."

He returns the nod. "Lord of Battle."

Caine blinks. "You know him?"

"You might recall how acute my perception can be."

"I sure as fuck recall now. What's this death cult problem of yours?"

"One you should stay out of."

"Sure. It's just, y'know, somebody started a death cult and it's not about me? I'm insulted. I think my feelings are hurt."

"It's about you enough," Kris says heavily. "It's a cult of Berne."

"You're pulling my dick. What do you call them, Bernies?"

"Bernites. It's not a joke. Sacrifices to St. Berne are gang-raped and tortured to death."

"Jesus Christ." He looks entirely disgusted. "So, what, I'm too tame for them? Starting wars and murdering gods just isn't, y'know, transgressive enough anymore?"

Duncan stares up at this man who looks like his son, and reflects that his feelings apparently really are hurt. He takes pride in the strangest things . . .

"Hari, we've got it, all right? Don't give it another thought."

"Ever change your mind, say the word. Anytime. Anywhere. I'm your guy."

"I'm hoping we can manage this without anything so . . . catastrophic."

"Hey, Ankhana was *not* my fault—"

"Ankhana?" Duncan asks. "What happened in Ankhana? Or did it happen *to* Ankhana?"

Hari and Kris give him identical glances and say in perfect unison, "It's complicated."

"I only ask because I'm trying, and failing, to imagine an event so monstrous that even Caine refuses to take any blame for it . . ."

"Yeah, funny. Shut up." He turns back to Kris. "Look, I know you're busy, y'know, running the Empire and shit, but I need you to do this one thing."

"If it lies within my power, and doesn't violate my obligations to the Empire and to Home."

"We've got bigger problems than Bernies."

"Bernites."

"I need to show you something that never happened."

"I'm sorry?"

"It's the past, but it's not *our* past. Not yet. The point is, we can *make* it our past."

"You want to change the *past*? Like an *Intervention*? You're Monastic—how can you even consider such insanity?"

"The governor chip on my *consider insanity* engine burned the fuck out a long time ago. It's not an exaggeration to say that the survival of the universe depends on it."

"Depends on it being done, or on you being stopped from doing it?"

"Look, we both know I sometimes jump into shit without checking all the angles and fields of fire."

"Sometimes?"

"But you're the opposite. And this could end up being about you. I need to know that you're okay with it."

"Do I need to remind you what happens when I let you talk me into something?"

"That's what I'm going to show you. What will happen if I talk you into this."

"If."

"Yeah. Everything's provisional. Contingent." He looks down at Duncan. "Everything I've shown you is the same. Contingent. It can all be wiped away with one snap of somebody's fucking fingers. I'm showing you the *best* outcome, you get it? What happens if I get everything I ask for and pull off everything I think I can do."

Kris still looks dubious. "What exactly is this *everything* you're after?"

"What if," Caine says softly, "you could take back the worst thing you ever did?"

tomorrow's yesterday

ELFSHOT

ELFSHOT

"*Apparently I should have taken a minute to think this through.*"

—DOMINIC SHADE

The bartender's primal, and his hair has more lacquer on it than his extravagantly long blush-pearl fingernails do. The hair sweeps up in three preposterous platinum waves like the tucked wings and stiff tail of a stooping peregrine. The black pearl studs on his pierced lower lip manage to suggest eyes and his chin is plenty pointed enough to be the beak. His cheeks have the waxy translucency of a longtime *lachrymatis* addict, and his hands show just a hint of the shivers—he's still a little high. His eyes are the color of stainless steel, and show only professional welcome and equally professional reserve, which is pretty impressive considering the accumulated filth of hard travel that stains my clothes, not to mention my generally shaggy smelliness.

I flip a gleaming royal onto the bar. "Brandy. Tinnaran, if you have it. I don't care about vintage."

The bartender looks distinctly offended. His professional smile widens until I can see his canines. From a fey, that's not friendly. Probably shouldn't have said *if you have it*.

He fishes a nondescript jug from somewhere in front of his crotch and turns toward the mirror, reaching for a snifter. "Will the gentleman have a steamed glass?"

"Fuck, no. And leave the snifters to the tourists," I tell him. "A cordial will do. Or a, y'know, a pony." Which I find obscurely amusing, but it's not a joke I can share.

Some of the piss drains out of his expression. He spins a tall slim pony onto the woven silk coaster and fills it from the jug, then watches expectantly as I sip. It's good. *Really* good; the only thing wrong with it is that it's not Scotch. He can read me well enough to know he got it right, and he gestures with his left hand. The royal disappears from the bartop and appears in his right. Probably so he wouldn't chip his nails.

"Thanks. Keep the change."

His feathery, near-white left eyebrow arches an additional millimeter. "Change, sir?"

I manage to not choke on the brandy.

"The gentleman *did* say he doesn't care about vintage . . ."

"Yeah. Where I'm from, that means give me the cheap shit."

"Ah. Apologies for the misapprehension." The gold royal chimes faintly as it reappears on the bartop. "Allow me to express the regret of the house by buying your brandy, sir."

"Hey, don't worry about it. I only wanted to leave a nice tip." A spectacular tip—an Ankhanan laborer might earn a couple royals a month, if he's got a good job—but the bartender's face frosts over. I've insulted him again.

Apparently here, two weeks' wage doesn't qualify as nice.

I put another royal on the bar. He looks a little more friendly. I stack a second on top of it. "Rith. Fermented. Six month at least. Twelve is better."

"Smoke or chew, sir?"

"Smoke. In fact—" I add another coin. "I hear your house blend is worth trying. Your leafmaster has a reputation."

"The gentleman has good sources." He's thawing. "I have the honor of serving Lady Kierendal in that position, sir. I would attest just how fine our house blend truly is, did modesty not forbid."

Leafmaster. On second look, his tall black-silk choker doesn't quite conceal a line of bruise that suggests somebody's been taking that *choker* thing a bit literally. Well, all right, then. That's convenient.

And it means I don't have to fake a scene with the smoke. Rith gives me a headache.

"Tell you what." The stack grows to four. "Make me happy, and I'll plaster the kingdom with unsolicited testimonials."

"I am always eager that my work be appreciated by the cognoscenti, sir. Please do not hesitate to call on me if there is *any* way I might further serve the gentleman's pleasure."

"Well, yeah, there is one thing." I lean toward him. "I skimmed the parlor talent on my way in, and I didn't see what I was looking for."

"Oh? It is a rare gentleman who finds our parlor staff lacking, sir."

"Yeah yeah, sure, whatever. Everybody's very pretty. Even that ogrillo bitch has her shit rolled and lit, which is not something I can say of many grills. I just had in mind something, y'know, specific."

Specific adds another millimeter to the arch of the bartender's eyebrow. "Here at the Exotic Love, we cater to the most *specialized* taste, sir. We are eager to accommodate a discerning client's most . . . detailed . . . request."

I lower my voice more to have an excuse to lean closer. "I'm looking for something sophisticated. Cultured. Possessed of particular skills. And tastes."

"How particular?"

"It's not complicated. Somebody who knows the harsh. All of it. Who likes it. And who isn't afraid to get, y'know, permanent."

"Ah . . ." His face sharpens a little. Now he's interested.

Go figure.

"And experienced. I mean, *experienced*. Permanent's in play; I want somebody who knows the game upside down and inside out."

"How experienced?"

"Decades. Centuries is better."

"Mmm . . ." His steel-colored eyes go over me in detail now, speculative, analytic, ticking off scars, calculating the curve of muscle and bone under my grey serge travel clothes, looking for signs of softness around my middle, tissue breakdown under my jaw, calluses on my hands, and what he finds squeezes a hint of appreciation through his professional's mask. "We may be able to meet your needs, sir. There is, however, a dress code."

"These clothes? Fucking burn 'em."

"Ah, no, apologies again, sir. It's not a question of clothing so much as it is hardware." His fingers flicker in a gesture my eyes can't quite resolve, and every blade in every sheath all over my body gives me a little jolt. Not unpleasant. Just enough to let me know that he knows where every single one of them is. "For the sort of entertainment we're discussing, only house equipment is permitted. I'm sure a gentleman of your refined tastes can appreciate why."

"I suppose I can defer to your expertise in the handling of hardware."

The corners of his mouth twitch. He might be suppressing a smile. Or maybe a retch. Or both. Doesn't matter.

You don't pay a whore to like you.

"So . . ." I rest both elbows on the bar, bringing my weight a span closer to him. "If a gentleman were to have someone specific in mind . . . and if this gentleman might want to share some of your fine house blend with this specific person—a person with an educated palate, who can appreciate its quality . . . ?"

This brings a playfully wicked twinkle to his eye. "This can indeed be arranged . . . but first, the gentleman will, ah, want a bath."

"Might a specific person be available to scrub a gentleman's back?"

The wicked twinkle trickled all the way down to the upcurving corners of his lips. "With my compliments."

I pick up the stack of gold coins and jingle them in my fist like I'm about to roll dice. "Got somebody to cover the bar?"

"Leave the arrangements to us, sir. It's what we do."

"Sure, sure. See you shortly." I hold out my gold-filled fist. "Thanks."

He reflexively extends his hand and I drop the gold, and while he's making sure he doesn't fumble any or chip his nails or in any other way mar the perfection of his service, I take his wrist and yank him toward me over the bar. He has time for just half a blink before my left cross smears his nose across his stratospheric cheekbones.

He seems to have trouble opening his eyes again, and instead of a shriek of alarm he says *muhaahgk* while I reach over and grab one of those lacquered peregrine wings and give it a wrenching twist that should be more than sufficient to rip away a handful, and it is. More than sufficient, because the whole fucking thing pops right off his head, which is shaved smooth except for some crosshatched scars the color of antique piano keys.

A wig. Of *course* it's a wig, dumbshit. Or he'd have to redo the fucking thing every fucking time he does any fucking. And then its weight registers, and I realize it's not a wig, it's jewelry, because what I'm holding isn't platinum-colored hair, it's honest-to-crap platinum. Made to *look* like hair.

Huh. I guess a royal really is a shitty tip in this place.

And in the second or so it takes this daisy-chain of dumbassitude to circle back and fuck itself, he's past the shock of the assault—huh, tougher than he looks, and goddammit I *knew* that—and he unleashes a godawful banshee wail that goes through my head like the screechers on a Social Police riot car. The sound makes me flinch and pull back, exactly like it's intended to, but that's no reason to let go of his wrist, so I don't, and half a second later I discover that the banshee wail isn't coming from his mouth.

This I discover because his mouth has latched onto my right wrist and those sharp fucking teeth of his are a lot sharper than they look and they look fucking sharp and the shriek keeps going even when he's chewing down to my ulna and I could reach over and snap his neck like a pencil except that's a *really* bad idea, so I have to settle for fishhooking his masseter with my thumb and prying his jaw open and it's time for me to fuck off out of here because I seem to recall that Kierendal favors chainmailed ogres for security.

But what am I gonna do for the hair? Pants him?

Do elves *have* pubic hair?

While I'm trying to puzzle this out, he pounces across the bar at me like a fucking mountain lion, all claws and teeth, and I fall back and get my guard up in time to intercept a *very* professional side kick and it still jolts me back and stabs the numb fire of a bone shot up my left arm and blood spurts and it's not his.

Oh, awesome. He's in stiletto heels.

Literally.

He snarls like a mountain lion too. "No fucking feral *scum* puts one filthy paw to me until I get fucking well *paid*!"

Or less like a mountain lion than a really, really pissed-off whore.

He lunges and he's all over me. Heel kicks, open hands—fuck, the *fingernails* are blades *too*—and he is lightning in a fucking bottle that somebody stuffed my stupid ass inside of. He's faster than me. He's faster than *Berne*. Hopped on *lachrymatis*, he's a fucking meat grinder—every other shot draws blood. The only reason I'm not dying already is that I'm twice his size and speed makes up for muscle only to a point, and because I know how to keep major arteries out of his way. I give ground, covering up, keeping those blades off my neck and away from my heart and liver.

Yeah, okay, maybe I should have realized a three-hundred-year-old rough-trade whore would pack a variety of sharps. And, yeah, son of a noble House, sure, decades of personal combat training, but I wasn't exactly planning to pull this in public and I *can't* kill him, but of course he doesn't have the same problem with me.

This would be the time to trot out my *Back off, fucker. I'm Caine* routine, but nobody in this town will hear that name for years.

Serves me right for improvising.

I have maybe ten seconds before security arrives, which is actually good because if this doesn't work I'll need them to save my life. I back to my left rear flank, a narrow angle that brings my ass in contact with one of the seats along the bar, because the first rule—the *only* rule—of defeating a superior opponent is *Never strike a striker. Never grapple a grappler. Never shoot a shooter.*

In other words, a century of knightly combat training might not prepare you for having a barstool busted across your face.

Worth the experiment, anyway.

I spin away from him and get the barstool and continue the spin with

the barstool whistling straight at those sharp fucking teeth of his, and his
knees bend and he lets himself drop under—*fuck*, he's fast—and I go with
the momentum into another full spin, this time at his knees, and he springs
straight up over the swing and uncorks a flying kick that stabs his heel at
my right eye but, y'know, I don't give a fuck how fast you are, you can't
dodge while you're in midair, so his flying kick chips the barstool's leg and
I knock his skinny elvish ass halfway across the room. He takes it in a back-
roll but by the time he's up I'm in full charge, the barstool in front of me
like a shield, all four legs toward him, because another thing knightly
training might not prepare you for is having somebody jabbing at you with
four different clubs at once.

He goes for a drop spinning heel kick that swivels him low, under the
stool and parallel to the floor at the height of my knee, which is what his
heel is whipping at but I take that shot on the kneecap without breaking
stride and dive on top of him with the barstool between us. The foot-brace
takes him across the bridge of his nose and one leg clips his shoulder and
one takes him right below the heart and his eyes roll up and oh holy crap
I wish I could just lie here on top of him and get my fucking breath, but I
can feel through the floor the approaching thunder of boots bigger and
heavier than any human being wears.

I grab his limp hand and use his razor-sharp thumbnail to slash the
choker. I get some skin with it, which frankly right now works for me. I wad
the choker and smear it across the blood pumping from his broken nose.
Should be convincing enough.

Jesus, it'll suck if I have the wrong whore.

The thumping from my left stops abruptly. I throw myself into a roll
toward it, one hand stuffing the choker inside my blouse while the other
slams that really remarkably durable barstool square into the groin of
nine-some-odd feet of ogre. It doesn't impress him.

Oh, sure, chainmail *and* a codpiece. Am I having fun yet?

Still, it could be worse: he doesn't want to chance damaging the elf,
and so instead of bashing my brains out with his cartoon-size spiked mace,
he reaches down to grab me, which he does slowly enough for me to throw
into a roll the other way and come to my feet and grab the barstool again.
Things back in his direction look grim—he's adjusted his grip on the
mace, and the door he came through is filled with a couple of capable-
looking stonebenders—and the other way, an even *bigger* ogre is moving
to occupy that exit, and why is nothing ever easy for me?

I think it was Clausewitz who said *when in doubt, blitz*. Or maybe
Lombardi.

I put my head down and charge for the only daylight I've got: the rapidly narrowing gap between the big fucker and the archway and I add a little stutter-step that lets me spin again and throw the barstool tumbling at his head. His hands come up to block and he turns a little as it whacks him and by then I'm already diving past his balls through the archway into a roll that puts me back on my feet pelting for the street door, and once I make that I should be okay because after all it's not like I killed anybody.

Shit, barely even drew blood. Except for mine.

Out in the street the day's so bright that at first I can't see much, but I can hear, and feel, and what I hear is a hot sizzle going past my head and what I feel is the breeze of something passing *way* too close to me and then there's a *spannng* from up ahead and a chunk of masonry from the storefront there basically explodes.

What the fuck?

I skid to a stop and look back in time to see a couple ogres coming after me full tilt and another one behind them winds up and just *throws* something round and shiny straight at my face and I barely get out of its way and this one catches the wall square and stone shrapnel goes all directions and what the fucker's throwing at me are steel spheres like fucking ball-bearings the size of my fist and Jesus a *glancing* hit could kill me.

I guess I'm not done running yet.

A meter or so of razor-sharp steel needle disagrees with me: it spears through the back of my knee and stabs straight through the joint to nick the inside of my kneecap. The needle is of the opinion I should go face-first into the cobbles, and it's real goddamn persuasive. Which is not a terrible thing, as it gets me out of the way of six or seven others that go past my ass with a sound like a million pissed-off dragonflies.

I turn the face-plant into a shoulder-roll and on the way over I yank the fucking thing out of my leg in time to keep impact with the street from jamming it all the way through the bone. I come up to my feet with the weapon in my hand and fuck my skull like a beanbag chair: it's a motherfucking *birdlance*.

Treetoppers. I *hate* treetoppers.

I'm not a bigot. We get along fine when they're not invisible and buzzing around my head trying to jam a yard of birdlance into my eye, but this is not one of those occasions. They can't be outrun; gotta get inside, somewhere tight, preferably steel-plated, and before I can spot a likely candidate the ogres remind me of their presence by clipping my right shoulder with one of those fucking steel baseballs, hard enough to spin me all the way around.

Shit.

If they'd give me half a fucking second I could detune myself from the treetoppers' Cloak, but that takes concentration that I really kind of need to duck, dodge, dive, and roll to get a horse trough between me and the ogres without getting my ass knocked to downtown fucking Thorncleft. The getting-inside-somewhere is looking problematic too, as this crowded street of busy storefronts transforms in seconds to a deserted ghost-town street lined by locked-down storefronts that look more like bunkers, which is another fucking crisis because clearing the street means my buddies out there don't have to worry anymore about hurting bystanders, and now from the general direction of the Exotic Love comes the regimented *chmp chmp chmp chmp* of hobnail boots in perfect step along with a syncopated clanging like steel drums played by overcaffeinated gorillas, and Jesus *wept* it's a troop of *stonebenders*. With at least one rockmagus.

All this for one damn elvish whore? They must really like him.

Or maybe Kierendal knows who he is.

A couple heavy thumps and a splintery ripping noise from the far side of the horse trough proclaim that nobody's forgotten about me. Higher ground. I need higher ground, treetoppers or not, because standing on a cobbled street is not how sane people confront rockmagi.

I roll from the trough up onto the boardwalk and keep rolling until I can get up with my back to the wall. One of those lethal bearings shatters the cedar planks less than a handspan from my left hip, but at least I'm on wood with wood at my back, which means the stonebenders can wait. The store two doors down is built out—a six-foot corner's worth of cover from the ogres—and I go for it in a high arching dive-roll with my arms wrapped around my head, a bit of tactical defense for which I pay by taking one of those steels into my right buttcheek hard enough that it spins me all the way over and my whole leg goes numb.

Sometimes it's worthwhile to hang your ass out in a firefight, because there's always some son of a bitch on the other side with a sense of humor who'll peg you there instead of your head, and while getting shot in the ass is no bushel of roses, it's better than most of the alternatives.

I come up into a one-knee crouch because my right leg refuses to co-operate, and I manage to wrench myself around to face straight back along the boardwalk, because that's the best flightpath for treetoppers to come at me full speed, and though experienced lancers go for the eyes, the one who spiked my knee was clearly trying to immobilize rather than maim, and Cloak is not the same as true invisibility; it doesn't affect light or space or anything outside your mind. So I keep my eyes wide and my arms loose and hands open, and let my reflexes take care of the rest, because even though my mind doesn't register them, my eyes work just fine.

Hands too.

My left flicks out in front of my knee, and half a birdlance blossoms from its back, stopped only by the grip of the lancer who jammed it through my palm. I get his legs with my right, half twist, and put his back in his partner's way. Her lance goes straight through him and stabs into the front of my left shoulder—through my subclavius deep enough to scrape my first rib, which doesn't improve my mood one tiny fucking bit—and since turnabout is more than fair play, I yank my left hand off the male's lance, reverse the steel, and impale her through the groin.

She snarls and grabs the lance and starts to pull herself along it toward my hand, shrilling what sounds like some really nasty curses from an enraged chipmunk. Her partner just screams. A treetopper's scream isn't all that loud, but it stabs into your ear like an audio feedback squeal of fingernails on slate.

"Shut up." I enforce my suggestion by wrapping both hands around both ends of the birdlances and squeezing them together, which turns shrieks and curses into thin grunts and wheezes. "Oh, I'm sorry, does that hurt? Well, so does my fucking *hand*. And my shoulder. And knee. And I will rip you off these lances sideways if you don't shut the fuck up."

They seem to get the message, because they quiet down and quit struggling. Or maybe they both just passed out. Or died in my hands. I can't find it in myself to worry much about it either way.

Now it's time to figure out just how deep this shitpool really is. "I'm coming out! I have hostages!"

Holding the two treetoppers in front of me, I step out onto the boardwalk to get a look at what I'm dealing with here. So: the three ogres, twenty-five or so stonebenders in armor, an unknown number of treetoppers, and at least one very, very angry elf. I nod to him. "Hey, sorry, man. It wasn't supposed to go like this."

"I am no *man*." His lips peel so far back, his face is nothing but eyes and bloody teeth, and that blood's mine. "Feral rapist scum. Kill him."

Rapist? "Now, hold on—"

"*Kill him!*"

"Fucking hold *on!*" I lift the treetoppers. "Nobody's dead. Tell them." I encourage them with a little shake. "Fucking *tell* them."

The female pipes reluctantly, "I yet live," and her male chimes in, "I as well."

"You get it?" I call. "I haven't killed anybody. Today. But it's not gonna be long before these two pass the point where kids can save them by clapping their fucking hands."

Everybody looks blank. Brilliant, dumbass—a Tinkerbell reference. That'll impress 'em. "Okay, look. If I was the bad guy here, some of you'd be dead already. These two for sure. And not just them."

I tip a nod toward the whore. "I could have had your life in the bar. At least twice. You can tell these fuckers whatever you want, but I've seen your skills. I know you're not a fool. You have an idea what I can do. You know you're alive because I left you that way. Twice. Shit, three times— I could have killed you before you came over the bar. But I didn't. Nobody's dead unless you decide to make them that way."

"And what then, should I *thank* you? Humans. Feral *scum*. You take and you take and you *take*, you rob and you reave and you *rape*, and you want *thanks* from us for having left a victim *alive!*"

"Yeah, humans suck, whatever. Except apparently not so bad that you weren't about to let me fuck you in the ass."

He goes even whiter—except for those red teeth and now eyes to match—and he raises his hands and the air around him crackles with white fire, and you know I really should try to remember that no matter what somebody does for a living, it's usually a good idea to be at least polite, because I think right now he doesn't care about the treetoppers or the stores or the whole fucking city as long as he burns my ass down.

One of the ogres, though, displaying a degree of good sense that we don't usually ascribe to them, touches his shoulder and leans down to speak a word or two in his pointy little ear, and those teeth go back in his mouth and his eyes turn back to violet and instead of blasting me into the next world, he just points at me and mutters, "Strength of limb I strike and slay—"

Lightning crackles between us. I shrug. "I think you missed."

He frowns, and power again gathers around him. "Light of eye to midnight pray—"

"Yeah, good luck with that too."

He snarls something in Primal, and the air around me suddenly sparkles like my head's inside a glitter rainbow, and my eyes water and my nose tickles. "Fairy dust? Seriously?"

And apparently he is serious and so is the fairy dust, because I uncork a sneeze so violent it doubles me over and I drop the treetoppers and try to get a breath which turns the tickle in my nose into a colony of hyperactive bullet ants marching around my sinuses, which unleashes another sneeze that sprays blood from my mouth and nose and drops me to my knees and my vision is mostly ragged splotches of black and the bullet ants have turned into a gallon of concentrated sulfuric acid which my convulsive whooping gasp sucks into my lungs and somebody says—

"Khryl bless you, my friend, and may Our Lord's Justice stand betwixt you and the fell magicks of darkling Folk."

—and apparently it will, now that she mentions it, because I can breathe again and even see a little.

I stand and wipe my face. The author of my blessing and cure stands a couple dozen feet back down the street, facing the ogres and stonebenders and elf and me with a kind of abstracted, skeptical bemusement on her face and a quarter-keg wooden barrel under her arm. "A few hairs of his head, says he," she says. "Only hairs. No fuss. No rumpus. Only a dozen royals and no trouble at all, says he. None of the slaughter that pursues him as crows follow an army. A few hairs of his head, says he."

"Um . . ." If I weren't so beat up I'd be blushing. "It's complicated."

"Oh, indeed? Strewth, from this scene no trusting soul would *suspect* complication."

"Holy shit." Now I'm scared. "You're *drunk* . . ."

"Holy shit," she replies, "you're bleeding."

I look from her to them and back again. "Um, I've got what we need. Maybe we can just, kind of, back away . . . ?"

"Flee? Surrender the field? For fear of these . . . animals?" She looks distinctly offended. "Have I then so misjudged your courage?"

"Everybody does." I shake blood out of my eyes. "They aren't animals. And they are a fuckload and a half more dangerous than they look."

"As am I."

Something about her bearing, about her simple, solid, unbreakable self-assurance brings Marade back to me so vividly—*You mean retreat? Run? Flee? I would mislike to use the C-word*—that I can't remember what I was going to say.

"Far fallen though I have, I am still to be numbered among the Lords Legendary."

Oh, yeah, that was it. "Yeah, like fifty fucking *years* from now—"

"I am what I am. Wherever—whenever—I am. My duty remains."

I'd like to tell her where she can shove her duty, but that seems a little ungracious considering her duty is why I'm breathing right now.

"This is no affair of yours, human cow," the elf spits. "He is a thief, a robber, and a rapist. Leave him to us."

"And I say he is not, and so I shall not," she replies equably. "Shall we here make trial of our respective convictions?"

"You're *mad*—"

"Perhaps. I am also a Knight of Khryl."

This gets everybody's attention. The ogres go decidedly uneasy, and the stonebenders exchange dark looks. Every variety of Folk knows the Order, at least by reputation.

They're an assload scarier than I am.

"You could not know this man stands in the Shield-shadow of the Lord of Battles. Thus I will not demand your life for having drawn his blood," she goes on. "Now, though, none can protest ignorance. The next who raises hand 'gainst him will raise no further hand in this world."

"You, a Khryllian Knight? Please," the elf sneers, and I can't really blame him, because just standing in the street in simple travel clothes of unbleached linen, she really looks like nothing more than a sexily butch twenty-something with dark auburn hair and an aversion to makeup—at least until you take in the cords in her neck and her suspiciously thick and powerful-looking wrists. "What's your name, then? Aren't you supposed to boast? Some bestial yammer about your family, your rank, and your lands?"

Which makes my stomach twist even tighter, but she fields it like a natural. "Were you a man here to face me, courtesy would require that I Declare the truth of my name, rank, and lands. As you are not human, I have granted already more than you deserve."

"If you're Khryllian, what are you doing walking around in public without your armor? Where's your fucking morningstar?"

She doesn't even blink. "I'm on vacation."

Like I said: natural. I smother a snort of laughter, because I don't want to remind anybody I'm still standing here.

"Vacation, my father's balls." He looks up at the ogre next to him. "Chase off this madwoman."

The ogre frowns dubiously, but he goes into his windup anyway.

She doesn't move.

He fires his steel ball so fast it's only a silvery blur, and she doesn't even flinch as the quarter keg under her arm explodes into splinters and soaks her leggings and boots with amber foamy liquid. Ale. Good ale, by the smell.

I look at the ogre. "Probably shouldn't have done that."

Not that I'll cry many tears for him—not when the mass of deep muscle bruise that is my right buttcheek weighs in—but the poor bastard really has no way to imagine how much trouble he's in.

She frowns down at the ruin of the cask and its contents, then bends down and picks up the steel ball. She weighs it in her right hand. "Interesting."

"Don't kill him."

She looks at me. "Should I not?"

I open my blood-soaked hands. "Could as easily have hit you in the face."

She nods judiciously and draws back her arm—but the ogre was ahead of us on this one, and his next shot shrieks through the air and takes her solidly at the joining of chest and right shoulder with shattering force. Splinters of bone rip through her skin and shred her sleeve. She staggers but stays on her feet. Now she looks annoyed.

And she didn't even drop the ball.

"Soundly struck, and well cast." She passes the ball to her left. "But I'm not right-handed."

This time there's no windup, just a blur of arm and hand and a scream of invisibly fast steel and the ogre's chest caves in around the impact, chainmail and all, and he goes down like she dropped a building on his head.

"Jesus *Christ*—what did I just *tell* you?"

"Your suggestion was noted."

"Goddammit—"

But she's already walking toward the other ogres and the stonebenders. She takes hold of her right wrist and shrugs her shoulder and tugs on the arm, and the splinters of bone withdraw back in through the rips, and the ogres and stonebenders start to give ground. She stops, standing over the dying ogre. "You fought with honor. Should we ever meet again, you may address me as some do in my native land. Vasse," she says gravely, though with quiet pride. "Vasse Khrylget. Mark it well."

I imagine he'll remember. I imagine they all will.

She lifts her head. "Khryl is Lord of Justice as well as Battles," she says generally. "This honorable creature need not perish. Nor need your sprit-ish comrades; Khryl's Love can restore even them. But I will implore the Lord of Justice only when the man and I are guaranteed safe passage from this place."

The elf just glowers at her, probably trying to figure a way he can still pull my guts out an inch at a time.

"Oh, for shit's sake, you vicious little cunt," I say, "how many of your friends have to die for your wounded fucking feelings?"

"You *robbed* me. You stole from me, and from the Exotic. By force."

"What, some scrap of black satin? Give me a fucking break."

"The privilege of touching my *flesh*, you disgusting feral slaughter-monkey."

"Nice. You should write greeting cards."

"I'm a *professional*. I am known, and *respected*, from one edge of this land to the other. Dukes of the *Cabinet* take a knee and *beg* I might deign to let them sniff my *ankle*."

Oh. Oh, shit, I get it.

I didn't go at him like his regular trade. I went at him like a grown-up been-around-the-block guy who wanted to have some sophisticated fun with another guy who turns him on—somebody who has similar tastes, and similar experiences, and who might actually take a step or two on the road to actual intimacy, like it wasn't so much a transaction as it would have been a date, and Jesus Christ, I *knew* better. Of course he's vulnerable to that pitch. That's what he's been hoping to find for centuries.

It's how he and Kris fell in love in the first place.

It's one thing to be an asshole. It's another to be a fucking idiot about it.

"Look, I'm sorry," I tell him. "I really am. More sorry than words can express. That was a shitty thing to do, and I really, sincerely regret it. If it means anything, there are still six or seven royals behind the bar—"

Now his face is nothing but bloody teeth. "You think this is about *money*—?"

"No, I know. I *know*. I just—I thought you wouldn't understand, that's all. I'm sorry. I should have trusted you."

Now he's starting to look puzzled, which is a hell of a lot better than homicidal. "Why should you trust me?"

"We . . . have an acquaintance in common."

"I find that implausible."

"His friends call him Rroni."

His mouth snaps shut so hard I can hear his teeth clack from across the street. "I know no one by that name."

"Maybe he goes by something else around here. Rroni, he's been in the wind for a while. His family's looking for him. And not just them. His family has enemies. These enemies would like to find Rroni too."

His eyes slit like knife wounds. "And?"

"Maybe I don't know where Rroni is. But I need to convince some people I do, you follow? I don't have to tell them. I just have to make them believe I can."

"And what happens to . . . your friend?"

"Nothing. Nothing at all. This isn't about him, it's about his family. Now, he doesn't have to trust me on this. Once somebody tells him what's going on . . . well, if he figures I won't keep his secret, he'll have plenty of time to run off and hide himself somewhere else. If he figures my word's good, he's got no reason to do anything at all."

"And why didn't you tell me this in the first place?"

"Well, y'know, if I'd had the faintest fucking clue how insanely dangerous you are, I would have done exactly that. On the other hand, you probably wouldn't have believed me. Now that you see I staked my life on it, I'm hoping you can take my word and we can all part as friends."

"The word *friends*," he says, sulky in the dregs of rage, "is an overstatement of breathtaking proportion. Vast beyond the concept of size."

And I can breathe a little easier still.

Angvasse has already knelt to examine the ogre's wound, but she looks over at me and her eyelids drift half-down while she gives one brief sketch of a nod, and it's kind of embarrassing for a general-purpose villain of my age and experience to go warm all over because some girl half his age gives him the *well done* wink.

Well, okay: she's not *some girl*. She's a hero. A real hero. The kind most people only hear about in stories. The kind most people don't even believe exists.

It's a fucking shame she has to die.

tomorrow's yesterday 2

TRUTH TO POWER

TRUTH TO POWER

"Hey, what can I say? I am who I am."

—CAINE

Blade of Tyshalle

ngvasse pays off the scow's captain and gravely thanks him, then shoulders her satchels and we take the gangway onto the Lyrissan quay through the lengthening shadows.

Lyrissan is decidedly strange. Weirder than anywhere else we've been; Ankhana will always be Ankhana, no matter what year it is, and even Harrakha has that English Midlands–village sort of tactile permanence. But the Lyrissan we walk into is only a collection of flops and whorehouses and taverns clustered around the big trading post in the middle of town. It doesn't even have streets. It's nothing but a stopover for hunters and trappers up in God's Teeth, where they can sell their take, then drink and gamble and whore away the money.

Forty-some-odd years from now, when the Overworld Company lays the seaward line of the Transdeian Railway, Lyrissan will become a wealthy market town, the first stop down from Khryl's Saddle. Right now, the hill where Countess Avery's manor will stand is a mound of trees two klicks off. There isn't even a road. Just the river.

And the river gives me the creeps.

I don't like looking at it. I sure as fuck don't plan to take a dip. Just knowing that this is part of what Shanna will become . . . It still makes me queasy, somehow, even after days on the scow. It's like finding a digigraph of your mom as a teenager and discovering she was high-grade fuckable, right? Anytime you think about it, it gets you again.

At least I don't have to worry about bumping into Shanna; as a Natural Power, She's as time-bound as I am. Huh. *More* time-bound than I am, right now.

Somehow that makes me queasy too.

Angvasse has found her way to the Lyrissan version of a market square. She looks from one flop to the next, distaste deepening her frown a little more each time. She casts that distaste in my direction. "Night falls slowly here, but fall it does," she says reluctantly. "We'll not have light sufficient to reach the next village."

"That's okay because there isn't a next village. Not where we're going."

"The least vile of these establishments inspires nightmare," she says heavily. "I suspect we'd find better rest among trees upriver."

"Glad you feel that way."

There's no actual stable or organized livery, just a couple of split-rail grass paddocks on the downstream side of town, and everybody in there looks pretty contented. A few others are ground-tied or hobbled a little farther out. A couple of them look pretty grumpy, but that won't do it. Only four horses are actually amidst the scatter of buildings, tied to hitching rails . . . and there's one on a rail by himself, a big old bag-of-bones black gelding going grey on the face.

He's still full-tacked, saddle and bridle and bags, and he's tied where he has to crank his neck around to even see the other horses nearby, and after a second or two I realize he's not looking at the horses, but at the water troughs beside them.

Because he doesn't have one of his own.

From the building in front of him comes firelight and ale-blurred laughter, and somebody's started to sing, and if I think too much more about some motherfucker having a few drinks and a leisurely meal while his horse is tied alone and thirsty in the dark outside I'll just kill the sonofabitch, of which Angvasse won't exactly approve.

"What do we have left for coin?"

She doesn't need to count. "Three royals, seven nobles, and a long dozen peasants."

I squint at the horse. "A royal should be plenty."

"You gave me to believe we're not staying," she says, holding one out for me. "And for an Ankhanan royal one might *buy* a better house than these."

"I'm not buying a house."

Inside, the tavern is basically a shack somebody built around a primitive kitchen. An earth-banked cookfire at the far end is most of the light. A handful of dirty lanterns provide spots of local ambience along the trestle tables and rude benches. Five guys lounge roughly together—four like they know one another and one an extra arm's length off, though they all seem friendly enough. A fair chunk of both walls is stacked with ale tuns, most of them with rusty iron cups hanging from hooks around their rims.

A guy with soot on his face and hands so grimy Lasser Pratt would have puked in his own beer beckons me in from the other side of the fire without getting up. "Whatcher pleasure, pal?"

"I'm just here to see a man about a horse."

He shrugs and sinks back down on his stool, clearly uninterested in anything that doesn't involve collecting coin.

I offer a friendly nod and trader's smile to the five guys at the table. "Who belongs to the black gelding at the rail outside?"

"Who's askin'?" This from the guy an arm's length off from the others, which is reassuring.

"What do you want for him?"

"Yuh-what?" He blinks like all of a sudden he doesn't see so well. "Yer wantin' to buy ol' Shandy?"

Having seen his horse, I understand his disbelief. "I'm not here to dicker, goodman. I'd like to take your horse, and I'd like to leave you with—" With a magician's flourish, I make the shiny royal appear between my first and second fingers. "This."

He's too lit to be subtle; his face goes slack for half a second, then tightens and his eyes go narrow. "I dunno, pal. I'm awful attached to him."

"Having your balls attached to my boot'll be more awful. This royal can buy four horses better than him. Take it."

"My balls to your boot, you little dried-up pissant?" He lurches to his feet. He's big. Big enough to have had a grill not too far back in his family tree. He pulls a knife that's not much smaller than he is. "You want to say that again?"

"Depends. You want to walk out of here with a royal in your hand, or get carried out with that knife up your ass?"

He hesitates, which is good and bad. It's good because we might get through this without me losing too much blood. It's bad because it means he's been around enough to know that a smaller, older, unarmed man who doesn't flinch with a knife in his face might be a little dangerous for a casual brawl. So if this starts, it won't be casual.

Works for me.

I lean around him to tip a nod at the other four guys. "This shit-hump mean anything to any of you? I'd like to know how many men I'm about to kill."

"Hard to know, freeman." One of them swings his legs over the bench and gets up. "Jafe don't mean much to anybody. But a fella who's got a royal to piss away on a broke-down old bag of grillshit might mean sumpin to the rest of us. Cuz there's gotta be more."

Now they're all getting up and this is not what I had in mind. I've had a dustup or three with mountain trappers and none of them was any fun at all, even though they happened back when I was a lot younger and a hell of a lot tougher. And I never took on five at once.

Apparently I should have taken a minute to think this through.

On the other hand, there are some tactical advantages to traveling with a Khryllian Knight. Speaking of—

"Oh, for the love of *justice!*" Angvasse's voice comes from the doorway behind me. "Does this happen *everywhere* you go?"

"Um . . . actually, yeah. Seems to be getting worse, though." I give a sideways nod and shrug and spread my hands, because he's looking past me at her now. "Sorry."

While I'm still half turning away, I snag his wrist with my left, his fist with my right, and drive his knuckles into the edge of the table hard enough to break any man's hand.

Well, almost.

Still, it springs his grip enough for me to strip the knife into an ice-pick grip and while he's yanking away and starting to cover against the backhand stab he's expecting in his chest or guts, I go overhand instead and give him the pommel square in the bridge of his nose. He still manages to get in a good solid knee just below my belt that's gonna need some attention from Angvasse before I walk straight again.

I jam the knife through his forearm and into the top of the table. He howls, and clouts me a solid star-shower upside my head with his free hand, so I wrench the knife back and forth deeper into the tabletop, which elicits more howling.

"Remember my boot?" I remind him by applying it a couple times to his testicles, and his howling chokes down to grunting.

The others are trying to maneuver to get at me. One manages to dive headlong over the table at my flank which would be more than trouble but Angvasse is there. With her customary uncomplicated display of terrifying power, she grabs the back of the guy's jacket, whips him over her head, and hurls him the length of the room so that he lands in the fire.

One-handed.

This gives the others sufficient pause that for a moment the only sounds in the room are the choking of my pal and the blistering cussing going back and forth between the publican and his medium-rare patron.

"Take 'im—jus' *take* 'im—!" my new best friend forces out. "Y'kin *have* 'im. Jus' lemme go!"

"You sure? Sure for sure? Because I'm thinking maybe you really want me to do you right now. With this nice big blade of yours. Save you the embarrassment of telling everybody about the little dried-up pissant who gave you that new scar."

Behind my shoulder, Angvasse says softly, "Don't."

Oh, sure. "Whatever." I let go of the knife with half a shrug and step back.

He's practically sobbing with gratitude as he takes the hilt and starts to work the blade out of the table. While he's still levering it back and forth, I drop the royal into the open palm of his nailed-down hand.

I'm still not a thief.

With Angvasse to cover my back, I take my time going out the door. Maybe one of them will try something. Even say something. Anything.

Give me an excuse.

But instead they just kind of huddle up and go quiet, and y'know maybe it'd be worth staying the night in this shit-hole town after all, considering what they're talking about back there is pretty much certain to be a plan that would give me that excuse.

Yeah, but never mind.

Deliann asked me once what I've ever done that didn't end in violent death. Maybe next time I see him, I'll have an answer.

Full dark now. The moon brushes silver across the mountaintops. The gelding doesn't even look up when I untie his reins and unbuckle his bridle. I cut the girth straps and pull the saddle and leave it where it falls.

Angvasse comes out the door behind me. "Khryl's Love has restored his arm, as well as the other's burns."

"Yeah, thanks." I shoot her a look. She's got one of those ale casks in a rope sling over her shoulder. "I see Khryl's Love has also restored your beer supply."

She sets it in the dirt. "And I have yet to assay its quality, which is as well. Alcohol seems to make me disinclined to overlook the imperfections of others."

"Was that supposed to be an insult? Better luck next time."

"You provoked that," she says. Softly. Without a trace of accusation. "If I hadn't been here, he'd be dead. So would you."

"If you hadn't been here, he never would have seen me coming."

"You decided to kill him before you went inside. And you attacked when you could have retired."

"Nobody made him pull that knife."

"No denial?"

"There's nothing to deny. He's alive. And temporarily wealthy. Who cares who started it?"

"Apparently you do."

I cut one of the saddlebags free and dump it. Some miscellaneous hand tools and a bundle of dried meat fall to the ground next to the saddle. "If you don't mind, check the other bags and the rest of the tack for grain or dried fruit or anything. I think my horse is hungry."

While she does that, I take the saddlebag to the nearest horse trough and scoop up a couple quarts. A third of it has already trickled out the seams before I can get it to the gelding, but it's just as well. Slow and steady with the water; I'm still not experienced enough with abused horses to be able to tell how dehydrated he is, but I know better than to give him too much at once.

"And what is this horse, that you would kill for it?"

"Him." I go back for another bag of water. "It's not about him. It's about somebody who would treat a horse that way. Anybody."

"It—he—appears to be in no great distress."

I hold the bag, and the gelding drinks again. "You don't know how to look."

"You'll forgive me, I hope, for pointing out that horses are after all only livestock. Cattle."

"That's how we treat them. It's not what they are." I give her a shrug. "If I treat you like some ignorant fucking slag hustling two-peasant blow jobs behind the bar, what does that make you?"

There's just enough light from inside that I can see her brows pull together.

"It makes you," I tell her heavily, so she doesn't have to guess, "a Lady Legendary of the Order of Khryl."

"Yes," she says softly. "I understand. I am what I am."

"Right. And what would treating you like that make me?"

The trace of a smile. "Unconscious. Possibly dead."

"That's why it's lucky most horses are nicer than you are." I shoot her a look sidelong. "Kind of makes me think about how Khryllians treat ogrilloi."

She stiffens. "Ogrilloi are not *nice*."

"Depends on what you think that word means."

"And they are not mistreated in the Battleground."

"No? Stop by your fucking jitney landing some night, then come and tell me that again."

"If ogrilloi ruled where Khryl does now—"

"Owning somebody is a knife that cuts both ways. It means one thing for them and a whole other thing for you. I don't know if it does you damage, or if it only displays shit that was already wrong with you, and I don't really care. It's ugly either way."

"If you truly care not, why do you speak of it?"

"Because *you* care." I drop the empty saddlebag. "You can't help it. You are what you are."

"This is a lesson from your horse-witch?"

"She's not mine. It's more like I'm hers. Well, not really. Mostly, she just doesn't try to run away."

"She must be extraordinarily patient."

"You don't know what patient looks like until you meet her." I pick a rope halter off one of the saddle pegs and slip it over the gelding's head. "Come on."

"Where do you think to go?"

"Upriver. Not far." I grab my satchel and shoulder it. "We need to be out of town."

"What of his equipment?"

"Leave it. Bring your pack. The cask too."

"What will you do without saddle and bridle? Let the horse go?"

I smile at her. "Come and see."

The gelding's balky on the lead; probably going extra-slow and careful because he's expecting a whipping whether he acts up or not. He's too hand-shy for me to pet him, and he won't even look me in the eye, so all I can do is hum to him a little. "It's okay, big guy. Come along. Just a little farther. Come on. It's okay."

I keep humming and murmuring and whatever because the words don't really matter anyway, just the sound of my voice, just a calm quiet human voice without anger or threat. A voice that doesn't belong to the ratfuck I took him from.

We don't have to go far. A hundred yards or so beyond the last of the buildings, we come across a broad swath of weeds and scrub along a little creek wending for the river. I take the halter off and step back, and the poor miserable fucking thing won't even lower his head to the grass. He just watches me out of the white rim of his left eye while he waits to find out how I'm going to hurt him.

I come around beside him, facing the other way, out of arm's reach, and give him my left eye while I talk. "Don't be afraid. I can't promise you'll never be hurt, but I will not hurt you. I will never hurt you. And if I might ease any of your pain, I will. That's not who I used to be, but it's who I am now. Don't be afraid."

"You speak to him as if he's a person," Angvasse says softly. "As if he understands."

"He understands. Not the way you understand, knowing what the words mean. At least, I don't think so. Hard to know for sure. Horses are deep."

"Then how do you know he understands at all?"

I shrug. "I've seen it. When you tell them the truth, they understand."

"Then why is he still frightened?"

"Probably expects me to change my mind."

Slowly, carefully, Angvasse lowers herself to sit on the ground a few yards away. "I begin to understand why you wanted to kill that man."

"You see what this horse is?"

"I see what he is to you," she says. "That suffices."

The gelding has relaxed a hair or two; looks like Angvasse has the right idea. I take a couple extra steps away from him and sit down on a rock. "The man I hurt because of you called you Shandy. That's just a word. You can pay attention to it or not. It's not you. You don't have to be anything but what you are. You can stay with us, or go where you please—though you should probably stick close for now, because there are wolves and bears and cougars in these hills, and we can protect you. But you don't have to stay. You're free."

"I don't understand," Angvasse murmurs. "You might have been killed to gain this horse—and now you cast him away?"

"That's not what this is." I look up into the moon-shadow pool of his eye. "So we're here. I know this time of year, you're usually south and west, but we need you. There are three of us, and we all need you. Please come when you can."

For a long moment, none of us moves. The only sound is the trickle of the creek, and the rustle of a small animal skittering through the scrub.

Then for the first time, the gelding makes a move I haven't ordered him to: he turns his head far enough that he can look me over with his other eye too, and apparently what he sees is reassuring, because his head lowers by his front hooves and he begins to munch the weeds.

Well, all right, then.

"What just happened here?" Angvasse speaks only a hair above a whisper. "Did you cast some glamour? Since when do you do magick?"

"It's not my magick," I tell her, just as softly. "It works best at dusk or dawn. Half-light. If you can't manage that, it's best to be outdoors, somewhere dark and quiet, without too many people around. Like here."

"To do what?"

I open my hands, a sort of gestural apology in advance for how this is gonna sound. "When you speak to a horse of the witch-herd, sometimes she can hear you."

"Witch-herd?" She pantomimes looking around in bafflement. "A herd of one? Through which you speak to a woman you won't meet for another fifty years?"

"It's complicated."

"Assuredly. And how long must we wait before you decide she's not coming?"

"We don't have to wait at all. If she's coming, she'll—"

The black gelding lifts his head and nickers softly. From somewhere back in the star-shadowed night, a horse nickers in reply.

"Like I was saying."

As the upper rim of the moon slips over the eastern peaks, she comes out of the darkness as if made of night. The horse is big, powerful, and in the moonlight I can't even guess his color. He walks slowly, easily, bare hooves making only the occasional knock when he steps on a stone. She is just another moon-silvered shadow, an outline, her face invisible within the haloed cloud of her hair.

Except for her witch-eye. Her witch-eye glitters like an ice dagger.

"I see I have underestimated you again." Angvasse gets up and starts toward her. "I give you greeting, good—"

"Angvasse. Don't."

She stops and frowns back at me.

I nod at the gelding. "Business first."

"But—"

"You don't need introduction. Just wait."

The big horse stops just short of the creek, and she swings down off him. She walks into the creek and stops in the middle. She stands there, watching the gelding. He snorts and tosses his head. He sidles one way, then the other, then takes a few steps backward, tosses his head and snorts again.

She just stands there.

He starts to move forward, still kind of sidling but the sidle's getting bigger, almost bouncing, stiff and gawky like some ancient geezer trying to show his grandchildren how he used to dance, and there's an arch to his neck now and he pulls himself up and gives a couple of big huffs like a stallion and stamps a forehoof.

She stands. Watching. Nothing else.

Angvasse moves close to me. "You've seen this before, but still you watch. She watches the horse. You watch her. As though to fix in memory every slightest detail."

"It's that obvious?"

"It's your smile," she murmurs. "I've never seen you smile. Not once. I've seen you grin. You bare your teeth like a dog about to bite—"

"I prefer to think it's a wolf."

"And I've seen that hard false smile you get when something hurts you. But this smile—"

"Shh. This is my favorite part."

The gelding reaches the bank of the creek. He snorts again, stamps a couple times, and leans away like he wants to run but some gravity, some magnetism, something draws him closer and closer, and the closer he gets the less he wants to get away, until he finally steps down into the creek beside her.

She lifts her hand toward his face.

He dances back from her, throwing his head, hand-shy and spooky. She doesn't move. Just stands there in the water up to her knees with her hand up and out and she watches him and she doesn't have anything more important than this to do, ever. She can stand there till the stars burn out if that's how long it takes, but of course it doesn't.

Sooner than I would believe if I hadn't seen this a hundred or a thousand times before, the gelding comes to her, takes a deep breath to gather every last scrap of his courage, and then just kind of leans forward against her hand.

They stand there together, neither moving except to breathe, like all he wants is to feel the warmth of her hand and all she wants is for him to feel it, and after a while he slips aside from her hand, lowers his head, and sets his face against her shoulder. She rests her cheek against his neck, and they stand together in the moonlight, and my hand to Jesus it's still the most beautiful fucking thing I ever hope to see.

"Does it—" Angvasse sounds a little choked up herself. "Does it always work?"

"No. Sometimes they're too damaged. Then the most you can do for them is leave them alone."

"But usually. Usually it works."

I recognize the need in her voice. I give her the best answer I have.

"It did on me."

Soon enough the gelding is calm, over cropping weeds alongside the horse she rode in on, and she comes out of the creek toward us. She looks us over silently.

Angvasse takes a breath like she's gonna say something. I lift a *no, just wait* palm, and she does.

Eventually the horse-witch sighs and nods to herself. She comes over to Angvasse. "I'm sorry," she says. "I know it hurts."

"What hurts?"

"It's possible I can help you someday. Not today. You're not ready."

"And I am grateful for your concern," she says. "I am Angvasse, Lady Khlaylock of . . ."

Her voice trails off because the horse-witch has already moved on. "You," she says. "I know you."

"You will. We're gonna meet about fifty years from now."

"I know you," she repeats. "You're the walking knife. The shape-shifter's echo. The shadow cast by darkness and scars."

I turn that over in my head for a few seconds, and discover I don't mind the sound of it at all. "I'm okay with that."

"You are now. You won't always be."

"Yeah, well, that's what you're gonna save me from."

"I'm glad to know it. What are you going to save me from?"

I manage to swallow instead of choking. Just barely.

She tilts a *just between us* smile toward me. "It must be I've already suggested we should rescue each other."

"It's come up in conversation."

"So well and well, then. Why are you here?"

"The fate of the world entire rests upon us, and we—" Angvasse begins.

"Yes, of course," the horse-witch says gently. "Except fate doesn't mean what you think it means. Please don't be offended, but I was asking him."

I take a deep breath. "I need a favor."

"Yes?"

"I need you to watch something for me."

tomorrow's yesterday 3

FATHER ISSUES

FATHER ISSUES

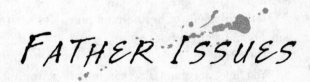

"And a man . . . a man can be excused . . . taking a certain amount of pride in his only son."

—DUNCAN MICHAELSON
Heroes Die

ater springs clear and sparkling from a crack in the rock and washes a broad lip of granite before it tumbles fifteen feet to the grassy streambed. My breath smokes in the morning chill. The horse-witch touches my arm. "It's beautiful."

I cough some knots out of my throat. "Yeah."

"It's beautiful every time you bring me here."

In her past. One or more of her pasts. Some of my futures. Potentially. In the disjointed time-stream of our relationship, it's most useful to stick close to present tense.

"When I'm here without you, it's not beautiful. Even a little."

By the time Berne's demon-mount corpse will drop me by this stream, it'll be fouled with oil and human waste and fuck knows what kinds of toxic runoff from the mines. This heather will be gone, and all the wildflowers, and the vast stand of aspen below us will be only blackened stumps left behind by Palatine Camp loggers.

But there's no point telling her that. Besides, I'm pretty sure I can't actually make myself say the fucking words. And she probably knows already anyway.

"I'm sad for you."

I take her hand off my arm and lace my fingers into hers. "I'm okay."

"I know. But this place makes you sad always. I know how much you love her."

"Loved."

She pulls my arm around her shoulders and snuggles in against my chest. "Don't pretend."

Her hair smells of heather and pine. "It's . . . it was, it's going to be, bad. For me. For Faith it's worse."

"Your daughter."

"You meet her about fifty years from now. You and she . . . have a lot in common. She adores you."

"I'm glad for that," she says. "Are we going down to the water?"

I shake my head. "I just wanted to look. To . . . I don't know. To have a different memory of this place."

She turns her doe eye up on me with a smile like summer rain. "One with me."

Now I feel bad about it. "Maybe I shouldn't have."

She sighs against my shoulder. "I'm sorry I won't be here then."

"You can't save her."

"And you won't need saving. I'm sorry anyway."

"Me too."

After a moment, she stirs and slips out from under my arm. She tips a nod at the mountain shadow's retreat upslope, toward where patient Angvasse waits with the horses below the crest of Khryl's Saddle. "It's a long road . . ."

" . . . and it won't get shorter till we start walking. Yeah."

It's a slow ride down to Thorncleft. The sun passes us going the other direction, and the shadow of Khryl's Saddle gathers us deep in a chill damp dusk for hours before sunset. Angvasse skirts the town with the horse-witch and our tiny witch-herd while I go in to see if I can winkle out a lead.

Thorncleft of this era is not far removed from the small city I will come to know; a bit smaller in these days, streets narrower and more crooked, smelling of garbage and horse shit rather than the coal smoke and petroleum grease of my native era. Lacking their future gaslights, the streets' thick shadows are only faintly brushed by the silver moon.

From the unpublished journals that will become the main source for his *Tales of the First Folk*, I know how he goes about hiring guides for these expeditions. A couple hours buying beers and brandies through a string of outlying pubs peels the necessary slim, and it's not good news. I cut short my evening's entertainment in favor of half an hour's friarpace down the

East Road out of town, until a horse knickers at me from the black gloom of the aspen forest and I stop, panting, my sweat-soaked shirt icy against my back. I wave, and beckon toward the trees. "We missed them. They're almost half a day ahead of us, and they're in trouble."

"Trouble?" Angvasse walks out into the moonlight, and behind her comes the horse-witch on the back of a thick-bodied mare. The rest of the horses trickle nervously into the open. "Are you certain?"

"The thing is, they're really just academics with guns. They were trolling the wayfarer pubs for guides to Diamondwell. They spent last night and part of this morning spreading around way too much silver, then a couple hardguys came up to them and claimed to know an overland shortcut to Shimmerrift Gap."

The horse-witch nods gravely and her gaze goes distant—I guess our hardguys don't take good care of their horses. Angvasse looks puzzled. "How is that 'trouble'?"

"There is no overland shortcut," the horse-witch murmurs. "Sharp thunder and red lightning and blood and man shit . . ."

Angvasse's fists curl. "Bandits."

The horse-witch nods at the northeastern shoulder of Mount Cutter: a jagged ridgeline descending away from us. Far below, a thin ghost-ribbon of smoke twists toward the moon. "They're not far. Greenwood campfire because they're not hiding. Two hours on horseback."

She turns her witch-eye on me. "Less on foot."

Their lookout picked a pretty comfortable spot on the top of the knoll, his back against the trunk of a small scrub oak. He's damn hard to spot, and whenever the clouds clear away from the moon he's got a good view of the road and the approaches to his pals' camp. If he had enough training or natural discipline to hold still, he might have lived through this.

But y'know, boys and toys—he can't stop playing with his new knife, because it's such a novel piece of technology: a spring-loaded tactical folder of a type that won't be seen again around these parts until a few get looted off the corpses of Social Police after Assumption Day. *Shhkck* he folds it closed, and *ksnpp* he clicks it open, then closed, then open, and he's having so much fun with it that he doesn't even know I'm there until my own knife—a long double-edged dagger of a much more traditional style, because I'm just old-fashioned that way—stabs into one side of his throat till its point comes out the other, its grip making a convenient handle for leverage while I quietly break his neck.

I close his knife and stick it in my pocket, because it really is a nice piece, action like silk, bead-blasted titanium nitride blacking, sharp as a ceramic scalpel—and besides, if the next ten minutes go well, I might get a chance to return it to whoever he stole it from.

I'm flat on the ground before my brain registers what put me there: a sharp and shockingly loud *pkow* from entirely too close by—gunshot, maybe a rifle. My heart beats twenty or thirty times while a couple of seconds pass. Then one more *pkow*, fractionally less loud, which is good, and a few seconds later a third, which is better. Probably just somebody playing with another new toy—a firearm is gonna look pretty impressive to a guy whose highest-tech weapon is probably a crossbow. Or they might be, y'know, executing prisoners, which would suck, but it could be worse.

At least they're not shooting at me.

Fifty or sixty yards away, a campfire lights trees above a tiny hollow in the side of a hill. I sing out before I get too close. "Heyo the fire!"

Some rustling, and a clank or two. "Heyo the woods . . ."

"Coming in. All I got's knives."

"How many are you?"

"Just me to come in. There's a couple more, but they favor darkness till I give them the shout."

"What's your business here?"

"Some folk of my acquaintance took this direction out of Thorncleft today. Should you come across any of them alive, I can arrange reward."

Crickets and soft breeze. For a long time.

Then: "What, like a ransom?"

Fucking amateurs. "If you want."

More crickets and soft breeze.

Eventually: "Come on in, then. Slow. Hands empty where we can see them."

So I do.

Amateurs can be dangerous. But usually only when you expect them to act like pros.

I drag the last corpse over to the rest of them. Another seven guys the world is better off without: filthy and unshaven, once-expensive clothes worn through and stained and obviously made for people who died wearing them. That is, *other* people who died wearing them. I safety both pistols and set them alongside the rifle and the shotgun. My ear still stings like a bastard, and the scorched hair around it reeks, but a powder-burnt cheek doesn't count as a serious wound. Besides, the girls are busy.

The horse-witch is off with their remuda, in the corral of rope strung between trees. A couple dozen nervous, spooky horses, snorting and stamping at her, at one another, at the wind. I go over by her because he's in the camp and I'm really not ready to face him.

"Hey."

The horse-witch comes to me and reaches across the rope to take my hand. "You look scared."

"Is it that obvious?"

"Probably only to me."

"I guess you've known me a lot longer than I've known you."

She smiles. "I've known you a lot longer than you've known anybody."

I'll give her that one. "What about my—uh, the girl?"

"I don't know." The horse-witch tilts her head. A trace of frown wrinkles her brow. "Sometimes she's here. This time she isn't."

"All right." A long sigh heaves some of the weight off my shoulders. "Maybe it's better this way."

"That's a matter too deep for me."

"You know how to get there from here, right? The whole place is probably concealed somehow. Glamour or something."

"I've been there before."

I blink. "You have?"

"I have been—"

"Unusual places, yeah, I remember. Listen, you and Angvasse can get him up there even if he's, well . . . if he has to be tied up or something?"

She looks thoughtful and shrugs with half a nod. "It'd be more convenient if you can talk him into cooperating."

"Yeah, except that'll involve, y'know, talking to him."

"Is that why you're scared? Is it him?"

"No, it's me. Well, it is him. And me. Hell, I don't know. It's just . . . it's like I can't make myself talk to him. Not here. Not when I'm . . . well, me." A heavy sigh. Letting it go doesn't make it any lighter. "I know what he thinks of men like me."

"He doesn't know any men like you. Except the one he sees in mirrors."

"That's not exactly a compliment. To either of us."

"It wasn't flattery." She squeezes my hand. I squeeze hers.

And smile.

In the camp, Angvasse cradles one survivor—Ridpath, if I'm remembering the right digigraph in *Tales*, a University cop on detached duty for field security—as she prays away his wounds. Nearby, the other survivor is on one knee, his shoulders bowed, his big square hand resting lightly on the brow of the one who didn't survive.

My heart lurches out of rhythm and thumps hard, twice, three times, and I barely stop myself from slipping my arm around those bowed shoulders of his. What he's gonna go through—what the rest of his life is gonna be . . . Christ, I wish I didn't know.

At least he doesn't. That's something. If this goes close enough to right, he still has five or six good years before reality fucks his dreams and shits on the last of his hope. Five or six good years is more than most people get.

He flinches when I clear my throat behind him. I give him a second to get hold of himself. "You're the professor, right?"

He takes a deep breath and comes to his feet without turning to face me, still looking down at his dead friend. "Instructor," he says, slow and distant. "This is . . . uh, I'm doing fieldwork. For my dissertation. That's like a—huh. Never mind. It's not important."

With a visible effort of will, he makes himself face me. He's pale as ice, and his eyes are clouded and wet, and he has to swallow before he can speak. I don't blame him for being nervy, even though I put away my weapons and he's damn near twice my size. He's seen a lot of men die today. He watched me kill most of them. Considering his entire previous experience with violent death comes from old movies and web games, it takes a lot of balls for him to look me square in the face from only an arm's length away.

"Are you a religious man?"

"Not really."

"Do you believe in God?"

"Depends on the god."

"He was Christian." A flick of a glance down at the corpse. "It's a faith of my native land. The One God makes of Himself a mortal man, and allows Himself to die on a cross to atone for the sins of humanity. I have just commended this man's spirit into His Hands."

"All kinds of people die on crosses. I'm mostly interested in the ones who survive."

The ghost of an acknowledging nod. "Why does it feel like a sin to pray to a God I don't believe exists?"

Okay, I'm over the scared. "Maybe it's a sin against your intellectual self-respect."

The clouds in his eyes evaporate, and his gaze sharpens like he's seeing me for the first time. "You're speaking English."

"So are you."

"Your accent—urban North America. West Coast. Downcaste with Professional overtone—Labor with elocution lessons. Oakland? How does an Oakland Laborer come to the eastern slopes of the God's Teeth?"

"Well, look at you. Henry fucking 'iggins."

"Ah . . . sorry—I'm sorry. It's a—well, it's a reflex. I can't believe I didn't notice already. But I'm a little . . ."

"You're having a tough day."

"I'm Duncan Michaelson." He sticks out a hand. "And you are?"

"Somebody you don't want to know that well."

He leaves his hand hanging there, so I put the folding knife in it. "This yours?"

"Yes—yes, it is. Thank you." He clutches it like he's grateful to have something to hang on to. "I've had it a long time."

"You carry a black knife." Like the universe just made a mild pun.

"I'm very fond of it." He tries out a warm smile while he puts it away. "You do seem familiar somehow."

Because I favor my mother, who he's already in love with, but telling him so won't do either of us any good. "I get that a lot."

"Well—thank you. I'm sorry I didn't thank you already. You saved our lives."

"We didn't do it for you."

"Oh—ah, of course." His eyes cloud over again. "I have some silver, of course, and our people will gladly pay you for our safe return."

"I want you to do something for me."

He takes half a step back, his face closed again, wary. "My gratitude extends only so far."

"Let's start with what I can offer you."

"Beyond our lives?"

"What if I could get you a one-on-one with T'ffarrell Mithondionne?"

"The Ravenlock?" His eyes widen, but then narrow again, skeptical. "I've begun to wonder if the whole King of the Elves business isn't just some combination of folktale and inside joke."

"Let's say it isn't. Hypothetically. If I could put you in a room with the Ravenlock, and he's willing to answer questions. To tell you any story you want to hear."

"Hypothetically . . ." He chuckles, shaking his head. "For a chance like that, I'd sell my hypothetical soul."

My turn to try the warm smile. "That's the answer I'm looking for."

It's a glade. I'm in a glade. I've been walking. I walked into this glade.

I must have, because I've been walking.

It's pretty. More than pretty: green-tinged sunbeams and gently whispering leaves, and somewhere nearby a waterfall hushes beyond the trees. Like I've walked into a painting. It smells more than nice too: wildflowers and clean rising sap, apples and pears and maybe even peaches, fresh black dirt, and I've been in a lot of forests and none of them actually smell like this. This place looks and smells and feels like I could turn around and bump into Snow White. I probably should know what I'm doing here.

I feel like I do know. But I don't know *what* I know.

Wait.

Fucking elves. Primals, feyin, whatever. I know this spell.

I close my eyes and turn in place, counterclockwise, and count off each revolution. "Three. Two. One."

It's not a counterspell, just a mnemonic to trigger a conditioned logic-cascade. Straightforward application of Control Discipline. If I hadn't been so distracted by how beautiful this place is, fucker never would have caught me in the first place.

I open my eyes. "Maybe you should come on out. On my best day, I'm not a patient man."

Dust motes swirling through the glade's green-shaded sunbeam organize themselves and coalesce into a tall fey whose face could have been chipped out of frozen limestone. He doesn't even pretend to be real; his voice is blended of wind and birdsong. *Feral humans are not welcome in this land.*

"I'm not feral."

He gives me an insufferably superior sneer. Reminds me of Kierendal. *The word* feral *means only that—*

"I know what it fucking means, jackass. I'm not feral. I'm from the Quiet Land."

What can you possibly know of the Quiet Land?

"That's what I'm here to talk about."

Your shallow puddle of amusement has now wholly evaporated. Go.

"Ooh, good one. You're like the three-year-old girl of smack talk."

You may depart unharmed.

"And with some luck I'll never have to bring up that you said so." Keeping my voice level is tougher than I expected. "I need to see the Ravenlock. Or really, y'know, he needs to see me. He just doesn't know it yet."

You can walk out freely. Or be made to walk out. Less than freely.

Hey, I know this tune. "Look, I'm not here to cause trouble. But you should know I won't mind."

The dust-mote elf extends an insubstantial hand, and power gathers around it. *Begone, beast! Back to your filth!*

"Um, well, when you put it that way . . ." I shrug. "No."

His eyes widen, his feathery brow compresses, and the shimmer of power around his hand brightens until the glare hurts my eyes. *Banished thou art. Leave this place now with all thine speed, and never think to return!*

"Some kinds of magick work on me," I tell him. "Other kinds."

His other hand comes up. The glow crackles lightning between them. *Then bide where you are. Wait without motion, without breath, without thought, a man of stone—*

"Nope."

Strike forever all light from your eye—

"Sorry." And I am, a little. Very little. "It's not your fault."

The elf's face goes pensive. He reluctantly lowers his hands. *Who are you, and what do you here?*

"You first."

I am Quelliar, Eldest of Massall. I ward this approach to the Living Palace, as have feyin of my House for ten thousand years.

He says that like he's proud of it. I guess I would be too. Something about his name, though . . . I've heard it before. Where? "You can call me Dominic Shade."

I can call you whatever I please, he says, a little tartly. *Is Dominic Shade your name?*

I shrug. "Today."

And your business, Dominic Shade Today?

"I told you already."

And yet have offered no reason you should be allowed to defile Mithondion with your reek of rancid sweat and breath of crow vomit. With your filthy human feet and—

"Yeah, yeah. Filthy human whatever." Ahh, got it. I know who he is.

I can't exactly tell him, since most of what I know about him is that forty-six or -seven years from now, Raithe will murder him in Vinson Garrette's reception chamber . . . but even a little knowledge is a dangerous thing. "Quelliar Massalle, huh? How's your little sister—what's her name, Finall?"

The simulated fey goes still. Absolutely still: a rabbit at the footfall of a wolf.

"And your father, the Massal. Querrisynne." Because I really don't like his attitude, I let him have one straight. "He's going to outlive you."

And how do you hope to even find my person, let alone do me harm?

"It's not a threat."

No? What then might it be?

"Prophecy."

From a feral?

"A man will kill you, but I am not that man." Abruptly my mind is made up. If it's gonna work at all, it should start working with this fucker.

I reach inside my tunic and pull out the black satin choker. The blood on it is long dry, brown and flaky. "See this? Take it to the Ravenlock. You fu—you, uh, people have magick and shit, you can tell who this belonged to, right?"

He looks at it like I'm offering a handful of dog turd. *Even immortal, I lack time to waste on feral mummery.*

Feral mummery this, fucker. "Tell the Ravenlock it's a keepsake from Torronell."

His eyes go all feline and slitty. *The Youngest of Mithondion has been dead for centuries.*

"For a corpse, he gives a pretty good blow job."

The breeze and birdsong voice does a pretty fair imitation of somebody gargling puke.

"I'm not the only human who knows where he is and how he makes his living, but I can and do guarantee absolute silence on these matters in exchange for ten minutes of T'ffarrell Mithondionne's attention. That's all. He needs to know what I'm here to tell him."

A subtle shift in his expression—he's finally decided to take me seriously. *Abide. Should your passage be permitted, I will come for you.*

"No more fucking spells either."

Abide, he says, and dissolves into a swirl of sunlight.

The Living Palace is kind of impressive, because, y'know, building a vast intricate castle out of stone is one thing. Takes a long time and everything, sure—but how long does it take to *grow* one?

Hundreds of trees—thousands—woven together as they grew. Sequoia or something. Old beyond years and vast beyond conception. Gently teased together, shaped, and polished, self-supporting in a branching structure hundreds of feet tall, far beyond the height of any trees on Earth, at least since there's been people around to look at them. It so ridiculously transcends description that the only useful comparison would be to Yggdrasil, and even that doesn't do it justice.

Deliann told me once that the Mithondion stronghold had been designed and begun by his grandfather Panchasell—the same fey who created the *dil T'llan*—ten thousand years ago. Until you actually see the fucking thing, those are just words. And then you walk in and somebody takes you to the Heartwood Hall, which is the formal audience chamber of the Mithondionne kings and just a hair too small for dragons to play rugby in, and you realize that you are standing inside a living being who is roughly the same age as human civilization . . .

Language fails.

It's worth mentioning that the place has kicked all my usual cocky so far up my ass that it's coming out my eyeballs. It's not an overstatement to say that awe doesn't have much hold on me, and *reverence* is a word I'd have to look up to be sure what it means, but when I walk up onto the Flame, a round red-gleaming disk inlaid in front of the royal gallery, it's all I can do to not fall to my knees.

Five primals up on the gallery, two males, two females, and one don't-make-me-pick. The Mithondionne is easy to spot; not only is he the tallest of them, his waist-length gleaming platinum fall of hair has one black swipe thick as my thumb that runs from his backswept widow's peak down over the front of his left shoulder, and ends exactly at the filigreed basket-hilt of his rapier.

Your name. He doesn't pretend he's actually speaking; his bloodless lips stay tight-drawn in a grim flat line, and the words have the dry-leaf rattle of that Whisper Kierendal favors.

"Dominic Shade."

Is not your name, feral. A flicker of annoyance from the Ravenlock at the other male—the "voice" is the same, but it's a good bet it's coming from the other guy. *Twist your heart and knot your will, your lips each dark truth bespill—*

"Yeah, keep trying." Already with the spells. So much for awe and reverence and shit. "Like I explained to that Quelliar guy, I'm not feral. I'm from the Quiet Land. And my name is whatever I say it is."

All of a sudden there's so much rustling it sounds like a burst of static inside my skull. The Ravenlock takes a step forward and cuts them off with an abrupt slice of one hand. He says aloud, "Speak to us of our son, and their brother."

His voice is dark and clear and inhumanly pure as the toll of an obsidian bell, and I can feel it clutch at my will—no subtlety there, a straightforward Dominate. I show him my teeth. "Ask me nicely."

His face goes even tighter. "The tricks you use to resist us? I myself taught those to your Ironhand half a millennium gone, friar. We have powers no Monastic Discipline can counter."

"First, I'm retired. Second, thanks for reminding me why I hate you fuckers. I came here to *help* you, goddammit. At considerable expense, and risk of my mortal fucking life, I found your son, and that was just to buy a chance to *talk* to you, because I know you arrogant shit-humping cunts treat humans like we're rats in your fucking bedrooms. And third—"

I spread my hands. "You want to do this with me? Make a move, elf-king. I've got powers of my own."

Before he can decide how much I might be bluffing, the taller of the two females steps up to his side and puts a hand on his elbow. "Peace, my lord," she says. "Humanity has done yeoman's service for House Mithondionne in former days. Presume, if you will, that this mortal may be himself an inheritor of the debt we owe the Ironhand and the Godslaughterer."

"Yeah, funny that you mention those guys—"

She turns her gaze on me, and some blinding grief behind her eyes cuts me off like a slap in the mouth. "If it please you, my lord Dominic Shade, share with me the news you have of my son."

"I'm no lord, and—" Oh, crap. Fuck me inside out. "*Your* son?"

"Two and a half centuries have passed since I last had word of my Torronell; I have mourned in private the death of my son, and carry that grief to this day. Lift it from my heart, and you will have the friendship of House Mithondionne as long as I yet walk the glades of day."

Which won't be as long as she thinks, but let that go. "I apologize, my lady. I . . . lost my own mother many years ago. Somehow it's always kind of a surprise that other people have mothers at all."

Which also leaves me completely unprepared to look Torronell's mother in the eye and say, *Oh, sure, your youngest son's a junkie rough trade cock-whore fucking humans in Ankhana.*

"Torronell is the leafmaster for a very exclusive entertainment establishment in a human city. He has a sterling professional reputation and a considerable following. I wouldn't call him happy, but he takes justifiable pride in his widely acknowledged expertise."

She inclines her head fractionally. "And if I 'ask you nicely' to share the rest of what you still conceal—?"

"I will respectfully decline, my lady."

"Will you—" She folds her hands and lowers her head. "Will you tell me where he is? How he can be found?"

"I won't. And before you start looking for him—if you send someone for him, or go yourself—you should probably first ask yourself how much truth you can bear to know."

Her eyes drift shut. "Ah."

"And, y'know, how much truth *he* can bear for you to know."

"Yes." Her voice has gone hushed, crumpled like a wad of paper. "Can you take a message to him?"

"No."

Her head comes up sharply. "You will not?"

"I'm in the middle of something."

Her lips peel back, and something sparks in her eyes that hints where Torronell gets his ferocious temper. "What business can a feral have more important than the life and honor of a prince of the First Folk?"

"I told you: I'm from the Quiet Land. We call it Earth." I nod at the Ravenlock. "When your father Bound the *dil T'llan*, there were a few hundred million humans in the Quiet Land. Right now there's almost thirteen *billion*. More every day. Not long ago, we figured out how to get to this world without using the *dillin* at all. The *dil T'llan* is useless. We're here, and it'll get worse. Within fifty years, your kingdom will be dust, and your people extinct."

Now all five of them might as well have been carved from alabaster.

"While I'm here, I should also mention that I know about Pirichanthe. I know the shit you tried to make sure nobody would ever learn. All of it."

The Ravenlock steps forward and the temperature in the Heartwood Hall drops twenty degrees. "This is impossible."

"Yeah, so am I."

He just looks blank.

"I'm only mostly human," I tell him. "Pirichanthe goes tits up a little less than fifty years from now. Which means various gods are busily back-chaining causality until pretty soon they're gonna unhappen the Deomachy."

"It cannot be done."

"Just trying will probably destroy the world."

"And what are you, that you know so much of what has not yet happened? A prophet? Some furtive godling escaped from beyond the walls of time?"

"I'm an angel."

I guess we're past the whole filthy human stuff, because they're all too polite to laugh in my face.

"Technically, I'm the theophanic fetch of a man who'll be born a little more than a year from now, in the Quiet Land. When he grows up, he's gonna be . . . well, involved . . . in the destruction of the Covenant. That's how I know all this shit. He's gonna make a deal with one of the gods to try and limit the damage. That god created me a couple of months ago, local time. He created me specifically to come here and see you, and tell you this."

"And why did this god not simply appear to me himself in a blare of celestial trumpets and a pillar of fire reaching to the stars themselves?"

"What part of *limit the damage* do you not understand? The god trusts me to do shit back here because I—well, him, the guy I look like—we have a couple of useful traits. You must have noticed my Shell."

His eyes narrow warily. "It's . . . unusual."

"Black, right? The only Flow that goes into or out of me is black. Remind you of anybody?"

He takes his time answering. Finally, all I get out of him is, "Yes. I knew him."

"Your Dominates and Charms and all the rest, I don't need Control Disciplines to break them. Not really. Read my mind. Try. Truthsense, divination, magickal detection, none of that shit works on me when I don't want it to. Not anymore."

"The Godslaughterer was thus," the Ravenlock admits. "But you are no Jereth."

"Believe it." I shrug at him. "I'm here because we know what you did. The whole story: the *dil T'llan*, the Butcher's Fist, and the Sword of Man."

"What you know is not remotely the whole story."

"Okay. But there's a part of the story I know that you don't. There's a fix. A little tricky, but you can do it."

"Fix the Covenant? Save Pirichanthe?"

"No. That's time-bound, and can't be changed. What we can do, though, is make it break the way *we* want it to, you follow? Like I said before: limit the damage."

"And how do you and your god suggest this be accomplished?"

"Bind a different Power. Pirichanthe is . . . kind of a blunt instrument, right? If Pirichanthe could have done what you needed it to do, the First Folk would still rule the planet. Instead, what's left of you is hiding out here in the woods."

"What sort of different power?"

"Back in the Quiet Land, there was a guy named Alexander Pope who wrote, 'An honest man is the noblest work of God.' And there was another guy a hundred years later, by the name of Robert Ingersoll, who had a better idea. He wrote, 'An honest god is the noblest work of man.' "

He stares in frank disbelief. "You want me to *create* a god?"

"All I need is a place for it to live. And I need it to be able to open or close the *dillin*. That's all."

"Do you have any conception of the magnitude of what you're asking?"

"And there's one more problem. It can't actually happen until fifty years from now."

"This is completely preposterous."

"I wouldn't believe it either, except for one thing."

"Which is?"

I shrug. "The god you'll make it for? He's the one I made the deal with."

The scene assembles itself from smoke, dust, and stars. Deep in an aspen grove, embers of a campfire banked with earth. A lean-to built of hide and bones bleached pale by the crescent moon. A shelter, round like a tepee, except with vertical walls six or seven feet high—I disremember what it's called. Not wigwam. Dad would know. Hell, he probably built this one.

Pacing a wide, slow circle around the little camp, Angvasse keeps watch.

Jesus. No wonder she drinks. How uptight do you have to be before you can't relax even in your dreams?

I close my eyes. When I open them again, I'm sitting beside the fire. "Angvasse."

Blue witchfire limns a girl-shaped shadow that moves warily toward me. "How did you get here?"

"I'm not here. Neither are you, really. We need to talk."

"Where did you come from?"

"Outside your head."

She stops. "I don't understand."

"You're asleep."

"This is a dream?"

"An altered state of consciousness. The First Folk call it the Meld."

"This is being *done* to me? By *elves*?"

"Done with you. Nothing will happen to you here that you don't consent to." My wave takes in the camp and the trees and the night around.

"This is all just, like, a frame of reference. I'm still in Mithondion. With the Ravenlock. He wants to meet you. He wants to talk with us. Together."

"To what end?"

"He needs to figure out if what we're asking him to do is even possible."

"What?"

"He says that without the Butcher's Fist and the Sword of Man, it can't be done."

"The Accursèd Blade and the Hand of Peace—"

"Whatever."

"—are in Purthin's Ford. What will be Purthin's Ford. In that place you call the *dil T'llan*."

"He says they're not. He's says they *can't* be. Creating the Covenant of Pirichanthe unmade them both."

"Yet they exist. The Blade, at least. Did you not tell him?"

"I told him everything."

A flicker of worry rumples her forehead. "Everything? Including—"

"He needs to know."

"Aren't you afraid that giving him knowledge of what is to come might change the future?"

"I'm afraid we *won't* change the future. All I could tell him is how things will go if we fail here." I spread my hands. "He found it pretty persuasive."

She considers this with a sober nod. "Yet if the Hand and the Blade are destroyed—"

"Not destroyed. Unmade. Or, like, un-Bound."

"There's a distinction?"

"He seems to think so." I beckon. "Come over here and close your eyes."

She does. I close mine too. "Okay, open them again."

When we do, the Ravenlock is with us.

He floats in the darkness, shining with power brighter than the moon. Huh—reminds me of how Kris used to talk about the *lios alfar*. His arms extend before him, fingers questing, eyes closed, on his face transcendent serenity. The light from his body pulses like a living thing and gathers itself upon Angvasse's brow into a halo of grace.

He's reading her. Whatever he finds, I hope he likes it.

She turns to him with grave dignity. "I give you greeting, good fey. I am honored by your presence. Are you to be addressed as Your Majesty?"

His eyes open, the light fades, and he settles silently to earth. "Your Ladyship may address me as Ravenlock."

She may? Son of a bitch.

"Your Majesty does me too much honor."

"On the contrary. May I call you Angvasse?"

What the hell is going on here?

She inclines her head fractionally. "Of course, Ravenlock. I am glad of this meeting, though I would have chosen to meet under less dire circumstance, had such a choice been offered. Please excuse the state of my garments, and please take no offense from my standing in your presence."

"You are well-spoken, for a Khryllian."

"Your Majesty is very kind to say so. You've had experience with the Order of Khryl?"

Jesus Christ. Get a fucking room.

"I've had experience of Khryl," he says softly. "I knew him well, and was proud to name him friend."

Okay, now that's interesting.

Angvasse stops, blinking. A frown gathers on her forehead. "Again, I apologize for my inattention, but I thought I heard you say you *knew* Our Lord of Battle?"

"I know your Lord of Battle only by His reputation—which among the First Folk is sadly unsavory, as one might imagine. But I did know Khryl, and admired him. You resemble him a great deal, did you know that?"

"I—" She sways, just a little. "May I sit?"

"Of course." He gestures, and out of the night coalesce three comfortable-looking armchairs, already arranged around the campfire. The Ravenlock takes the big one, and we settle in and the chairs are as comfortable as they look and if I think about this too much I'll probably fall right through the seat.

"What Khryl was, and what he is thought to have been, are not the same," the Ravenlock says. "The political ambitions of the Lipkan Empire required a Lord of Battle, to be the obedient son and handboy of Dal'kannith Wargod, and so thus He has been worshipped, and so thus He has become. In life, Khryl hated Dal'kannith with a loathing that beggars my powers of description; war was the opposite of everything Khryl valued. The opposite of everything he stood for."

Angvasse looks like her whole life just collapsed around her ears. "But—if Khryl was no Lord of Battle and never hoped to be . . . what *was* He?"

"He was a hero, child," the Ravenlock says gently. Almost regretfully. "Very like yourself."

"Like . . ." Her eyes are wide and they start to glisten with tears. "I? A hero . . . like *Khryl*? I am only a mortal woman—"

"At the end, he too was only a mortal man. He surrendered deity when he began what men now call the Deomachy."

I sit forward. "*Khryl* began the Deomachy? That's not how we learn it in the Monasteries."

"Because thus was his will," the Ravenlock says. "He surrendered his name with his immortality, as did his twin."

"Twin . . . ? *Wait* a second—are you trying to tell me—"

"*Jantho* and *Jereth* are, in a tongue so ancient not even the First Folk still speak it, words for *dawn* and *dusk*."

"Dawn and dusk . . ." I hear myself mutter. "Light and dark."

"Yes. Also beginning and end."

"Jantho—Khryl—began the Deomachy . . ."

"Because the other gods would have destroyed all existence with their infantile squabbling. Khryl was always the protector of humanity—he it was who, in human tales of the time, stole fire from the sun, and taught men its secrets."

"And Jantho—*Khryl*—founded the *Monasteries*?"

"After his maiming and the loss of his brother, he hoped that he might teach men to turn to each other, instead of to gods."

"His maiming . . . the Butcher's Fist . . ."

"Thus he earned his epithet Ironhand, for of such was forged its replacement."

"Holy shit. And all this time, we never suspected . . ."

"As he intended. The enchantment to conceal the truth of Pirichanthe was to conceal the truth of Khryl and his brother as well."

"And Jereth—?"

The Ravenlock's eyes go distant. "Before he chose mortality, Jereth was called only 'the Dark Man.' If he ever had a name, I do not know it; no human being would willingly speak it, for fear of drawing his gaze."

"What, like a god of death?"

"A god of murder. The god of massacre. Of every kind of killing, and the black despair that attends both victim and villain. The bitterest enemy of Khryl's light and hope."

"Twins. Opposites." Dad would recognize the trope instantly: Osiris and Set. No, wait—Nissyen and Evnissyen. "Why would a god of murder give up immortality to fight beside his worst enemy?"

"He never said." The Ravenlock shakes his head just barely enough that I can see it. "When I spoke of it to Jantho, he would say only that dark knows love even as does light, and love's power springs as much from despair as from hope."

Angvasse's eyes have gone dark as the sky. "And His loving brother maimed Him forever."

"It was the price of Pirichanthe. And he devoted the rest of his mortal days to the service of what he believed was the best hope for humanity. He gave up eternity to help men who would never know him. Who would, he hoped, someday come to curse his name."

"Curse him . . ."

"And then to make of his name a thing of derision. Contempt and scorn, and finally only an empty, obscure jest."

"I cannot imagine . . . and you claim my heart resembles . . . You do not understand. He might have chosen scorn, as you say. But I *deserve* it. You—you have no . . . I am so desperately unworthy . . ."

Her voice fails and she turns away, and the horse-witch is there, at her shoulder, sitting on her heels in Angvasse's shadow like a Fantasy conjured by the night and the stars, and her voice is too soft to be heard across the fire but in the ember-glow I can read her lips.

Hero is a word. You are more than a word. Don't be afraid.

Be who you are.

I blink, blink again, and frown at her. "What the hell are you doing here? When did you get here? *How* did you get here?"

She gives me the witch-eye, cold as frozen milk. "I go where my work takes me."

I'll have to take that for an answer. I know better than to argue with the witch-eye.

"Greeting to you," the Ravenlock says softly, coaxingly, like he's calming a spooked horse. "And well-met."

"Thanks. Likewise."

"How are you called in this time?"

"The horse-witch. I don't mind."

"I have not seen you since the Binding, I think. Some five hundred years."

The Binding . . . ? Wait—*five* hundred years?

She shrugs. "I don't like forests."

"As well I recall," he says, and they go on and make chitchat for a while during which I entirely lose the thread of their conversation, because I really can't get my fucking mind around it.

Eventually I can't hold it in. "You were *there? You?*"

"I have been to interesting places," the horse-witch says, "and seen—"

"Exotic things, yeah, I know, but—hot staggering *fuck*! Were you ever gonna tell me?"

"I didn't think I had to."

"Jesus Christ, you're worse than Angvasse! What in eight ways to ass-fuck would make you think you didn't need to, y'know, mention in *passing* that you happened to be *present* at the Binding of the Covenant of moth-erfucking *Pirichanthe*?"

She shrugs at me. "You were there too."

I sit there. For a long time. Just sit.

It doesn't help. There's no way I'm gonna convince myself she's just making that up.

And the really fucking appalling thing is that I'm the only one ap-palled.

I can give Angvasse a pass, I guess; she's kind of going through some-thing of her own right now. The Ravenlock just frowns at me, then says to the horse-witch, "I don't see it."

"That's because you think he's a person."

"*Excuse* me?"

"I'm sorry, did you not know this?" She looks like she really is sorry. She looks like it hurts her to upset me. "You said yourself how the god built you and the girl for this purpose."

"Well, yeah, but—I mean, you didn't say anything about me not being a person. Not being human. I mean, you won't. When I meet you."

She shrugs. "It may be that recalling how I've upset you tonight will make me avoid the subject, because I'm not good at tact. Or it may be that the you I will meet will actually be a human person. He'll have to ask me then."

"Oh." The Ravenlock stares at me, his voice gone small with awe. "I see it now—and I ken now why he cannot be read as men are read. He was the Weapon . . ."

"I was the—wait, *what* weapon?"

"I understand now," the Ravenlock says slowly. "Many things begin to make sense. Black Flow—joined with Jereth, not part of him. Lunatic confidence. Inhuman self-possession. Single-minded ruthlessness. With-out fear, without doubt. Without regret and without mercy."

"Yeah, okay, except I've got my share of self-doubt, and I get scared all the time. Shit, I'm scared right *now*—"

"That's because you still think you're human," the horse-witch says. "You'll get over it."

"Oh, for fuck's *sake*."

"And self-loathing is not self-doubt."

"Well, okay, self-loathing, then. What kind of weapon hates itself?"

"A knife that thinks it's a spade," the Ravenlock replies gently.

Angvasse looks thoughtful. "A sword that can't understand why it's such a poor plowshare."

Now I can't even really fucking breathe.

"There is what a thing is thought to be," the Ravenlock says, "and there is what a thing is. You can't be intimidated. You can't be bargained with. You can't be diverted, or persuaded, or deceived. Your every gesture displays the elegance of pure destruction."

And again, all I can do is sit there.

It still doesn't help.

Professional Tallman, my personal combat instructor at the Studio Conservatory, was mostly an idiot, but he knew a thing or two about swordplay, and he could throw down the kenjutsu like nobody I've ever seen. When we started on basic sword, he opened the class by asking us what, exactly, a sword is.

Because, y'know, sure, you can use a sword to clear brush, but you're better off with a scythe and an axe. And you can use it to loosen dirt, but a pick does it better. You can use it to cut fabric or rope, or even carve wood; you can use it for all kinds of shit, but none of those are what it's for. None of those are what it *is*.

The answer Tallman was looking for was "A sword is a tool for killing."

No matter what you try to make it do.

"Very well then," the Ravenlock says. He inclines his head toward the horse-witch. "Thank you for your insight. Will you be there when we arrive?"

The horse-witch shrugs. "Ogrilloi make me nervous."

"Arrive?" I frown at him. "We're going?"

"The attempt will be made."

He fades into darkness, and Angvasse evaporates along with the forest and the campfire and as the stars go out, the last thing I see is the witch-eye, pale as the moon.

Permission to be who you are.

Standing by the figurehead of the Mithondion flagship, looking out upon the Ravenlock's landfleet spreading across a fair chunk of the northern Boedecken, I can't help reflecting for the thousandth or millionth time that the Living Palace should have been my first clue that this family doesn't do anything small.

The flagship isn't really the size of an aircraft carrier, or even a battleship, but it still kind of feels like one because it's the biggest fucking thing I ever thought to see rolling over grassland. The main deck would make a fair approximation of a football field, and the abbey, my mansion from my superstar days in San Francisco, could get lost in a corner of the main hold. I don't know how the gigantic rollers it rides on are engineered, but the sheer size of the thing gives it an almost ridiculously smooth ride—not to mention flattening and compacting the earth over which we roll into a reasonable facsimile of pavement. Where we pass, we leave a road.

The landships aren't built, they're grown, woven of living trees—some kind of banyan, I think, given that the massive hawsers trailing from its hull are braided of peripheral rootlike tendrils that seek out the earth whenever we stop, and dig into the ground to nourish the ship as well as anchor it. Those same hawsers connect to the yokes of the landships' motive power: instead of engines, we have ogrilloi.

Lots of ogrilloi.

The flagship complement alone must be four or five thousand. They make a solid mass just barely wider than the flagship and almost a mile long—maybe two thousand to haul at any given time, with some insanely complicated substitution system, continuously moving fresh grills in to take over so tired grills can fall out and rest . . . which they do by jogging along our freshly flattened trail.

I can't even guess how fast we're actually going; I mean, I know how fast unburdened ogrilloi can run, but judging by how the distant mountains are getting visibly less distant, we're going a *lot* faster than that. The Ravenlock—in his cabin preparing the ritual—can't be bothered to explain how, and none of the rest of the bastards will talk to me at all. To be fair, they're all busy too—over a hundred primal mages on the flagship alone, all conjuring like hell, throwing out so much power I can see it even without mindview: heat shimmer and miragelike mirror flashes and somehow it's like every step counts for ten or something. Twenty. So fast I start to worry we'll get there before the horse-witch, Angvasse, and Dad.

I really don't want the Ravenlock to think we've been stood up.

Needn't have worried—when the sun one morning sparks the cliffline into view, the trail of smoke twisting up into the sky's blinding blue is visible even to me. It comes from the tip of the escarpment, probably right by the little passage that is the only way from the vertical city into the upland.

The landfleet spreads out like a wave that'll break against the base of the cliff.

We're here.

Dusk shades blue into the softly falling snow. My knees hurt from sitting here on the ground so long, at the tip of the escarpment, but I don't feel inclined to move.

Spread below me is the vast Mithondion landfleet, ground-tethered, campfires and roasting meat and tens of thousands of ogrilloi. Bigger than the Black Knife Nation. Smaller than Purthin's Ford. A couple hundred yards behind my left shoulder, the flagship looms like a Mission District Labor tenement.

Everything comes back to here.

There's enough snow on the ground now that Angvasse's boots crunch a little as she comes up behind me. "Are you well?"

"I'm all right." Not really, but what's the point yapping about it? "I wish she was here."

"Ogrilloi make her witch-herd nervous."

"They make me nervous too."

Angvasse lowers herself to the white-dusted grass beside me, with a sigh as faint and hopeless as the wind. "It is . . . eerie," she murmurs, staring down at the badlands. "To see the lights, and know that they are not lamps and hearths of goodmen in city windows, but instead campfires of elves and their brutish warriors . . ."

"Yeah." I twitch a nod back toward the yurt that stands alone beyond our tiny fire. "Any progress? Anybody say anything? Anything at all?"

"Nay. No sound. No motion. Doubtless some eldritch magicks let them commune in silence."

"Or they both fell asleep."

She tilts her head. "Do elves sleep?"

I shrug. "When they want to, I guess."

They're not asleep. Whatever else T'ffarrell Mithondionne and Dad have been doing in there all these hours, it hasn't been sleeping. I don't even really want to know.

I just want it to be over.

"I never . . ." Angvasse gives another of those faint sighs, and starts again. "I never knew my father."

For a while I watch her, while memories of Dad—some good—unspool behind my eyes. I can't imagine my life without him.

Eventually all I can say is, "I'm sorry."

She nods, pensive rather than melancholy. "But I did know love, in my uncle's house. I was loved."

I match her nod. "So was I. In my father's."

"Somehow it seems that should make things easier."

"Yeah." I stare out into the darkening snow. "Except it's mostly the opposite."

Sometime later, a subtle shift in the light draws her eyes. She glances over her shoulder, then heaves herself to her feet. "He's coming out."

I don't look. "Okay."

"I'll withdraw."

Which tells me which him we're talking about. "Okay."

The crunch of his footsteps is uneven, almost erratic—like he keeps stopping but then keeps deciding he should come a little closer. "That was . . . quite the conversation."

I don't bother to answer.

"The Ravenlock . . . well, he's an extraordinary creature. What he proposes to do . . ."

"Did you agree? Are you going through with it?"

"I . . . didn't want to."

"But you will."

"What we talked about—"

"Yeah, I know, all the lore and shit. You can write a fucking book."

"He says I *will* write a book. *Tales of the First Folk*."

It's kind of like being slapped on the top of my head. Now I do turn and look without knowing really what the fuck I'm expecting to see. All I get is his big shadow silhouetted against the campfire behind him . . . but I can read his posture like most people read road signs. "You want to give me that again?"

"We didn't talk about lore," he says. "The lore—he put it in my head. He says it's the only thing I'll remember. He says I'll wake up back in Thorncleft with the worst headache I'll ever have, but I'll be able to transcribe everything he gave me. Which will get me my doctorate and a professorship, and marriage to the woman I love. And a son."

"So you were really talking about—"

"My future. *Our* future." His silhouette shifts like he wants to reach for me but he's afraid I'll rip his arm off. "He told me who you are."

Fuck.

My head gains a couple tons.

"I'm not your son."

"He explained that. May I sit?"

"No."

"I'm sorry?"

"Want me to spell it?" Now I'm on my feet and I don't remember getting up. I don't remember getting angry either. "No, we're not having this fucking conversation. We're not gonna talk about my childhood. We're not gonna talk about Mom. We're *not*."

"But—" His shoulders droop, and his weight rocks back on his heels. "But I don't even know your name . . ."

"Fucking make one up when I'm born. It doesn't matter. You won't remember me when you wake up, and by tomorrow morning I'll be fucking dead. Leave it alone."

"Dead—? He didn't say anything about anyone . . . well, dying . . ."

"I'm not anyone. I'm any*thing*. And I shouldn't say dead. It's more like destroyed."

"I don't understand . . ." His palms turn upward as though he can cup comprehension and drink it like water from his hands. "A thousand primal mages. Twenty-five thousand ogrilloi. And me. For a day, and then he puts me back where you got me from, with a book's worth of stories in my head. That's the deal. He didn't say—"

"He didn't say anything about the True Relics?"

"What, the Sword and the Hand? Well, yes, he said they'll be destroyed in the ritual—but they're mostly symbolic, aren't they? Like pieces of the True Cross, or the Holy Grail."

"Not symbolic. Metaphoric. It's not the same thing."

"Of course it isn't, but I'm not sure about the pertinence of the distinction you're making here."

"It's pretty straightforward." I wave a hand toward Angvasse, a dim ghost-shape in the snow. "Angvasse there. You probably got to know her a little on your way up here. Notice anything strange about her?"

"Beyond being a superhero?"

"She's not human. Neither am I."

"What is she, then?"

"She's the Hand of Khryl."

"The hell you say."

"And me . . ." A little sigh, and little shrug, and an all-over weird-ass chill from finally, after all this time, actually saying it out loud . . .

"I'm the Sword of Man."

the now of always 7

THE ART OF UNHAPPENING

THE ART OF
UNHAPPENING

"Some of our theoretical thaumatologists have speculated that unhappened events cast a shadow on reality—an echo—that might be expressed as fiction, or legend, or myth."

—READING MASTER OF THORNCLEFT

Kris kneels in the snow, his head lowered. He neither moves nor speaks, and from his face drip tears that chime faintly as they strike ground, where they become a scatter of glittering gemstones.

Duncan watches him for some considerable time before he turns his head back toward Caine. "You're the Sword of Man?"

"Maybe." He shrugs. "A lot depends on who you let draw that blade from your chest. Those conversations with the Ravenlock might be among the consequences. Besides, the Sword-of-Man thing—remember how I was talking about metaphors? I think it's close enough to say I might be—potentially—a physical expression of the same metaphysical energy that the Sword of Man expressed."

"Kind of a mouthful."

"It gets worse from here."

"He's just warming up," the horse-witch says. "He thinks that the more words you use to explain something, the better you understand it."

Duncan lifts an eyebrow at her. "A little hard on him, aren't you?"

She smiles. "He likes that in a woman."

And when he looks at Caine, the killer wears a smile so fond and happy and playfully wicked all together that Duncan finds himself smiling with them. "He probably gets that from my side of the family."

"Of course."

"Hari . . ." Kris is there, a hand on Caine's shoulder.

Caine rises, and Kris gathers him into an embrace. "Whatever happens, Hari, thank you for this. No matter what. Just to . . . see my family again. Just once. To see them whole and hale . . . it means more to me than I can say."

"You're welcome," Caine says. "It gets better."

"It does?"

"You ain't seen nuthin' yet."

"The . . . project . . . you asked my father to attempt . . . did he succeed?"

"Dunno."

"It's one of those, then."

"Yeah. We'll find out when we try. It'll work, or it won't."

"The Power you hope to Bind, to control the *dil T'llan* . . . what is it?"

"I'm not telling."

"Hari—"

"No. Sorry."

"You told me once that there were only three people you ever really trusted. One of them was your father and the other two were me."

"Still true." He nods toward the horse-witch. "Except now it's four."

"Four?"

"Five. You remember Orbek."

"Yes, of course."

"Six. Avery Shanks."

"Oh, come *on*."

"Seven. Raithe."

"*Raithe?*"

"It's complicated. Look, I didn't tell any of them either, all right? All I need from you is a yes or a no. Go or no go. What you saw? I can make that real."

"You treated Rroni very badly."

"Yeah, and I paid for it."

"You were very cruel and demeaning. And you thought worse than you said."

"Soliloquy. Not thought."

Kris nods, and a gentle smile takes over the sadness in his face.

"Rroni . . . I suppose it might be worth allowing to happen. Just for your astonishment when he kicked the shit out of you."

"I wouldn't go *that* far—"

"He beat you like a rented mule he rode to an old-fashioned country ass-whuppin'."

"All right, all right." Caine waves a hand. He's done playing. "You need to take this seriously, Kris. You need to think it through. It's not a choice you get to take back. And you're just about the only person in recorded history who can say 'Caine, don't do that,' and have the slimmest chance I won't."

"I can't imagine why I would say no."

"That's because you haven't thought it through. The issue for you here isn't my plan. It's not what I want the Ravenlock to do. Succeed or fail or something in between. The issue for you is what I did by accident."

"By accident?"

"I got in a fight with your brother."

"I don't understand."

"Rroni's got skills. He also had an assload of sharps that ended up with my blood all over them."

His eyes pop wide. "Your blood . . ."

"I asked you if you'd take back the worst thing you ever did," Caine says darkly. "What's in my blood?"

"Oh, my heart . . ." Deliann's knees buckle. Caine catches him and helps him sit down instead of fall down. "Rroni . . ."

"Yeah. So entirely due to my own fucking stupidity, I potentially infected the most sought-after whore in Ankhana with Pallas Ril's countervirus to HRVP."

"He'll never catch it at all . . ." Deliann whispers. "Ever . . ."

"Yeah. Neither will Kierendal, or Tup. Or Toa-Sytell. Or anyone else. And after Torronell meets you thirty years later, you take him back to Mithondion . . ."

"Oh, my god."

"You understand this isn't exactly good news. When you get to that village, all your friends will already be immune. Hell, the feyin in the village might be immune already. They might never get it in the first place. No HRVP outbreak might mean you never kidnap J'Than. I never recognize you. Caine never returns to Overworld. And there's no way to know what comes after that."

"Hari, my god—my *god*! You could *unhappen* Shanna's *murder*!"

"Maybe. There's no way to know. This is what the Giant Brains at the Monasteries call an acausal loop. Curing HRVP before anybody here catches it might mean Pallas Ril never creates the countervirus in the first place."

"What happens then?"

"Nobody knows for sure. There are theories. People think most likely the unhappening will itself unhappen . . . though there are complications there too, and basically nobody agrees with anybody else. Best case? She or somebody else still creates the countervirus for some other reason, and the rest of the shit goes close enough to the previous events that we end up more or less here."

"Except my family will be alive. My people."

"They might die from something else."

"Deliann." The horse-witch gives him an infinitesimal *don't worry* headshake. "There are better best cases."

"Don't help." Caine scowls out into the snow like something's wrong. "Kris, we're up against it. Yes or no."

"Up against it? Up against what?"

"It's stopped snowing."

Duncan twists his neck to look around. Not only has it stopped snowing, there is grass softening what had been naked rock, and wildflowers uncoil new blossoms toward the sun.

"Company." Angvasse sounds grim.

"Oh, you think?"

"Caine. I await your word."

"Don't wait. If this goes south, nail that bitch to the fucking ground. I'll sort it out later."

"Hari—Caine," Duncan says, "what bitch? What's happening?"

"The gods have found us. They're sending an enforcer. To stop us. To kill me, probably."

Angvasse puts on her helm. "You shouldn't have spoken Her name."

"An *enforcer*? Are you in danger? Are we?"

Up from the grassy earth spring saplings that creak and groan as if in agony as they twist upward, flowering and leafing and multiplying into the distance: hickory, birch, and elm and maple and walnut and oak, and the escarpment has become a glade filled with green, sunbeams, and birdsong.

"Um, yeah." Caine sighs. "It's my wife."

"Late wife," the horse-witch says.

Now in that glade a Presence arises, gathering Itself of sunlight and blossom and the dark earth rich with every life returning, and here She is in the midst of them.

devices and maneuvers

RUN AND GUN

RUN AND GUN

> *"Because there is a time to be smart and careful and look*
> *before you leap, and there is a time to just rock and fucking*
> *roll."*
>
> —CAINE
>   *Blade of Tyshalle*

The sign on the padlocked roller gate read—

CLOSED FOR THE JUSTICE
REOPEN TWO HOURS PAST SUNSET

—in Westerling, Lipkan, and English. He thought this was uncharacteristically generous of the Actors and Social Police who ran this place, as all but the overseers were grills and thus had virtually no rights at all. On the other hand, Tourann had implied that the miners at BlackStone were Intacts, which might mean that the mine had been closed in self-defense. Keeping a couple thousand ogrilloi away from the show could turn ugly in a hurry. The extra two hours were probably cushion to give management enough time to see if there would be riots.

Didn't matter who won and who lost. Riots either way.

The fences were only anodized chain link with coils of razor wire at top and bottom—they wouldn't stop a determined invader, but they'd slow people down. Most people. Somebody preternaturally strong and fully armored—like, say, Tyrkilld—could go through razor wire and chain link without breaking stride.

The gatehouse was Earth-style: a small cinder-block box with windows all around. Gaslights were already on inside; clouds like sheets of granite cast gloom thick as dusk. Looked like five or six guys in there, which meant that some guys who should have been walking the wire had instead decided to hang out and grouse about being stuck here working while everybody else had the afternoon off.

He stopped at the gate, scuffed up a handful of loose gravel, and tossed it, not gently, against the gatehouse's nearest window. Very shortly a door opened and a pissed-off gatekeeper stomped out, already yelling about not throwing shit at his gatehouse before he made it far enough out to see who was throwing.

He was pretty sure the guy would recognize him. A saddler in River-dock had been so impressed by the unexpected appearance of Lady Khlay-lock at his workshop that he had enthusiastically donated several yards of soft black leather. Kravmik was nearly as accomplished a seamster as he was a chef; he'd built the whole outfit from cuffs to collar in no more than an hour. A few minutes had sufficed to attach the various sheaths to hold his various knives. It didn't fit very well, and it wasn't comfortable—had his leathers ever been?—but fit and comfort weren't issues. Not today.

He had ditched Jonathan Fist's comfortably sturdy travel clothes at the Pratt & Redhorn, and left his name with them.

The gate guy jolted to a stop, squinting disbelief. "Sweet mother of crap," he said. "It's you."

"It's me."

"Guys! Guys, you have to come *out* here—it's fucking *Caine!*"

The guys piled out the door and very shortly they had reached a general consensus that it was, in fact, Caine. Immediately after that, they all wanted to know how he'd gotten there and what he was doing and what had he been up to these last three years and did he know they'd opened Earthside transit and—

"Yeah, thanks. I had no fucking clue what you people do here," he said. "That's why I came. Because I had no fucking clue. Open the gate."

A couple of them jumped to it. Being a celebrity didn't always suck.

While they rolled the gate door aside, he had a chance to look these clowns over. All six wore sidearms. Four were in clothing bulky enough to conceal body armor, and a couple went back and picked up the light assault carbines they'd leaned against the gatehouse wall.

Yeah: Actors. They all looked familiar to a greater or lesser degree, and a couple tried to remind him of some occasion or other when they had supposedly met. One, though, he knew by description—a tall slender guy with red hair and pale skin who wore his pistol in a breakaway holster strapped to his thigh. "Yeah, I remember you," he said. "Your name's . . . Dale, maybe? Frank? Help me out."

"Deacon Tucker," the tall redhead said. "Call me Deak."

"Yeah, Deak. Sure. You played . . . an assassin? No, that's not right. Some kind of killer, though . . ."

"Duelist," Tucker said. "Blades, magick, bare knuckle, you pick. Choose your weapon and I'm your guy. Mostly contract work. Here on Overworld, people call me the Ember."

"Right, sure, the Ember. Good to see you again."

He nodded amiably. "I'm flattered to be remembered. And it's great to see you. Everybody thinks you're dead."

"Not everybody. Listen, I need to get into your Earth Normal vault—there's a report I have to deliver to management personally."

Tucker nodded just as amiably as before. "Something you couldn't tell them last night? When Tarkanen dragged in your naked bleeding ass and booted it Earthside?"

"I *told* you it wasn't him last night," somebody said to somebody else. "See? What did I tell you? I *told* you."

Tucker fixed him with a level stare that didn't look all that amiable anymore. "Maybe you could tell me who that guy was."

"My evil twin. Who gives a fuck? I'm still on your detain-and-report list, right? That's where you're supposed to take me anyway, so they can tell you what to do with me."

"That's most of why I don't like this shit anymore." He took two steps back and pulled the pistol so smoothly it didn't look fast. It looked magickal. There was nothing magickal, though, about the view down the inside of the barrel. "Toss him a couple strips."

One of the other guys flipped two stripcuffs to the ground at his feet.

"Cuff yourself," Tucker said. "Behind your back. The second cuff hooks the first one to your belt. Tight. Benson—stand behind and watch. Make sure he does it right."

He picked up the cuffs. "It doesn't have to be like this."

"It has to be exactly like this. I haven't shot you already only because I don't want to carry your ass, old man. Hawk was a friend of mine."

"You have shitty taste in friends." He sighed and cuffed himself as directed. "Happy now?"

"I'll be happy when you're dead or Earthside. Until then, I'm figuring you're about to kill me."

He shrugged. "Maybe you should have been nicer."

"Benson, you're with me. The rest of you clowns spread out and get everybody onsite up and ready. *Everybody*. Caine wouldn't be here unless shit's about to get hairy. Clear the buildings. Get people in the hardpoints and snipers on the stacks. Faller's Earthside. I'll report to management."

One guy scowled at him. "Who put you in charge, newbie?"

"You did. When you stood there with your thumb up your ass instead of doing your fucking job." Tucker swung wide to keep his pistol and himself more than ten feet back while letting his prisoner pass. "Benson, cover him. Stay out of my line of fire and for fuck's sake don't shoot *me*. Let's go."

They made cautious progress among the hulking buildings. More and more people came out with more and more weapons. Eventually they reached the mine's office complex. There was only one guy still in there, and Tucker told him to grab a rifle and head up high. They went through Faller's office. The rug was gone, but the walls still showed plenty of fresh-ish bloodspatter. Benson picked up a gas lamp and lit it.

Beyond the office was a straightforward freight cage with two control chains running through the floor.

"Keep him away from the chains." Tucker pulled one and the freight cage lurched into motion. Steam hissed somewhere above, and stacked counterweights clattered upward on braided chains as the cage descended.

They went down for a while. At the bottom, Tucker pulled a stiletto out of his sleeve and spiked the chain to the cage to lock it in place. "In case we have to leave in a hurry."

The tunnels were lined with darkened gaslights. Most were short, connecting enormous low-ceilinged chambers, featureless save for huge hewn pillars left in place during excavation. The floors were level and clean. For short chamber-to-chamber transit there were stairs, or steel ladders bolted to the stone. Longer descents were slants. Down at the bottom of one long descending spiral was a large armored hatch. "Benson—make sure we got no guests down here. I don't want any surprises."

Benson set down the gas lamp, undogged the hatch, and went in. Light from inside was the coolly bluish color of modern fluorescents. A few seconds later he came back out. "It's cool. Nobody home but Anders. It's his watch."

"Good. Thanks," Tucker said, and shot him in the face.

Benson's head snapped back and forward again like it couldn't decide whether to tag along with the burst of blood and bone and brain behind him or run the other way. From inside the office came a shout of *What the fuck?* and the sound of knocked-over chairs and Tucker squealed, "*Anders! Oh, holy shit, Anders—oh my god—*"

From inside the office: "What is it? What's going *on*?"

Tucker fired twice in *very* rapid succession. "Nothing."

From inside the office: a dull sack-of-potatoes thud.

"Jesus Christ."

"He liked little girls," Tucker said darkly. "Really little girls. I couldn't think of any reason he should live through this."

"And Benson?"

He shrugged. "Cheated at cards."

"He cleaned you out and you couldn't figure how."

"I said he cheated, not that I don't."

"What happened to the real Deak Tucker?"

"Couple years ago, he took a gimme—a duel with an aging, slightly dim-witted elder son of a Paqulan baron, who wasn't as old and dim-witted as he pretended." Tucker reholstered his pistol. "Wasn't the baron's son either."

"Nice. Do him yourself?"

"Oh, he's not dead," Tucker said. "Seems somebody Earthside decided to cancel Actors' deadman blocks. Amazing what you get out of people once you start them talking. Not out of any obligation to you for sparing my life or anything, but you should know some people argue you and Deak ought to be neighbors. Next-door neighbors."

"What's your opinion?"

"Well, I ain't much for disputation, Jonnie—"

"Don't do that, huh? It's creepy hearing Tanner's voice come out of your mouth."

Tucker shrugged. "For what it's worth, I keep telling everyone who'll listen that we don't want your kind of trouble."

"Thanks."

"It's self-defense. I'm nervous just being on the same planet."

"Look, Tanner—"

"Tucker." He held up a hand. "Call me by the name of the guy I'm dressed like. And talk like. It's only polite."

"Nice accent you've picked up."

"Figures you'd like it. It's yours." Tucker swung around behind him. "It was hard enough learning English. I don't have time to fuck around with regional dialects. Hold still."

He did. The cuffs went tight, then a single sharp report freed his hands. He rubbed his wrists and shook the knots out of his shoulders. "Good to be on the same side for a change."

"I delivered your message to Damon," he said. "How's life in the witch-herd?"

"Tense. T'Passe read you in?"

"Some. Got actual business in this vault?"

"Some."

"I'll wait out here."

"Okay."

"Place gives me the creeps. Been making excuses to stay out of it all month. No offense, but it's hard to think of any way in which Earth does not suck."

"Plus I might see what you really look like."

"Don't insult me. Like I'd be working an Actor legend wearing nothing but a Seeming."

"Seemings don't work too well on me anyway. What is it?"

"Classified." He nudged the corpse with his toe. "Drag this on in, would you? I can clean up out here."

He picked up Benson's pistol and stuck it behind his belt, then took the dead man's ankles. "Back in five."

BlackStone's Earth Normal vault didn't look like the one in Thorn-cleft's Railhead, naturally enough. The Railhead office was powered by microtransfer imbalance, a source of energy that requires working Winston units; this one . . . hard to say. His first guess had been steam, but the turbine would have to be practically inside the room. Twelve screens distributed among five workstations, and not a single manual keypad among them—hard to believe this room was shielded well enough to make touch-screens reliable—and all of them seemed to be made of the same black composite material, almost like carbon fiber. And all of them appeared to be powered down, including the one the man's corpse lay in front of.

To either side of the screens on each desktop were inset disks of what looked like the same composite, nine or ten inches in diameter. He brushed his fingers across one, to feel the texture, and the screen beside it lit up.

"Oh, like that, is it?" he muttered. He took his fingers off the inset—there was no one on Earth he really wanted to talk to, and actually if Earth found out he was here it would be a serious fucking problem in and of itself—and ducked under the counter to get a look at the workstation from below.

No power cords. Nothing like them. Instead he found a branching array of dark tubing—something disturbingly almost-but-not-quite random about their arrangement. Yeah: blood vessels.

Apparently shit gets weird in the vicinity of the gate.

He stuck one of his boot knives into one of the smallest tubes, about the same size as an I.V. line . . . and it came back out with its tip painted in black oil that was already beginning to smoke.

"Huh." Scratch the *apparently*. "All right, then."

A couple minutes later, he was back out in the corridor with Tucker. He swung the hatch shut and dogged it from the outside. "Time to go."

"What about the office?"

"They're about to have a fire."

An only half-muffled *boom* emphasized his point—and it came with a shock they could feel through the stone, and the hatch buckled and smoke leaked out around the seal and he said, "Okay, more than a fire."

"Now the gate?"

"Can we do it?"

"Hard to say. The gate area is NFP without a Social Police escort."

"NFP?"

"No fucking people. And they've got a couple guys posted at an armored hatch to enforce it. Real armor, not this shit here."

"Not much point hanging around, though."

Tucker shrugged. "This way."

The accessway to the gate itself was down another two and a half levels. The final thirty yards was a corridor-like tunnel, straight and flat and only six or seven feet wide. At the far end, Tucker reported, would be posted a pair of Social Police in full anti-magick armor, assault rifles, grenades, night vision, the works.

"That's fucking inconvenient."

"They're not there to be easy."

"What's your plan?"

Tucker shrugged and handed him something round and heavy. "It may be that stealth has outlived its usefulness."

It was a grenade. "Cool. I'm sick of sneaking around."

"Which is why you'll always be a better Actor than you are an operative."

"So?"

"So nothing. Set down the lamp. It's only another hundred yards."

"Um, I can't Nightsee. All I've got is Discipline."

"I'll point you in the right direction. After that, we can see by the light of burning Social Police."

"Jesus, it's like talking to myself."

"Stop it. You'll hurt my feelings."

"I'm starting to get why nobody likes me."

"Shh."

It was darker than dark. After almost a minute of silently cautious creep, he felt a hand on his left arm. He stopped. His arm was directed to a corner just ahead. He explored it only with his fingertips. Then on his wrist: three fingers, then two, then one, then he triggered his grenade and whipped it sharply around the corner, then flattened himself against the wall and covered his ears with both hands as he felt Tucker do the same. One of the soapies had time to yell *Grenade!* before twin detonations blasted fire all the way back out the mouth of the corridor.

There was a less-welcome sound too: assault rifles on autoburst, suppressing fire. Slugs shrieked out the mouth and shattered against the corridor wall.

"I really have to get myself some of that armor," Tucker said as he leaned around the corner and sprayed fire with his pistol on full auto—two seconds at ten rounds per—and the rifle fire stopped. Tucker slapped in a fresh clip. "Come on."

Flames still licked upward from the residue of whatever the hell the incendiary had been. The two soapies lay like abandoned maquettes, every muscle locked in rictus so extreme that they didn't even look like people—magickal Hold, or something like it. "Holy shit."

Tucker flashed him a grin. "Custom ammo."

"No, really?"

"How about you lend me one of those toadstickers of yours?"

He pulled one of the long fighting knives from inside his tunic. Tucker took it and slid its point under one soapy's helmet below his ear, then jammed it all the way in and gave a twist for good measure. He did the same to the other, then wiped the blade on one's armor and returned it. "When Tucker disappears instead of coming back out, somebody's gonna remember he didn't take away your knives. Now if I need to be him again sometime, all I need is a harrowing story of my narrow escape."

"So if you're loading wildcat rounds that pop their armor, how come the grenades?"

"Knocking on the door," he said. "It only opens from the other side, and I don't know the passcode."

"What if they're not curious? Or too smart to go for it?"

"Hey, you don't like my plan, take over."

"Huh." He looked down at the dead soapies. "Check it out."

Their blood was on fire.

"What the fuck?" Tucker dropped to one knee, and tentatively sniffed the twisting coils of black smoke that came up from beneath their helmets and through rents in their chest armor. Even the swath where he'd wiped the blade was smoldering. "That's not blood. It's not oil either. Not any oil I've ever smelled. Aren't these guys human?"

"More or less." He bent down and put his hand to one's neck wound. The fire went out, and when he pulled his hand back, his fingertips were painted with familiar black goo. "Shit gets weird near the gate."

"What is that gunk?"

"Blood. More or less."

"Like they were more-or-less human?"

"Yeah. It's not their blood. It's their god's. More or less."

"Um . . ."

"You might want to step back." He stuck both hands back down into the oil, and leaned on the dead man's chest to squeeze an extra couple ounces out. "This could get a little entertaining."

"Yeah, good thing. I was about to doze the fuck off."

He stood, raising his hands before him like a scrubbed-in surgeon, and let the black oil roll down his wrists toward his elbows. A couple drops spattered the floor, and instantly kindled greasy flames. Tucker turned kind of sidelong, leaning away as if he hadn't quite made up his mind whether he should bolt. "How come it doesn't burn when it's on you?"

"Same reason it didn't burn those soapies from the inside out. The energy's being used for something else."

"Like what?"

"Shh." He closed his eyes. "This is trickier than it looks."

"It'd have to be."

"Quiet." He breathed himself into mindview. It didn't take long. He'd been practicing.

Images swam into focus inside his head. "Four soapies farside—full enforcement squad, which means one capture-and-detain guy with sticky-foam and tanglefoot and who knows what else, a primary striker and a reserve striker, and one heavy support guy. Not to mention they're behind two dedicated hardpoints."

"Not the best news I've heard today."

"They haven't breached the door because they're waiting for somebody."

"Backup?"

"Front-up. Whoever it is, they're scared. Hot staggering fuck. Make that *what*ever it is. They're about to piss themselves, and I'm not making that up."

And now inside his head, as he sought to slide deeper into the oil after the source of their fear, a vast and ancient consciousness tasted his mind.

And winked at him.

He withdrew with a lurch, and opened his eyes. "Know what it takes to frighten Social Police?"

"Not a clue."

"Me neither. This looks like serious fucking trouble."

"Can you—do whatever it is you're doing—deeper in? Get a look?"

He shook his head. "It fought back. Whatever the fuck it is, it felt me going in, and it wasn't happy about it. Not one little bit. It's stronger than I am. A lot. It's probably what they're expecting."

"You are a fountain of good news. Except not for us."

"It gets better." He had to take a breath and swallow to untie a knot of nausea in his guts. "It knew me."

"Knew you as in knows you? This just gets better and better. Do you know *it*?"

Muscle bunched along his jaw. "Nothing on the short list will cheer you up. Listen, Tucker—Tanner, whateverthefuck your name really is—you can still make it out of here. You've done a great job today. Go live long enough to do others."

"Now you're having me on, and I don't much admire your sense of humor." It was Tanner's voice.

"The Monasteries need people like you. Being human on the other side of this door is about to be a bad idea."

"You're going."

"I don't have a choice. You do. Make the right one."

He rotated his shoulders, cracked his neck, and checked the loads in his pistol's clip. "In the words of an old pal of mine—Jonnie, his name was, you'd like him," he said through a lopsided smile. "He used to say 'I wouldn't have come to the party if I didn't want to dance.' "

"Whatever." He closed his eyes again. "Give me another couple quiet seconds. I'll handle the Social Police."

"Seriously?"

"Shh."

Mindview came on instantly. The enforcement squad was barely perceptible now, three-quarters buried in imaginary trans-real muck. No time to be subtle.

Also no inclination.

He made his left hand a fist as if he could grab and hold his perception. Then he did the same with his right. The Social Police vanished from his mind. Something behind him made a muffled, raggedly wet *fwaptch*, and the greasy smoke thickened into a choking cloud.

Tucker yelped and jumped away to flatten himself against the wall. "Sweet mother of fuck my god's *asshole*," he gasped. "Whyn't you *warn* a guy?"

He frowned down at the corpses of the two soapies. As near as he could tell, the *fwaptch* had been the sounds of their heads exploding inside their helmets. "Could have been worse."

"Worse?"

"Could have taken off their helmets first. Stand back."

There was still enough oil on his hands to make him look like he'd been greasing wagon wheels. He again made fists, and the edges of the steel door caught fire, eye-burning white.

"Holy shit." Tucker stared. "Second coming of Lazarus fucking Dane . . ."

"Yeah, off by an order of magnitude or three. But thanks anyway."

"It wasn't a compliment," he said with feeling. "I can't wait to file my History. They will fucking lock me up."

A swift side kick into the center knocked the door flat. On the far side, the helmets of four fallen Social Police belched billows of smoke. "Um, listen," Tucker said faintly, "anything I have ever done that you don't like—anything at all—I just want to say I'm sorry. I am very, very sorry. I apologize unreservedly—"

"Which way to the gate?"

"Weren't you just down here?"

"Unconscious with a bag on my head, smart guy."

Three archways opened into corridors. The only light came from the burning Social Police in the hall outside. No doors in this little chamber, just a table with black bags on it—he couldn't help wondering if one of them still had chunks of his puke in it—along with some fruit, sliced meats and cheeses, and a plate of cookies. A watercooler stood to one side. Tucker saw him frowning at it. "What's the matter?"

"Cookies," he said slowly. "Somebody put out cookies for the Social Police."

"Looks like they ate some too. What do you care?"

"I can't explain. It's just . . . I don't know. Wrong." He shook himself back to business. "Listen, this is your last chance to bail, Tucker. Go."

"What part of 'I wouldn't have come to the party' did you not understand?"

"Cut it out. You're after the Butcher's Fist."

He took it without a blink. "*If* that's true—and nobody's saying it is—a chance to stuff the Hand of Khryl inside a Vault of Binding is worth more than both our lives," he said easily. "However many you actually have."

"You don't get it. Everything I told t'Passe? Just a come-on. I'm not here to recover the Fist."

"Then you won't mind if somebody packs it off to Thorncleft, right?"

"Trying will get you killed. If you're lucky. There are worse things than dying."

"So I hear. If I ever come across one, I'll let you know."

"Fuck it. I don't like you enough to argue." He went to the closest archway. It ran straight and level as far as he could see. At regular intervals—every ten yards or so—a hand-size patch of the ceiling glowed pale green. "Huh. Elf-light."

Tucker headed over to check one of the others. "So?"

"So Social Police helmets have built-in night vision. They don't need elf-light. And these aren't bright enough for regular people."

"Ogrilloi," Tucker said hollowly from the other arch.

"Yeah. We're getting close."

"Not what I meant. Um, the big nasty your playmates were waiting for—would it be coming from the direction of the gate?"

"Maybe. What do you have?"

"I think it's the Smoke Hunt."

He looked over Tucker's shoulder. The hallway descended and widened as it went, fanning out in the far distance into what might have been some kind of large open chamber, and from what he could see there might have been firelight or torches, but mostly he was just looking at the giant crowd of bare-ass ogrilloi.

Every square inch was packed shoulder to shoulder and cock to butt-crack with naked ogrilloi. Just standing there. Those scarlet flames that cast no light flickered and played over them, and there were elf-lights here too, but there was no way to know if the ogrilloi down there needed them or not.

They all had their eyes closed.

And they weren't ogrilloi so much as they were a thousand-plus identically dough-faced manikins—ogrillokins—like full-size clay figures still only half-shaped. "Put your weapon down."

"Are you fucking kidding me?"

"They're not Smoke Hunters." A tilt of the head. "Not yet."

"Then what are they?"

"Blanks. Ever do armoring? Like knife blanks, except they're fetch blanks."

"I get it—Black Knife blanks."

"Yeah, funny. Put your weapon down, goddammit. Want to live through this?" He put Benson's pistol on the floor and started pulling knives to lay beside it. "You used the pistol and grenades on the Social Police, so it knows what those are, if it didn't already. Any spells you've used on the Battleground, ever—those have to go too."

"You are batshit insane."

"So?"

"So I've always admired that about you." He knelt to disarm. Along with his pistol and three knives, he laid out a handful of differently shaped and colored crystals, several tiny metal figurines of unlikely-looking creatures, and three coin-size disks of dark wood inlaid with delicate traceries of gold.

"That's everything?"

Tucker shrugged. "Everything you'll find without a body-cavity search."

"I'm sure you've still got enough shit stashed to perpetrate ten or twelve different flavors of stupid. Don't. I mean it. Play anything but straight low and you will not walk out of here."

"Ain't I always been the brains of this team, pappy?"

"I told you cut it out." He stepped forward to the front rank of the half-cooked Smoke Hunters. He touched one on the chest and said, "All right, I'm ready. Let's do this."

The fetch blanks pressed themselves back from him, parting enough to give him space to walk. Tucker said, "Um . . . you kind of said that like you know what's happening."

"Come on."

The blanks pushed themselves against the walls as they passed, then filled in the corridor behind them.

He shrugged. "I still don't have it all. But every step we take sharpens the focus."

"That doesn't tell me as much as you seem to think it does."

"It's not deep. Look, I don't know how much t'Passe told you about my situation here, and I don't have time to explain. I have detailed intelligence about this place on this day, but it's not reliable. At all. For reasons I can't really go into right now either. I have an idea of what's happening, but it's provisional. More than provisional. Probabilistic. Shit, if they taught quantum mechanics in abbey school, it'd be easier to explain. It's close enough to say that nothing here is entirely real until I see it."

"You're talking about time-binding."

He shot Tucker a sharp look. Tucker spread his hands. "After our last conversation, I was debriefed by the Thorncleft Inquisitor."

"Figures."

"He said you parted on friendly terms."

"More so than most. So look: cutting What Might Be down into What Actually Is works kind of like analytic elimination. That you were t'Passe's inside guy cut off a whole universe of possible. The Earth Normal vault was powered by the black oil; that carved away more. Social Police at the door to the gate told me a lot—and having more soapies inside than outside, and the inside having fucking defensive hardpoints, told me more. Then Soapy bleeds the blind god's oil. Then Smoke Hunt fetch-blanks come from the gate. Then the blanks don't attack. They wait."

"Like they were expecting us." Tucker's eyelids fluttered. He nodded to himself, resigned. Suddenly tired. "Not us. You."

"I told you to go."

"I swear to you on any kind of sacred whateverthefuck you favor: if I live through this I will absolutely start taking your advice."

"That'll look nice on your headstone." He sighed. "There's one other thing you should probably know. When I was telling you about the big nasty monster that scared the fuck out of the Social Police? Some of that was less than entirely true. It was mostly to convince you to fuck off and live homicidally ever after somewhere else."

"What, they weren't scared? There's no monster?"

"Oh, they were scared. There is a real monster. That's all true."

"So what's the lie?"

He shrugged apologetically. "I said it wasn't happy to see me."

The corridor opened into a huge ovoid chamber. It was full of ogrilloi.

"*Rint diz Ekt Perrog'k, Nazutakkaarik.*"

"Oh, crap. Hi." Caine waved. "And, y'know, fuck yourself."

This could have been going better already.

" 'Welcome to our place, Skinwalker'? Seriously?" Tucker murmured. "You two know each other?"

"Shut up."

The ceiling was a huge dome, deep enough to echo a raised voice. The floor was polished until it gleamed like travertine in the rain. The topmost level, where they stood, was at least fifteen yards deep; in the center of the cavern, the polished stone descended in shrinking steplike rings nine or ten feet wide and a couple feet high, ten levels down to a central disk like the bull's-eye on a target. The bull's-eye looked to be twenty-some-odd feet across, some kind of crystal, glowing with a soft yellow light of its own. The ceiling was a mirror of the floor. The walls were polished like the floor and ceiling, and were engraved with elegantly artistic renderings of ogrillo petroglyph clan-sign.

"Look at this fucking place . . ." Tucker breathed.

"Yeah, they've remodeled since the last time I was here."

"You were here?"

"Long time ago."

The uppermost floor was packed with the fetch blanks. He couldn't guess how many. Two other archways spread wide as the avenue down which they'd come, and there was nowhere not full of half-made grills.

Two steps above the bull's-eye stood fifty or sixty ogrillo bucks, clearly real, warts and all, scowling like they knew who he was. Across the dome from where he stood rose a stepped pyramid that appeared to have been carved out of the wall. Ten steps up. Every other step had been fashioned into seats. Below the apex sat three bitches. Two steps down sat nine more. Then what was probably twenty-seven, because the threefold thing seemed to be the order of the day, which wasn't good news.

Asshole estimation: over three hundred and fifty bitches. The entire Black Knife priesthood, give or take. In their holiest sanctum. Instead of being out to watch Khryl's Justice.

Sometimes shit just is what it is. Sometimes you do what you do, and let the rest go.

He walked toward the first ring. "Come on. Act like you know what you're doing."

"You look worried."

He nodded toward the pyramid. "She's not who I was hoping to find."

"The top bitch? Who were you expecting?"

"Anybody else."

He jumped down. Tucker dropped in right beside him. "If she's a problem for us, I can drop her from here. Nobody'll know. Looks like a heart attack."

He kept moving. "Make a move on her and I'll kill you myself."

Tucker kept up. "What's she to you?"

"My sister-in-law."

"You are pulling my dick."

"Do not harm her. Don't even think it too loud." He jumped down another level. "You think coming at me sucked? Wait till I come at you."

"But—I mean, your *sister-in-law* is the head of the fucking *Smoke Hunt*? You *have* to be pulling my dick." Tucker sounded distinctly offended. "Is there anything about you the Monasteries actually has right? One fucking thing?"

"Sure. Lots." He jumped down to the next lower ring. "Probably."

He came to the step above the one the bucks stood on. Christ, these bucks were big—he stood two feet up, and the grill in front of him still came up to his nose—and they didn't seem inclined to get out of his way. He looked up at the apex of the pyramid.

She scowled down at him for a second or two, then snapped an abrupt bark. The bucks parted to let him and Tucker pass.

He jumped down into the bull's-eye and looked back. Tucker had stopped one ring up.

"You coming?"

"I'm good here, thanks."

The bull's-eye was smooth as glass. Hairs on his arms and the back of his neck lifted and crackled with blue sparks. "All right, goddammit, a hint, huh?" he muttered under his breath. "You didn't Call me here to enjoy my fucking company."

Kaiggez barked something in Etk Dag. He ignored her. "Tucker, make yourself useful," he said, low. "There's a Triple Aspect here. Somewhere."

"A *Triple*?"

"Yeah, we hit the trifecta. Outside/Ideational/Natural. Find it."

"Names might help."

He took a deep breath. "The Natural Power doesn't have a name. Call it the Blind God. The other two are Pirichanthe and Khryl."

"Khryl, sure, the Fist and all. Who's the other again?"

"Pirichanthe."

"Somehow I'm not understanding you."

Kaiggez barked again. He didn't even look up. "You read my History of the Breaking of the Black Knives. The Outside Power that was Bound in the vertical city—the entity that maintains the *dil T'llan*. It's *Pirichanthe*."

"Sorry." Tucker looked baffled. "I still can't figure out what you're trying to tell me."

"Yeah." Of course. That would have been too easy. "Listen, it's the Smoke God, all right? The Power that animates the Smoke Hunt."

"Whyn't you say so? This Smoke whatever of yours—don't you know its name?"

"Never mind."

Kaiggez was leaning forward on her throne, and her barking had gone thick with anger.

Finally he looked up at her. "You know I don't speak that shit."

"*Paggallo?*" she said. "*Paggannik ymik, paggtakkuni,*" which he was pretty sure would be Etk Dag for *Say what? See what you say in a minute, cockroach.*

More or less.

"Kaiggez. We can stand here while everybody listens to you yammer and watches me get bored, or you can grow the fuck up and speak Westerling."

"Grow up?" She sounded even more icily contemptuous when she spoke Westerling. "What does Skinwalker know of *grow up* except to burn cubs so they never do?"

"Huh." He caught the accent. "You're Ankhanan."

She lurched to her feet. "I am *Black Knife!*"

"Sure, okay. Whatever. Where's the Hand?"

She showed him a grin full of tusks and made a fist. "Here? Only *my* hand."

"The longer this takes, the less you'll like it."

"I shove you through *taggannik* once already. I can shove you again."

"What, the gate? I don't think so."

She raised her fist and her eyes flashed the same sunlight yellow of the bull's-eye. The crystal's glow became radiance that flared to blinding in a single eyeblink. It entirely erased the chamber and the bucks and the bitches and even his own body . . . but there was something he saw when he was blind to everything else. Below his feet, half-buried in the impossible brilliance, hung a shadow.

A human-shaped shadow.

"Huh," he said under his breath. "Well, all right, then."

The radiance faded as suddenly as it had arisen. Everybody looked kind of surprised that he was still there.

"Here's the thing," he said. "You're not in charge here anymore. Black Knives, Butt Sporks, whatever. You're done. Pack up your bitches and get the fuck out. Take the females too."

Kaiggez was still on her feet and still had her fist clenched. She growled, "What voice do you have here to say what I am? What voice do you have here to even speak?"

"It's not a debate. It's an order."

"*You?* Order *me?*"

"Isn't that what I just said?"

"You still have tongue to speak only from respect for my buck. You breathe only from respect for his love for you."

"Well, there's a coincidence."

"How do you get out from True Hell where I put you, little bitch?"

"You're gonna have to get used to shit not depending on what you do or don't do."

"What I do? I speak with Voice of God Itself. One *word* from me crushes light from your eye forever."

"Yeah, big talk. You want to do this with me?" He opened his arms as though offering a hug. "Make a move."

This got a dangerous rumble out of the bucks, right up until Kaiggez made her move, which cut off the rumble like a punch in the throat. She leaned forward and peeled back her lips around her long and impressively sharp tusks, and her yellow eyes burned with furious triumph.

She raised her fist. Around her upraised fist gathered power that was visible mainly in how it made everything else less real.

He'd seen that power before, the ball of Reality: the power that had allowed Crowmane to bend time and space like a fever nightmare. He had felt it on the Purificapex, when the Living Fist of Khryl laid her hand upon the Sword of Man.

He had felt it at the west end of God's Way in Ankhana, as he watched the Incarnate Ma'elKoth descend from the heavens.

Tucker was edging back. "This is you not being stupid?"

"Shut up."

He lifted his fist and extended his middle finger up toward her, then waggled his fist to make sure she got a good look. "To avoid any, y'know, cross-cultural misunderstanding: this gesture—the one I'm making at you right now—this gesture has a meaning, where I come from, that translates roughly as *Try me and I will fuck your asshole with my fighting claw.*"

"God can hurt you and leave you alive," Kaiggez growled. "My first word can make you *beg* for death—"

"Your entire fucking vocabulary can't mess up my hair."

Tucker said from the side of his mouth, "You sure about that?"

He replied the same way. "We're about to find out."

"When I apologize to Orbek later, he forgives because he knows you. Knows how you can be hornets in God's own Cunt."

"Okay."

"How do we hurt you, little bitch? Do we make you ancient so your bones snap like reeds? Do we make you rot so we hear you scream as your parts fall off?"

"Look, is this gonna happen or not? I've got shit to do."

"Then it happens," she snarled, and snapped her fist toward him. "*Burn.*"

"Oh, that's original." He didn't burn. He didn't even move, except to raise his left hand.

On that upraised left hand coalesced a shimmering nonsphere of Reality. By the time it assembled itself, it was the only Reality in the chamber. Her fist was now only the flesh and bone it had always been.

"See, here's another thing," he said. "I know your god, and your god knows me. And it likes me better than you."

Her eyes popped wide as saucers. She made a faint choking noise.

He smiled at her. "Hey, want to see a trick?"

"Better be a good one," Tucker muttered.

He lifted the Reality and stared into and through it, reaching out with mindview.

Something winked at him again. An encouraging wink.

He said through his teeth, "Get my back."

"What's about to happen here?"

"I don't know. That's why you need to have my back. If we survive, I'll make you glad you did."

"Well, when you put it that way . . ."

This time, he sought the level of mind that could show him the connections and currents of black Flow. Slowly, cautiously, he teased loose a fiber of Flow from his own Shell; the last time something like this had happened it just about blew his head off, so this time he figured to sort of ease into it . . .

He let the tiny fiber brush Reality, and his head exploded.

No . . .

Felt like it, though.

He thought he might be on his knees. He smelled a bitter stink of burning hair. He remembered one of the Smoke Hunter Leisure brats talking about how cool it looked when your eyeballs explode, and he figured now he kind of knew what the little fucker had been talking about. There was an awful racket, all kinds of shouting and cheering and derisive catcalls and shit, and it seemed logical to him that if he could still hear with exploded ears, he could probably see with exploded eyes.

He looked around. He was on his knees after all; his eyes had apparently not only failed to explode, they seemed to be working better then they had before, because he was looking down into the yellow glow of the crystal beneath him and now he could again see the shadow below—

And now he knew what that shadow was.

"Tucker." He coughed, and gagged, and barely managed to swallow vomit instead of spewing it. "Am I on fire?"

"Not anymore. Probably want to replace your leathers. And maybe shave your head." Tucker was crouching beside him. "What just happened?"

"Uh . . . remember when I . . ." He gagged again, and again swallowed. "When I told you . . . detailed intelligence and shit?"

"Yeah . . . ?"

"I think this just now is when I actually learn it."

"I'm not gonna ask how exactly *that* works, but I hope you got good shit," Tucker said, "because the HMS *Cowed Black Knives* weighed anchor right about when your knees hit the floor. You might recall that she told you to burn."

He lifted his head. "I got more than good shit," he said as he rose to his feet. "I got all the shit there is."

"Maybe God is like you say," Kaiggez purred. "Maybe it takes pity on you. Or maybe it just wants to give me more time to play."

He made a show of dusting himself off while he considered how to make her game into his.

"Your god," he said at length, "is not what you think it is. It didn't just spring out of the universe's asshole. Your god was created. Designed and put together in a specific way to accomplish a specific task. Your god does not love you. You're not its children. Most of the time it doesn't remember you exist. It was here long before there was such a thing as a Black Knife Nation, and I'd tell you that it'll be here long after you're all gone, if, y'know, it will. But it won't.

"Where I come from, there was a guy who made a splash saying *God is dead*—and that was in a world where nobody could even be sure that god had been real in the first place. Yours, on the other hand? Real, sure. But it's dead too."

"*You* say." She raised her fist and more Reality gathered around it. "Tell me *again* God is dead!"

He said, "Give me that."

The Reality vanished from her hand and reappeared in his. She swayed and her knees buckled. The three bitches below her leaped up and eased her back into her seat.

"Thanks." He meant it, because he didn't have attention to spare for Control Disciplines and his burns were starting to really fucking hurt. He understood now: he didn't even need mindview. Not here.

His burns healed. His hair grew. So did his beard.

His leathers changed.

Gone was the supple new leather. Gone was the clean lanolin smell and Kravmik's careful stitching. What he wore now was scuffed and worn and crusted with white salt rings of ancient sweat, and the threads that held rips and slashes together had been stained brown with old blood. It wasn't exactly trading up, but at least now he was comfortable.

And for the first time he could remember, no part of him hurt.

Not anymore.

"Um, yeah . . ." Tucker murmured beside him. "That's a little, uh, different . . ."

"Just a costume." He shrugged it into a perfect fit. "And shut up."

There was plenty of Reality left. More than enough to go around. He turned his palm upward, as though he balanced Reality upon it like a ball.

"Temporal discharge," he said. "It might go on a few days. Even a month or two. Then it's all over. No Smoke Hunt. No gate. No power. No god." He shrugged. "Sorry. If you're nice to me, maybe I won't kill your next god."

She leaned on the polished stone armrest like it was all that stopped her from falling out of the chair. "You say *you* kill *God?*"

"Not on purpose."

"Your brain rots till even humans smell it."

"It died on Assumption Day." He tilted his head and righted it again. "It just hasn't stopped twitching yet."

He hefted the Reality as if it had weight. "Like I said: temporal discharge. It sent power forward in time to maintain its consciousness while it waited."

"And God's wait is *over.*" Her voice rose, and she shifted forward. "Black Knives rule Our Place again from *today. There's* its power. More than any god needs. Our god lives *forever.*"

"Have you not been paying attention? It never needed you. Nothing you do can save it. It's already done. What we're doing here today is working out how shit is gonna be afterward, you follow?"

"For what God waits all this time, then?"

He lifted the ball of Reality so that he was looking through it at her. "Me."

She made some more of those choking noises.

He nodded sympathetically. "I know it's kind of hard to take in. Imagine it from my side. I spent my whole life fighting it. Running from it. I destroyed everyone who ever cared about me because I couldn't face what I really am. A little while ago I learned some hard lessons about being myself, and they got me thinking. Some things we don't get to choose. Like Orbek said, 'No one chooses their clan. Born Black Knife, you're Black Knife.' So your god and me, we reached an understanding."

"What are you, then? What do you claim to be?"

"I am master of this place," he said. "I am master of you."

All the bitches leaped up then, shouting and shaking their fists. The bucks roared, raising their arms and flipping fighting claws forward over their fists.

"God is not the only power here, little bitch." Kaiggez lowered her fist and turned her snarl on the fifty or sixty enormous ogrillo bucks who stood a couple rings above him and Tucker. "Kill them. Hurt them first. You will live forever."

He could read Tucker's lips. *This must be why nobody put you in the Diplomatic Service.*

He mouthed back: *Watch this.*

He raised the ball of Reality, and his voice was the peal of thunder. "Silence."

And his will was done: instant silence, so absolute that his ears rang.

Good so far.

He turned to the bucks. "Want a piece of me? Step on up, fuckers. One at a time or all in a rush."

The bucks looked at one another. Finally, the largest, most scarred, hardest-ass-looking one shrugged and stepped forward.

"You're today's lucky winner." He lowered the ball of Reality to his side and just stared at the huge buck. "Die."

The buck snorted and went to take another step, but swayed instead. His eyes went wide, and he clutched at his chest in growing disbelief. Then his legs gave out and he dropped to his knees. He made a choking, gagging kind of sound, then pitched forward onto his face and lay still.

"Did anybody not see that? Does anybody need it explained?"

He looked around the chamber, meeting each Black Knife's eyes in turn.

Then he looked at the fallen buck. "Rise and walk."

After one stretching silent second, the buck convulsed, whooping great gasps of air. He pushed himself up to his knees . . . and instead of rising, he lowered his face to the floor. And stayed there.

Tucker murmured, "Nice."

"None of you need to bother with submission," he said. "You're already mine. What you have is mine. What you are is mine. At my word, you come out. At my word you go in. At my word you walk the world. At my word you lie in darkness. At my word you live. At my word you die.

"My word is your law. You have no law but my word. Break the law and you suffer. Defy the law and you beg for death.

"To affront me is to die. To affront my people is to affront me. Take care that you do neither.

"These are my words. This is your law."

"Your *people*?" Veins bulged in Kaiggez's thick neck. "Slavers who whip us? Murderers who destroy our people along with Our Place? Men who cannot stand without a boot on Black Knife necks?"

"No."

"That's all you say? No?"

"Your neck is my neck."

She rocked back, suddenly pensive.

"My brother is Orbek Black Knife: Taykarget. Your buck. Your husband. I have been called Caine, and Dominic, and Shade and Jonathan Fist and K'Thal and Hari Michaelson and many other names, and I am proud to bear every one. But those names are not me."

He bared his teeth up toward Kaiggez. "You know who I am. Tell them."

She looked like she was snarling something under her breath.

He squeezed the ball of Reality. "*Tell* them."

Reluctantly she rose. Reluctantly she drew breath. "He is *Nazutak-kaarik . . . Nazutakkaarik* of Hell's nightmare."

She lowered her head. "He is Skinwalker. There is no other."

Silence.

The silence deepened while he looked around the chamber until he met every single pair of yellow eyes. "Anybody wants to get stupid with me, first go find somebody who lived through the Horror. Ask what happens when I get angry."

He raised his left hand and regarded the crackling swirl of Reality he held. Somehow he felt like he should be able to see his future in there. But all he saw was power.

So he used it because, y'know, what the hell else is power for?

When at length he looked again to the motionless, silent Black Knives, he said, "Why are you still here? Fuck off. All of you. Now."

As though they had suddenly awakened from a dream, the ogrilloi slowly, unsteadily bestirred themselves to leave. He looked at Kaiggez. "Not you."

He beckoned. "We need to talk."

The Black Knives filed out, leaving behind only the fetch-blanks and Kaiggez, who reluctantly climbed down toward them.

"You do put on a show," Tucker said.

"Thanks. Nice catch on the die business."

"You're welcome. Rise and walk was a bit of a trick, though. That's not easy magick to cancel on short notice. On no notice."

"I have nothing but confidence in your ability."

"Thus proving yourself to be a gentleman of taste and discernment, but what would you have done if I'd dropped it?"

He shrugged. "Something else. Better this way."

"Yeah?"

"With me, the rise and walk part isn't a happy ending."

"I take your meaning."

Kaiggez slipped down from the last ring. She lowered herself to one knee and bowed her head. "What does Skinwalker wish to say?"

"The Skinwalker wants to—" He stopped, and made a face. "Oh, for fuck's sake, Kaiggez. Get up. And if I do start talking about myself in third person, you have my permission to stab me in the face."

She rose, but still averted her eyes. He let it go; to ogrilloi, a level stare is a dominance test, and he didn't want to invite any more of that shit. Not now. Instead he reached over and laid his right hand on the top of her head. "I called you down here to say I'm sorry."

Her head jerked up, and for a glancing second she looked straight into his eyes before averting her face again. "Sorry for just now, or sorry for everything?"

"For just now."

"Just now ain't much."

"It's what you get. The rest? That was war. Including the cubs. Even your cubs. It's okay that you hate me for it. Just now, though . . . well, I'm sorry to bitch-slap you in front of your friends."

"My *family*," she growled, low.

"Our family." He put his hand on her head again, and lightly stroked the brush of hair that sprang up from her spinal ridge. "These things should be private. I'm sorry it wasn't. And I want to make it up to you."

She stepped back and cocked her head so she could look at him side-long. "Make up how?"

"By having you help."

"Help you kill last Black Knives?"

"I need you to look after our family. More. I need you to *lead* them."

Her eyes slitted, and she did not respond.

"Yeah, I'm the boss of you now. Now I say you're the boss of everybody else."

"And this man?" She twitched a shoulder at Tucker. "What is he to stand at Skinwalker's side?"

"He's nothing. If you see him again, kill him."

"Hey now," Tucker said. "That's not friendly."

"If you got orders to put a bullet in the back of my head, you wouldn't even hesitate."

"But I'd feel bad after. Doesn't that count for something?"

"No."

He turned back to Kaiggez. "The whole city is gonna know what happened here by sundown, and it's likely to cause a bit of a stir. Keep the clan calm but ready to move. All of you. I know a lot, but I don't know what's gonna happen at the Justice. We might need to fight. We might need to run. We might need to hold shit together and wait. That's gonna be your call."

"Mine." She looked thoughtful, though still wary. "I can do this."

"You've been fighting to give our clan power. To give us freedom, and a future here in Our Place. Now it's less complicated. Your job now is only to protect us. Do you understand me?"

She didn't answer.

"This is my word. This is your law. Do you understand? Say it."

Softly. "I understand."

"You and your bitches—your priesthood, whatever the fuck you call yourselves—your duty now is to care for the Black Knife Nation as a bitch cares for her cubs. The rest isn't your problem anymore."

"Bitches *fight*."

"I know," he said. "But Black Knife bitches fight only to *defend* the cubs. To defend the family. This is law. From now till forever."

"Then who destroys our enemies? Who bitches the world to keep it down scared? Who?"

He gave her half a self-deprecating smile. "When Orbek adopted me, he said I had put dishonor on the Black Knives. He said now that I am Black Knife, I share dishonor. And I do. He also said that what honor I win, Black Knives share. And you will."

"You say . . ." A fierce yellow light kindled in her eyes. "You say Skinwalker fights for *us* now."

"You have seen me make war against Black Knives. Now see me make war *as* Black Knife."

She whispered with something resembling reverence, "*Nazutakkaarik terkallaz keptarroll ymik kaz tash . . .*"

She ducked her head, then whirled, scrambled up the rings, and sprinted out into the tunnel toward BlackStone. He watched her go, reflecting that he really would have to learn Etk Dag someday, then turned to Tucker. "So?"

"Sounded like a proverb." Tucker looked singularly thoughtful. "She said 'The Skinwalker becomes his kill.' "

"Huh." He couldn't decide whether the coincidence was significant or not. "Funny how shit comes together."

"Funny?"

"You speak Lipkan. Ever read their poetry? There's a traditional metaphoric reference, especially in epodes—they refer to Tyshalle with imagery about night, unlit caverns, inside the tomb, y'know, all that shit. In older works—especially in the early epics where Tyshalle is used as a character—He's often tagged with an epithet that translates roughly as 'the permanent dark.' Sometimes just with a capital-D Dark, right?"

"Holy shit."

"Yeah. The Blade of Tyshalle," he said heavily, "is basically a poetic usage for *the black knife.*"

"That's what you call funny?" Tucker looked appalled. "You have a peculiar sense of humor."

"I get that a lot." He went over to the lowest ring and sat. "Time for you to go."

"How many times do we have to have this conversation?"

"Not that kind of go."

Tucker went still. "Hey, y'know," he said slowly, "if this is about the Hand—"

"This is about you," he said. "I'd let you walk out of here if I could make myself believe you'd actually do it."

Tucker sighed. "Well, if you're gonna be that way about it—"

"You've done me a lot of good," he said. He leaned back on his elbows, then scooted farther back so he could draw up his knees. "You helped me get with the horse-witch, and you helped me get with myself. You helped me get down here today. I know you didn't do any of it *for* me, but I owe you anyway. That's why I don't kill you where you stand."

"Well, I'm plain damn sad you feel like that, Jonnie. You think maybe we could come to some flavor of accommodation?" He scratched absently at his arm, and a lance of scarlet power blasted through the air—

And exactly at the perimeter of the bull's-eye, it evaporated as if it had never been.

"Don't insult me."

"I had sort of thought to arrange a surprise," Tucker said.

"Nifty Firebolt. How'd you grave the enchantment? A tattoo?"

"If you really want to know," Tucker said, "maybe you'd like to step on in here and have a look for yourself."

"I should kill you. I know I should. If our positions were reversed—"

"Never happen." He sat down on the crystal. He sounded tired. "I'm a professional. You're not. You never were."

"That's true enough, I guess."

"A pro would have finished me at the bluffs."

He shrugged. "The thing is, I admire you."

"Skip the blow job."

"Not just your skill. Your commitment. Devotion to your craft. And I like you."

"Not enough to let me walk out of here."

"Because getting people to like you is part of your job. And you're just as good at it as you are at everything else."

"We done yet?"

"How about you answer one question? Just one, for no reason but to satisfy my curiosity, since you'll never see this world again."

"Hate to leave you unsatisfied." Tucker shrugged. "How about we trade? Since I'll never see this world again."

"Sure."

"What do you figure to do with the Hand? Take it for yourself?"

"Oh, hell no."

"It's a lot of power."

"Not any kind I want."

"Then what? Must be extreme. Since you're about to smoke a guy you like just in case he might get in your way."

"Extreme enough," he said. "I'm gonna give it back to Khryl."

Tucker stared.

And stared.

And stared some more.

And finally said, "You're right to kill me."

"I'm not gonna kill you."

"Does t'Passe know about this?"

"Of course not. Jesus Christ. She'd have blown my head off before I finished the sentence."

"She's not as sentimental as you."

"You might say."

Tucker sighed. "All right. Ask."

"Your name."

"Come again?"

"Your name. That's all. Your real name. For when I tell people this story."

He seemed to think this over for some few seconds, then he sighed a nod and shrugged. "All right," he said reluctantly. "No harm, I guess. You can call me Heywood, Lord Jablohmie, Marquess of—"

The rest vanished into the blinding yellow flare of power. When the power was gone, so was Tucker.

The chamber was quiet then, so quiet that he could hear the synchronized breathing of the thousands of immobile fetch-blanks that still crowded the topmost level of floor. He looked up. Well . . . not *quite* immobile . . .

Their eyes were open.

All of them.

And all of those eyes were fixed on him.

"Yeah, all right. I can take a fucking hint."

He pushed himself to the edge of the ring and stood up. Out in the center of the crystal there was no trace Tucker had ever been there. No trace any of them had been there.

Except for the shadow in the crystal below. A bug in amber.

He took a knee in the center of the bull's-eye, and laid his palm flat upon it. "Hey," he said softly. "You ready?"

A reply came—not in voice, nor even language—but in silent understanding.

Since before either of us was born.

"This is not what I wanted for you. Not even close. I wanted to hurt you. I wanted to hurt you so badly you'd remember me every hour of every day for the rest of your life. But not like this."

You swore that when I woke up in Hell, you would already be killing me again.

"I wasn't talking about this Hell. Or how you woke up. Or even this kind of killing."

Does your meaning exist? Your words still do. I can hear them now. Forever.

"Not forever. I'm taking care of forever right here."

Forever, my beloved, does not mean what you think it means.

"Yeah, okay, I should have known better than to talk to you anyway."

He reached out with his mind and found Reality, and he put his will upon it. "Skaikkak Neruch'khaitan, come forth! Or, y'know, rise and walk. Whatever."

In the depths of the crystal, the shadow moved.

It grew, gathering solidity as it did, coalescing in the soft yellow glow, and the clearer it became, the less human it appeared. The crystal's surface parted and from it like a goddess from the sea foam rose an ancient and withered ogrillo bitch, wholly hairless, only crumpled stumps where her legs should be, a knot of scar where her right eye and cheekbone had been, and her remaining eye burned with ferocious madness that was yellow as the crystal below.

"Hey there, you shit-crazy old bat. Been awhile."

It has been forever, little rabbit. But in forever, I see you always.

Where her right hand had once been—where her hand had been blasted to smoldering shreds by her once-borrowed power—was instead a mailed fist, its steel chromed like curves of mirror, flawless and pristine. It was this she extended toward him as though offering to shake his hand.

Care for our people, little rabbit.

"You know I will."

He clasped the mailed fist with his hand of flesh. "Good night, Crowmane. Sleep well."

I will dream of you, my beloved.

"And in that dream I'll be skull-fucking your eye socket with a barbwire cock."

I'll miss you too.

"You're still a festering slab of rat cunt," he said. *"Ch'syavallanaig Khryllan'tai."*

When the flame of Khryl's Authority from his hand met the Flesh of His Fist, white fire incinerated the universe.

When he became aware once more of his surroundings, the Hand of Khryl was gone, and the only light in the chamber came from the flames licking up from Crowmane's corpse. He lay on the smooth cold crystal and tried to figure out how to get to his feet, because he couldn't exactly remember how to move his arms and legs. His hand hurt. So did his arm, his shoulder, chest, ear, face—even after taking some time to think about it and really search, he couldn't find a single part of his body that was not shivering with pain.

"Oh, sure," he muttered. "Forgot to mention this part, huh?"

His leathers weren't in much better shape than he was. He reached once more with his mind to touch Reality, to repair his body and restore his clothing . . . but he found no Reality he could touch. He couldn't even register the fetch-blanks, who lay lifeless in jumbles like a mass grave.

He sighed. Sure, this was how it was supposed to work . . . but somehow that didn't make any of him hurt any less.

He managed to push himself up to hands and knees. Then he had to stop and catch his breath. His nose was bleeding. His blood dropped to the crystal and in the firelight it was black.

Black?

Blood doesn't look black in firelight. He touched his face, and his hand came away blackened with oil that dripped from within his nose. He stared at his reflection in its iridescent obsidian, and like the ball of Reality in which he'd sought a glimpse of his future, what he saw was power.

But in the oil, he saw his future too.

He nodded to himself. "Showtime."

the now of always 8

A DARKLING WOOD

A DARKLING WOOD

*"Nel mezzo del cammin di nostra vita
mi ritrovai per una selva oscura,
ché la diritta via era smarrita."*

— DANTE ALIGHIERI
  Inferno

S he is not seen, nor is She heard or felt, smelled or tasted, but She is
  here, for Here is She Everlasting.

"And amen," Duncan murmurs, acutely grateful to be pinned to the
ground, as it relieves him of an unconquerable necessity to kneel. And
within his head whirls a vertiginous existential dread: that he is only a fig-
ment of Her Imagination, a passing fancy that at Her slightest distraction
would evaporate into nothing that had ever existed at all.

Kris Hansen, Deliann Mithondionne, Emperor of Ankhana and
human king of the elves rests on his knees with lowered head. Even
Angvasse Khlaylock, Lord of Battle, has taken a respectful knee. Only the
horse-witch has not moved; still she sits at Duncan's side, now idly braiding wildflowers into a garland.

Caine walks out into the center of the glade and says, "Fucking cut it
out."

The Presence replies, not in words, or even sound at all, but in meaning.

As ever, you demand I be less than I Am.

"If I could demand, I'd demand you take a fucking hike. How's Faith?"

She worries for you. As do I.

"And I'm just fine. See? Now the hike."

A shimmer of power gathers in the air beside Duncan. The power becomes light, which shapes itself into a figure resembling his son's wife. "Shanna."

Pallas Ril. I am glad to meet you again, Duncan. Let me help you.

"Help me?"

I can ease your pain.

"It doesn't hurt."

Not the pain of your flesh, Duncan.

He feels Her Power upon him, warm as a kitchen on winter's day, safe and comforting as the memory of his mother's arms.

Caine says, "Remember what I told you."

"I haven't forgotten." He turns a regretful half-smile upon the goddess's shimmering form. "Thank You for Your concern, Pallas Ril," he says with deliberate formality. "But without that pain, I wouldn't know who I am."

Is that a dreadful fate? I tell you now: forgetting is calm, and quiet, without suffering, without fear, without desire. Only rest.

He finds tears gathering at the corners of his eyes. "You are very kind. But no. I can't. Not yet." He opens his hands toward her. "Hari still needs me."

Hari is dead. That man is not your son.

"He's somebody's son. He's the son of a father who loved him without reservation. The son of a mother whose fondest dream in life was to see her son become a man." Now his tears spill over. "That's son enough for me."

Then in respect for the memory of love we share for Hari, let me at least free you from this prison. The shimmer gains substance as it reaches for the hilt of the black sword.

Angvasse Khlaylock says, "Stay."

Without transition, Angvasse's kneeling form has translated from across the glade to between the Sword and the goddess's Hand. Still on one knee, still without weapon, head still inclined in reverence, she says, "One touches the Sword by invitation only. You are not invited."

You would oppose Me, little godling? I am as far beyond you as you are beyond these mortals you hope to defend.

"I know full well the depth of Your Might. My duty remains." She lifts her head to regard the shape of power that was the goddess's face. "I do not set Myself beyond mortals, Wild Queen, but beside them. My Shield is and always shall be faced against all who would do them harm."

Mortal harm from mortal hand.

"Not this time."

You forget to whom you speak.

"There are two ways only to resolve a threat 'gainst any who bide in shadow of My Shield. One of these ways is that you withdraw." Angvasse stands and faces square the Power. "That is the way without violence."

Had I the power to stop you all while harming none, please believe I would.

"I believe what I am shown. If you would neither do harm nor suffer it, withdraw."

I can see why Caine admires you so. Good-bye, little godling.

The Hand of the Power stretches forth to touch the armored chest; a silent blinding flash wipes the god who took the form of Angvasse Khlaylock from the glade as though neither had ever existed.

Now I will have the Sword, and this will end with its destruction.

"No." It was Kris Hansen who had knelt; it is Deliann Mithondionne who rises. "Now I see why Caine doesn't trust You."

You, creature? You pathetic created thing—you would seek to defy My Will? You are not a fraction of what Khryl is, and I banished Him with a thought. A flick of my eyelash would destroy you forever.

"Good luck explaining to Ma'elKoth." He looks over his shoulder at Caine. "You know my answer."

A blast of thunder darkens the sky and forking branches of lightning converge on Deliann; when vision returns, the earth where he had stood is burned to the rock.

Caine says, "I always did."

The Power reaches again for the Sword.

Duncan grimaces, finding himself aghast at what he was about to say, but he says it anyway. "No."

You dare?

"Save the *You dare* shit for the tourists," Caine says.

You would set your will against Mine?

"Caine says you can't take the Sword unless I give it to you."

Then give it to Me.

"I already said no." He sets his jaw. "I don't like the way you ask."

It was not a request.

"That's what I don't like."

I can make of this pretty glade a hell beyond imagination—

"It is a hell, you silly bitch," the horse-witch says, still absently weaving her wildflower garland. "Haven't you been paying attention?"

The Attention of the Power wheels on her.

You. What are you? So insignificant I can barely see you. A gnat buzzing around matters beyond your comprehension. Less.

"I'm the horse-witch." She sighs, lays the garland in her lap, and folds her hands over it. "Do you know why he hasn't killed you yet?"

You're as tiresome as Khryl.

"It's Faith. He loves her, and he doesn't know what destroying you will do to her. But I do, and it's not much, so you should be nicer to people."

You're insane.

"You should understand that I'm trying to help you, even though you don't deserve it. Eventually he'll believe me about Faith, and then he might just execute your slag ass, River Bitch. After that he'll find out I was right. She'll barely even miss you."

"Um," Duncan says, "are you sure you want to take that tone? With Her?"

I know of your rutting with the man who once had been My Husband. I have no reason to harm you, but I also have no reason to endure your company. The Power gathers almost to physicality. *Begone.*

The horse-witch shrugs and goes back to braiding wildflowers.

How are you still here? The sky darkens again, and once more thunder rolls. *Begone!*

The horse-witch rolls her eyes without bothering to look up. The Presence gives now only a sense of being flabbergasted into immobility.

"She doesn't like you," Caine says to the Power. "She doesn't get angry often, and she never holds a grudge. Except for you."

This is impossible!

"Apparently it isn't."

It's inconceivable . . .

"Look, first, she can't be forced. You can kill her, but you can't make her do anything she doesn't want to. And second, you can't kill her."

Watch me.

"It's not even about you and me, or You and me," he goes on. "It's because she, um, some people, some of whom looked like her, used to run away and pray to You for help to hide in forests and shit. Prayed for even a chance at freedom. And you didn't help."

And don't.

"Yeah. She doesn't hate Shanna. She knew about Shanna. She even helped some of the *tokali* escape, when she was down along the river that fall. She knows Shanna Leighton would give her life without hesitation to help these people You ignore. The human Pallas Ril *did* give her life to help people like them. But You can't be bothered. So the horse-witch is angry, and probably still will be even if I kill you."

Kill Me? You?

"You don't understand what's going on here. Ma'elKoth—Home, whateverthefuck—sent you after the Sword because you're the only god in His pantheon who had a physical Aspect before Assumption Day. You're the only one who can't be unhappened."

Unhappened . . . ?

"Believe it."

You truly think it is even vanishingly possible to unhappen the Mind of Home?

"There's one way to find out."

You're insane.

"I get that a lot. I know you're thinking you should probably warn Him or something, or maybe just run the fuck away, but you can't. He can't either, because you aren't wholly separate entities. You express a part of His whole, right? So while I hold You here, I'm holding Him."

And how do you hope to hold Me?

"You're kidding, right? Have You completely fucking forgotten everything You ever knew about me? It's already done."

Done . . .

"I know You're a Natural Power, so you don't have the whole temporal omnipresence shit, but somebody should have told you who Khryl was. Who the *real* Khryl was. Angvasse, if you wouldn't mind, bring Kris on out here."

In the depth of shadow under the trees, the tent-flap of the yurt pulls back, and out from it walks Angvasse Khlaylock, now dressed in a simple tunic and pants, and at her side walks Kris Hansen.

Kris said, "Next time *warn* me. I thought I really was about to die."

"I figure that's a feeling you immortals need to be reminded of, every so often. Besides, you'd have blown it. You are a man of many talents, Kris, but you can't fucking act."

Kris looks like he can't decide whether to scream or weep. "Do you have any idea how hard it is to be your friend?"

Caine turns back to the Presence. "Just between You and me and Ma'elKoth, Khryl was the one who Bound all You Fuckers in the first place. You touched him with Your Power; his power touched you. Worked out well, considering Lord Fair Fucking Play over there wasn't willing to just bushwack Your Ass."

You don't—you can't possibly even hope—

"No? So, the last time I had a little disagreement with You and Ma'elKoth, how did I make him come after me?"

Oh—oh, the black knife . . . the oil . . .

"Sucks to fall for the same fucking trick all over again, doesn't it?"

Thunder becomes words:

AND THUS WE SHALL NOT.

When they look up, the sky from horizon to horizon is the Face of Ma'elKoth, with clouds His Beard, mountains His Teeth, and the sun and moon His Eyes.

"Oh, hey," Caine says. "Thanks for stopping by. There's something I want you to see."

devices and maneuvers 2

JUSTICE

JUSTICE

"*Let me quote you: 'I believe in justice, as long as I'm holding a knife at the throat of the judge.'*"

—SHANNA LEIGHTON MICHAELSON
  Heroes Die

*H*e stared down the face of Hell into the Ring of Justice, and he had to give the fuckers credit.

The Order of Khryl had a refined appreciation of the power of show-manship. They had arranged a spectacle on the order of the Nuremberg Rally in *Triumph of the Will*. Arguably even better, as the Nazis had been too fastidious to build a national event around mortal combat between race-champions. The Khryllians would have had Hitler do the intro for a cage match between Joe Louis and Max Schmeling with spiked cesti and no referee. To the death. Now, *that's* showbiz—

And pretty much what they were going for with this particular Khryl's Justice.

This Ring of Justice had been raised and consecrated especially for this particular event. A circular platform a dozen feet tall and some fifty paces in diameter stood at exactly the intersection between Purthin's Ford and Hell, positioned for maximum exposure to both: erected upon the jitney landing at the foot of the vertical city, between the base of the Spire and the lowest tier of Hell. The disk was covered and draped with several layers of thick, absorbent linen, white and spotless to absorb and show every drop of blood; blood shed in Khryl's Justice is sacred to the Lord of Battle.

Two rings encircled the platform, one at three feet and the other at six. On the tallest, one hundred outward-facing armsmen stood shoulder to shoulder, riot guns at parade rest, eyes invisible within gleaming helmets. On the ring below stood one hundred and twenty. On the flagstones below them stood two hundred more. Public sentiment had been running high for some time, and the devastation of not only the previous night's Smoke Hunt but the morning's bombing in Weaver's Square had the massed assemblage of Oath-bound Soldiers and Civility in a dangerously unstable mood.

The Spire bristled with sharpshooters. While nearly all of them directed their attention straight across to the tiers of Hell, a surprisingly large fraction scanned the massed humanity below. The officers of Khryl's Own understood all too well the risk of a general riot, and the dire outcome should such riot spread to become general disorder.

Simple arithmetic:

Five hundred Knights. Ten thousand armsmen. Thirty thousand sworn Soldiers of Khryl, and as many again of the unsworn Civility . . .

And over two hundred thousand ogrillo slaves.

Nobody wanted to find out what the final sum would be.

At the moment of Shortshadow, as noon is called on the Battleground, a young and powerfully built ogrillo hung with weighted chains had been brought up onto the Ring and there directed, as is traditional, to kneel and await the Knight Accusor. Words passed between him and the armsmen who had accompanied him, but the young ogrillo kept his feet.

This had not made the crowd any happier. Now as dusk approached, the mutterings among the spectators took on a darker tone, and were punctuated by occasional shouts of defiance, as the younger, less disciplined, and less sober encouraged one another to rush the Ring and settle this Broken Knife bastard whether Lady Khlaylock showed up or not.

He stood on the sill of a low window on the east face of the third tier, not far from the parapet from which Caine and the partners had watched the approach of the Black Knife Nation. Leaning back into a corner where this building met the next, the blood-rimmed shadows swallowed all of him save the whites of his eyes. The retaining wall in front of him was packed knife to knife with silent ogrilloi. None of them seemed to mind him watching over their shoulders.

Be different if they knew who he used to be.

Be more different if they knew who he was now.

He squinted up at the white-painted framework of the main crane's boom as it swung out from the cargo aerie on the topmost tier. He thought he could pick out a white-clad figure near the tip, but he might have been kidding himself. His eyes weren't what they'd once been, and the latticed steel of the boom made effective camouflage.

He could see plenty well enough to register the seething streets around the Spire. Freedom's Face had done their job well. As the afternoon had worn on, more and more of the assembled crowd had drifted away in disappointment, dismay, and boredom. No one understood why the Champion had not already appeared, and no one was certain what her disappearance would mean for the ogrilloi, the Khryllians, and the Battleground itself.

Things were different now.

An hour before, Kierendal's agents had scattered throughout Purthin's Ford to spread the word:

The Champion arrives at sunset. The last of the Black Knives will give submission to the Living Fist of Khryl, or he will die. Khryl's Justice will be served. The Smoke Hunt will end.

And everybody wanted to see it happen.

Funny: that was exactly what he intended to show them.

A small dais had been erected back against the wall where the two switchback ramps met in the middle. Seven chairs. Men wearing the mirror-polished full plate of Khryllian Lords sat in six of them—these would be the Lords Legendary. Every single one of them a former Champion of Khryl, and each very high on the list of people who should under no circumstances, ever, be fucked with. The empty chair in the middle was for the remaining Lord Legendary, who also happened to be Justiciar of the Order of Khryl. But he had a prior engagement.

Hosting a banquet for crows, maggots, and worms.

He wondered if any of those fuckers even knew Khlaylock was dead. It was possible Markham's balls had finally dropped and he'd 'fessed up. Didn't seem likely; actual testicles would be a little too human.

Maybe later on, he'd pants the sonofabitch and see for himself.

He stared down at the top of Markham's head. The fucker was just standing there, perfectly calm in parade rest, behind and to the right of the empty chair, his helm under one arm, and jeez, if only he'd kept the Automag—

Huh. Yeah, maybe better he wasn't strapped. He probably couldn't have stopped himself.

While Markham might have been carved out of limestone, the Lords Legendary seemed restive—leaning toward one another as if to speak only for one another's ears, looking around, probably wondering whether

Angvasse would show up after all—because if she was gonna make it before sundown, her processional should be already visible, and they should have been hearing the Khryllian Call of Justice anthem for the last ten minutes.

Yeah, processional. Just wait, fuckers. He had a processional for them right here.

"Kierendal," he said softly between his teeth. "How we doing?"

In position. Her Whisper was faint, half-buried in a breathy rustling of breeze. *T'Passe says everything is in place. One supposes we must trust her, despite her unfortunate loyalties.*

"To the Monasteries or to me?"

You pick.

"She's a hell of a lot more trustworthy than I am."

Everyone is. It's not her intentions that worry me; I warned you magick is erratic here.

"Shit, Kier, if magick's the only thing that doesn't work today—"

I'm only saying that when this whole preposterous charade goes tits up, don't count on me to save your life.

"And that's different from the other crazy shit we've done together exactly how?"

A long empty pause.

Die fighting, Caine.

"Um—you do know that's supposed to mean *good* luck, right?"

For both of us.

"Always the charmer." He looked to his left, to his right, and once more down the face of Hell. "I don't see any reason to wait."

Is that a go?

"Yeah. Go."

A shattering detonation split the sky.

Everyone in Hell and Purthin's Ford felt the explosion in their chests like a thump from a fist. A sheet of writhing silver fire whited out the sun, then shattered into thousands of blazing stars trickling down like hot rain.

Down through the storm of stars came a figure in gleaming white, brilliant and blazing, one foot in a stirrup at the bottom of a rope that reached up through the flaming sky above.

Lower, darkness gathered around the figure, which made it shine ever more, brighter and brighter until it seared the eye—but eyes adjust, and as they did a cheer went up from the crowd, answered by an oceanic roar of rage and hunger from the face of Hell.

To welcome Angvasse Khlaylock.

She received the cheers and the roars with only stillness, impassive, incalculable, until the rope reached down fully to the Ring of Justice and she stepped forth upon the linen and finally, only then, acknowledged the storm of voices by raising her right hand.

For a single breath, all voices stilled.

Her raised hand became a fist.

The answering roar rocked the Battleground from Riverdock to the Purificapex atop the Spire.

Sure, the Order of Khryl understood spectacle. They were even pretty good at it. But there is a world's difference between knowing showmanship and being the show.

He'd been the show for half his life.

He didn't mind somebody else taking center stage for a change. Briefly. But even that showed personal growth, he figured. A little. Maybe.

He squinted out at the unarmed woman standing where everyone expected to see the Living Fist of Khryl. He wondered briefly, for the hundredth or thousandth time, if he should have told Angvasse what lay beneath the jitney landing—what was underneath the Ring of so-called Justice: the ruins of the ancient gate to the vertical city, where once upon a time a small band of Aktiri ambushed a Black Knife scouting party and lit the fuse on this whole clusterfuckbomb in the first place.

Too late now.

He reached back over his head for the lip of the window above. With a single smooth heave he drew himself up high enough that he could kick off the wall and swing his legs up through the window and slide the rest of him after.

He went flat on the floor and rolled to the side before standing. He came up with his back to the wall and knives in his hands.

Nobody home. Which was how it was supposed to work, but he hadn't lived this long by taking that kind of shit for granted. He moved deeper into the apartment, away from the light of the windows, and entered the webwork of halls and tunnels, back into the rock.

He didn't bother to put away the knives.

On the Ring, Angvasse Khlaylock paced toward Orbek Black Knife with a stately ceremonial deliberation. She beckoned for the waiting pair of Knights Attendant to enter the ring and unlock the heavy chains that bound him.

Orbek peeled lip from tusk, seized chain with both hands, and with a ripple of muscle and bulge of tendon snapped them in two. The crowds, human and ogrilloi alike, unleashed a roar. He let his broken chains fall and stepped forward, leaning into the thunder as though it had weight, and raised his fist to the tiers of Hell above. As the roar subsided, he answered it with one of his own.

"*I am Black Knife! Orbek Black Knife!*"

BLACK KNIFE! The echoing roar from the tiers of Hell made the rock tremble. ORBEK BLACK KNIFE!

"*I am Orbek! Buck of God! Terror of Our Place! Today Orbek Black Knife breaks Khryl's Own Fist. When Khryl FALLS before BLACK KNIFE, all world will know!*

"*From now till forever, BLACK KNIVES DON'T KNEEL!*"

At his side, Angvasse warned off the Knights Attendant with a glance, then spoke only loud enough for Orbek's ears alone. "And yet you are not Orbek," she said, "and you are not Black Knife *kwatcharr*. Khryl punishes the faithless."

He turned his tusks toward her. "What Khyl does or doesn't, who fuck me cares? What I am is your death."

"You're not that either. Neither of us is who we thought to be, in this Ring on this day. Must this be done?"

"Do you yield?"

"Of course not."

"Then you die."

"It's unlikely."

"Don't you Declare Yourself, or whatever fuck-me stupid shit you gotta do before I kill you?"

She nodded, and turned to the Lords Legendary on their dais. She lifted her hand, and waited for the crowds to quiet. When they had, she spoke slowly, precisely, and so clearly that she could be heard without raising her voice.

"I am Angvasse Khlaylock of Lockholm, Lady Legendary and Knight Accusor in this matter. I will see this supposed ogrillo kneel, or I will see it dead."

No roars greeted her, only a rustling that gathered like stormwinds stirring fallen leaves.

She turned back to Orbek. "Ready?"

Orbek wore a frown that was developing toward a scowl. "Where's your armor? Where's your weapon?"

Her eyes softened momentarily, as though she restrained a tolerant smile. "Do I need them?"

"And what's that *supposed* mean? Supposed ogrillo. You know my name. What do you play at?"

"If this is a game, you have lost. You are not *kwatcharr* of the Black Knives. You are barely Orbek. You're not even an ogrillo, any more than were the Smoke Hunters."

Cords in his neck drew his chin down, and the brush of hair on his spinal ridge stood straight out from his body, and he did not reply.

The rustling from the crowds began to develop voice, puzzled, quizzical, some astonished and more derisive. Markham Tarkanen stomped to the front of the Lords Legendary dais and raised his arms. "Silence! In the Name of Khryl Battlegod, I will have *silence!*"

"What's up *his* ass?"

"I have a message from your brother," she said softly. "He asked me to tell you before the Justice."

"What, he says I should die fighting?"

"His exact words were *Once we're done with your beat-down, get your stupid dog ass out of that goddamn simichair and fuck off for the gate. There's a guy coming through. He doesn't look it and he won't smell it, but he's Tanner. Play nice. We need him. I'll be in touch.*"

Orbek said, "Fuck *me* . . ."

"He worried that you—your body, this body, this Smoke Hunt fetch you're controlling by technology from Earth—will die before he can tell you himself."

"Yah? He must know something I don't."

"He is singularly well informed."

As the crowds settled back down, Markham came stomping out into the Ring. "Lady Khlaylock!" he boomed. "How is it you do not declare your title?"

"Hm," she said softly, nodding to herself. "He said this would happen."

She stepped forward to address the Lord Righteous, and all the assembled crowds. "My Lord, I have declared every title I lawfully hold."

"But—" Markham blinked as though she were a blinding light. "But you are Khryl's Own Fist!"

"No more."

"You have been Champion longer than any Lord in two hundred years!"

"I was." Her voice rang like a brass bell. "This noontide I ventured to assault an Armed Combatant. I was defeated, and thus hold no formal title beyond my rank and my uncle's lands."

"Defeated?" Markham looked dazed. "You?"

"I have said so." Her balance shifted subtly, and a dangerous spark glittered in her eyes. "Do you undertake to doubt a Khlaylock's word? In public?"

The Lord Righteous stiffened. "This Justice—this was to be Khryl's Fist against the—"

"I have no interest in what this Justice *was to be*. My sole concern—the sole concern of every *true* Soldier of Khryl—is to ensure that Justice assayed is justice *done*. Neither less nor more."

Markham reddened to the roots of his hair. She swept past him and opened her arms to the Lords Legendary and the assembled ogrilloi of Hell above them. "Many here believed that you would today see the Lord of Battle's affirmation, or denial, that enslaving ogrilloi was and is a righteous act. And some would have argued the question based upon an outcome of trial between the chieftain of the Black Knives and Khryl's Living Fist. There will never be such outcome. I am not Khryl's Champion, and this creature is not *kwatcharr* of the Black Knives."

This brought a dangerous rumble up from the humans and down from the ogrilloi both.

She raised her hand. "Must I kill or die to reveal a truth that every living creature here today already knows? Must I shed blood to defend crime? Hazard my skill, my life, and Khryl's Strength in service to contemptible injustice? Were Our Lord of Battle among us today, He would weep with shame at what has been done in His Name."

Markham's eyes bulged and cords twisted in his neck. "What are you *doing*?"

"Speaking truth, as I am Sworn to do." Scalding contempt joined the dangerous glitter in her indigo eyes. "What are *you* doing?"

He wheeled on Orbek. "Say that you are *kwatcharr*."

Orbek's head winched downward.

"*Say it!*"

"I am Orbek, Black Knife *kwatcharr*."

Markham flinched like he'd been slapped.

"You hear. Khryl hears." Angvasse lifted her chin along with her voice. "Every Sworn Knight and Lord within the sound of his voice knows Khryl hears this lie! Whatever you all hoped to see today will not happen. Will *never* happen."

"You cannot do this," Markham growled.

"I can. I do."

"The Black Knife must submit to Khryl."

"It will not happen."

"How can you say this?"

"Khryl's Champion affirmed it to me himself, as did the Black Knife. There will be neither submission nor battle. Ever."

" 'Affirmed it' to you *alone*?"

"Should you think I have been misled, or have mistaken his meaning, you are welcome to ask him yourself."

"Him? Which one?"

"There is only one."

With a curiously pleasurable frisson—one that gave her a hint of why the new Champion was so fond of theatrics—she waved toward the retaining wall of Hell's first tier, above and directly behind the dais where sat the Lords Legendary.

"He's right up there."

As all eyes turned to the face of Hell, there came a peal of thunder that blasted away all other sound, and the city fell into midnight as though some god had extinguished the sun. The shocked blind silence lasted only as long as taking a breath, and then the darkness was sliced open by a ragged pillar of lightning that danced and writhed and crashed into thunder . . . and with this second peal light returned to the city, and on the spot she had indicated—still smoking from the lightning's fury—stood a slim man with salted black hair and greying beard, clad in tunic, pants, and boots of stained, half-faded black leather, and each of his hands held a black-bladed knife.

"Sorry I'm late," he said in a tone of cheerful mockery. "Did I miss anything?"

"What—but—what—?" Markham sputtered. "You can't—this can't be—"

Orbek only stood and stared with a sullen scowl.

"Give the Champion his due," Angvasse Khlaylock murmured. "He does know how to make an entrance."

He took one step for momentum and hurled himself headlong into space to execute an elegant flip and land with a resonant *boom* on the dais of the Lords Legendary. "Hi, boys. Don't get up."

"Seriously. Don't," he said, as a couple of them were rising, hands to their weapons. "I haven't killed any good guys today. Don't be first."

He backflipped off the dais and landed on the Ring of Justice in a three-point kneel, head inclined, and took just a second to reflect how much better he was at pretty much everything when he was showing off.

Maybe Kollberg had been right, all those years ago: maybe the only power he needed was star power.

"My Lords," he said gravely, and when he rose, the riot guns of several hundred armsmen were pointed in his general direction. He lifted his right hand. *"Lady Khlaylock!"*

Amplified until it seemed the shout had come from the world entire, his words boomed back from the face of Hell and thundered through the whitestone streets of Purthin's Ford.

"Who is Champion? Who is the Living Fist of Khryl?"

She stepped forward. *"You are, my Lord!"*

He stood and waited until the roars of disbelief and outrage began to fade. *"What is my name?"*

"Men call you Caine, my Lord!"

Silence dropped like a boulder big enough to crush the city.

"What is my *full* name?"

Angvasse Khlaylock took a knee.

Rumblings from the crowds like a distant earthquake.

"My Lord Champion, you are Caine Black Knife, *kwatcharr* of the Boedecken ogrilloi."

In later years, it would come to be said that the roar from the crowds present on that day to witness the Declaration of Caine swelled until it cracked the world.

This was only a metaphor, of course—a poetic exaggeration invented to underscore the significance of the event—and it would later come to be a commonplace cliché for any cataclysm to be referred to as "like another Declaration of Caine." Eventually, the reference would be applied to anything loud, even if not dramatic. During a severe thunderstorm, for instance, someone would customarily say words to the effect of "Well, Caine's Declarin' the hell out of us today"; someone who wished to underscore implacable determination might say, "Let Caine Declare what he may." In the fullness of time, the phrase would be used most often with derision, as a sarcastic hyperbole for something merely trivial.

It would also be said, among the common run of superstitious folk, that the Declaration of Caine cracked not the world, but the heavens above and all hells below, and that the roar greeting the Declaration came not from the throats of humanity and ogrilloi, but from the fear and despair of every living god and demon and angel and deva as they first heard the name of the Black Knife.

Unlike the proverbial expressions above, however, this was not only a metaphor.

. . .

He waited for the roar to fade.

He turned then, gazing out into the crowds, slowly, as though to meet every pair of eyes in turn. He cast the knives down so that they stabbed into the Ring of Justice at his feet, and shivered there. Then he unlaced his tunic, and as he took it off, he spoke.

"Any man, woman, buck, or bitch who would deny me either title, step up and get in line. I want to count how many people I have to kill today."

Now bare to the waist, his webwork of scars on full display, he went over to where Markham and Orbek stood, and Angvasse knelt.

Angvasse lowered her head. "My Lord Champion."

He touched her shoulder. "Good evening and well met, Lady Khlay-lock. Rise."

Even in a normal tone, his words boomed across the Battleground.

Orbek growled under his breath, "Fucking Kierendal. Go figure. Elf slag sells me out."

"Nobody's selling anybody, big dog. Shut up and sit down."

"Don't take your orders, me. Not anymore."

"Like that, is it?"

"You know it is."

"Yeah, whatever." He looked around. "Anybody else?"

No one seemed to be leaping in.

"Come on, some fucking idiot around here has to be brain-dead enough to think he can take me."

"I can take you, little fucker," Orbek growled.

"Yeah, except you're not a fucking idiot."

Markham's face darkened and hardened. He paced away toward the center of the Ring.

"I am Markham Tarkanen of Purthin's Ford, Lord Righteous of the Order of Khryl," he said distinctly, "and I proclaim that this supposed Caine Black Knife is not Khryl's Champion, has never been Khryl's Champion, and will never be Khryl's Champion. If any dispute this proclamation, I will undertake to prove its truth upon their bodies in this place and at this time."

"That's what I'm talking about. Thanks, Markham." He grinned. "I knew I'd have to kill a Knight today. I'm glad it's you."

"I have defeated you before."

"By ambush, you Craven Recreant whateverthefuck. Raise a hand to me here, and I will smoke your Knight ass like a cheap cigar. In this place and at this time. Believe it."

The Lord Righteous touched his mailed hand to his brushed-steel breastplate. "Shall I disarm?"

"Nobody wants to see you naked."

"Very well." Markham set his helm upon his head. "Choose your weapon."

"I have every weapon I need right here. Use whatever suits you."

Markham strode over to the dais of the Lords Legendary. One of them handed him a morningstar. "At your pleasure."

"Hey, I've got an idea. Orbek, you think you can whip me and become the Black Knife, right?"

"You know I can, little human fucker."

"And you, Markham, think you can whip me and become the Champion."

"Should Khryl so decree."

"Sure. How about instead I whip both of you? At the same time. It's getting late and I've got shit to do."

Orbek's face darkened too, and his eyes took on a suspicious slant. "What trick you think you play, little fucker?"

"You've got an easy way to find out."

He pulled his two blades out of the Ring floor and tossed them casually near Orbek's feet. "What do you think? Just like a story, huh? The ogrillo with black knives, the Knight with the morningstar in his hand, and me with the only pair of balls in the Ring. I'm thinking after I kill both of you, everybody else will probably shut the fuck up."

Orbek picked up the knives and weighed them in his hands. "What do you do for weapon?"

"I'm pretty sure I know where to put my hands on two or three. If I need them."

"This is ridiculous." Markham turned toward the Lords Legendary. "He makes a mockery of Khryl's Justice."

"Khryl's Justice was mockery already."

"It's *unprecedented*—"

"Oh, sure, and you've had a Monastic assassin Champion plenty of times. Come on, bitches. What are you afraid of? Losing, or winning? Because, y'know, if you win you'll be Champion and he'll be *kwatcharr* and you two sissies will get to stage your precious fucking pillow fight."

Orbek tilted his head to one side, then the other, cracking his neck with a sound like a drumroll. "If Khrylbitches are ready, Black Knives are ready."

The Lords Legendary weren't having any, of course; maintaining tradition, dignity, and decorum was their job. But he saw the dangerous glitter within the eye-slits of Markham's helm, and he knew he could make this happen.

Besides, nobody in the crowd could hear a word the Lords Legendary said.

"I'm *kwatcharr,* and I say to hold back is submission!" he barked at Orbek, then turned to Markham. "I am Khryl's Champion, and I proclaim Lord Tarkanen's hesitation displays the same *cowardice* for which *I killed Purthin Khlaylock!*"

And when those words thundered out across the Battleground, there was no one not on their feet, no one not shouting, no one not craving blood, and he went to the center of the Ring of Justice, exactly between Orbek and Markham, spread his arms, and said, "Come on, then."

Markham lowered his head, roared, *"For the glory of Khryl!"* and charged; Orbek just roared, and charged twice as fast. In the middle of the Ring, exactly between them, Caine Black Knife said only one word.

"Angvasse."

With preternatural speed, the former Champion's right hand slipped up under the back of her tunic to the holster fixed to her trouser belt at the small of her back.

The knives in Orbek's hands exploded into blinding white fire as though they'd been forged from thermite, too intense to even register as heat. *"Gahhh—"*

He reeled to one side, frantically whipping his hands to cast away the blades, but they had burned themselves into his flesh and into his bone and his feet tangled and he went down on his face, rolling in hopes of smothering the insatiable flame.

Markham shouted, *"Tashonnall!"* and blue witchfire erupted over his armor and his velocity instantly tripled, turning his body into a lethal missile that would certainly have splattered Caine into bloody gobbets of flesh and sprayed them over half of Purthin's Ford had Caine not snatched neatly from the air the large black pistol that Angvasse had tossed to him and then put a couple tristack shatterslugs precisely through Markham's eyeballs.

The shatterslugs didn't penetrate the back curve of the Lord Righteous's helm, and thus when his corpse went facedown skidding across the Ring, the streak it left was a pudding of Markham's face, brain, and skull. Caine stepped back to let the corpse slide on past him. He couldn't help smiling.

Jesus, it felt great to get off a good one once in a while.

"Orbek."

"Wha—?" The dazed ogrillo made it up to his knees, burning hands jammed into his now-also-burning armpits. His jaw hung slack.

"*That's* how you do a pitch-out, big dog. Maybe you should take notes."

"Fucker. You *fucker*. What fucking happens to you being a fucking crappy fucking *shot*?"

"You believed that? Shit, I guess I *can* act." Caine shook his head, chuckling. "Say hi to Tanner," he said, and shot Orbek in the face.

The three shatterslugs snapped Orbek's head back, then he fell forward and lay on the Ring, still on fire, as was now the Ring itself around him.

He cast aside the pistol, and did not mark where it fell. "And three rounds is plenty."

The crowds fell so suddenly silent that for some seconds birdsong and the soft plash of ripples in the Caineway could be heard.

He stepped back into the center of the burning Ring, threw wide his arms, and shouted at the top of his considerable lungs, further amplified by the magicks of Kierendal.

"*Did anybody NOT see that? Does anybody need it EXPLAINED?*"

Nobody volunteered a question. The Lords Legendary looked to be arguing about what Khryl wanted them to do now. A couple hundred armsmen fiddled nervously with their riot guns, swinging them back and forth trying to get a clear line of fire at him and control the crowds at the same time.

Well, all right, then.

"*Twenty-five years ago, I stood in this place. I told the Black Knife Nation that this place is MINE. I told them that here for them is DEATH. I told them their bitches will HOWL and their pups will STARVE.*

"*I said for Black Knives, this place is HELL.*

"*Some of you heard me on that day. Many more know some who did. Did I LIE? Was I MISTAKEN? Was I JOKING?*"

The answering roar made the Ring shudder like a drumhead.

"*What is my WORD? Is it FALSE? Is it EMPTY?*"

This time the answer had words, a rhythm, becoming a chant.

Skinwalker's word is LAW

Skinwalker's word is LAW

He couldn't help smiling. Kaiggez, all over the job. Nice.

The Lords Legendary seemed to have come to some kind of decision, as every one of them was now on his feet, unlimbering weapons and affixing helms.

He held up a hand, and the chanting fell away.

"*Then, I warned Black Knives.*"

"*Now I warn SOLDIERS OF KHRYL.*

"*This place is NOT THE BATTLEGROUND. This place is NOT PURTHIN'S FORD.*

"*This place is MINE.*"

He gave them half a breath for effect.

"*Whose PLACE is this?*"

The answer from two hundred thousand throats:

YOUR PLACE

"*Who AM I?*"

SKINWALKER

"*What is my name?*"

CAINE

"*What is my NAME?*"

CAINE

"*WHAT IS MY NAME?*"

And now the roar did seem as though it might break the world.

CAINE BLACK KNIFE

"*I am CAINE BLACK KNIFE!*"

CAINE BLACK KNIFE

"*I am BLACK KNIFE, and I say—this is OUR PLACE!*"

Hell erupted in a hurricane of rage and triumph.

Angvasse caught his eye and nodded. She mouthed, *Good one.*

Into the hurricane of rage leaped all six Lords Legendary. Their simultaneous landing on the Ring sounded like the continent had exploded. It blasted the city into silence.

One of the Lords stepped forward. "This . . . *monstrosity* . . . ends now! You both will surrender yourselves. Until we decide how best to undo this horror."

"Horror. Huh. Y'know, when Black Knives talk about meeting me, that's exactly the word they use. The Horror." He bared his teeth. "Maybe it'll work out better for you."

The other Lords Legendary began to spread out around the circle. The spokeslord said, "A thousand rifles are on you as we speak. One word from me and Khryl Himself won't recognize your bodies."

"Khryl knows His Own," Angvasse said sadly. "You are not among them."

The Lord raised a mailed fist. "Armsmen! Take aim!"

"It is as you have said, my Lord Champion. Holding the Battleground has broken our honor, and stained the name of Our Lord of Battle forever."

He smiled. "Our Lord of *Battle's* a fucking punk. Make of Him instead the Lord of Light and Love and that kind of shit, you might get an Order who'd use the Might of Khryl for something better than holding slaves and killing people."

"As you said: to have better gods, be better people."

"Yeah." He looked at the spokeslord. "You want to shoot us, punk ass? Go ahead. Let me just say one thing first."

"And that is?"

He spread his hands. "You were warned. All of you. Warned."

"That's all?"

"That's all."

"Then yield. Take a knee, and live."

He exchanged a look with Angvasse. She said, "Brothers together. To the end."

"Oh, sisters too," he said with a smile. "And this isn't the end."

"*Yield!*"

"Fuck yourself."

The Lord's mailed fist came down. "*Fire!*"

And fire is exactly what he got.

A thundering blast of white flame leaped up from the whole Ring. Armsmen on the galleries of the Spire above poured volley after volley into the fire, and several Lords Legendary managed to reel out of the flames in red-hot armor, and at the instant of the Lord's command, Angvasse Khlaylock shouted *Tashonall* and gathered Caine Black Knife into her arms as she streaked for the dangling cabled chain she had ridden down into the Ring, leaping high to burst out from the flames in a blue streak of witch-fire.

She caught the chain. Far above, a counterweight plunged, and the two flashed upward through the storm of bullets as though they'd been shot from a cannon. On Angvasse, the splattering impacts of rifle rounds made no impression beyond causing her to fix a loop of the chain to her wrist, so they wouldn't fall if she lost consciousness; the Love of Khryl sustained her and restored her shredded flesh. Every time one hit Caine, he snarled a curse—largely from force of habit—as power from the oil in his arteries flashed each slug into nonexistence, because the burns hurt more than the bullets would have, and his leathers were on fire everywhere they had not been blown off.

Angvasse shouted into the wind, "*There must have been easier ways!*"

His arms tightened around her, and he put his lips against her ear. "What's the matter? Aren't you having fun?"

the now of always 9

FUCK GOD

FUCK GOD

*"Fear God, and keep his commandments: for this is the whole
duty of man."*

— *Ecclesiastes* 12:13

"Y ou might as well come on down in person," Caine says to the sky
full of Face. "I mean, seriously. You know me. The harm I intend
to do you is already done."

HOW CAN WE POSSIBLY BELIEVE ANYTHING YOU SAY?

"Jesus Christ, how can you *not*? Besides, the entire sky thing is not a
good look for you. Nose hair. And, holy shit—try flossing sometime, man.
Yikes."

AND HAVE YOU LURED US HERE FOR JUVENILE ABUSE?

"Oh, hell no. The juvenile abuse is strictly for my personal entertainment. I have a real reason. Remember the afternoon of the day we slagged
Kosall?"

VIVIDLY.

"Remember what I told you?"

**WE CONVERSED AT SOME LENGTH, ON A VARIETY OF
SUBJECTS.**

"Y'know, if I wanted, I could summon it up so we could all watch it
together. But it's not that important. You were talking about being my
friend."

AND I AM.

"Swell. Remember what I told you? I told you I'm not *your* friend. You
killed my wife, fucker. You hurt my *daughter*."

AND FROM THOSE CRIMES, WE SAVED THE WORLD.

"See? You do remember. I said, 'I don't care if you save the mother-fucking *universe*, it won't get you off the hook with me. I don't care if you are God. Someday, somehow, I'm gonna fuck you up.' Remember?"

OF COURSE.

"Well, this is the day."

YOU'RE MAD.

"Crazy too. I unhappened your discarnate ass. Welcome to the rest of your fucking afterlife."

WHAT?

"Funny thing is, I didn't even do it on purpose. But once I figured out what I'd done, I ran with it. It's kind of my style."

ANYTHING YOU'VE DONE CAN BE UNDONE. WITH A SHRUG OF INTENTION, WE CAN REHAPPEN ANYTHING YOU CAN UNHAPPEN.

"Yeah, maybe. If you weren't kind of tied up here right now. The instant I pull that Sword—the instant Duncan *decides* I can pull the Sword—you'll blow away like a bird fart."

AND YET YOU STAY YOUR HAND.

GLOATING HAS NEVER BEEN YOUR STYLE.

Caine nods. "This isn't nearly as much fun as I thought it would be."

WHY DO YOU POSTPONE THE INEVITABLE?

"Because I'm sorry."

The Face that is the sky falls silent.

"Ma'elKoth, goddammit, come down here and be a man again. Just for a while. I want to apologize face-to-face. Please. Out of respect for the friendship we could have had."

"Then I am with you, Caine."

And He is.

Wreathed in majesty like the sun, God cannot be regarded with mortal eyes. Even with his arm thrown across his face, the figure of God scalds Duncan's eyes and crushes breath from his lungs.

"Fucking cut it out."

There follows some byplay that Duncan does not clearly hear—some words of the Sword, of the horse-witch, and of Duncan himself—and then at length the furious majesty passes through and beyond him, and Duncan can breathe again. He takes his arm from his face, squinting cautiously, to find seated on the grass some distance away a figure he knows well: Tan'elKoth, dressed as he had appeared on Earth, in his formal Artisan shirt and tie, clean-shaven, his lush curls gathered back into a conservative ponytail. Caine stands by his side, and the two men stare gravely into the middle distance, and though they are well away and speak together only softly, Duncan is aware of their words.

"I wish shit could have been different," Caine is saying. "I wish *I* could have been different."

Ma'elKoth doesn't seem to hear. "What changed?"

"What, about me? About me and you?"

Ma'elKoth shrugs diffidently, and looks away.

Caine sighs and lowers himself to the grass beside him. "I just got thinking, that's all. Like you said that day in the Cathedral, we both did what we had to do to protect what we most loved."

"You weren't impressed by the sentiment at the time."

"I was angry."

"Now you're not?"

"You know I am. I just—I don't know. Most of the really shitty things you did were at least partly because of shitty stuff I did. But that's not really it either. It's not easy to talk about."

"I have never known you to be inarticulate—though I frequently wished you so."

"Yeah, okay, fair enough. Look, in the Vault of Binding in Thorncleft, they have at least one History of Caine where I really was the son of a blacksmith in Pathqua—where my fake background was real. Somehow it got unhappened, and became only fiction. I don't know how or why, but it doesn't really matter. It just got me thinking about how my life would have been different if I hadn't been an Actor, you know? If I really was who I've been pretending to be."

"And you suspect your life would be so very different?"

"I don't know. But I'm fucking positive *your* life would be different."

Ma'elKoth goes thoughtful.

"Seriously. You never get kidnapped to Earth. The history of both worlds looks different. And it's more than that . . . if I weren't an Actor, if I really was Dominic Smith, really was Caine, when you went looking for me you would have found me. Then I could have been your loyal leg-breaker instead of Berne. Imagine how much shit *that* might have saved. If I'd been more dependable—and easier to find—Hannto might not have felt like he had to hire Berne for the Dal'kannith thing in the first place."

"And do you imagine this hypothetical life to be greater than the one we have shared?"

"Greater? Probably not. Calmer? Happier? Less cataclysmic? Seems a safe bet."

Ma'elKoth greets this with a solemn nod. "That it does."

"And . . ." Now Caine looks away. "And something happened that made me understand you. Really understand you. Understand why you made yourself what you are."

"Were."

"Yeah. I get it now. I get you."

"I can't imagine why you felt a need to tell me this."

"Let me show you. Let me show all of you." Caine rises, and moves back among the others. "What you're about to see is what this is all about. Not why it started, or when—but why *I* started. The fights, the killings, the double-crosses, my career—hell, my whole life, all that shit—none of it means anything without this.

"I used to say *why* is bullshit. Well, y'know, live and learn. This right here . . .

"This is why."

the horse-witch 4

HORSE TIME

HORSE TIME

"Sometimes eating an apple can last all day."
—THE HORSE-WITCH
Occasionally

*H*e woke to twilight among trees and stone. A soft rush of falling water came from not far, and also not near. Earth rose up before him, and behind and beside. Far above, indigo sky glittered with stars framed by outcrops of sun-bleached rock.

Ah: a canyon.

He remembered walking into a canyon. He wasn't sure it had been this one. It had twisted and curved in upon itself until he'd entirely lost track of any notion of north, south, east, or west. This didn't worry him. Compass points are half-imaginary anyway, useful mostly to those who don't know the road. Here the only directions were this way and that way, up and down. These seemed to be enough.

He woke also to the understanding that he had not been sleeping. He had been walking. He wasn't sure for how long or how far, and he wasn't sure it mattered. He also wasn't sure why he was now walking awake, where before he had walked somewise else.

He rounded a sharp angle and found her there, beside an earth-banked fire on a sward that filled a long slow bend in the river. Two horses were with her. One placidly cropped grass. The other, larger horse dipped its head and nickered as if to say *I see you, I know you, and I am not afraid,* and he recognized the young stallion he and the ogrillo had followed into the south.

The woman by the fire said, "He likes you."

"He does?"

"He wants to know if you like him back. He wants to know if you want him to be yours. He asked me to find out because you don't speak horse."

He stopped across the campfire from her and lowered himself to the grass. "I'll have to think it over."

She nodded. "It's a serious matter."

"I get that."

"He likes you because you're strong and fierce, and because other men fear you and do what you say. He thinks that together you and he would be the wind, and laugh at fences and chains and castle walls; he thinks that together you would be the thunderbolt, that men would tremble and hide their faces, and pray to you to spare their lives."

"That's kind of dramatic."

"He's very young. And very male." She smiled at him. "What was your dream, when you first became a man?"

He had to smile back. "Well, yeah. Okay."

"Also—and this is very important—he likes you because I like you. He believes I'm very wise, and that I see deeply into the hearts of others."

"I kind of believe that myself."

"Because I like you, he believes that strong and fierce is not all you are. He believes you can be gentle. He believes you can be kind, and that you will care for him. He believes you understand what it is to love, and to be loved."

He had to look away.

"He's young, and full of extravagant fantasy; his heart holds more dream than reality. Young of that type are fragile. If you take him to be your horse, you are making a sacred vow—to both of us—that he's right about you. That I'm right about you."

"That's why I have to think about it," he said, barely above a whisper. "It's kind of an intense relationship."

"There are horses who pass their lives cheery and carefree, who play with their herds and are not troubled by the imperfections of riders, however many there may be. Many horses, most horses, don't need a single person on whom to rest all their trust and devotion."

She met his eyes across the fire. "Horses like those don't join the witch-herd."

He drew up his knees and wrapped his arms around them. "Pretty much the same for people, huh?"

"I've been waiting for you to understand that."

They were silent then for a time, letting the fire's crackle and the ripples on the river speak for them. A brush of wind and cricketing of frogs and the mare's contentedly methodical rip-and-crunch of the grass, and he said, "That sound. The river and the frogs. The grass. Mostly the grass. Something about hearing her eat grass . . ."

"Lets you be calm," she said. Slowly. Quietly.

"Better than a tranquilizer."

"Even an ordinary horse's senses are a hundred times sharper than ours. Prey animals. Fear is their life. Sight, scent, sound. These are what keep them alive. And the senses of the witch-herd horses are a hundred times sharper still. They've learned that ordinary fear isn't enough. A horse can eat while she's afraid . . . but not slowly. Not evenly. For more than a hundred thousand years, your ancestors have known a placidly chewing horse means safety."

"You talk more than you used to."

She shrugged. "You live on words. You don't understand until it's explained, to you or by you."

"Everybody's like that."

"I'm not."

"Yeah, but you're the horse-witch."

She smiled, and her smile warmed him like a kiss of fire.

He looked back to the young stallion. "Fucking grass. Shit, if I'd known that years ago . . ."

"If you'd known that years ago, you'd be somebody else."

"Better?"

"Different."

"Still—grass. Just grass."

"Food is powerful. Shared food is more powerful. Here."

She tossed him a carrot she must have gotten out of that same otherplace where she kept her knives and rasps and medicines. "Take a bite. Take two."

He did. The carrot was perfect: sweet and crisp and earthy. It made him smile.

"Give the rest to him."

He looked up and saw that the young stallion was behind him, sidling up warily, watching him sidelong. He offered the rest of the carrot on a flat palm. Gravely, decorously formal, the stallion took the carrot from his hand and began to chew it. The man chewed too. They watched each other chew. The stallion stared intently, long enough to be sure no more carrots might unexpectedly appear, then turned slightly aside and joined the mare in crunching grass.

"You made him happy just then."

"More like he made me happy."

"If you're with him, what makes him happy will make you happy. What makes you proud will make him proud. In lands to the south, from Kor to Yalitrayya, the wise women say your horse is who you are without your name."

"It's like magick."

"It is magick," she said. "Good magick. Magick that does no one harm."

He discovered he was hungry. He chanced to look down into the campfire, and found a pair of spits, on which were roasting the limbs and torsos of some small animals. Jackrabbit, probably. And a substantial-looking camp oven, cover off, in which boiled a thick pottage of beans and barley. "Was that always there?"

"Yes."

"Always as in from before I came walking up, or always as in, y'know, always?"

She shrugged.

"Smells good," he said, because it did.

"I hope you'll like it."

"When will it be ready?"

"When would you like to eat?"

He looked around. The twilight made the rocks and trees and grass and river seem alive somehow, changeable and permanent together. The grass smelled like a hayfield after the rain. Some twilight-blooming flowers were opening upstream on the riverbank, and the water carried their delicately inviting scent. He rubbed his fingers together, scowling faintly at the grime caked under his nails, and slowly he became aware of how stiffly sweat-salted and greased he was, and he imagined how he must smell. "Will it keep long enough for me to take a bath? Maybe wash my clothes?"

"If the hare overcooks, I'll strip its meat into the pottage and we'll have stew. If you're too tired to eat tonight, it will still be warm in the morning."

He nodded and went to rise, but the weight in his heart made him pause on one knee. "Have I been here for a long time?"

"You've been here since you got here."

"No—I mean, it *feels* like a long time. And like a short time. And somehow the light doesn't change . . ."

"That's why I like canyons," she said. "Dusk feels like forever. Dawn too."

He nodded again. "Things take as long as they take. They last as long as they last. Horse time."

Her doe eye twinkled at him. "I like my apple better."

"I guess I do too." Again he went to rise, and again the weight surpassed his strength. "Seems like I walked a long way to get here. A really long way."

"Three or four days, probably. Unless you walk very fast."

"No, I mean like . . . like twenty-five years. More. My whole life."

"When did I go literal and you metaphoric? Aren't we supposed to work the other way around?"

"Now you're teasing me."

"Only a little." She smiled fondly. "Myself a little too."

Sometime later, he stirred himself to speak again.

"I just wish . . ." He shook his head. "I wish we could have met a long time ago. Then maybe everything would be different."

"We did meet a long time ago," she said, "and everything is different."

"That's not what I mean."

"But it is. You just don't know it yet."

He looked pained. "None of that, huh? No more gnomic epigrams."

"Gnomic epigrams!" She laughed delightedly. "Oh, I *like* that."

"Stop. No games, all right? This is serious."

"Come at this with solemn resolve and it will eat you alive. Forever. And its teeth aren't even sharp."

"What the hell are you talking about?"

"Powers have been loosed upon the world who make the future more frantic than a lunatic's nightmare, and make the past less than words you might write with your finger on the surface of this river."

"Um, actually . . ." He frowned. "Yeah, actually that's pretty much it. How do you know about this?"

"There are ways in which I'm very like a mortal woman," she said. "There are ways in which I'm more like a horse. Horses never forget. They can't. Teach a colt a trick and forty years later the aged gelding he's become will know that trick without reminder. Every smile, every frown, every caress. Every slap. Every whipping. Always there. Always. That's how I am. I remember. I remember more than even horses. I remember things that didn't happen."

"You remember—?"

"The past is in motion. In these days, nothing is certain. Anything can change. This moment itself may evaporate like a dewdrop in summer sun. But I remember what is lost when the world is changed."

"That's a . . . um, interesting power."

"It's not power. Only memory. I mention it because you should know some things *don't* change."

"Really?" The more he thought about that, the more important it sounded. "Because you've lived—"

"Mostly forever," she said lightly. "I have been to interesting places, and seen exotic things. Witnessed events small and events vast. Some of which are still real."

"I guess it's those still-real ones I should know about."

"Most things that don't change are inconsequential; they mean so little to the wider world that no god can be bothered to change them. Then there are others that have stood so eternally themselves, I believe they *can't* be changed."

"Tell me."

"I have seen a man-god with a sword strike the hand from an arm of a god-man. I have seen a man-god with a sword drive a thousand thousand gods into a crack in the universe. I have seen a man throw himself upon a sword to slay his dearest enemy and save his bitterest love. I have seen a sword slay a goddess, transubstantiate a god, and bring forth upon this guilty world an empire of immortal justice."

"Um . . ." He frowned, swallowed, coughed, and started again. "A couple of those, I was there."

"I saw you."

"I didn't see you."

"You seemed a little distracted."

"Did we—did I ever meet you before—wait. Here. Did I ever meet someone who wasn't you yet? Someone who wasn't the horse-witch?"

"Why?" Something dark and wary in her tone caught him and turned him toward her. She had drawn back from the fire, and the twilight had thickened enough to shadow her face. "What can the answer to that question mean to you?"

"A woman in Faltane. A slave at the manor. She died in the fire."

"That didn't happen. You didn't meet her."

"I know. Please. You remember?"

"Yes."

"Tell me about her."

"I would prefer not."

He nodded. "I won't try to make you."

"It's a dark tale," she said. "A perilous road, one that will take you somewhere you may not like."

"Pretty much the same as any road."

She sighed. "Yes."

"I can't think of a road I've walked that *isn't* perilous."

She said, "She is gone, and no one remembers her except me. This will take a woman and make her into a story. There was more to her, more in her, than can be told. She deserves a better story than I can give her."

"Most people do," he said. "Start with her name."

"Slaves don't have names. She was called by whatever word pleased her master that day."

"Oh. It's that kind of story."

"Of slavery, yes. But mainly: rape."

He looked down. *Rape* was a hard word. Harder when it's someone he knew. And cared about. The sick twist in his guts booted denial right the fuck out of his head.

Maybe if he kept his eyes on the ground he could stand here and take it.

"No," she said. "You're not allowed to look away. Not from this story. If you want to know this, you have to take it face-to-face."

"I have to know."

"And I'm sorry for that."

"Me too." He lifted his head and made himself gaze square into the distant gleam of eyes within the shadows of her face. "Whenever you're ready."

"Then listen," she said. "This is her story. It's the only one she gets."

"Her first master was a man who may have been her father, or may have bought her from her family, or stolen her. He may have found her in a wood; it was not uncommon, in the land of her birth, for impoverished families to expose and abandon infants they could not afford to feed. Some things can't be known. What is known is that her earliest memory was of rape."

"Jesus."

"Is that a name or a curse?"

"Both."

She nodded. "All right."

After a bit, she went on.

"It is known that this man used her as another man might use a hand-kerchief: a receptacle for his casual lust. When she could, she would run. When she was caught, she would be whipped.

"When she had grown sufficiently tall that his attentions were diverted by younger children, her master sold her to a whorehouse in a neighboring town. There, being still young and slender, she was taught how to feign virginity. Not virginity as it is, but virginity as lustful men dream it might be—virginity of the sort for which these men were willing to pay a great deal. She lost her maidenhead several times a day for some years.

"When she grew into womanhood, she became instead a young wife whose husband was off in the war—whatever war was handy—selling her body to pay rent on the farm they tilled, and to provide for her little daughter, or her little son. Sometimes both. Who were also available, for the right price.

"She was never given money of her own, of course, nor were the dozens of girls who were occasionally her daughter, or the boys who were occasionally her son; their reward for their labor was scant food and barely enough rest that they might continue the next day. She did not have friends there. Very few of the children lived more than a few weeks. Very few of the slaves lived more than a year."

Her face showed only dispassion, but still it hurt him to look at her. "How could you—she—live through that? How could anybody?"

"Some things cannot be known," the horse-witch repeated severely. "As a child, she survived by feats of imagination, spinning endlessly romantic dreams about other lives—of adventure, drama, of exotic places and exotic creatures, and she dreamed at first that the dream was her real life, and her real life was only nightmare. When she could maintain that fantasy no longer, she fancied instead that in some other life she must have been wicked. Greatly wicked. An avatar of evil power, transforming the life she was forced to live from unreasoning horror into a just and reasonable punishment for crimes she could not remember, and only barely imagine.

"She turned to this latter fancy after one of her attempts to escape, when she was perhaps nine years old. She had reached a temple to the local goddess of harvest, and had thrown herself on the mercy of the priestesses. She told them of the life she had fled, and begged to be allowed to sweep their floors, muck out their kitchens, anything at all that might keep her safe from rape and the whip. The priestesses took her in, bathed and fed and clothed her, and then returned her to her master.

"They were the first to tell her what she would hear again and again, from priests, wise women, holy hermits, sacerdotes and hieresiarchs and everyone else who claimed to know or work the will of the gods. They told her everything happens for a reason. They told her the gods work in mysterious ways. They told her she wouldn't be a slave unless that was the fate the gods had decreed for her. The gods had made her a slave, and their will was not to be questioned. Those were the words they used.

"What those words meant was this: The gods decided she *should* be raped. Should be whipped. Should starve and live in pain and covered in scabs. Every day it was ordained she should scream to the gods for mercy. That never came. That would never come.

"Some said that the endless horror she suffered was punishment for crimes she had committed in some forgotten previous existence. Others said her endless horror was purifying some invisible part of her so that she might have ease and station in an imaginary existence after her death. Some even told her that she was being punished for someone *else's* crime—that an unknowable ancestor had burdened her with an inheritance of evil.

"Sometimes the godfolk did try to help her, but they were few and weak; their only power was condemnation and moral outrage. Her masters, who profited by the continual rape of her and of those like her, were many and strong; if they had been the sort of people to be moved by moral outrage, they would never have become merchants of rape.

"This was how she passed her childhood and her young womanhood. In the fullness of time, privation and horror took from her the power to seem a young wife, and so she was given over to the men who enjoy pain. Receiving pain, but more often inflicting pain.

"This was when she discovered it was possible to enjoy her work.

"She learned many ways to hurt men, and many ways to survive being hurt by them. She developed a reputation for ingenuity, as well as durability. She could take a considerable beating, and could inflict a very credible beating even on a man much larger than herself. She healed quickly, and she never lost her enthusiasm for hurting the whorehouse's clientele. She became sought after, requested, well regarded by her fellow slaves, and even pampered with small privileges from her masters and their guards; somehow this made her even more unhappy. She had been punished for being bad. Did being rewarded mean she was now good?

"If a horse can't make a connection between good behavior and reward, bad behavior and punishment, this can break their mind. Horses need stories even more than people do; this causes that, something else causes the other thing. Simple stories, but they need them. Something like that may have happened to her: her mind may have broken. Or perhaps being valued had somehow given her the notion that she had value. This is another thing that cannot be known.

"What is known is that during an otherwise routine exercise in sexual humiliation, she took up the instruments of pain and killed several men. She crippled, maimed, or disfigured several more, and she ran.

"She had run before, and had been always caught and whipped for it—but she was older now, more wily, and she had well-honed skills of both deception and violence, but most of all she believed that she deserved to get away. This may have made the difference.

"She moved by night, and hid during the day. Sometimes she hid in outlying barns, or in tall grass of hay meadows, and in these places she first met horses. They feared her, because she was strange, and human, and stank of blood and desperation. But though they feared her, they did not despise her; they had not been taught that some humans are to be worshipped, while others are vermin to be destroyed, or objects to be used and discarded. She found, across the months of her flight, that to approach horses with kindness made them approachable, and that horses receive gifts with gratitude and give affection in return.

"She found someone she could love who would love her back.

"Weeks and months went by, and in time she was recaptured, of course. Slavery was blazoned in the whip scars on her back. But now she was far from the lands of her former masters, and she had skills more useful than submission to men's lust. In Faltane County, she became a stablehand, which to her was a gift of the mercy she had never received for all her prayers; to shovel horse shit all day was to her a blessing of peace. Later she became a groom, permitted now to handle her master's mounts, and later still a retrainer of horses damaged by the ignorant brutality of their masters.

"Soon her reputation reached the ears of the Faltane himself. The Faltane was a bad rider, and a bad man. It is known that once when he was riding to hounds, his horse stumbled and nearly pitched him from the saddle. He dismounted, had his footmen untack the horse, then drew his sword, slashed the horse through its belly, and left it in the field to die.

"He had ruined many horses, and scarred many more, and when he heard of a slave woman skilled with damaged horses, he let it be known that he desired her service. She was given to him as a gift. And thus was her life for some years, until the Faltane looked around his lands and saw those of his neighbors, and he looked upon those lands with lust. He hired mercenaries of tremendous power, who drove the Faltane's neighbors before them like deer before a wildfire."

"And that's where I came in."

"You didn't. You were never there."

"That's why I started asking you about this stuff. Because I was there."

"You weren't. With the mercenaries came a man who looked like you, and who spoke with a voice like yours, and who may have behaved, in some ways, as you might. This man was not you.

"He was a sad man, a tired man, a man whose youth was horror and whose maturity was worse. He was broken in ways impossible to describe. He was scarred deeper than his face and form could reveal, and many of his scars were from his own hand. Perhaps it was his damage that called to her, or hers to him. This too cannot be known.

"What is known is that he and she spoke together from time to time, and some of what they spoke of was how each of them had been hurt. Not much, but little needed saying. He felt bad for her. She felt bad for him. Speaking together awakened pain, but silence would have been worse. Soon she came to understand that he was her friend, and she was his friend, and this was a curiosity to her, as she'd never had a friend who was human, much less a man.

"When he did not have killing to do in the Faltane's service, he would come and watch her work the horses. He brought meals down to the stables and shared them with her. At the last of these shared meals, he asked what she might do if she could leave Faltane. What she might do if she were free.

"She told him she could never be free. Her life had become her master, and her past was its whip. He said he understood, and that *free* was a made-up word, one that didn't really mean what it is supposed to mean, and he apologized for using it.

"He wanted to know, he said, if he asked her, would she come away with him? He said his daughter had many horses, and none of the men who trained them were as good as she was, and she would have her own cottage and her own garden, even her own horses, and she would be paid for her work, in real gold, and she began to weep.

"She said he was almost as kind as a horse, but no kindness could take her from there. The horses in the manor stable were her only friends other than him—and worse, she was their only human friend at all. She could never abandon them to torturers.

"He asked then, what if all the horses could come with them? and she said that the world does not work in such ways, and he said *Fuck the world. Just say yes and we will make this happen.*

"But he was wrong about the world, and she was right. Before she could answer, the stable was on fire. The mercenaries had turned their hand against the Faltane, and their leader could with a glance strike fire hot enough to ignite stone.

"The man told the slave to free the horses, and he raced away to fight whatever battle he might have thought important. She did what she could, but horses panic in fires, and when frightened, a horse will return to its stall; many must be led from their stalls individually and the stalls closed behind them. Then there were men with armor and swords who wanted to take the horses she had freed and ride them into battle. She killed some of these men, and the others ran away.

"The man who was her friend returned to bring her away from the fire, for now all the manor was ablaze, and he said that soon there might be no escape. He took her knife, and he held her even though she fought against him, and would have carried her away. But horses—"

For the first time, the horse-witch's voice broke, and for a time she could not speak. When she could, she went on.

"But horses were screaming. And some of the horses she had freed were screaming in reply, screaming to their beloved companions trapped in the fire, and she told her friend that she could not leave them to die in agony and terror. He held her and he spoke to her, and when he saw she understood, he let her go, and came into the burning stable at her side."

"He went in with her," he murmured. "That makes sense."

"It is not known if together they saved any horses. It is not known whether he survived the fire. She didn't. The last thing she said to him was, *After the horses, we can rescue each other.*"

"Son of a bitch."

"Yes."

Night had gathered darkness around them. "He made it out. Survived," he said. "That's what he does."

"Were she able to know this, it would make her glad."

"Horses too. They saved some. Not all. But some. I don't know if it was enough to be worth dying for."

"What's worth dying for, and what isn't, is too deep for me. Such matters must be left to mortals."

"Can I look away now?"

"If you must."

"Did he—uh." He swallowed and tried again. "You said he spoke to her. Is it, uh, known what he said?"

"It is known."

"Will you tell me? Please."

"You may find this difficult to hear."

"That'll be a damn shame, considering how the rest of it was a fucking carnival."

No moon yet peered above the canyon rim, and the firelight did not reach her face. He could see only glistening highlights where her cheeks would be and the faint silver gleam of her witch-eye.

"These are his words, exactly as he spoke them.

"He said, *What you call yourself, what others call you, what you have done and what has been done to you—none of this touches what I know. I know you. You met me days ago. I have known you since the world was born.*

"*Everything you are is what you should be. Everything you should be is what you are.*

"*I know all of you, and there is nothing in you I do not love.*"

The fire showed only embers. The night was very dark, and very still. Even the frogs had gone quiet; there was no sound of any living thing.

Then eventually, slowly, finally: "Holy shit."

"Yes."

"Fuck me inside out."

"You were warned."

"Does that mean—? Wait, or did we—? Huh. I can't make that into anything that even looks like sense." Every way he tried to think about it only spun the whirl inside his head faster and higher. "Son of a bitch."

He looked up and found a sliver of moon creeping over the canyon's rim. "I just don't fucking know anymore."

"Nobody knows," she said. "Except me. And I don't know everything. Only what I remember."

"But I knew about her. Somehow I knew. I didn't remember her. Still don't. But I knew."

"There are ways in which you are very like a mortal man," she said. "There are ways in which you are more like something else."

His head jerked up. "I'm not mortal?"

"I don't know. I'd rather not test it," she said. "Now you understand why I worried for you."

"No shit. So when we first met, and I said I didn't know why I was even talking to you, you said—"

" 'I could tell you.' " She sounded like she might be smiling, just a bit, as she quoted herself. " 'But you wouldn't believe me.' "

"That. Yeah. This was what you were talking about."

"Some of it."

"I was drawn to you because of what happened between . . . that guy who looked like me, and the slave woman."

"You're drawn to me because you need forgiveness and permission. And, I think, a girlfriend. The other?" A shrug in her voice. "There was a stable fire in your Faltane County War, but no horses died. Why?"

"How do you—yeah, never mind. Dumbass question. The manor stables were empty—I had Tanner drive the horses off just before . . ."

"*You* had," she said. "You decided to empty the stables. Why?"

"Well . . . I mean, y'know, to deny remounts to Faltane's cavalry, obviously."

"Which the stable fire would have accomplished. Obviously."

"Well, yeah, but after meeting you, I wasn't about to . . . oh. Holy shit."

"Again: yes."

"It's making me dizzy. Does this ever get less fucked-up?"

"I don't know."

"Are you doing this? Making this happen?" He shook his head, helpless in the whirl. "Am I?"

"I don't know that either."

"Do you know anything more? Anything at all that might help us make sense of all this shit?"

"Yes," she said. "I know you'll smell better after you take that bath."

The moon hung silver on the riverbanks and splashed the water with platinum sparks. The water was lazy, too slow to be cold, and the scent of flowers upstream reminded him of something. A dream he'd had, maybe. Or maybe he had been here before.

He'd scrubbed out his clothes and boots with sand from a small bar a few yards out. Now they hung on a twisted dwarf cedar just back from the water's edge, and he went back out for more sand to scrub himself down. The water was deeper just beyond the bar, and after scraping off his top couple layers of grime, he anchored himself with one hand and let himself float.

The canyon, the river, the moon. Calm. Clean. All of it.

In this place, it was hard to imagine a world where the slave woman's life and death could happen. But it did. Every day. In every land. The slave's life, and worse. Girls suffered. Boys suffered. Women and men. At least she had the horses, at the end. That was a lot more than a lot of people ever get.

He thought then that he finally understood what Ma'elKoth had been about all along. How can you know such things and not want to make the world better? Shit, if *he* were God, he'd have burned this motherfucker down a long time ago.

And started over with people who don't do that shit.

"You're sad now," she said from somewhere not far away.

"I guess."

"Do you remember ordering me to not be sad for you?"

He felt himself smile. "Sometimes I talk faster than I think."

"Not anymore."

"That's a nice thing to say."

"It's also true."

"Well, thanks."

"You wondered once why there should be such a creature as a horse-witch. The only answer I have is the answer I am. I only know I'm grateful for it."

"Me too," he said to the stars. "The world would be a better place with more of you and less of everything else."

"And thanks in return."

Then for a while there was only the night and the water, until she said, "I still like you."

Something inside him stirred, rousing from a decade's hibernation, and it woke up hungry. But the darkness inside him wouldn't let it out. "I don't see how you can like anybody, much less a man. Much less me. After everything that happened—"

"It didn't happen to me," she said. "It happened to the slave woman. I am not her. I look like her because her human friend looked like you."

"But—"

"She was a slave. I can't be caught, much less chained. She was alone. I have friends without number. She was damaged; every part of her that wasn't scar was open wound. If I live a million million years, I will never take another mark upon my flesh. She lived in fear. I barely recall such a feeling. She was killed, and she died. I am killed, and I live. For a man, she had Dominic Shade a few days. For a man, I have you forever."

"Forever," he echoed, because he discovered he liked the sound of the word. "It's like we—wait. Dominic . . . *Shade*? What the hell?"

"That's the name her friend gave to her. It's how he was called by the mercenaries, and the Faltane's men."

"Nobody's called me Dominic in thirty years," he said slowly. "And I haven't used *Shade* since I left Kirisch-Nar. Why the hell would I go by that?"

"You didn't. He did."

"Still," he said. "I wonder. Dominic Shade instead of Jonathan Fist."

"Maybe he hadn't yet made the bargain you can't get out of."

He sat upright in the river. "Holy shit."

He turned to look at her. She was on the riverbank. Her clothes were somewhere else. The moon on her skin was the most dazzling vision ever to grace his eye. He tried to say *holy shit* again, but the sight of her had left him no breath with which to speak.

"I told you I still like you," she said. "And I know you still like me."

"You do?"

She pointed. "Looks like you like me a *lot*."

"Uh . . ."

"Just say yes," she said, "and we will make this happen."

"That's what I—I mean, he—said, when . . ."

"I warned you the story could take you somewhere you might not like."

"No—that's not . . . I mean, of course I—but I think I kind of need to . . ."

She folded her arms across her breasts in a way that somehow subtly altered the curve of her shoulder and hip from sublimely erotic to frankly pornographic.

"What you need is to make up your mind," she said. "I'm immortal. You, on the other hand, aren't getting any younger, tough guy."

the now of always 10

REASONS FOR PEASANTS

REASONS FOR PEASANTS

"A religion that teaches you God is something outside the world—something separate from everything you see, smell, taste, touch, and hear—is nothing but a cheap hustle."

—DUNCAN MICHAELSON
Tales of the First Folk

Caine and Ma'elKoth converse softly, some distance away. Kris and Angvasse walk together idly among the trees. The horse-witch braids her garland, and Duncan finally gets it.

"Ah . . ." He sighs into the dappled green. "Ah, of course."

He understands now, or thinks he does. Someone unhappened the slave woman, and now there is a horse-witch . . . which means she can be unhappened too.

He rolls his head to look up into the horse-witch's face. "So it really is all about the girl."

She holds her wildflower garland out, squinting critically. "Too much? Maybe more subtle in the shades of blue?"

"He's done this—is doing this, is . . . rewriting the entire structure of reality—for *you*?"

She smiles past the flowers. "That's very romantic."

"Capital R as well."

"He doesn't believe in happy endings."

Duncan nods. "He has reason."

"He's not doing this for me. He's doing it for love."

"He loves *you*. I see it every time he even thinks about you."

"Oh, yes. But I don't need defending. I need nothing. We have an uncomplicated relationship."

"Compared to his others, I daresay it is."

"This may be difficult for you to understand, because it's not easily expressed in the words you and your son still need. You could say that he's doing it for Love in the abstract sense—for the right to love, and the chance to be loved. Not for himself. For everyone. He would deny this, angrily, because he thinks the abstract is where good things turn bad, and he may be right. That is a matter too deep for me. I can tell you that there is nothing abstract in his love; his love is specific, and concrete. Love is his law. His only law."

She smiles at Duncan, and hangs the garland of wildflowers from the guard of the Sword. "I think he gets that from you."

"I beg your pardon?"

"Duncan. I don't know you well, but him I know *very* well. I've known him a lot longer than you have. When he thinks of love, he thinks of you. You're the example he's trying to live up to."

"That's . . ." He shakes his head. "I know better than to argue with you, but I want to. I want to deny it. I wish I could make *that* unhappen. He deserves better."

"If you mean by *deserve* what I think you mean, everyone does."

"I was a *terrible* example. Of practically everything."

"You were what you were. Now you can be what you are. You did what you did. Now you can do what you do."

"I don't understand."

She nodded, and for a moment her brows drew together in thought. At length she said, "I don't love horses."

"You don't?"

"Of course not. Horses are large smelly dim-witted creatures who serve no higher purpose than processing grass into shit."

"Then—"

"But there is a one-eyed mare, with a white scar just here, for whom I would give all my lives if it might keep her happy forever. Your son's horse, the one he calls Carillon, is so bright and playful that I start to laugh when I first smell his approach. There's a medicine-hat paint, who has a cast in one eye—sometimes I look at her and think I'm seeing myself. One old gelding, who used to be black, follows her around like a body servant, because she won't let the younger geldings and stallions pick on him."

"You don't love horses. You love each horse," Duncan says slowly, with a distantly thoughtful nod. "Personally."

"He doesn't love people. He doesn't even *like* people. He dislikes everyone he meets, on principle, because it gives him an excuse to be an asshole. But he loves you. He loves me. He loves Kris, and Deliann. Angvasse. Even Pallas Ril. Ma'elKoth. Personally."

"Yes."

"He loves the slave woman in Faltane most of all."

Duncan frowns. "A woman he never met? One who never really existed . . . ?"

"I told you," she says lightly, "some things he loves are more unlikely than you."

"Still."

"He grieves for her. Not for her death. For her life. He grieved for her before he had any idea there was such a person. He grieves for everyone like her. For everyone like you."

"Me?"

"What hurts him most is imagining how she begged and prayed and pleaded for mercy, and mercy never came. She screamed and no one listened. She bled and no one cared. He would have helped her. He wanted to help her. His heart is still broken because he didn't. He'll never get over it."

"I think I understand."

"For more than forty years, you begged and prayed and pleaded for mercy, and mercy never came. You screamed and no one listened. You bled and no one cared."

"*He* cared," Duncan says fiercely.

"Yes. And you cared about him. And both your hearts are still broken because you didn't save each other."

Sometime later, Caine gathers them all together around Duncan and the Sword. When he sees the garland hanging from the guard, he smiles at the horse-witch. "Nice."

"Thank you."

"So here it is," he says. "Here we are. We're up against the hard shit now. The Sword can't stay here forever, and neither can we. I need everyone together on this. It's gonna be fucking hard enough with everybody pitching in; we can't afford to have anybody working at cross-purposes. Am I being clear?"

He looks from one to the next, meeting every gaze. Ma'elKoth. Pallas

Ril. Deliann Mithondionne. Angvasse Khlaylock. The horse-witch, and Duncan.

"This all happens at the instant the Sword is moved. Actually, at the instant the decision is made. Your decision, Duncan."

He nods. "I understand."

"This is the outcome I've been playing for. In Purthin's Ford, Angvasse and Jonathan Fist fight our way up to the Purificapex, to rejoin the power of the Sword and the Hand. We're not gonna survive—probably—but that's not important. Both Powers exist outside time, so every version of us will be able to tap in."

"In theory," Ma'elKoth rumbles.

"In the vertical city, T'farrell Mithondionne will use part of the Power Rejoined to re-purpose the *dil T'llan* to Bind a different consciousness. To put somebody else in charge of the *dillin*. Somebody we can trust to manage traffic between Earth and Home. On Earth, Dominic Shade will Bind the power of the blind god to our new *dil T'llan*, to give the, whateverthefuck, the Gatekeeper, I guess, plenty of power to open or close the gates."

Duncan suddenly feels lost again. "You're using the *blind god?*"

Caine shrugs. "Fifteen billion people on Earth want to live just as much as anybody else. We already know we can't stop traffic between the universes; they'll always find a way around any wall we can build. So our next best option is to manage it. We can make being responsible and respectful of Home *profitable*. As soon as people start making money off being good guys, the market for bad guys dries the fuck up, right?"

"It's . . . possible," Duncan says. "That's as much as I can say for sure. You won't know till you actually do it."

"And that's the big one, right there. Up to now, we've had a little wiggle room with this. It's how I've got it as close to fine-tuned as it can be. But the instant the Sword's in play, everything's for keeps. We can use it to time-bind Ma'elKoth, at least for a while, so He won't unhappen right away; it'll limit Your power, but You'll still be in the game."

"A superior option to nonexistence, one supposes."

"You always wanted the power to help people. You'll still have some. You'll need it. I'm pretty sure the Spire's coming down."

"The *Spire?*"

"Probably. Since we're about to steal the whole power of both True Relics that hold it up. Look, I told Kierendal that I'd break the Khryllians like I broke the Black Knives. If You don't pitch in, that's gonna get way too literal."

Ma'elKoth looks appalled—and then distantly thoughtful . . .

"Cut it out," Caine says. "Don't even have that idea."

"I can't imagine what you might be—"

"Behave yourself. Same goes for you, Pallas. And all your fucking deific ass-buddies. We're moving into uncharted territory here. You all understand that, right?"

Again he meets each pair of eyes in turn.

"We all know what the world was like *with* the Covenant of Pirichanthe. A shithole. Since the True Assumption, it hasn't been much better. From here on out, all bets are off. People turn to gods to make the world better. Shit, we make 'em up right and left. So we'll give them a little room to work. As long as they're, y'know, helping more than they hurt, fine. But if shit starts to get out of control . . . Well, the gods—*all* the gods—need to understand that there are consequences now."

"Consequences?" Duncan's still lost. "What kind of consequences?"

Caine shows them his teeth. They appear very white, and singularly sharp. "My kind."

Ma'elKoth says, "The Sword of Man."

"Fucking right."

"Pure destruction. Permanent destruction."

He shrugs. "My whole life, I can't remember a single thing I ever managed to take back."

"The power to punish gods . . ." Deliann murmurs, then he shrugs too. "I like it."

Duncan shakes his head. "It seems like a dark life."

"I'll try to bear up. One more thing. When Angvasse and I spontaneously combust—or whatever—from joining the Powers on the Purificapex . . . well, look. It's gonna put us into the Gatekeeper, and some of Him into us. Like when Deliann joined with the river. So listen, I've been over this with Angvasse, and she's in favor. Because she's a hero. A real hero, who has the power to do great things, and who lives to help people. To protect people who can't protect themselves. So if we ever need a hero, the Gatekeeper can *make* one. As long as the Gatekeeper's in charge, a brand-spankin' new Angvasse Khlaylock can come walking right out of any *dil* in the world. Either world."

"An inexhaustible supply of heroes," Duncan murmurs. "How did you manage to arrange this?"

"It was a negotiation. To get a little, you give a little."

"What did you give?"

Caine shrugs. "My retirement."

"I'm sorry?"

"I sold my soul to Pirichanthe."

"Your *soul?*"

"Or whatever. Look, Pirichanthe was Bound to keep a lid on human gods. That was its whole reason for being. Literally. But it couldn't really do it—we keep finding ways to fuck with the world—so it decided the next best thing was to find somebody who wasn't afraid to get up on his hind legs and smack a god in the balls."

"Metaphorically."

"You think so? Ask Ma'elKoth."

Duncan squints at him. "So in exchange for a permanent hero . . ."

"It got a monster down the block."

"The only reason civilized Atticus has the luxury to be civilized," Duncan murmurs, "is that he's got a monster watching his back."

"You must be quoting someone smart."

"You frighten me, Caine."

"I should." He looks to each of them. "I should frighten all of you."

"Except for me," the horse-witch says.

"Except for you. Everything is except for you."

"I like it that way," she says. "It makes me feel special."

"Just before I killed him, Purthin Khlaylock told me *fear of God is the beginning of wisdom.* I think he was wrong. I think the more you fear God, the scarier God gets. Fear His Anger, and He starts tossing thunderbolts and earthquakes and whatever. Fear His punishment, and He gives you eternal damnation. People need to know they don't have to be afraid. It's *God* who has to be afraid."

The horse-witch smiles fondly. "For God, fear of Caine is the beginning of wisdom."

Caine returns her smile as a fierce grin. "Somebody should write that down."

Duncan frowns at her. "Caine doesn't scare you?"

"Of course he does," the horse-witch says. "Caine's a monster who gives monsters nightmares."

"But then—?"

"We don't use that name," she says. "Call a monster's name and it remembers where you sleep."

"Exactly," Caine says. "As soon as the fuckers understand they need to check their closets and under their beds for Caine before they turn out the lights, a lot of potential problems become self-correcting."

"Consequences."

"Believe it."

"And the Gatekeeper—"

"Can dropkick Caine out of any given *dil*. Just like Angvasse. Wherever and whenever he decides he needs Somebody hurt."

"You're giving this Gatekeeper a great deal of very dangerous power."

"That's why I got somebody I can trust."

"And that would be—?" Duncan says, and then he realizes everyone is looking at him. "Oh, no—come on, you can't *possibly* ask—"

"The world needs you, Duncan. I need you."

"But I'm the *last* man who'd want—"

"I know. 'The only man who can be trusted with power is a man who doesn't want it.' Wait—who said that?"

"But—you can't—"

"You've been here. You've seen. You know the need is real. Jesus Christ, Duncan, who would *you* trust?"

"Well, I . . . well, I . . ."

"I'll let you call me Hari."

"What? You will?" He frowns, just a bit. "Will you call me Dad?"

Caine smiles. "Are we haggling now?"

"I just . . . I don't know. There's just so much I wish could be different. Should be different."

"I told you before that we don't get should, we get is—except right now, right here, we've got a chance to take an is and make it *into* a should."

"Don't be afraid," the horse-witch says, so softly he can barely hear her. "Be what you are."

"What if," Caine says slowly, almost solemnly, "what if the worst thing you ever did wasn't you?"

"What?"

"What if. You don't remember the beating that killed Mom, do you?"

"I remember plenty of others."

"Me too. But what if. What if it wasn't you?"

"What do you mean?"

"What if she got mugged? Hit by a Businessman's car?" He crouches at Duncan's side. "What if she didn't die?"

Duncan can no longer breathe. "Are you . . ." he croaks. "What are you saying?"

"The old guy at the clinic that day—the one who looked like me. What was he doing there? What was inside that crutch he was carrying?"

"I . . . I don't . . ."

"Think about it. What if somebody Healed her that afternoon? What if somebody took her away?" He lowered his voice to a whisper. "What if she's sitting inside that yurt over there, waiting for you to decide whether to take the chance?"

"Is she?" The words scrape his dry throat so hard he tastes blood. "Is she there?"

"Maybe."

"*Maybe?*"

"The only way you'll ever know is if you say yes."

"Yes."

"That's right. Just yes. A simple word."

"No, you don't understand. That *was* the word. Yes."

Caine stands. "Well, all right, then. Go take a look."

The Sword is gone. Duncan is free. There isn't even a slice in his serape. He stares, half-frozen with incomprehension.

Caine shrugs. "I told you: a metaphor."

"You are the Sword."

"Yeah. And you just pulled me from the stone. Welcome to your kingdom."

"My—?"

"Whose else?" Caine says. "I think we should call it Duncan's Gate."

"If I didn't just now destroy the universe."

"Well, yeah. Too late to start worrying about it now."

On Duncan's chest lies the wildflower garland. He gathers it to himself and stands, then goes to return the garland to the horse-witch.

"Take it with you," the horse-witch says with a tiny hint of smile. "Girls like when you bring them flowers."

the happiest of all the infinite
possible endings

POKE THE BEAR

POKE THE BEAR

"If you're gonna play Poke the Bear, you better keep in mind the bear doesn't give a shit it's just a game."

—UNKNOWN

I've been thinking about this moment, in broad outline, off and on for a long time. Before I was kidnapped by the Knights of Khryl. Before Assumption Day. Before *For Love of Pallas Ril.* If I had to pick a moment when it first crossed my mind, it'd be the end of *Servant of the Empire*—on the platform with Shanna, when Kollberg's emergency transfer got us Earthside in time to save my life, and in my lap I still held the severed head of Toa-Phelathon, a pompous, slightly dim old man I had murdered for the crime of taking bad advice. I was in the middle of passing out from blood loss, having a few minutes previously taken one of the worst wounds of my career, but even with night falling on the universe around me, I could see the look on Shanna's face.

I can still see it.

We had our share of problems, Shanna and I. Most were of our own creation. We were never happy together. Never. Not when we met. Not when we married, not even when I kidnapped a god and ignited civil war and crippled myself to save her. She was in love with the guy she thought was inside Caine—the sad, suffering soul who'd forged a monster mask to defend his pain against the bleak realities of Earth.

Me? I was desperate to prove her right.

Pretending there was a decent guy lurking somewhere in the vicinity of my heart gave me a narrative I thought I could live with. I didn't much like myself in those days.

Still don't, really. I just don't mind so much anymore.

Shanna and I both told ourselves—with hysterical insistence—that Caine was just an act. A character played by Hari Michaelson, international superstar and bon vivant. And on the platform, the look on her face . . . I was watching her finally understand that the character had been Hari Michaelson. From the beginning.

She knew the man she'd married had been Caine all along.

And even then, neither of us understood who—what—Caine really is.

Shanna became an Actress because it gave her the chance to help people, really help them. *Save* them. Being born into a Tradesman family meant she'd never be able to do much for people on Earth; Acting for her was the power, every day, to make a positive difference in someone's life.

Acting for me was getting rich because I like to hurt people.

But not just any people.

I was already in my sixth straight year in the worldwide Top Ten, and Shanna's numbers would never get her even a whiff of what Top Ten smelled like. And all this and all that and everything else and I wasn't thinking real clearly at the time, but I distinctly recall one last fleeting thought skating across the surface of unconsciousness.

Somebody ought to burn this motherfucker down.

I thought that burn-down would happen on its own after *For Love of Pallas Ril*, with Kollberg's trial and the L-Con hearings into the Studio's abuse of contract law. I thought the burn-down would happen after Assumption Day.

I thought roasting Marc Vilo alive on real-time video would make my point. Show, don't tell, right?

But some people are too stupid to believe even their own fucking eyes.

Including me.

I finally figured it out: I don't like hurting people. I never did. What I like is hurting people in *charge*.

There's a reason kings hide when they hear I'm in town.

I like hurting people who think they can't be hurt. Who think that money or power or God or whateverthefuck makes them invulnerable. Invincible. Omnipotent.

I really, really like proving them wrong.

Check off a list of my Greatest Hits: Purthin Khlaylock. The Black Knife Nation. The Khulan G'thar. Toa-Phelathon. Kollberg. Toa-Sytell. Marc Vilo. Even the ones that didn't rule anything: Berne. Dane and Blackwood. Calm Guy, Whistler, and Hawk. Adder in the Pit. Even Ballinger. Doesn't matter: the guys I aim for are the guys who have the power to make shit better, but they don't.

Because keeping things shitty gets them what they want.

Me too.

It seems like whenever I smoked somebody for some other reason—*any* other reason—the universe fucked me for it. Killing Creele put Raithe on my tail. Killing Karl bought Faith a date with Avery Shanks. We all know how that turned out. I hated Berne because he tortured Marade and Tizarre to death, down in Yalitrayya. He hated me because I did the same to his lover t'Gall.

I could go on for hours. Days. And then there's the big one.

Ma'elKoth.

I had him beat. I had Shanna safe, I had Berne dead and Kosall in my guts. I had Kollberg by the balls. I could have left Ma'elKoth there. Should have left him there.

Instead I took his hand, and dragged him with me into Hell.

Not that he was an angel, or a saint. But he truly, sincerely devoted his larger-than-life existence to making the Ankhanan Empire a better place. He didn't have to. He had unimaginable power, limitless wealth, a perfection of human form that you just don't see outside of Michelangelo. And instead of kicking back to enjoy all that shit, he put everything he had achieved, everything he'd become, into a job that was not only mostly impossible but would eventually put him in the crosshairs of a homicidal sociopath with serious anger issues.

Jesus, I wish I'd left him alone.

And yeah, it was my job. That was part of it. But mostly it was because he pissed me off. Because I could break him and there wasn't the first fucking thing he could do about it. My job was just an excuse.

And that's why—I really think this is true—that's why I just about drank myself to death after *For Love of Pallas Ril*. Because I let the fuckers co-opt me. I traded them everything I've ever done—everything I've ever been—for a nice house, money, and something resembling a normal family. I let them make me into the kind of fucker I had spent the best of my life destroying.

I left this shitty world shitty, because it got me what I wanted.

That's about to change.

"Hari?" Gayle looks up from the pad and nods to me. "Showtime."

All right, then. I got your fucking showtime right here.

. . .

Now I'm up against it and I still don't know how to put words to this. There's too much. So I start small. "It didn't have to be like this."

Gayle cocks his head, frowning. "What? I mean, I don't—"

"Not talking to you."

I raise my eyes to the moiré face shields of the Social Police anti-magick helmets. "I'm talking to you guys. And to everybody who's watching the video link through your helmets. And everybody who'll watch the recording. All you fuckers. Board of Governors. Social Police. Leisure Congress.

"All of you and every other poor bastard who's gonna have to die because you brain-dead sacks of shit are too fucking stupid to make one fucking deal."

"Hari—"

"You could have had it all. Everything. And you *know* it. Jesus staggering Christ, have any of you been paying attention these last twenty-five years? I have carved across the faces of two worlds proof that my word is *absolute*. Even my *lies* become truth. What I said I'd give you is what you would have gotten. All you had to do was say yes.

"That's all. Yes.

"I would have handed you an entire fucking planet in exchange for peace between us. But peace isn't what you chose, and peace isn't what you'll get.

"And thanks for that."

I shake my head at myself, just a little. I really don't want to go on. But I have to. People need to know. They need to understand.

"I mean it: thank you. Thank you because I am sick to fucking death of this pus-crusted open sore of a world. And I am sick to fucking death of every one of you. Because you know what this world is, and you have the power to change it. And you don't. Because you *like* it this way. So thanks.

"Now I'm gonna kill you for it."

Gayle looks like he just choked on his own tongue.

"This is not a threat. It's not a warning. We're way the fuck past all that. You're already dead, and pretty soon people won't be able to ignore the smell.

"Days from now, months, years, when your entire fucking world is burning down, somebody's going to create a narrative to explain it. To tell people why their whole lives are on fire. This narrative will feature me as the bad guy.

"You probably already know I'm okay with that.

"This narrative will explain to people that their families are dead and their world's dying because I'm an evil motherfucker. And sure, fair enough. I am.

"The thing is, you knew it.

"You've known for decades just exactly what kind of evil motherfucker I am. You knew it when you made me an Actor.

"You knew it when you murdered my wife.

"You knew it when you raped my daughter, and you knew it when you ripped the eyes from my father's face.

"You knew it twenty-five years ago, when I committed honest-to-fuck-my-ass *genocide* to boost my fucking career.

"You might remember how I gave warning to the Black Knife Nation. How I told them what would happen if they came after us. They didn't believe me.

"You didn't believe me either.

"For the record: you were warned. Again and again. I warned you in my offer. I warned you when I killed Marc Vilo. I warned you twenty-five fucking years ago, talking to Arturo Kollberg in a conference room in the San Francisco Studio.

"I don't rescue people. I don't do nonviolent resistance, and I don't work to change the system from within. You need to remember what I am. What you wanted me to be.

"Remember. Remember when I come for you.

"Remember it didn't have to be this way."

The secmen shift their balance and adjust their grips on their power rifles just enough for me to read their body language like a fucking head-line. *This fucking guy—this broke-down cripple stripcuffed to a bed in a massively fortified installation that nobody even knows exists—expects somebody to believe he's ever going to do anything other than lie there and wait to die? Yeah, right.*

Maybe in his next life.

And they're right. Except this is my next life.

I lift my gaze once more to the distorted blur of my own face reflected in their helmets. "If anybody had given my father a choice, he would have lived and died a gentle man. He believed—believes—that the use of force degrades, and eventually destroys, civil society. He believes that hands are for helping people up, not for knocking them down.

"You're probably aware that I do not share this opinion.

"My father believes that human life is sacrosanct, and that a human being may be harmed only reluctantly, gravely, as a last resort, when there is no other way to defend the health and lives of others. For Dad, that's a law of nature, quantifiable and absolute, like gravity and momentum and entropy.

"Except for you fuckers."

I nod at moiré smears of my own face. "He hates you. All of you. Every single one of you. Personally. If every soapy on Earth was on fire, he wouldn't piss on one to put him out.

"He admits this is a failure of principle. He admits it makes him a hypocrite, but he can't help it. The closest he can come to rationalizing it is deciding you're not really human anymore. He says humanity can't be taken from a person, but it can be surrendered. He says every one of you surrendered your humanity when you became the willing tool of oppression. Get it? You're not even really alive. You're tools. Inanimate objects. Hammers. Saws. Whatever. You should know that I don't share this opinion either.

"He's giving you fuckers too much credit.

"You're people just like anybody else. Bad people, but people. That's all. I don't hate you. You don't hate slime buildup in your bathroom drain, y'know? But sooner or later you've got to clean that shit out.

"My father dreamed of a society that valued people for what they are instead of what they have. He dreamed that government of the people, by the people, and for the people had not perished from the Earth. He dreamed *with liberty and justice for all.*

"He didn't have the power to bring forth even an echo of these things. He didn't have the power to save his wife, or his child, or himself. He didn't even have the power to control his own body.

"There's tragic irony for you: the greatest accomplishment of this idealist, this civilized man of peace, was to father the living negation of everything he believes in. A human weapon of mass destruction.

"That would be me.

"He didn't mean to. He didn't want to. If you could put him back together and wake him up, he'd probably try to stop me. He would never, never *ever*, raise his fist against you. His fists were for my mother, and for me.

"His fists raised against his will. If he could have stopped himself, he would have. But he couldn't. He can't. He couldn't stop his fists then.

"He can't stop his fist now.

"Against his will he has raised me up, and I am going to beat this world until your entire fucking planet can't do anything except lie there and bleed."

. . .

Finally one of the soapies breaks. His helmet's digitizer turns his derisive snort into a burst of static. "*Nice speech,*" he says. "*Too bad nobody will ever hear it.*"

In his mask, my smile looks wider than the span of my hand. "That's not what I hear."

"*From who? The voices in your head?*"

"Um, actually, since you ask? Yes. Exactly that." I shrug at him. "Voices in my head. Funny, huh?"

"*What's more funny is that your father is part of the system that isolates and deletes seditious transmissions. He might be the exact component that has flagged your whole little rant for deletion.*"

"That *is* funny," I admit. "Want to see something even funnier than that? Gayle, you'll like this one too. What's the call code on that palmpad?"

"Why?"

"Just read it out."

He does, and then I say, "Jed? Get everything? How's it look?"

When the palmpad's annunciator chimes, Gayle jerks so hard he almost drops the thing. I nod to him. "It's all right. Answer it. Hold it so we can all see."

The soapies shift and tighten up on their weapons. I wonder if they can see the looks they're giving one another. I wish I could. Merciful Jesus, if I could only see the looks on their faces as Gayle taps the accept and a frame-in-frame box pops up and Jed Clearlake says, "Pretty good, Hari. It'll take some editing, and I'll have to cut in reaction shots."

All six soapies lurch into combat stances and their rifles twitch back and forth like none of them can decide whether to shoot me or the palmpad or both.

I grin at them. "Those voices in my head? He's one of them."

"It's kind of over the top," Jed says.

"Practically my trademark."

"The 'government of the people' et cetera stuff is Abraham Lincoln, right? Dictator of the American Federal Union?"

"Hey, good catch. Except the title was President of the United States of America."

"Depends on who you read. Anyway, what's this 'liberty and justice for all'? Is that some kind of historical reference? Nobody knows what it's supposed to mean."

"Leave it in."

"You're the boss. We done?"

"Miles to go before we sleep."

"Is that another—"

"Forget it. Yeah, we're done. Get to work."

"Then I'm out. Give 'em Hell, Hari."

"Believe it."

A couple of the soapies are tapping away on their sleevepads.

"Don't bother. You can't trace that signal."

"There's no such thing as a signal we can't trace."

"Really? No kidding. People used to say there's no such thing as magick. That's what educated people call irony, huh?"

They stop tapping. I wave a hand. "Hey, don't let me spoil your fun. Take your best shot."

I look over at Gayle. His face has gone almost as grey as Faller's was, and his lips are white and he keeps mouthing *oh my god oh my god.* "Recognize that guy? Know what he does for a living?"

"That's Jed . . ." He has to cough his throat clear. "That was Jed *Clearlake*—the, uh, the . . . the Studio Affairs anchor for *Adventure Update*—"

"Used to be. Now he's the information minister for the Free State of Caine."

"The *what?*"

"Even the Social Police and the Board of Governors would be surprised by everything we can do on Earth with magick these days. Monitor my thoughtmitter, for example."

Gayle jerks again. I smile at him. "Thought I didn't know about that one, huh? That while you fuckers were putting my skull back together, you went ahead and jammed in a new thoughtmitter. A convenient tool to keep tabs on me. It may be that there is such a thing as a tool that can't be used as a weapon, but I've never met one."

I open my hands. "I'm kinda proud of myself. You know I like books. One of the oldest, cheesiest gags in the history of the novel is the concealed recorder—hell, it's older than the novel. Before they had the technology, it was somebody hiding in the bushes or behind an arras. What I think is cool is I didn't have to worry about you finding mine. You fucking *put* it here."

Gayle can't get his mind around it. "But how can you *possibly* have done *any*—"

"Oh, I didn't. It took me a few years—a few decades—to figure out that I don't have to do everything myself. That's why it's good to have friends. I don't have many, but they're good ones to have.

"Like, say, if you have friends who can Whisper or Speak, they can tell you shit privately—not even a thoughtmitter can pick it up. And if one of your other friends can, say, Meld, well then, you can actually have a whole conference just in your mind. So you don't have to, say, actually talk. Or even monologue. But that's kid stuff. We can hijack whole data streams. And upload viral—literally viral—video. Not to mention crown me king of my own virtual nation, but let that part go. It's not easy, but all kinds of shit can be done if your friends are powerful enough. If you stop and think about it, you might remember who some of my friends are."

One of the soapies jams his rifle at my face. *"Can they bring you back from the dead?"*

"Actually, yes. Sort of. It's complicated."

Another rifle joins the first. *"Killing you isn't."*

"Have you been listening at all? Uh, wait. Hang on a second. Voices again . . ."

Stillness.

"You're *sure* you have him? Raithe, we have to do this right the first time."

Gayle says, "Raithe?"

"Shh."

An electric rush all over me inside and out, skin and bone and guts and blood, dry ice and thermite.

A tear rolls from my eye and tracks down my face and scorches stink up from my beard. It splashes iridescent black on the front of my prisoner's gown and it starts to burn and I don't care.

One of the soapies leans in for a better look. *"What the fuck?"*

"Raithe. Thank you. Anything. Ever. Just ask."

A second or two of stillness, and I nod to myself. "Thanks. Tell Orbek: go on my signal."

"Signal? Orbek and Raithe?"

Gayle backs away. "Maybe you should shoot him."

"Too late."

Another rush, bigger, harsher, and it's not the love of some incomprehensibly oceanic thing I'm feeling now.

It's concrete. And specific.

"Oh God . . . Jesus, if you could only know . . ."

More tears roll, and if I don't cut this out I'll set my fucking beard on fire. "Yeah. I know. I do. I love you, Dad. See you soon."

Now all six of them have their power rifles aimed at my face. *"What the fuck are you playing at?"*

"I really think you should shoot him," Gayle says unsteadily. He's backed himself all the way to the wall. "I really do."

"Yeah, go ahead. One thing first."

"*Shoot* him!"

"*It's not your call*," one of the soapies says, then aims his mask at me. "*Start talking. You know what happens if you don't.*"

"Talk? Sure. Regards from my father," I tell them. "He says good-bye."

I make a fist and five of their heads explode.

Really explode: blood and brains and shreds of their helmets and pretty much all of it's on fire and Gayle's screaming at the last one to *shoot him fucking shoot him*, and the sixth soapy lowers his rifle and shakes his head.

"*Fuck me upside down*," he says. "*I tell you, Jonnie, I will never get used to that.*"

"Let's hope you don't have to," I tell him. "Have everything you need?"

He nods, kneeling to go through the other guys' armor. "*Anything I don't have, I can get as I go. Think you could cut it a little closer next time? Like, say, after they actually open fire?*"

"Timing is everything."

"*Would it be rude to mention that breathing is everything too?*" He pockets the secmen's personal pads and spare charge packs. "*Useful talent, Jonnie. Leaves all their gear intact. Well, not the helmets. But still not bad. For an amateur.*"

"Is anybody ever gonna explain how the fuck this all came off?"

"*If somebody tries, don't expect it to make sense.*" He gets up and heads for the door, but stops with his hand on the lever. "*It really is Tanner.*"

"What is?"

"*My name. The one I was born with.*" His face is unreadable in his helmet. "*Not Hackford, though. Mark.*"

"Mark Tanner?"

"*You—uh, somebody who looked like you—asked me one time. Since we both figured we wouldn't see each other again.*"

"Shit, Tanner, if I *killed* you I'd figure to see you again."

"*I guess.*" He pushes open the door and heads on out. "*Take care of yourself, Jonnie. I ain't so friend-heavy I can afford to lose any.*"

I'd tell him to take his friend and shove it up his ass, except he might be able to make me fit. If he chops the pieces small enough.

Besides, I like the guy. "Luck to you, Tanner."

"*Thanks.*" The helmet twists back toward me. "*Die fighting, Caine.*"

"Seems likely. Thanks."

And he's gone.

Gayle is mostly huddled in a corner, but he's getting his nerve back. "Who was that? An Actor?"

"Best I've ever seen. But he works for somebody else."

"There's no way he can successfully impersonate a Studio secman."

"That's his problem." I stare at my stripcuffs for a second until they kindle white fire and melt away. Gayle doesn't seem to notice. "We need to talk about the future."

"Future? You don't have a future. There is a whole division of Social Police out there—"

"Not anymore." I swing my legs over the edge of the bed and stand up. Jesus, that feels good. I stretch, pull the I.V. out of my feeding port, and walk over to the armorglass windows. "A report should come through any second."

"You can *walk*?"

"Here, yeah. It's a little tricky—the oil is a different kind of power from Flow, and there's some boundary effect—but I'll get the hang of it."

The palmpad's annunciator chimes again. I pick it up and give it a tap, and the screen wipes to a shadowy side-lit image of my brother's face. *"You look like shit."*

"Good to see you, big dog. How we doing?"

"You do good work for a human," he says. *"All clear so far."*

"Good. Don't kill anybody."

"Yah yah. Survivors are maybe friendlies, hey?"

"On the ground, yeah. The lockout codes?"

"Fire control dick is up hard," he says. *"We ain't gonna be sharp as Soapy for a while, though."*

"Are you kidding? If I ever find a gun ogrilloi can't shoot better than humans, I'll fucking eat it."

"How's our air cover? Whole lotta bad guys up there."

"On its way."

"Yeah well, maybe they get their way on fucking faster, hey? I don't want to eat a nuke when Deliann's not here to turn the fucker off."

"Me neither. Stand by." I look over at Gayle. "Maybe you want to come watch, huh? This is not gonna be something you see every day."

He dazedly pulls himself up and stumbles over by me. "Can you tell me—explain to me—any of this . . . ?"

"Glad to. Because the Board of Governors is monitoring my thought-mitter, and this is shit they need to understand. It's pretty straightforward."

"Straightforward?" He gives a bleak laugh. "That's a joke, yes?"

"Mostly it's what I already said. It's just that none of you fuckers believed me. Because you dumb shits think this is just another Caine Adventure, so it has to end with some kind of giant fucking Bond movie battle. So okay. This was it."

Gayle looks baffled.

"That giant battle? You just saw it," I explain patiently, because I can afford to be patient. "You lost."

Gayle goggles at me.

I'd feel sorry for him, except there's that whole smug-weasel, unctuous-little-fuck thing. "It's like this. What I did to those secmen is a nifty feature of what happens when I come in contact with your black oil blood-of-the-blind-god shit. Well, you pumped an assload of it into me today. So just now, I exploded the heads of all the soapies within a couple miles of here."

Gayle's jaw drops and just hangs there. "You—?"

"Yeah. This close to the *dil*, they've got oil in their blood too. My oil can talk to their oil. My oil told their oil to ignite, and their oil wants to stay on my oil's good side, so they did me this favor. I guess it's more accurate to say it's all my oil, but I don't think that clarifies the situation."

"I have no clue what you're talking about."

"The Bog does. So, you're a reader. Ever come across a story called 'Br'er Rabbit'?"

He turns a whiter shade of pale.

"Now, I can't reach out farther than a mile or two because the farther you go, the more local physics goes Earth Normal. So all those riot cars on station up there are out of range. That's okay. We have an unpleasant surprise for them too.

"See, none of you really understands what the black oil is. The Bog *thinks* it knows . . . but then, the Bog thought mainlining that shit would turn me into whatever kind of psycho zombie monster Kollberg was, so we don't have to pay much attention to their opinion, right? Other than me and a few Monastic scholars and operatives, the only person who really understands the oil—who understands the true nature of the blind god—is my dad. He called it the shared will of the human race, and that's closer to true than, y'know, any of those elvish legends he got the name from. The blind god is an expression of human nature, and the black oil is only an expression of the blind god's power. It's not evil. *People* are evil.

"That's the whole thing, right there. Good and evil has nothing to do with gods. It has to do with us. The blind god destroys because we do. But we also create.

"Now look, Gayle. Don't blame yourself for any of this. There's a lot of shit you don't know about what happened after my wife was murdered. Though you'd think the Bog would clue you in, because they *do* know some of that shit. I mean, come on. They must have suspected. Seriously. Black hair. Black beard. Black eyes. Black clothes. Black Knife. Black Flow."

I spread my hands to apologize for how fucking obvious this is. "Black oil."

Gayle sits down. There's no chair. He doesn't seem to notice. He draws his knees up and wraps his arms around them.

"You'll be interested in some of the, y'know, peculiarities about my current situation, excuse the planet-size understatement. One of them is how those voices in my head can tell me about shit that hasn't happened yet. They're not always right—they never really capture the details—but some things are clear. Hell of an edge in planning, right? This installation was clear. That black oil is another, because without your black oil I.V. today, the whole seeing-the-future thing never comes about in the first place. In fact, it's probably fair to say my whole career might have unhappened."

Gayle shakes his head blankly.

"Yeah, well, I don't really understand either. Point is, we knew what you fuckers were going to try, and we knew when, and we were ready. You lost. I won."

"You've won . . . what?" He looks around, still baffled. "Anything? You can't go anywhere. You can't do anything. All you've done is murder a few thousand innocent men in the middle of a radioactive wasteland."

"It's not murder. It's war. Well, it *was* war. Now it's an occupation."

"By the ogrilloi? What, five hundred? A thousand?"

"More than ogrilloi, Gayle. Black Knives. A thousand Black Knives with modern weapons? Take my word for it. A thousand is a *lot.*"

"Black Knives *hate* you—"

"They worship me." I spread my hands again. "Things have changed."

"You're insane."

"I get that a lot. You—you the Board, and you the Leisure Congress, and you the Social Police—need to understand. It's over."

"What's over? What exactly do you think you're going to be able to do?"

"It's already done. The gate's been under our control for weeks."

"We get regular reports—"

"From Monastic agents. We're good at this."

"And there has been *traffic*—"

"Yeah, that's the good part. We took down the *dil T'llan.*"

"You *what?*"

"Well, sort of. Maybe I should say, we took it over. It was in the way."

"Oh, my God."

"Yeah, mine too. Now you fuckers go to Home only when we decide to let you. That's what's been going on for a couple of weeks now."

"And the transit—the operation of BlackStone—"

"Like I said: the Monasteries are good at this."

"You're bluffing. You have to be."

"People keep telling me that. What they never get around to telling me is if they remember the last time I was bluffing. Or any time I was bluffing. Even one. Go ahead and think it over. There's nowhere I have to be."

He doesn't say anything for a long time. He has his eyes closed.

When he speaks, he speaks very softly, and very clearly, overenunciating as though talking's painful. "What about me? What happens to me now? I can't imagine I have any value as a hostage. And it seems the Overworld Company no longer requires a Director of Operations for this installation."

"That pretty well sums it up."

"So. Is this when you . . ." He coughs. Sounds like that hurts too. "Is this when you kill me?"

"I thought about it."

He opens his eyes. "Past tense?"

I shrug. "I can't think of any plausible harm you can do. And I know you're not a ratfuck just for the sake of being a ratfuck."

"That might be the closest you've ever come to giving me a compliment."

"What I'd like to give you," I tell him, "is a job."

His eyelids droop in a long, slow blink, like he's about to faint.

"Think about it, Gayle. I'm pretty sure you're currently unemployed."

He just lowers his face into his doubled knees. "Nothing makes any sense to me anymore."

That's all right. He's not the one who needs to understand this. You do.

I do not bluff.

Watch.

"Hey, Gayle, check it out. Did you know the collective noun for dragons is *conflagration?* I love that word. A conflagration of dragons. Beautiful. Almost poetic, don't you think?"

He lifts his head, frowning. "Dragons? Why are you talking about—"

Then the shadow, vast and dark, sweeps over us and ripples across the emplacements outside, and Gayle chokes on the word. He lurches to his feet and presses his face against the window, mouth hanging open.

And I'm right next to him doing the same thing. I'd be cooler about it, but occasions like this transcend dignity. Fuck being cool.

This is *awesome*.

It's too big to really see as it swoops low over the installation. The shadow is too dark and my eyes just refuse to take it all in, because after all the only one I've ever seen in person was Sha-Rikkintaer in the San Francisco Curioseum and live ones are kind of fucking scarier. Maybe a quarter mile out it folds its wings—dragons don't need to flap their wings any more than a jet fighter does—and blasts straight up. I mean, *straight* up. Like a fucking rocket.

I can just get a hint of a colorful scale pattern like a reticulated python and it fires up its Shield and sun-colored flame blossoms around it, and here's another Merciful Jesus moment, because I so wish I could see the looks on the soapies' faces as they listen to their threat monitors try to figure out just what kind of vehicle is coming for them at just below the speed of sound. If only.

Oh, my god, if only.

Just as I spot a tiny dark speck near its haunches, Gayle says, "There's a man on the back of that dragon" in a perfectly calm, slightly bemused ordering-dinner tone.

He's got better eyes than I do. "Facing backward, right?"

"Could be."

"Probably Ankhanan military. Thaumaturgic Corps. Could be Monastic."

"But facing backward?"

I shrug. "Tail gunner."

And now the two behind it roar past and hit parallel verticals, and Gayle says, "Oh, my *God* . . ."

"A different god this time. Wait for it."

The third rank, three more, swings wide to take the slant.

"My late wife," I tell him, "can be very, very persuasive."

"Holy *shit* . . ." I don't think I've ever heard him use vulgar language before. Except when he's quoting me.

And when flashes and flares begin to expand around the intersecting vectors of six dragons and a couple dozen riot cars and it's riot cars that come spiraling down, spewing smoke and flame as they tumble into the badlands, Gayle whispers, *"Fuck my ass like a chicken pot pie . . ."*

Okay, that one's a quote.

I catch my own eye in my reflection on the armorglass.

So.

Does anybody not see what is happening here? Does anybody need it explained?

The badlands belong to us now. It's a no-fly zone. It's also a no-drive, no-march, no-missile, no-bomb no-whateverthefuck-else zone. Just in case you doubt our ability to enforce this . . .

"Hey, Gayle, trivia question. How many dragons do you think there are on Overworld?"

He shakes his head. "I have no idea."

"Me neither," I tell him. "But I bet it's a *lot* more than six."

"Uh. Mm." He nods thoughtfully. "Yes."

He turns to me with a quizzical frown. "So all this time—ever since you woke up in the Buchanan Social Camp—you've been planning this?"

"Me plan? Are you kidding? I have people for that. Some of my friends are *really* fucking smart."

"And if the Board had surprised everybody by accepting your offer?"

"Exactly what I said." I shrug. "If nothing else, I am a man of my word."

"Apparently so," he murmurs. "But still—all this time—you knew. You knew what their answer would be. You knew about this installation. About the black oil. About your *father.*"

"People get so used to listening to me monologue, they forget that what my thoughtmitter transmits isn't actually thought. It's narration. Like I'm talking, except softer."

"But—how you went pale. The trembling. The tears. The flush of rage—"

"Oh, the rage is real enough. So's the rest. It's not about faking shit. It's about using shit that's already there."

"Still—"

I spread my hands. "There's a reason it's called Acting."

Now another shadow sweeps over us, and into the rocks and sand outside settles a huge iridescent black sphere, like an obsidian marble for somebody with a thumb the size of the Spire.

"What's that?"

"The sphere? That's a Shield. She's probably having a little trouble retuning it to let visible light through without letting in the less friendly radiation. So listen, about the job?"

"Yes. I, ah . . . I'm not sure either of us would be comfortable with me working for you again."

"You won't be working for me. You'll be working for Faller. He won't be working for me either."

"Faller?"

"Yeah. I'm promoting him. And the new management here doesn't give a shit about return on investment, so we'll take care of that cancer first thing. He's going to be in charge of Earthside operations. We need a liaison to the Leisure Council. Interested?"

He nods again, back with the distant and thoughtful. "Mm. Yes. I believe I am. The, ah—the Shield?"

The obsidian shimmer pales, slowly revealing what stands within the Shield, which is a lion the size of an elephant with the head of an eagle and wings roughly the span of a city block. Just below the feather-line, it has a multisaddle harness buckled across its back and around its forelegs, and standing in the stirrups waving wildly to me is the most beautiful ten-year-old girl who has ever lived. In either universe. And who has a smile that makes everything right with the world. Worlds.

"Wait . . ." Gayle squints through the window. "Is that—?"

"Yeah," I say with a smile of my own. "That's my ride."

afterword

TO THE MASTERS OF EARTH

TO THE MASTERS OF EARTH

"You should have known better than to fuck with my family."

—CAINE

Blade of Tyshalle

So one more thing.

Just between you fuckers and me, this is a gesture of goodwill. Seriously.

We currently command more than enough power to conquer your world, but to tell you the truth we don't fucking want it. And an awful lot of people—human and otherwise—would get killed along the way. Which is, believe it or not, exactly what I'm trying to prevent. And it's brutally fucking clear that if you were the kind of people who gave a shit about whether anybody else lives or dies, you wouldn't be you. Earth wouldn't be Earth. So a billion people die. Five billion. Ten. It's no skin off your ass. I'm not gonna get anywhere by threatening them. So I'm threatening you.

Personally.

I want to be clear on this. Crystal fucking clear. That man in the Studio Security armor, who introduced himself as Mark Tanner—he's a Monastic Esoteric. An assassin. I've been telling people for *decades* that I'm not even close to the best killer the Monasteries have.

Him? He's close.

Compared to him, I'm about as dangerous as day-old bread. He's the best assassin I've ever met. The thing is, I haven't met that many assassins. There might be dozens—hundreds—even better than he is.

This is pertinent because we now control the *dil T'llan,* which allows us to do more than move through this particular *dil.* It allows us to move through *any* of them.

Get it?

This place, here in this fucking radioactive wasteland, is the only place you can come at us. We, on the other hand, can come at you from any *dil.* At will. All over the world. Do you know where all these *dillin* are?

Do you know where *any* of them are?

We do.

And, y'know, that's not all we know.

Know that kids' story about the country mouse and the city mouse? That's us in reverse. Your technology on Overworld can fuck us up pretty good. Our magick on Earth can fuck you up better.

Like your Social Police? Guess what? Their identities, postings, and files are, as of right now, freely available on the net. And nothing you do can change that. So when Soapy goes to strike back, he's gonna get a nasty fucking surprise.

So are you.

There is nothing on any computer, *anywhere,* that we can't get to. For example: I have recently been informed that the Board of Governors currently has, ah, sixteen members, isn't it? Let's go through some names off the top of my head . . .

Edward Charles Windsor. Theresa Dayton Walton. Ruhollah Mohammed Ahmedinajad. Adrej ibn Saud.

You get the idea, I imagine.

We know who you are. We know where you live. Shit, we know where you are *right now.*

We can find you. We can hurt you. We can kill you.

You *personally.*

I know you still don't really believe we can touch you. One of you is going to be the first to die. Two of you will be second.

Third, it's all of you.

If you want to live through this, you need to follow the rules. Some of you may not be familiar with them. Pay attention. There's gonna be a quiz.

Rule One: fuck with me and you die. This is your only warning.

Rule Two: what I say goes. Break Rule Two, you get hurt. Break it again, you die. Again: this is your only warning.

Rule Three: fuck with my family or my friends, and you're fucking with me. When in doubt, see Rule One.

Just so you know: my family and friends now includes everybody who isn't you.

So.

Any fucking questions?

This story is about what happened after the end of the world.

The end of the world had passed unmarked by most who lived in those days. How could they notice? The sun still shone yellow and hot, the winds still blew from thunderstorm to blizzard and back again, the silver moon still sailed across a starlit sky. There were fish in the sea, cattle in the fields, birds in the air, deepwood glens still rustling with the dry-leaf laughter of the fey, mountain mines ringing with the steely chime of stonebender tools, treetoppers fluttering and ogres growling and dragons slumbering in forgotten lairs.

For a long time, the only people who knew the world had ended were certain clever men and clever women whose lives were devoted to knowing clever things of this nature, and even they weren't certain; the end of the world was a serious matter, and they didn't want to be wrong.

One of the ways in which they were clever was in the naming of things. They were very concerned with comprehending what they named, to ensure the name they gave it was the name it should have. They knew that names are masks, but they also knew masks can reveal truth that might otherwise remain occult. The names we give to things channel how we think of them, and because the end of the world began small and subtle and slow to burgeon—despite being locally dramatic—at first they called it by the wrong name.

They called it the True Assumption of Ma'elKoth.

The Age of Gods had lasted five hundred years, from the Feral Rebellion—when the human gods overpowered the combined might of the Folk of Home, and set humanity free—until the Deomachy, when Jereth of Tyrnall, called the Godslaughterer, rose up against his gods and those of all humanity, and his brother Jantho, called the Ironhand, crafted the Covenant of Pirichanthe to bind the human gods beyond the walls of time, and together these brothers ushered in the Age of Man.

The Age of Man lasted also five hundred years, until Ma'elKoth—who Himself once had been, briefly, a man—became a god and took all Home to be His Body and worked His Will upon it, and thereby rent the Covenant that had been Jantho Ironhand's greatest work. The Age of Man was over, and the world it had shaped was gone forever.

This is the story of how the end of the world gave birth to the Age of Caine.